Sketches from a Hunter's Album

The Complete and Uncensored Edition

IVAN TURGENEV

*Translated from the Russian
by Constance Garnett*

Seven Treasures Publications

D1203168

Published by
Seven Treasures Publications
SevenTreasuresPublications@gmail.com
Fax 413-653-8797

Printed in the United States of America

ISBN   9781441405555

CONTENTS

I   HOR AND KALINITCH

Anyone who has chanced to pass from the Bolhovsky district into the Zhizdrinsky district, must have been impressed by the striking difference between the race of people in the province of Orel and the population of the province of Kaluga. The peasant of Orel is not tall, is bent in figure, sullen and suspicious in his looks; he lives in wretched little hovels of aspen-wood, labours as a serf in the fields, and engages in no kind of trading, is miserably fed, and wears slippers of bast: the rent-paying peasant of Kaluga lives in roomy cottages of pine-wood; he is tall, bold, and cheerful in his looks, neat and clean of countenance; he carries on a trade in butter and tar, and on holidays he wears boots. The village of the Orel province (we are speaking now of the eastern part of the province) is usually situated in the midst of ploughed fields, near a water-course which has been converted into a filthy pool. Except for a few of the ever- accommodating willows, and two or three gaunt birch-trees, you do not see a tree for a mile round; hut is huddled up against hut, their roofs covered with rotting thatch.... The villages of Kaluga, on the contrary, are generally surrounded by forest; the huts stand more freely, are more upright, and have boarded roofs; the gates fasten closely, the hedge is not broken down nor trailing about; there are no gaps to invite the visits of the passing pig.... And things are much better in the Kaluga province for the sportsman. In the Orel province the last of the woods and copses will have disappeared five years hence, and there is no trace of moorland left; in Kaluga, on the contrary, the moors extend over tens, the forest over hundreds of miles, and a splendid bird, the grouse, is still extant there; there are abundance of the friendly larger snipe, and the loud-clapping partridge cheers and startles the sportsman and his dog by its abrupt upward flight.

On a visit to the Zhizdrinsky district in search of sport, I met in the fields a petty proprietor of the Kaluga province called Polutikin, and made his acquaintance. He was an enthusiastic sportsman; it follows, therefore, that he was an excellent fellow. He was liable, indeed, to a few weaknesses; he used, for instance, to pay his addresses to every unmarried heiress in the province, and when he had been refused her hand and house, broken-hearted he confided his sorrows to all his friends and acquaintances, and continued to shower offerings of sour peaches and other raw produce from his garden upon the young lady's relatives; he was fond of repeating one and the same anecdote, which, in spite of Mr. Polutikin's appreciation of its merits, had certainly never amused anyone; he admired the works of Akim Nahimov and the novel Pinna ; he stammered; he called his dog Astronomer; instead of 'however' said 'howsomever'; and had established in his household a French system of cookery, the secret of which consisted, according to his cook's interpretation, in a complete transformation of the natural taste of each dish; in this artiste's hands meat assumed the flavour of fish, fish of mushrooms, macaroni of gunpowder; to make up for this, not a single carrot went into the soup without taking the shape of a rhombus or a trapeze. But, with the exception of these few and insignificant failings, Mr. Polutikin was, as has been said already, an excellent fellow.

On the first day of my acquaintance with Mr. Polutikin, he invited me to stay the night at his house.

'It will be five miles farther to my house,' he added; 'it's a long way to walk; let us first go to Hor's.' (The reader must excuse my omitting his stammer.)

'Who is Hor?'

'A peasant of mine. He is quite close by here.'

We went in that direction. In a well-cultivated clearing in the middle of the forest rose Hor's solitary homestead. It consisted of several pine-wood buildings, enclosed by plank fences; a porch ran along the front of the principal building, supported on slender posts. We went in. We were met by a young lad of twenty, tall and good-looking.

'Ah, Fedya! is Hor at home?' Mr. Polutikin asked him.

'No. Hor has gone into town,' answered the lad, smiling and showing a row of snow-white teeth. 'You would like the little cart brought out?'

'Yes, my boy, the little cart. And bring us some kvas.'

We went into the cottage. Not a single cheap glaring print was pasted up on the clean boards of the walls; in the corner, before the heavy, holy picture in its silver setting, a lamp was burning; the table of linden-wood had been lately planed and scrubbed; between the joists and in the cracks of the window-frames there were no lively Prussian beetles running about, nor gloomy cockroaches in hiding. The young lad soon reappeared with a great white pitcher filled with excellent kvas, a huge hunch of wheaten bread, and a dozen salted cucumbers in a wooden bowl. He put all these provisions on the table, and then, leaning with his back against the door, began to gaze with a smiling face at us. We had not had time to finish eating our lunch when the cart was already rattling before the doorstep. We went out. A curly-headed, rosy-cheeked boy of fifteen was sitting in the cart as driver, and with difficulty holding in the well-fed piebald horse. Round the cart stood six young giants, very like one another, and Fedya.

'All of these Hor's sons!' said Polutikin.

'These are all Horkies' (i.e. wild cats), put in Fedya, who had come after us on to the step; 'but that's not all of them: Potap is in the wood, and Sidor has gone with old Hor to the town. Look out, Vasya,' he went on, turning to the coachman; 'drive like the wind; you are driving the master. Only mind what you're about over the ruts, and easy a little; don't tip the cart over, and upset the master's stomach!'

The other Horkies smiled at Fedya's sally. 'Lift Astronomer in!' Mr. Polutikin called majestically. Fedya, not without amusement, lifted the dog, who wore a forced smile, into the air, and laid her at the bottom of the cart. Vasya let the horse go. We rolled away. 'And here is my counting-house,' said Mr. Polutikin suddenly to me, pointing to a little low-pitched house. 'Shall we go in?' 'By all means.' 'It is no longer used,' he observed, going in; 'still, it is worth looking at.' The counting-house consisted of two empty rooms. The caretaker, a one- eyed old man, ran out of the yard. 'Good day, Minyaitch,' said Mr. Polutikin; 'bring us some water.' The one-eyed old man disappeared, and at once returned with a bottle of water and two glasses. 'Taste it,' Polutikin said to me; 'it is splendid spring water.' We drank off a glass each, while the old man bowed low. 'Come, now, I think we can go on,' said my new Friend. 'In that counting-house I sold the merchant Alliluev four acres of forest-land for a good price.' We took our seats in the cart, and in half-an-hour we had reached the court of the manor- house.

'Tell me, please,' I asked Polutikin at supper; 'why does Hor live apart from your other peasants?'

'Well, this is why; he is a clever peasant. Twenty-five years ago his cottage was burnt down; so he came up to my late father and said: "Allow me, Nikolai Kouzmitch," says he, "to settle in your forest, on the bog. I will pay you a good rent." "But what do you want to settle on the bog for?" "Oh, I want to; only, your honour, Nikolai Kouzmitch, be so good as not to claim any labour from me, but fix a rent as you think best." "Fifty roubles a year!" "Very well." "But I'll have no arrears, mind!" "Of course, no arrears"; and so he settled on the bog. Since then they have called him Hor' (i.e. wild cat).

'Well, and has he grown rich?' I inquired.

'Yes, he has grown rich. Now he pays me a round hundred for rent, and I shall raise it again, I dare say. I have said to him more than once, "Buy your freedom, Hor; come, buy your freedom." ... But he declares, the rogue, that he can't; has no money, he says.... As though that were likely....'

The next day, directly after our morning tea, we started out hunting again. As we were driving through the village, Mr. Polutikin ordered the coachman to stop at a low-pitched cottage and called loudly, 'Kalinitch!' 'Coming, your honour, coming' sounded a voice from the yard; 'I am tying on my shoes.' We went on at a walk; outside the village a man of about forty over-took us. He was tall and thin, with a small and erect head. It was Kalinitch. His good-humoured; swarthy face, somewhat pitted with small-pox, pleased me from the first glance. Kalinitch (as I learnt afterwards) went hunting every day with his master, carried his bag, and sometimes also his gun, noted where game was to be found, fetched water, built shanties, and gathered strawberries, and ran behind the droshky; Mr. Polutikin could not stir a step without him. Kalinitch was a man of the merriest and gentlest disposition; he was constantly singing to himself in a low voice, and looking carelessly about him. He spoke a little through his nose, with a laughing twinkle in his light blue eyes, and he had a habit of plucking at his scanty, wedge-shaped beard with his hand. He walked not rapidly, but with long strides, leaning lightly on a long thin staff. He addressed me more than once during the day, and he waited on me without, obsequiousness, but he looked after his master as if he were a child. When the unbearable heat drove us at mid-day to seek shelter, he took us to his beehouse in the very heart of the forest. There Kalinitch opened the little hut for us, which was hung round with bunches of dry scented herbs. He made us comfortable on some dry hay, and then put a kind of bag of network over his head, took a knife, a little pot, and a smouldering stick, and went to the hive to cut us out some honey-comb. We had a draught of spring water after the warm transparent honey, and then dropped asleep to the sound of the monotonous humming of the bees and the rustling chatter of the leaves. A slight gust of wind awakened me.... I opened my eyes and saw Kalinitch: he was sitting on the threshold of the half-opened door, carving a spoon with his knife. I gazed a long time admiring his face, as sweet and clear as an evening sky. Mr. Polutikin too woke up. We did not get up at once. After our long walk and our deep sleep it was pleasant to lie without moving in the hay; we felt weary and languid in body, our faces were in a slight glow of warmth, our eyes were closed in delicious laziness. At last we got up, and set off on our wanderings again till evening. At supper I began again to talk of Hor and Kalinitch. 'Kalinitch is a good peasant,' Mr. Polutikin told me; 'he is a willing and useful peasant; he can't farm his land properly; I am always taking him away from it. He goes out hunting every day with me.... You can judge for yourself how his farming must fare.'

I agreed with him, and we went to bed.

The next day Mr. Polutikin was obliged to go to town about some business with his neighbour Pitchukoff. This neighbour Pitchukoff had ploughed over some land of

Polutikin's, and had flogged a peasant woman of his on this same piece of land. I went out hunting alone, and before evening I turned into Hor's house. On the threshold of the cottage I was met by an old man--bald, short, broad-shouldered, and stout--Hor himself. I looked with curiosity at the man. The cut of his face recalled Socrates; there was the same high, knobby forehead, the same little eyes, the same snub nose. We went into the cottage together. The same Fedya brought me some milk and black bread. Hor sat down on a bench, and, quietly stroking his curly beard, entered into conversation with me. He seemed to know his own value; he spoke and moved slowly; from time to time a chuckle came from between his long moustaches.

We discussed the sowing, the crops, the peasant's life.... He always seemed to agree with me; only afterwards I had a sense of awkwardness and felt I was talking foolishly.... In this way our conversation was rather curious. Hor, doubtless through caution, expressed himself very obscurely at times.... Here is a specimen of our talk.

"Tell me, Hor," I said to him, "why don't you buy your freedom from your master?"

"And what would I buy my freedom for? Now I know my master, and I know my rent.... We have a good master."

'It's always better to be free,' I remarked. Hor gave me a dubious look.

'Surely,' he said.

'Well, then, why don't you buy your freedom?' Hor shook his head.

'What would you have me buy it with, your honour?'

'Oh, come, now, old man!'

'If Hor were thrown among free men,' he continued in an undertone, as though to himself, 'everyone without a beard would be a better man than Hor.'

'Then shave your beard.'

'What is a beard? a beard is grass: one can cut it.'

'Well, then?'

'But Hor will be a merchant straight away; and merchants have a fine life, and they have beards.'

'Why, do you do a little trading too?' I asked him.

'We trade a little in a little butter and a little tar.... Would your honour like the cart put to?'

'You're a close man and keep a tight rein on your tongue,' I thought to myself. 'No,' I said aloud, 'I don't want the cart; I shall want to be near your homestead to-morrow, and if you will let me, I will stay the night in your hay-barn.'

'You are very welcome. But will you be comfortable in the barn? I will tell the women to lay a sheet and put you a pillow.... Hey, girls!' he cried, getting up from his place; 'here, girls!... And you, Fedya, go with them. Women, you know, are foolish folk.'

A quarter of an hour later Fedya conducted me with a lantern to the barn. I threw myself down on the fragrant hay; my dog curled himself up at my feet; Fedya wished me good-night; the door creaked and slammed to. For rather a long time I could not get to sleep. A cow came up to the door, and breathed heavily twice; the dog growled at her with dignity; a pig passed by, grunting pensively; a horse somewhere near began to munch the hay and snort.... At last I fell asleep.

At sunrise Fedya awakened me. This brisk, lively young man pleased me; and, from what I could see, he was old Hor's favourite too. They used to banter one another in a very friendly way. The old man came to meet me. Whether because I had spent the night under his roof, or for some other reason, Hor certainly treated me far more cordially than the day before.

'The samovar is ready,' he told me with a smile; 'let us come and have tea.'

We took our seats at the table. A robust-looking peasant woman, one of his daughters-in-law, brought in a jug of milk. All his sons came one after another into the cottage.

'What a fine set of fellows you have!' I remarked to the old man.

'Yes,' he said, breaking off a tiny piece of sugar with his teeth; 'me and my old woman have nothing to complain of, seemingly.'

'And do they all live with you?'

'Yes; they choose to, themselves, and so they live here.'

'And are they all married?'

'Here's one not married, the scamp!' he answered, pointing to Fedya, who was leaning as before against the door. 'Vaska, he's still too young; he can wait.'

'And why should I get married?' retorted Fedya; 'I'm very well off as I am. What do I want a wife for? To squabble with, eh?'

'Now then, you ... ah, I know you! you wear a silver ring.... You'd always be after the girls up at the manor house.... "Have done, do, for shame!"' the old man went on, mimicking the servant girls. 'Ah, I know you, you white-handed rascal!'

'But what's the good of a peasant woman?'

'A peasant woman--is a labourer,' said Hor seriously; 'she is the peasant's servant.'

'And what do I want with a labourer?'

'I dare say; you'd like to play with the fire and let others burn their fingers: we know the sort of chap you are.'

'Well, marry me, then. Well, why don't you answer?'

'There, that's enough, that's enough, giddy pate! You see we're disturbing the gentleman. I'll marry you, depend on it.... And you, your honour, don't be vexed with him; you see, he's only a baby; he's not had time to get much sense.'

Fedya shook his head.

'Is Hor at home?' sounded a well-known voice; and Kalinitch came into the cottage with a bunch of wild strawberries in his hands, which he had gathered for his friend Hor. The old man gave him a warm welcome. I looked with surprise at Kalinitch. I confess I had not expected such a delicate attention on the part of a peasant.

That day I started out to hunt four hours later than usual, and the following three days I spent at Hor's. My new friends interested me. I don't know how I had gained their confidence, but they began to talk to me without constraint. The two friends were not at all alike. Hor was a positive, practical man, with a head for management, a rationalist; Kalinitch, on the other hand, belonged to the order of idealists and dreamers, of romantic and enthusiastic spirits. Hor had a grasp of actuality--that is to say, he looked ahead, was saving a little money, kept on good terms with his master and the other authorities; Kalinitch wore shoes of bast, and lived from hand to mouth. Hor had reared a large family, who were obedient and united; Kalinitch had once had a wife, whom he had been afraid of, and he had had no children. Hor took a very critical view of Mr. Polutikin; Kalinitch revered his master. Hor loved Kalinitch, and took protecting care of him; Kalinitch loved and respected Hor. Hor spoke little, chuckled, and thought for himself; Kalinitch expressed himself with warmth, though he had not the flow of fine language of a smart factory hand. But Kalinitch was endowed with powers which even Hor recognised; he could charm away haemorrhages, fits, madness, and worms; his bees always did well; he had a light hand. Hor asked him before me to introduce a newly bought horse to his stable, and with scrupulous gravity Kalinitch carried out the old sceptic's request. Kalinitch was in closer contact with nature; Hor with men and society. Kalinitch had no liking for argument, and believed in everything blindly; Hor had reached even an ironical point of view of life. He had seen and experienced much, and I learnt a good deal from him. For instance, from his account I learnt that every year before mowing-time a small, peculiar-looking cart makes its appearance in the villages. In this cart sits a man in a long coat, who sells scythes. He charges one rouble twenty-five copecks--a rouble and a half in notes--for ready money; four roubles if he gives credit. All the peasants, of course, take the scythes from him on credit. In two or three weeks he reappears and asks for the money. As the peasant has only just cut his oats, he is able to pay him; he goes with the merchant to the tavern, and there the debt is settled. Some landowners conceived the idea of buying the scythes themselves for ready money and letting the peasants have them on credit for the same price; but the peasants seemed dissatisfied, even dejected; they had deprived them of the pleasure of tapping the scythe and listening to the ring of the metal, turning it over and over in their hands, and telling the scoundrelly city-trader twenty times over, 'Eh, my friend, you won't take me in with your scythe!' The same tricks are played over the sale of sickles, only with this difference, that the women have a hand in the business then, and they sometimes drive the trader himself to the necessity--for their good, of course--of beating them. But the women suffer most ill-treatment through the following circumstances. Contractors for the supply of stuff for paper factories employ for the purchase of rags a special class of men, who in some districts are called eagles. Such an 'eagle' receives two hundred roubles in bank- notes from the merchant, and starts off in search of his prey. But, unlike the noble bird from whom he has derived his name, he does not swoop down openly and boldly upon it; quite the contrary; the 'eagle' has recourse to deceit and cunning. He leaves his cart somewhere in a thicket near the village, and goes himself to the back-yards and back- doors, like someone casually passing, or simply a tramp. The women scent out his proximity and steal out to meet him. The bargain is hurriedly concluded. For a few copper half-pence a woman gives the 'eagle' not only every useless rag she has, but often even her husband's shirt and her own petticoat. Of late the women have thought it profitable to steal even from themselves, and to sell hemp in the same way--a great extension and improvement of the business for the 'eagles'! To meet this, however, the peasants have grown more cunning in their turn, and on the slightest suspicion, on the most distant rumors of the approach of an 'eagle,' they have prompt and sharp recourse to corrective and preventive measures. And, after all, wasn't it disgraceful? To sell the hemp was the men's business--and they certainly do sell it--not in the town (they would have to drag it there themselves), but to traders who come for it, who, for want of scales, reckon forty handfuls to the pood--and you know what a Russian's hand is and what it can hold, especially when he 'tries his best'! As I had had no experience and was not 'country-bred' (as they say in Orel) I heard plenty of such descriptions. But Hor was not always the narrator; he questioned me too about many things. He learned that I had been in foreign parts, and his curiosity was aroused.... Kalinitch was not behind him in curiosity; but he was more attracted by descriptions of nature, of mountains and waterfalls, extraordinary buildings and great towns; Hor was interested in questions of government and administration. He went through everything in order. 'Well, is that with them as it is with us, or different?... Come, tell us, your honour, how is it?' 'Ah, Lord, thy will be done!' Kalinitch would exclaim while I told my story; Hor did not speak, but frowned with his bushy eyebrows, only observing at times, 'That wouldn't do for us; still, it's a good thing--it's right.' All his inquiries, I cannot recount, and it is unnecessary; but from our conversations I carried away one conviction, which my readers will certainly not anticipate ... the conviction that Peter the Great was pre-eminently a Russian-- Russian, above all, in his reforms. The Russian is so convinced of his own strength and powers that he is not afraid of putting himself to severe strain; he takes little interest in his past, and looks boldly forward. What is good he likes, what is sensible he will have, and where it comes from he does not care. His vigorous sense is fond of ridiculing the thin theorising of the German; but, in Hor's words, 'The Germans are curious folk,' and he was ready to learn from them a little. Thanks to his exceptional position, his practical independence, Hor told me a great deal which you could not screw or--as the peasants say--grind with a grindstone, out of any other man. He did, in fact, understand his position. Talking with Hor, I for the first time listened to the simple, wise discourse of the Russian peasant. His acquirements were, in his own opinion, wide enough; but he could not read, though Kalinitch could. 'That ne'er-do-weel has school-learning,' observed Hor, 'and his bees never die in the winter.' 'But haven't you had your children taught to read?' Hor was silent a minute. 'Fedya can read.' 'And the others?' 'The others can't.' 'And why?' The old man made no answer, and changed the subject. However, sensible as he was, he had many prejudices and crotchets. He despised women, for instance, from the depths of his soul, and in his merry moments he amused himself by jesting at their expense. His wife was a cross old woman who lay all day long on the stove, incessantly grumbling and scolding; her sons paid no attention to her, but she kept her daughters-in-law in the fear of God. Very significantly the mother-in-law sings in the Russian ballad: 'What a son art thou to me! What a head of a household! Thou dost not beat thy wife; thou dost not beat thy young wife....' I once attempted to intercede for the daughters-in-law, and tried to rouse Hor's sympathy; but he met me with the tranquil rejoinder, 'Why did I want to trouble about such ... trifles; let the women fight it out. ... If anything separates them, it only makes it worse ... and it's not worth dirtying one's hands over.' Sometimes the spiteful old woman got down from the stove and called the yard dog out of the hay, crying, 'Here, here, doggie'; and then beat it on its thin back with the poker, or she would stand in the porch and 'snarl,' as Hor expressed it, at everyone that passed. She stood in awe of her husband though, and would return, at his command, to her place on the stove. It was specially curious to hear Hor and Kalinitch dispute whenever Mr. Polutikin was touched upon.

'There, Hor, do let him alone,' Kalinitch would say. 'But why doesn't he order some boots for you?' Hor retorted. 'Eh? boots!... what do I want with boots? I am a peasant.' 'Well, so am I a peasant, but look!' And Hor lifted up his leg and showed Kalinitch a boot which looked as if it had been cut out of a mammoth's hide. 'As if you were like one of us!' replied Kalinitch. 'Well, at least he might pay for your bast shoes; you go out hunting with him; you must use a pair a day.' 'He does give me something for bast shoes.' 'Yes, he gave you two coppers last year.'

Kalinitch turned away in vexation, but Hor went off into a chuckle, during which his little eyes completely disappeared.

Kalinitch sang rather sweetly and played a little on the balalaeca. Hor was never weary of listening to him: all at once he would let his head drop on one side and begin to chime in, in a lugubrious voice. He was particularly fond of the song, 'Ah, my fate, my fate!' Fedya never lost an opportunity of making fun of his father, saying, 'What are you so mournful about, old man?' But Hor leaned his cheek on his hand, covered his eyes, and continued to mourn over his fate.... Yet at other times there could not be a more active man; he was always busy over something--mending the cart, patching up the fence, looking after the harness. He did not insist on a very high degree of cleanliness, however; and, in answer to some remark of mine, said once, 'A cottage ought to smell as if it were lived in.'

'Look,' I answered, 'how clean it is in Kalinitch's beehouse.'

'The bees would not live there else, your honour,' he said with a sigh.

'Tell me,' he asked me another time, 'have you an estate of your own?' 'Yes.' 'Far from here?' 'A hundred miles.' 'Do you live on your land, your honour?' 'Yes.'

'But you like your gun best, I dare say?'

'Yes, I must confess I do.' 'And you do well, your honour; shoot grouse to your heart's content, and change your bailiff pretty often.'

On the fourth day Mr. Polutikin sent for me in the evening. I was sorry to part from the old man. I took my seat with Kalinitch in the trap. 'Well, good-bye, Hor--good luck to you,' I said; 'good-bye, Fedya.'

'Good-bye, your honour, good-bye; don't forget us.' We started; there was the first red glow of sunset. 'It will be a fine day to-morrow,' I remarked looking at the clear sky. 'No, it will rain,' Kalinitch replied; 'the ducks yonder are splashing, and the scent of the grass is strong.' We drove into the copse. Kalinitch began singing in an undertone as he was jolted up and down on the driver's seat, and he kept gazing and gazing at the sunset.

The next day I left the hospitable roof of Mr. Polutikin.

II   YERMOLAI AND THE MILLER'S WIFE

One evening I went with the huntsman Yermolai 'stand-shooting.' ... But perhaps all my readers may not know what 'stand-shooting' is. I will tell you.

A quarter of an hour before sunset in spring-time you go out into the woods with your gun, but without your dog. You seek out a spot for yourself on the outskirts of the forest, take a look round, examine your caps, and glance at your companion. A quarter of an hour passes; the sun has set, but it is still light in the forest; the sky is clear and transparent; the birds are chattering and twittering; the young grass shines with the brilliance of emerald.... You wait. Gradually the recesses of the forest grow dark; the blood-red glow of the evening sky creeps slowly on to the roots and the trunks of the trees, and keeps rising higher and higher, passes from the lower, still almost leafless branches, to the motionless, slumbering tree-tops.... And now even the topmost branches are darkened; the purple sky fades to dark-blue. The forest fragrance grows stronger; there is a scent of warmth and damp earth; the fluttering breeze dies away at your side. The birds go to sleep--not all at once--but after their kinds; first the finches are hushed, a few minutes later the warblers, and after them the yellow buntings. In the forest it grows darker and darker. The trees melt together into great masses of blackness; in the dark-blue sky the first stars come timidly out. All the birds are asleep. Only the redstarts and the nuthatches are still chirping drowsily.... And now they too are still. The last echoing call of the pee-wit rings over our heads; the oriole's melancholy cry sounds somewhere in the distance; then the nightingale's first note. Your heart is weary with suspense, when suddenly--but only sportsmen can understand me--suddenly in the deep hush there is a peculiar croaking and whirring sound, the measured sweep of swift wings is heard, and the snipe, gracefully bending its long beak, sails smoothly down behind a dark bush to meet your shot.

That is the meaning of 'stand-shooting.' And so I had gone out stand- shooting with Yermolai; but excuse me, reader: I must first introduce you to Yermolai.

Picture to yourself a tall gaunt man of forty-five, with a long thin nose, a narrow forehead, little grey eyes, a bristling head of hair, and thick sarcastic lips. This man wore, winter and summer alike, a yellow nankin coat of German cut, but with a sash round the waist; he wore blue pantaloons and a cap of astrakhan, presented to him in a merry hour by a spendthrift landowner. Two bags were fastened on to his sash, one in front, skilfully tied into two halves, for powder and for shot; the other behind for game: wadding Yermolai used to produce out of his peculiar, seemingly inexhaustible cap. With the money he gained by the game he sold, he might easily have bought himself a cartridge-box and powder-flask; but he never once even contemplated such a purchase, and continued to load his gun after his old fashion, exciting the admiration of all beholders by the skill with which he avoided the risks of spilling or mixing his powder and shot. His gun was a single- barrelled flint-lock, endowed, moreover, with a villainous habit of 'kicking.' It was due to this that Yermolai's right cheek was permanently swollen to a larger size than the left. How he ever succeeded in hitting anything with this gun, it would take a shrewd man to discover--but he did. He had too a setter-dog, by name Valetka, a most extraordinary creature. Yermolai never fed him. 'Me feed a dog!' he reasoned; 'why, a dog's a clever beast; he finds a living for himself.' And certainly, though Valetka's extreme thinness was a shock even to an indifferent observer, he still lived and had a long life; and in spite of his pitiable position he was not even once lost, and never showed an inclination to desert his master. Once indeed, in his youth, he had absented himself for two days, on courting bent, but this folly was soon over with him. Valetka's most noticeable peculiarity was his impenetrable indifference to everything in the world.... If it were not a dog I was speaking of, I should have called him 'disillusioned.' He usually sat with his cropped tail curled up under him, scowling and twitching at times, and he never smiled. (It is well known that dogs can smile, and smile very sweetly.) He was exceedingly ugly; and the idle house-serfs never lost an opportunity of jeering cruelly at his appearance; but all these jeers, and even blows, Valetka bore with astonishing indifference. He was a source of special delight to the cooks, who would all leave their work at once and give him chase with shouts and abuse, whenever, through a weakness not confined to dogs, he thrust his hungry nose through the half-open door of the kitchen, tempting with its warmth and appetising smells. He distinguished himself by untiring energy in the chase, and had a good scent; but if he chanced to overtake a slightly wounded hare, he devoured it with relish to the last bone, somewhere in the cool shade under the green bushes, at a respectful distance from Yermolai, who was abusing him in every known and unknown dialect. Yermolai belonged to one of my neighbours, a landowner of the old style. Landowners of the old style don't care for game, and prefer the domestic fowl. Only on extraordinary occasions, such as birthdays, namedays, and elections, the cooks of the old-fashioned landowners set to work to prepare some long-beaked birds, and, falling into the state of frenzy peculiar to Russians when they don't quite know what to do, they concoct such marvellous sauces for them that the guests examine the proffered dishes curiously and attentively, but rarely make up their minds to try them. Yermolai was under orders to provide his master's kitchen with two brace of grouse and partridges once a month. But he might live where and how he pleased. They had given him up as a man of no use for work of any kind—'bone lazy,' as the expression is among us in Orel. Powder and shot, of course, they did not provide him, following precisely the same principle in virtue of which he did not feed his dog. Yermolai was a very strange kind of man; heedless as a bird, rather fond of talking, awkward and vacant-looking; he was excessively fond of drink, and never could sit still long; in walking he shambled along, and rolled from side to side; and yet he got over fifty miles in the day with his rolling, shambling gait. He exposed himself to the most varied adventures: spent the night in the marshes, in trees, on roofs, or under bridges; more than once he had got shut up in lofts, cellars, or barns; he sometimes lost his gun, his dog, his most indispensable garments; got long and severe thrashings; but he always returned home, after a little while, in his clothes, and with his gun and his dog. One could not call him a cheerful man, though one almost always found him in an even frame of mind; he was looked on generally as an eccentric. Yermolai liked a little chat with a good companion, especially over a glass, but he would not stop long; he would get up and go. 'But where the devil are you going? It's dark out of doors.' 'To Tchaplino.' 'But what's taking you to Tchaplino, ten miles away?' 'I am going to stay the night at Sophron's there.' 'But stay the night here.' 'No, I can't.' And Yermolai, with his Valetka, would go off into the dark night, through woods and water-courses, and the peasant Sophron very likely did not let him into his place, and even, I am afraid, gave him a blow to teach him 'not to disturb honest folks.' But none could compare with Yermolai in skill in deep-water fishing in spring-time, in catching crayfish with his hands, in tracking game by scent, in snaring quails, in training hawks, in capturing the nightingales who had the greatest variety of notes. ... One thing he could not do, train a dog; he had not patience enough. He had a wife too. He went to see her once a week. She lived in a wretched, tumble-down little hut, and led a hand-to-mouth existence, never knowing overnight whether she would have food to eat on the morrow; and in every way her lot was a pitiful one. Yermolai, who seemed such a careless and easy-going fellow, treated his wife with cruel harshness; in his own house he assumed a stern, and menacing manner; and his poor wife did everything she could to please him, trembled when he looked at her, and spent her last farthing to buy him vodka; and when he stretched himself majestically on the stove and fell into an heroic sleep, she obsequiously covered him with a sheepskin. I happened myself more than once to catch an involuntary look in him of a kind of savage ferocity; I did not like the expression of his face when he finished off a wounded bird with his teeth. But Yermolai never remained more than a day at home, and away from home he was once more the same 'Yermolka' (i.e. the shooting-cap), as he was called for a hundred miles round, and as he sometimes called himself. The lowest house-serf was conscious of being superior to this vagabond —and perhaps this was precisely why they treated him with friendliness; the peasants at first amused themselves by chasing him and driving him like a hare over the open country, but afterwards they left him in God's hands, and when once they recognised him as 'queer,' they no longer tormented him, and even gave him bread and entered into talk with him.... This was the man I took as my huntsman, and with him I went stand-shooting to a great birch-wood on the banks of the Ista.

Many Russian rivers, like the Volga, have one bank rugged and precipitous, the other bounded by level meadows; and so it is with the Ista. This small river winds extremely capriciously, coils like a snake, and does not keep a straight course for half-a-mile together; in some places, from the top of a sharp declivity, one can see the river for ten miles, with its dykes, its pools and mills, and the gardens on its banks, shut in with willows and thick flower-gardens. There are fish in the Ista in endless numbers, especially roaches (the peasants take them in hot weather from under the bushes with their hands); little sand-pipers flutter whistling along the stony banks, which are streaked with cold clear streams; wild ducks dive in the middle of the pools, and look round warily; in the coves under the overhanging cliffs herons stand out in the shade.... We stood in ambush nearly an hour, killed two brace of wood snipe, and, as we wanted to try our luck again at sunrise (stand-shooting can be done as well in the early morning), we resolved to spend the night at the nearest mill. We came out of the wood, and went down the slope. The dark-blue waters of the river ran below; the air was thick with the mists of night. We knocked at the gate. The dogs began barking in the yard.

'Who is there?' asked a hoarse and sleepy voice.

'We are sportsmen; let us stay the night.' There was no reply. 'We will pay.'

'I will go and tell the master--Sh! Curse the dogs! Go to the devil with you!'

We listened as the workman went into the cottage; he soon came back to the gate. 'No,' he said; 'the master tells me not to let you in.'

'Why not?'

'He is afraid; you are sportsmen; you might set the mill on fire; you've firearms with you, to be sure.'

'But what nonsense!'

'We had our mill on fire like that last year; some fish-dealers stayed the night, and they managed to set it on fire somehow.'

'But, my good friend, we can't sleep in the open air!'

'That's your business.' He went away, his boots clacking as he walked.

Yermolai promised him various unpleasant things in the future. 'Let us go to the village,' he brought out at last, with a sigh. But it was two miles to the village.

'Let us stay the night here,' I said, 'in the open air--the night is warm; the miller will let us have some straw if we pay for it.'

Yermolai agreed without discussion. We began again to knock.

'Well, what do you want?' the workman's voice was heard again; 'I've told you we can't.'

We explained to him what we wanted. He went to consult the master of the house, and returned with him. The little side gate creaked. The miller appeared, a tall, fat-faced man with a bull-neck, round-bellied and corpulent. He agreed to my proposal. A hundred paces from the mill there was a little outhouse open to the air on all sides. They carried straw and hay there for us; the workman set a samovar down on the grass near the river, and, squatting on his heels, began to blow vigorously into the pipe of it. The embers glowed, and threw a bright light on his young face. The miller ran to wake his wife, and suggested at last that I myself should sleep in the cottage; but I preferred to remain in the open air. The miller's wife brought us milk, eggs, potatoes and bread. Soon the samovar boiled, and we began drinking tea. A mist had risen from the river; there was no wind; from all round came the cry of the corn-crake, and faint sounds from the mill-wheels of drops that dripped from the paddles and of water gurgling through the bars of the lock. We built a small fire on the ground. While Yermolai was baking the potatoes in the embers, I had time to fall into a doze. I was waked by a discreetly-subdued whispering near me. I lifted my head; before the fire, on a tub turned upside down, the miller's wife sat talking to my huntsman. By her dress, her movements, and her manner of speaking, I had already recognised that she had been in domestic service, and was neither peasant nor city-bred; but now for the first time I got a clear view of her features. She looked about thirty; her thin, pale face still showed the traces of remarkable beauty; what particularly charmed me was her eyes, large and mournful in expression. She was leaning her elbows on her knees, and had her face in her hands. Yermolai was sitting with his back to me, and thrusting sticks into the fire.

'They've the cattle-plague again at Zheltonhiny,' the miller's wife was saying; 'father Ivan's two cows are dead--Lord have mercy on them!'

'And how are your pigs doing?' asked Yermolai, after a brief pause.

'They're alive.'

'You ought to make me a present of a sucking pig.'

The miller's wife was silent for a while, then she sighed.

'Who is it you're with?' she asked.

'A gentleman from Kostomarovo.'

Yermolai threw a few pine twigs on the fire; they all caught fire at once, and a thick white smoke came puffing into his face.

'Why didn't your husband let us into the cottage?'

'He's afraid.'

'Afraid! the fat old tub! Arina Timofyevna, my darling, bring me a little glass of spirits.'

The miller's wife rose and vanished into the darkness. Yermolai began to sing in an undertone--

'When I went to see my sweetheart,

I wore out all my shoes.'

Arina returned with a small flask and a glass. Yermolai got up, crossed himself, and drank it off at a draught. 'Good!' was his comment.

The miller's wife sat down again on the tub.

'Well, Arina Timofyevna, are you still ill?'

'Yes.'

'What is it?'

'My cough troubles me at night.'

'The gentleman's asleep, it seems,' observed Yermolai after a short silence. 'Don't go to a doctor, Arina; it will be worse if you do.'

'Well, I am not going.'

'But come and pay me a visit.'

Arina hung down her head dejectedly.

'I will drive my wife out for the occasion,' continued Yermolai 'Upon my word, I will.'

'You had better wake the gentleman, Yermolai Petrovitch; you see, the potatoes are done.'

'Oh, let him snore,' observed my faithful servant indifferently; 'he's tired with walking, so he sleeps sound.'

I turned over in the hay. Yermolai got up and came to me. 'The potatoes are ready; will you come and eat them?'

I came out of the outhouse; the miller's wife got up from the tub and was going away. I addressed her.

'Have you kept this mill long?'

'It's two years since I came on Trinity day.'

'And where does your husband come from?'

Arina had not caught my question.

'Where's your husband from?' repeated Yermolai, raising his voice.

'From Byelev. He's a Byelev townsman.'

'And are you too from Byelev?'

'No, I'm a serf; I was a serf.'

'Whose?'

'Zvyerkoff was my master. Now I am free.'

'What Zvyerkoff?'

'Alexandr Selitch.'

'Weren't you his wife's lady's maid?'

'How did you know? Yes.'

I looked at Arina with redoubled curiosity and sympathy.

'I know your master,' I continued.

'Do you?' she replied in a low voice, and her head drooped.

I must tell the reader why I looked with such sympathy at Arina. During my stay at Petersburg I had become by chance acquainted with Mr. Zvyerkoff. He had a rather influential position, and was reputed a man of sense and education. He had a wife, fat, sentimental, lachrymose and spiteful--a vulgar and disagreeable creature; he had too a son, the very type of the young swell of to-day, pampered and stupid. The exterior of Mr. Zvyerkoff himself did not prepossess one in his favour; his little mouse-like eyes peeped slyly out of a broad, almost square, face; he had a large, prominent nose, with distended nostrils; his close-cropped grey hair stood up like a brush above his scowling brow; his thin lips were for ever twitching and smiling mawkishly. Mr. Zvyerkoff's favourite position was standing with his legs wide apart and his fat hands in his trouser pockets. Once I happened somehow to be driving alone with Mr. Zvyerkoff in a coach out of town. We fell into conversation. As a man of experience and of judgment, Mr. Zvyerkoff began to try to set me in 'the path of truth.'

'Allow me to observe to you,' he drawled at last; 'all you young people criticise and form judgments on everything at random; you have little knowledge of your own country; Russia, young gentlemen, is an unknown land to you; that's where it is!... You are for ever reading German. For instance, now you say this and that and the other about anything; for instance, about the house-serfs.... Very fine; I don't dispute it's all very fine; but you don't know them; you don't know the kind of people they are.' (Mr. Zvyerkoff blew his nose loudly and took a pinch of snuff.) 'Allow me to tell you as an illustration one little anecdote; it may perhaps interest you.' (Mr. Zvyerkoff cleared his throat.) 'You know, doubtless, what my wife is; it would be difficult, I should imagine, to find a more kind-hearted woman, you will agree. For her waiting-maids, existence is simply a perfect paradise, and no mistake about it.... But my wife has made it a rule never to keep married lady's maids. Certainly it would not do; children come--and one thing and the other--and how is a lady's maid to look after her mistress as she ought, to fit in with her ways; she is no longer able to do it; her mind is in other things. One must look at things through human nature. Well, we were driving once through our village, it must be--let me be correct--yes, fifteen years ago. We saw, at the bailiff's, a young girl, his daughter, very pretty indeed; something even--you know--something attractive in her manners. And my wife said to me: "Koko"--you understand, of course, that is her pet name for me-- "let us take this girl to Petersburg; I like her, Koko...." I said, "Let us take her, by all means." The bailiff, of course, was at our feet; he could not have expected such good fortune, you can imagine.... Well, the girl of course cried violently. Of course, it was hard for her at first; the parental home ... in fact ... there was nothing surprising in that. However, she soon got used to us: at first we put her in the maidservants' room; they trained her, of course. And what do you think? The girl made wonderful progress; my wife became simply devoted to her, promoted her at last above the rest to wait on herself ... observe.... And one must do her the justice to say, my wife had never such a maid, absolutely never; attentive, modest, and obedient--simply all that could be desired. But my wife, I must confess, spoilt her too much; she dressed her well, fed her from our own table, gave her tea to drink, and so on, as you can imagine! So she waited on my wife like this for ten years. Suddenly, one fine morning, picture to yourself, Arina--her name was Arina--rushes unannounced into my study, and flops down at my feet. That's a thing, I tell you plainly, I can't endure. No human being ought ever to lose sight of their personal dignity. Am I not right? What do you say? "Your honour, Alexandr Selitch, I beseech a favour of you." "What favour?" "Let me be married." I must confess I was taken aback. "But you know, you stupid, your mistress has no other lady's maid?" "I will wait on mistress as before." "Nonsense! nonsense! your mistress can't endure married lady's maids," "Malanya could take my place." "Pray don't argue." "I obey your will." I must confess it was quite a shock, I assure you, I am like that; nothing wounds me so-- nothing, I venture to say, wounds me so deeply as ingratitude. I need not tell you--you know what my wife is; an angel upon earth, goodness inexhaustible. One would fancy even the worst of men would be ashamed to hurt her. Well, I got rid of Arina. I thought, perhaps, she would come to her senses; I was unwilling, do you know, to believe in wicked, black ingratitude in anyone. What do you think? Within six months she thought fit to come to me again with the same request. I felt revolted. But imagine my amazement when, some time later, my wife comes to me in tears, so agitated that I felt positively alarmed. "What has happened?" "Arina.... You understand ... I am ashamed to tell it." ... "Impossible! ... Who is the man?" "Petrushka, the footman." My indignation broke out then. I am like that. I don't like half measures! Petrushka was not to blame. We might flog him, but in my opinion he was not to blame. Arina.... Well, well, well! what more's to be said? I gave orders, of course, that her hair should be cut off, she should be dressed in sackcloth, and sent into the country. My wife was deprived of an excellent lady's maid; but there was no help for it: immorality cannot be tolerated in a household in any case. Better to cut off the infected member at once. There, there! now you can judge the thing for yourself--you know that my wife is ... yes, yes, yes! indeed!... an angel! She had grown attached to Arina, and Arina knew it, and had the face to ... Eh? no, tell me ... eh? And what's the use of talking about it. Any way, there was no help for it. I, indeed--I, in particular, felt hurt, felt wounded for a long time by the ingratitude of this girl. Whatever you say--it's no good to look for feeling, for heart, in these people! You may feed the wolf as you will; he has always a hankering for the woods. Education, by all means! But I only wanted to give you an example....'

And Mr. Zvyerkoff, without finishing his sentence, turned away his head, and, wrapping himself more closely into his cloak, manfully repressed his involuntary emotion.

The reader now probably understands why I looked with sympathetic interest at Arina.

'Have you long been married to the miller?' I asked her at last.

'Two years.'

'How was it? Did your master allow it?'

'They bought my freedom.'

'Who?'

'Savely Alexyevitch.'

'Who is that?'

'My husband.' (Yermolai smiled to himself.) 'Has my master perhaps spoken to you of me?' added Arina, after a brief silence.

I did not know what reply to make to her question.

'Arina!' cried the miller from a distance. She got up and walked away.

'Is her husband a good fellow?' I asked Yermolai.

'So-so.'

'Have they any children?'

'There was one, but it died.'

'How was it? Did the miller take a liking to her? Did he give much to buy her freedom?'

'I don't know. She can read and write; in their business it's of use. I suppose he liked her.'

'And have you known her long?'

'Yes. I used to go to her master's. Their house isn't far from here.'

'And do you know the footman Petrushka?'

'Piotr Vassilyevitch? Of course, I knew him.'

'Where is he now?'

'He was sent for a soldier.'

We were silent for a while.

'She doesn't seem well?' I asked Yermolai at last.

'I should think not! To-morrow, I say, we shall have good sport. A little sleep now would do us no harm.'

A flock of wild ducks swept whizzing over our heads, and we heard them drop down into the river not far from us. It was now quite dark, and it began to be cold; in the thicket sounded the melodious notes of a nightingale. We buried ourselves in the hay and fell asleep.

III   RASPBERRY SPRING

At the beginning of August the heat often becomes insupportable. At that season, from twelve to three o'clock, the most determined and ardent sportsman is not able to hunt, and the most devoted dog begins to 'clean his master's spurs,' that is, to follow at his heels, his eyes painfully blinking, and his tongue hanging out to an exaggerated length; and in response to his master's reproaches he humbly wags his tail and shows his confusion in his face; but he does not run forward. I happened to be out hunting on exactly such a day. I had long been fighting against the temptation to lie down somewhere in the shade, at least for a moment; for a long time my indefatigable dog went on running about in the bushes, though he clearly did not himself expect much good from his feverish activity. The stifling heat compelled me at last to begin to think of husbanding our energies and strength. I managed to reach the little river Ista, which is already known to my indulgent readers, descended the steep bank, and walked along the damp, yellow sand in the direction of the spring, known to the whole neighbourhood as Raspberry Spring. This spring gushes out of a cleft in the bank, which widens out by degrees into a small but deep creek, and, twenty paces beyond it, falls with a merry babbling sound into the river; the short velvety grass is green about the source: the sun's rays scarcely ever reach its cold, silvery water. I came as far as the spring; a cup of birch-wood lay on the grass, left by a passing peasant for the public benefit. I quenched my thirst, lay down in the shade, and looked round. In the cave, which had been formed by the flowing of the stream into the river, and hence marked for ever with the trace of ripples, two old men were sitting with their backs to me. One, a rather stout and tall man in a neat dark-green coat and lined cap, was fishing; the other was thin and little; he wore a patched fustian coat and no cap; he held a little pot full of worms on his knees, and sometimes lifted his hand up to his grizzled little head, as though he wanted to protect it from the sun. I looked at him more attentively, and recognised in him Styopushka of Shumihino. I must ask the reader's leave to present this man to him.

A few miles from my place there is a large village called Shumihino, with a stone church, erected in the name of St. Kosmo and St. Damian. Facing this church there had once stood a large and stately manor-house, surrounded by various outhouses, offices, workshops, stables and coach-houses, baths and temporary kitchens, wings for visitors and for bailiffs, conservatories, swings for the people, and other more or less useful edifices. A family of rich landowners lived in this manor-house, and all went well with them, till suddenly one morning all this prosperity was burnt to ashes. The owners removed to another home; the place was deserted. The blackened site of the immense house was transformed into a kitchen-garden, cumbered up in parts by piles of bricks, the remains of the old foundations. A little hut had been hurriedly put together out of the beams that had escaped the fire; it was roofed with timber bought ten years before for the construction of a pavilion in the Gothic style; and the gardener, Mitrofan, with his wife Axinya and their seven children, was installed in it. Mitrofan received orders to send greens and garden-stuff for the master's table, a hundred and fifty miles away; Axinya was put in charge of a Tyrolese cow, which had been bought for a high price in Moscow, but had not given a drop of milk since its acquisition; a crested smoke-coloured drake too had been left in her hands, the solitary 'seignorial' bird; for the children, in consideration of their tender age, no special duties had been provided, a fact, however, which had not hindered them from growing up utterly lazy. It happened to me on two occasions to stay the night at this gardener's, and when I passed by I used to get cucumbers from him, which, for some unknown reason, were even in summer peculiar for their size, their poor, watery flavour, and their thick yellow skin. It was there I first saw Styopushka. Except Mitrofan and his family, and the old deaf churchwarden Gerasim, kept out of charity in a little room at the one-eyed soldier's widow's, not one man among the house-serfs had remained at Shumihino; for Styopushka, whom I intend to introduce to the reader, could not be classified under the special order of house-serfs, and hardly under the genus 'man' at all.

Every man has some kind of position in society, and at least some ties of some sort; every house-serf receives, if not wages, at least some so-called 'ration.' Styopushka had absolutely no means of subsistence of any kind; had no relationship to anyone; no one knew of his existence. This man had not even a past; there was no story told of him; he had probably never been enrolled on a census-revision. There were vague rumours that he had once belonged to someone as a valet; but who he was, where he came from, who was his father, and how he had come to be one of the Shumihino people; in what way he had come by the fustian coat he had worn from immemorial times; where he lived and what he lived on--on all these questions no one had the least idea; and, to tell the truth, no one took any interest in the subject. Grandfather Trofimitch, who knew all the pedigrees of all the house-serfs in the direct line to the fourth generation, had once indeed been known to say that he remembered that Styopushka was related to a Turkish woman whom the late master, the brigadier Alexy Romanitch had been pleased to bring home from a campaign in the baggage waggon. Even on holidays, days of general money-giving and of feasting on buckwheat dumplings and vodka, after the old Russian fashion--even on such days Styopushka did not put in an appearance at the trestle-tables nor at the barrels; he did not make his bow nor kiss the master's hand, nor toss off to the master's health and under the master's eye a glass filled by the fat hands of the bailiff. Some kind soul who passed by him might share an unfinished bit of dumpling with the poor beggar, perhaps. At Easter they said 'Christ is risen!' to him; but he did not pull up his greasy sleeve, and bring out of the depths of his pocket a coloured egg, to offer it, panting and blinking, to his young masters or to the mistress herself. He lived in summer in a little shed behind the chicken-house, and in winter in the ante-room of the bathhouse; in the bitter frosts he spent the night in the hayloft. The house-serfs had grown used to seeing him; sometimes they gave him a kick, but no one ever addressed a remark to him; as for him, he seems never to have opened his lips from the time of his birth. After the conflagration, this forsaken creature sought a refuge at the gardener Mitrofan's. The gardener left him alone; he did not say 'Live with me,' but he did not drive him away. And Styopushka did not live at the gardener's; his abode was the garden. He moved and walked about quite noiselessly; he sneezed and coughed behind his hand, not without apprehension; he was for ever busy and going stealthily to and fro like an ant; and all to get food-- simply food to eat. And indeed, if he had not toiled from morning till night for his living, our poor friend would certainly have died of hunger. It's a sad lot not to know in the morning what you will find to eat before night! Sometimes Styopushka sits under the hedge and gnaws a radish or sucks a carrot, or shreds up some dirty cabbage-stalks; or he drags a bucket of water along, for some object or other, groaning as he goes; or he lights a fire under a small pot, and throws in some little black scraps which he takes from out of the bosom of his coat; or he is hammering in his little wooden den--driving in a nail, putting up a shelf for bread. And all this he does silently, as though on the sly: before you can look round, he's in hiding again. Sometimes he suddenly disappears for a couple of days; but of course no one notices his absence.... Then, lo and behold! he is there again, somewhere under the hedge, stealthily kindling a fire of sticks under a kettle. He had a small face, yellowish eyes, hair coming down to his eyebrows, a sharp nose, large transparent ears, like a bat's, and a beard that looked as if it were a fortnight's growth, and never grew more nor less. This, then, was Styopushka, whom I met on the bank of the Ista in company with another old man.

I went up to him, wished him good-day, and sat down beside him. Styopushka's companion too I recognised as an acquaintance; he was a freed serf of Count Piotr Ilitch's, one Mihal Savelitch, nicknamed Tuman (i.e. fog). He lived with a consumptive Bolhovsky man, who kept an inn, where I had several times stayed. Young officials and other persons of leisure travelling on the Orel highroad (merchants, buried in their striped rugs, have other things to do) may still see at no great distance from the large village of Troitska, and almost on the highroad, an immense two-storied wooden house, completely deserted, with its roof falling in and its windows closely stuffed up. At mid-day in bright, sunny weather nothing can be imagined more melancholy than this ruin. Here there once lived Count Piotr Ilitch, a rich grandee of the olden time, renowned for his hospitality. At one time the whole province used to meet at his house, to dance and make merry to their heart's content to the deafening sound of a home-trained orchestra, and the popping of rockets and Roman candles; and doubtless more than one aged lady sighs as she drives by the deserted palace of the boyar and recalls the old days and her vanished youth. The count long continued to give balls, and to walk about with an affable smile among the crowd of fawning guests; but his property, unluckily, was not enough to last his whole life. When he was entirely ruined, he set off to Petersburg to try for a post for himself, and died in a room at a hotel, without having gained anything by his efforts. Tuman had been a steward of his, and had received his freedom already in the count's lifetime. He was a man of about seventy, with a regular and pleasant face. He was almost continually smiling, as only men of the time of Catherine ever do smile--a smile at once stately and indulgent; in speaking, he slowly opened and closed his lips, winked genially with his eyes, and spoke slightly through his nose. He blew his nose and took snuff too in a leisurely fashion, as though he were doing something serious.

'Well, Mihal Savelitch,' I began, 'have you caught any fish?'

'Here, if you will deign to look in the basket: I have caught two perch and five roaches.... Show them, Styopka.'

Styopushka stretched out the basket to me.

'How are you, Styopka?' I asked him.

'Oh--oh--not--not--not so badly, your honour,' answered Stepan, stammering as though he had a heavy weight on his tongue.

'And is Mitrofan well?'

'Well--yes, yes--your honour.'

The poor fellow turned away.

'But there are not many bites,' remarked Tuman; 'it's so fearfully hot; the fish are all tired out under the bushes; they're asleep. Put on a worm, Styopka.' (Styopushka took out a worm, laid it on his open hand, struck it two or three times, put it on the hook, spat on it, and gave it to Tuman.) 'Thanks, Styopka.... And you, your honour,' he continued, turning to me, 'are pleased to be out hunting?'

'As you see.'

'Ah--and is your dog there English or German?'

The old man liked to show off on occasion, as though he would say, 'I, too, have lived in the world!'

'I don't know what breed it is, but it's a good dog.'

'Ah! and do you go out with the hounds too?'

'Yes, I have two leashes of hounds.'

Tuman smiled and shook his head.

'That's just it; one man is devoted to dogs, and another doesn't want them for anything. According to my simple notions, I fancy dogs should be kept rather for appearance' sake ... and all should be in style too; horses too should be in style, and huntsmen in style, as they ought to be, and all. The late count--God's grace be with him!-- was never, I must own, much of a hunter; but he kept dogs, and twice a year he was pleased to go out with them. The huntsmen assembled in the courtyard, in red caftans trimmed with galloon, and blew their horns; his excellency would be pleased to come out, and his excellency's horse would be led up; his excellency would mount, and the chief huntsman puts his feet in the stirrups, takes his hat off, and puts the reins in his hat to offer them to his excellency. His excellency is pleased to click his whip like this, and the huntsmen give a shout, and off they go out of the gate away. A huntsman rides behind the count, and holds in a silken leash two of the master's favourite dogs, and looks after them well, you may fancy.... And he, too, this huntsman, sits up high, on a Cossack saddle: such a red-cheeked fellow he was, and rolled his eyes like this.... And there were guests too, you may be sure, on such occasions, and entertainment, and ceremonies observed.... Ah, he's got away, the Asiatic!' He interrupted himself suddenly, drawing in his line.

'They say the count used to live pretty freely in his day?' I asked.

The old man spat on the worm and lowered the line in again.

'He was a great gentleman, as is well-known. At times the persons of the first rank, one may say, at Petersburg, used to visit him. With coloured ribbons on their breasts they used to sit down to table and eat. Well, he knew how to entertain them. He called me sometimes. "Tuman," says he, "I want by to-morrow some live sturgeon; see there are some, do you hear?" "Yes, your excellency." Embroidered coats, wigs, canes, perfumes, eau de Cologne of the best sort, snuff-boxes, huge pictures: he would order them all from Paris itself! When he gave a banquet, God Almighty, Lord of my being! there were fireworks, and carriages driving up! They even fired off the cannon. The orchestra alone consisted of forty men. He kept a German as conductor of the band, but the German gave himself dreadful airs; he wanted to eat at the same table as the masters; so his excellency gave orders to get rid of him! "My musicians," says he, "can do their work even without a conductor." Of course he was master. Then they would fall to dancing, and dance till morning, especially at the ecossaise-matrador. ... Ah-- ah--there's one caught!' (The old man drew a small perch out of the water.) 'Here you are, Styopka! The master was all a master should be,' continued the old man, dropping his line in again, 'and he had a kind heart too. He would give you a blow at times, and before you could look round, he'd forgotten it already. There was only one thing: he kept mistresses. Ugh, those mistresses! God forgive them! They were the ruin of him too; and yet, you know, he took them most generally from a low station. You would fancy they would not want much? Not a bit--they must have everything of the most expensive in all Europe! One may say, "Why shouldn't he live as he likes; it's the master's business" ... but there was no need to ruin himself. There was one especially; Akulina was her name. She is dead now; God rest her soul! the daughter of the watchman at Sitoia; and such a vixen! She would slap the count's face sometimes. She simply bewitched him. My nephew she sent for a soldier; he spilt some chocolate on a new dress of hers ... and he wasn't the only one she served so. Ah, well, those were good times, though!' added the old man with a deep sigh. His head drooped forward and he was silent.

'Your master, I see, was severe, then?' I began after a brief silence.

'That was the fashion then, your honour,' he replied, shaking his head.

'That sort of thing is not done now?' I observed, not taking my eyes off him.

He gave me a look askance.

'Now, surely it's better,' he muttered, and let out his line further.

We were sitting in the shade; but even in the shade it was stifling. The sultry atmosphere was faint and heavy; one lifted one's burning face uneasily, seeking a breath of wind; but there was no wind. The sun beat down from blue and darkening skies; right opposite us, on the other bank, was a yellow field of oats, overgrown here and there with wormwood; not one ear of the oats quivered. A little lower down a peasant's horse stood in the river up to its knees, and slowly shook its wet tail; from time to time, under an overhanging bush, a large fish shot up, bringing bubbles to the surface, and gently sank down to the bottom, leaving a slight ripple behind it. The grasshoppers chirped in the scorched grass; the quail's cry sounded languid and reluctant; hawks sailed smoothly over the meadows, often resting in the same spot, rapidly fluttering their wings and opening their tails into a fan. We sat motionless, overpowered with the heat. Suddenly there was a sound behind us in the creek; someone came down to the spring. I looked round, and saw a peasant of about fifty, covered with dust, in a smock, and wearing bast slippers; he carried a wickerwork pannier and a cloak on his shoulders. He went down to the spring, drank thirstily, and got up.

'Ah, Vlass!' cried Tuman, staring at him; 'good health to you, friend! Where has God sent you from?'

'Good health to you, Mihal Savelitch!' said the peasant, coming nearer to us; 'from a long way off.'

'Where have you been?' Tuman asked him.

'I have been to Moscow, to my master.'

'What for?'

'I went to ask him a favour.'

'What about?'

'Oh, to lessen my rent, or to let me work it out in labour, or to put me on another piece of land, or something.... My son is dead--so I can't manage it now alone.'

'Your son is dead?'

'He is dead. My son,' added the peasant, after a pause, 'lived in Moscow as a cabman; he paid, I must confess, rent for me.'

'Then are you now paying rent?'

'Yes, we pay rent.'

'What did your master say?'

'What did the master say! He drove me away! Says he, "How dare you come straight to me; there is a bailiff for such things. You ought first," says he, "to apply to the bailiff ... and where am I to put you on other land? You first," says he, "bring the debt you owe." He was angry altogether.'

'What then--did you come back?'

'I came back. I wanted to find out if my son had not left any goods of his own, but I couldn't get a straight answer. I say to his employer, "I am Philip's father"; and he says, "What do I know about that? And your son," says he, "left nothing; he was even in debt to me." So I came away.'

The peasant related all this with a smile, as though he were speaking of someone else; but tears were starting into his small, screwed-up eyes, and his lips were quivering.

'Well, are you going home then now?'

'Where can I go? Of course I'm going home. My wife, I suppose, is pretty well starved by now.'

'You should--then,' Styopushka said suddenly. He grew confused, was silent, and began to rummage in the worm-pot.

'And shall you go to the bailiff?' continued Tuman, looking with some amazement at Styopka.

'What should I go to him for?--I'm in arrears as it is. My son was ill for a year before his death; he could not pay even his own rent. But it can't hurt me; they can get nothing from me.... Yes, my friend, you can be as cunning as you please--I'm cleaned out!' (The peasant began to laugh.) 'Kintlyan Semenitch'll have to be clever if--'

Vlass laughed again.

'Oh! things are in a sad way, brother Vlass,' Tuman ejaculated deliberately.

'Sad! No!' (Vlass's voice broke.) 'How hot it is!' he went on, wiping his face with his sleeve.

'Who is your master?' I asked him.

'Count Valerian Petrovitch.'

'The son of Piotr Ilitch?'

'The son of Piotr Ilitch,' replied Tuman. 'Piotr Hitch gave him Vlass's village in his lifetime.'

'Is he well?'

'He is well, thank God!' replied Vlass. 'He has grown so red, and his face looks as though it were padded.'

'You see, your honour,' continued Tuman, turning to me, 'it would be very well near Moscow, but it's a different matter to pay rent here.'

'And what is the rent for you altogether?'

'Ninety-five roubles,' muttered Vlass.

'There, you see; and it's the least bit of land; all there is is the master's forest.'

'And that, they say, they have sold,' observed the peasant.

'There, you see. Styopka, give me a worm. Why, Styopka, are you asleep --eh?'

Styopushka started. The peasant sat down by us. We sank into silence again. On the other bank someone was singing a song--but such a mournful one. Our poor Vlass grew deeply dejected.

Half-an-hour later we parted.

IV   THE DISTRICT DOCTOR

One day in autumn on my way back from a remote part of the country I caught cold and fell ill. Fortunately the fever attacked me in the district town at the inn; I sent for the doctor. In half-an-hour the district doctor appeared, a thin, dark-haired man of middle height. He prescribed me the usual sudorific, ordered a mustard-plaster to be put on, very deftly slid a five-rouble note up his sleeve, coughing drily and looking away as he did so, and then was getting up to go home, but somehow fell into talk and remained. I was exhausted with feverishness; I foresaw a sleepless night, and was glad of a little chat with a pleasant companion. Tea was served. My doctor began to converse freely. He was a sensible fellow, and expressed himself with vigour and some humour. Queer things happen in the world: you may live a long while with some people, and be on friendly terms with them, and never once speak openly with them from your soul; with others you have scarcely time to get acquainted, and all at once you are pouring out to him--or he to you--all your secrets, as though you were at confession. I don't know how I gained the confidence of my new friend--any way, with nothing to lead up to it, he told me a rather curious incident; and here I will report his tale for the information of the indulgent reader. I will try to tell it in the doctor's own words.

'You don't happen to know,' he began in a weak and quavering voice (the common result of the use of unmixed Berezov snuff); 'you don't happen to know the judge here, Mylov, Pavel Lukitch?... You don't know him?... Well, it's all the same.' (He cleared his throat and rubbed his eyes.) 'Well, you see, the thing happened, to tell you exactly without mistake, in Lent, at the very time of the thaws. I was sitting at his house--our judge's, you know--playing preference. Our judge is a good fellow, and fond of playing preference. Suddenly' (the doctor made frequent use of this word, suddenly) 'they tell me, "There's a servant asking for you." I say, "What does he want?" They say, "He has brought a note--it must be from a patient." "Give me the note," I say. So it is from a patient--well and good--you understand--it's our bread and butter. ... But this is how it was: a lady, a widow, writes to me; she says, "My daughter is dying. Come, for God's sake!" she says; "and the horses have been sent for you." ... Well, that's all right. But she was twenty miles from the town, and it was midnight out of doors, and the roads in such a state, my word! And as she was poor herself, one could not expect more than two silver roubles, and even that problematic; and perhaps it might only be a matter of a roll of linen and a sack of oatmeal in payment. However, duty, you know, before everything: a fellow-creature may be dying. I hand over my cards at once to Kalliopin, the member of the provincial commission, and return home. I look; a wretched little trap was standing at the steps, with peasant's horses, fat--too fat--and their coat as shaggy as felt; and the coachman sitting with his cap off out of respect. Well, I think to myself, "It's clear, my friend, these patients aren't rolling in riches." ... You smile; but I tell you, a poor man like me has to take everything into consideration.... If the coachman sits like a prince, and doesn't touch his cap, and even sneers at you behind his beard, and flicks his whip--then you may bet on six roubles. But this case, I saw, had a very different air. However, I think there's no help for it; duty before everything. I snatch up the most necessary drugs, and set off. Will you believe it? I only just managed to get there at all. The road was infernal: streams, snow, watercourses, and the dyke had suddenly burst there--that was the worst of it! However, I arrived at last. It was a little thatched house. There was a light in the windows; that meant they expected me. I was met by an old lady, very venerable, in a cap. "Save her!" she says; "she is dying." I say, "Pray don't distress yourself--Where is the invalid?" "Come this way." I see a clean little room, a lamp in the corner; on the bed a girl of twenty, unconscious. She was in a burning heat, and breathing heavily--it was fever. There were two other girls, her sisters, scared and in tears. "Yesterday," they tell me, "she was perfectly well and had a good appetite; this morning she complained of her head, and this evening, suddenly, you see, like this." I say again: "Pray don't be uneasy." It's a doctor's duty, you know--and I went up to her and bled her, told them to put on a mustard-plaster, and prescribed a mixture. Meantime I looked at her; I looked at her, you know--there, by God! I had never seen such a face!--she was a beauty, in a word! I felt quite shaken with pity. Such lovely features; such eyes!... But, thank God! she became easier; she fell into a perspiration, seemed to come to her senses, looked round, smiled, and passed her hand over her face.... Her sisters bent over her. They ask, "How are you?" "All right," she says, and turns away. I looked at her; she had fallen asleep. "Well," I say, "now the patient should be left alone." So we all went out on tiptoe; only a maid remained, in case she was wanted. In the parlour there was a samovar standing on the table, and a bottle of rum; in our profession one can't get on without it. They gave me tea; asked me to stop the night. ... I consented: where could I go, indeed, at that time of night? The old lady kept groaning. "What is it?" I say; "she will live; don't worry yourself; you had better take a little rest yourself; it is about two o'clock." "But will you send to wake me if anything happens?" "Yes, yes." The old lady went away, and the girls too went to their own room; they made up a bed for me in the parlour. Well, I went to bed--but I could not get to sleep, for a wonder! for in reality I was very tired. I could not get my patient out of my head. At last I could not put up with it any longer; I got up suddenly; I think to myself, "I will go and see how the patient is getting on." Her bedroom was next to the parlour. Well, I got up, and gently opened the door--how my heart beat! I looked in: the servant was asleep, her mouth wide open, and even snoring, the wretch! but the patient lay with her face towards me, and her arms flung wide apart, poor girl! I went up to her ... when suddenly she opened her eyes and stared at me! "Who is it? who is it?" I was in confusion. "Don't be alarmed, madam," I say; "I am the doctor; I have come to see how you feel." "You the doctor?" "Yes, the doctor; your mother sent for me from the town; we have bled you, madam; now pray go to sleep, and in a day or two, please God! we will set you on your feet again." "Ah, yes, yes, doctor, don't let me die.... please, please." "Why do you talk like that? God bless you!" She is in a fever again, I think to myself; I felt her pulse; yes, she was feverish. She looked at me, and then took me by the hand. "I will tell you why I don't want to die; I will tell you.... Now we are alone; and only, please don't you ... not to anyone ... Listen...." I bent down; she moved her lips quite to my ear; she touched my cheek with her hair--I confess my head went round--and began to whisper.... I could make out nothing of it.... Ah, she was delirious!... She whispered and whispered, but so quickly, and as if it were not in Russian; at last she finished, and shivering dropped her head on the pillow, and threatened me with her finger: "Remember, doctor, to no one." I calmed her somehow, gave her something to drink, waked the servant, and went away.'

At this point the doctor again took snuff with exasperated energy, and for a moment seemed stupefied by its effects.

'However,' he continued, 'the next day, contrary to my expectations, the patient was no better. I thought and thought, and suddenly decided to remain there, even though my other patients were expecting me.... And you know one can't afford to disregard that; one's practice suffers if one does. But, in the first place, the patient was really in danger; and secondly, to tell the truth, I felt strongly drawn to her. Besides, I liked the whole family. Though they were really badly off, they were singularly, I may say, cultivated people.... Their father had been a learned man, an author; he died, of course, in poverty, but he had managed before he died to give his children an excellent education; he left a lot of books too. Either because I looked after the invalid very carefully, or for some other reason; any way, I can venture to say all the household loved me as if I were one of the family.... Meantime the roads were in a worse state than ever; all communications, so to say, were cut off completely; even medicine could with difficulty be got from the town.... The sick girl was not getting better. ... Day after day, and day after day ... but ... here....' (The doctor made a brief pause.) 'I declare I don't know how to tell you.' ... (He again took snuff, coughed, and swallowed a little tea.) 'I will tell you without beating about the bush. My patient ... how should I say?... Well, she had fallen in love with me ... or, no, it was not that she was in love ... however ... really, how should one say?' (The doctor looked down and grew red.) 'No,' he went on quickly, 'in love, indeed! A man should not over-estimate himself. She was an educated girl, clever and well- read, and I had even forgotten my Latin, one may say, completely. As to appearance' (the doctor looked himself over with a smile) 'I am nothing to boast of there either. But God Almighty did not make me a fool; I don't take black for white; I know a thing or two; I could see very clearly, for instance, that Alexandra Andreevna--that was her name--did not feel love for me, but had a friendly, so to say, inclination--a respect or something for me. Though she herself perhaps mistook this sentiment, any way this was her attitude; you may form your own judgment of it. But,' added the doctor, who had brought out all these disconnected sentences without taking breath, and with obvious embarrassment, 'I seem to be wandering rather--you won't understand anything like this.... There, with your leave, I will relate it all in order.'

He drank off a glass of tea, and began in a calmer voice.

'Well, then. My patient kept getting worse and worse. You are not a doctor, my good sir; you cannot understand what passes in a poor fellow's heart, especially at first, when he begins to suspect that the disease is getting the upper hand of him. What becomes of his belief in himself? You suddenly grow so timid; it's indescribable. You fancy then that you have forgotten everything you knew, and that the patient has no faith in you, and that other people begin to notice how distracted you are, and tell you the symptoms with reluctance; that they are looking at you suspiciously, whispering.... Ah! it's horrid! There must be a remedy, you think, for this disease, if one could find it. Isn't this it? You try--no, that's not it! You don't allow the medicine the necessary time to do good.... You clutch at one thing, then at another. Sometimes you take up a book of medical prescriptions--here it is, you think! Sometimes, by Jove, you pick one out by chance, thinking to leave it to fate.... But meantime a fellow-creature's dying, and another doctor would have saved him. "We must have a consultation," you say; "I will not take the responsibility on myself." And what a fool you look at such times! Well, in time you learn to bear it; it's nothing to you. A man has died--but it's not your fault; you treated him by the rules. But what's still more torture to you is to see blind faith in you, and to feel yourself that you are not able to be of use. Well, it was just this blind faith that the whole of Alexandra Andreevna's family had in me; they had forgotten to think that their daughter was in danger. I, too, on my side assure them that it's nothing, but meantime my heart sinks into my boots. To add to our troubles, the roads were in such a state that the coachman was gone for whole days together to get medicine. And I never left the patient's room; I could not tear myself away; I tell her amusing stories, you know, and play cards with her. I watch by her side at night. The old mother thanks me with tears in her eyes; but I think to myself, "I don't deserve your gratitude." I frankly confess to you--there is no object in concealing it now-- I was in love with my patient. And Alexandra Andreevna had grown fond of me; she would not sometimes let anyone be in her room but me. She began to talk to me, to ask me questions; where I had studied, how I lived, who are my people, whom I go to see. I feel that she ought not to talk; but to forbid her to--to forbid her resolutely, you know--I could not. Sometimes I held my head in my hands, and asked myself, "What are you doing, villain?" ... And she would take my hand and hold it, give me a long, long look, and turn away, sigh, and say, "How good you are!" Her hands were so feverish, her eyes so large and languid.... "Yes," she says, "you are a good, kind man; you are not like our neighbours.... No, you are not like that. ... Why did I not know you till now!" "Alexandra Andreevna, calm yourself," I say.... "I feel, believe me, I don't know how I have gained ... but there, calm yourself.... All will be right; you will be well again." And meanwhile I must tell you,' continued the doctor, bending forward and raising his eyebrows, 'that they associated very little with the neighbours, because the smaller people were not on their level, and pride hindered them from being friendly with the rich. I tell you, they were an exceptionally cultivated family; so you know it was gratifying for me. She would only take her medicine from my hands ... she would lift herself up, poor girl, with my aid, take it, and gaze at me.... My heart felt as if it were bursting. And meanwhile she was growing worse and worse, worse and worse, all the time; she will die, I think to myself; she must die. Believe me, I would sooner have gone to the grave myself; and here were her mother and sisters watching me, looking into my eyes ... and their faith in me was wearing away. "Well? how is she?" "Oh, all right, all right!" All right, indeed! My mind was failing me. Well, I was sitting one night alone again by my patient. The maid was sitting there too, and snoring away in full swing; I can't find fault with the poor girl, though; she was worn out too. Alexandra Andreevna had felt very unwell all the evening; she was very feverish. Until midnight she kept tossing about; at last she seemed to fall asleep; at least, she lay still without stirring. The lamp was burning in the corner before the holy image. I sat there, you know, with my head bent; I even dozed a little. Suddenly it seemed as though someone touched me in the side; I turned round.... Good God! Alexandra Andreevna was gazing with intent eyes at me ... her lips parted, her cheeks seemed burning. "What is it?" "Doctor, shall I die?" "Merciful Heavens!" "No, doctor, no; please don't tell me I shall live ... don't say so.... If you knew.... Listen! for God's sake don't conceal my real position," and her breath came so fast. "If I can know for certain that I must die ... then I will tell you all--all!" "Alexandra Andreevna, I beg!" "Listen; I have not been asleep at all ... I have been looking at you a long while.... For God's sake! ... I believe in you; you are a good man, an honest man; I entreat you by all that is sacred in the world--tell me the truth! If you knew how important it is for me.... Doctor, for God's sake tell me.... Am I in danger?" "What can I tell you, Alexandra Andreevna, pray?" "For God's sake, I beseech you!" "I can't disguise from you," I say, "Alexandra Andreevna; you are certainly in danger; but God is merciful." "I shall die, I shall die." And it seemed as though she were pleased; her face grew so bright; I was alarmed. "Don't be afraid, don't be afraid! I am not frightened of death at all." She suddenly sat up and leaned on her elbow. "Now ... yes, now I can tell you that I thank you with my whole heart ... that you are kind and good-- that I love you!" I stare at her, like one possessed; it was terrible for me, you know. "Do you hear, I love you!" "Alexandra Andreevna, how have I deserved--" "No, no, you don't--you don't understand me." ... And suddenly she stretched out her arms, and taking my head in her hands, she kissed it.... Believe me, I almost screamed aloud.... I threw myself on my knees, and buried my head in the pillow. She did not speak; her fingers trembled in my hair; I listen; she is weeping. I began to soothe her, to assure her.... I really don't know what I did say to her. "You will wake up the girl," I say to her; "Alexandra Andreevna, I thank you ... believe me ... calm yourself." "Enough, enough!" she persisted; "never mind all of them; let them wake, then; let them come in--it does not matter; I am dying, you see.... And what do you fear? why are you afraid? Lift up your head.... Or, perhaps, you don't love me; perhaps I am wrong.... In that case, forgive me." "Alexandra Andreevna, what are you saying!... I love you, Alexandra Andreevna." She looked straight into my eyes, and opened her arms wide. "Then take me in your arms." I tell you frankly, I don't know how it was I did not go mad that night. I feel that my patient is killing herself; I see that she is not fully herself; I understand, too, that if she did not consider herself on the point of death, she would never have thought of me; and, indeed, say what you will, it's hard to die at twenty without having known love; this was what was torturing her; this was why, in despair, she caught at me--do you understand now? But she held me in her arms, and would not let me go. "Have pity on me, Alexandra Andreevna, and have pity on yourself," I say. "Why," she says; "what is there to think of? You know I must die." ... This she repeated incessantly.... "If I knew that I should return to life, and be a proper young lady again, I should be ashamed ... of course, ashamed ... but why now?" "But who has said you will die?" "Oh, no, leave off! you will not deceive me; you don't know how to lie--look at your face." ... "You shall live, Alexandra Andreevna; I will cure you; we will ask your mother's blessing ... we will be united--we will be happy." "No, no, I have your word; I must die ... you have promised me ... you have told me." ... It was cruel for me--cruel for many reasons. And see what trifling things can do sometimes; it seems nothing at all, but it's painful. It occurred to her to ask me, what is my name; not my surname, but my first name. I must needs be so unlucky as to be called Trifon. Yes, indeed; Trifon Ivanitch. Every one in the house called me doctor. However, there's no help for it. I say, "Trifon, madam." She frowned, shook her head, and muttered something in French--ah, something unpleasant, of course!--and then she laughed--disagreeably too. Well, I spent the whole night with her in this way. Before morning I went away, feeling as though I were mad. When I went again into her room it was daytime, after morning tea. Good God! I could scarcely recognise her; people are laid in their grave looking better than that. I swear to you, on my honour, I don't understand--I absolutely don't understand--now, how I lived through that experience. Three days and nights my patient still lingered on. And what nights! What things she said to me! And on the last night--only imagine to yourself--I was sitting near her, and kept praying to God for one thing only: "Take her," I said, "quickly, and me with her." Suddenly the old mother comes unexpectedly into the room. I had already the evening before told her--the mother--there was little hope, and it would be well to send for a priest. When the sick girl saw her mother she said: "It's very well you have come; look at us, we love one another--we have given each other our word." "What does she say, doctor? what does she say?" I turned livid. "She is wandering," I say; "the fever." But she: "Hush, hush; you told me something quite different just now, and have taken my ring. Why do you pretend? My mother is good--she will forgive --she will understand--and I am dying.... I have no need to tell lies; give me your hand." I jumped up and ran out of the room. The old lady, of course, guessed how it was.

'I will not, however, weary you any longer, and to me too, of course, it's painful to recall all this. My patient passed away the next day. God rest her soul!' the doctor added, speaking quickly and with a sigh. 'Before her death she asked her family to go out and leave me alone with her.'

'"Forgive me," she said; "I am perhaps to blame towards you ... my illness ... but believe me, I have loved no one more than you ... do not forget me ... keep my ring."'

The doctor turned away; I took his hand.

'Ah!' he said, 'let us talk of something else, or would you care to play preference for a small stake? It is not for people like me to give way to exalted emotions. There's only one thing for me to think of; how to keep the children from crying and the wife from scolding. Since then, you know, I have had time to enter into lawful wed-lock, as they say.... Oh ... I took a merchant's daughter--seven thousand for her dowry. Her name's Akulina; it goes well with Trifon. She is an ill- tempered woman, I must tell you, but luckily she's asleep all day.... Well, shall it be preference?'

We sat down to preference for halfpenny points. Trifon Ivanitch won two roubles and a half from me, and went home late, well pleased with his success.

V   MY NEIGHBOUR RADILOV

For the autumn, woodcocks often take refuge in old gardens of lime- trees. There are a good many such gardens among us, in the province of Orel. Our forefathers, when they selected a place for habitation, invariably marked out two acres of good ground for a fruit-garden, with avenues of lime-trees. Within the last fifty, or seventy years at most, these mansions--'noblemen's nests,' as they call them--have gradually disappeared off the face of the earth; the houses are falling to pieces, or have been sold for the building materials; the stone outhouses have become piles of rubbish; the apple-trees are dead and turned into firewood, the hedges and fences are pulled up. Only the lime-trees grow in all their glory as before, and with ploughed fields all round them, tell a tale to this light-hearted generation of 'our fathers and brothers who have lived before us.'

A magnificent tree is such an old lime-tree.... Even the merciless axe of the Russian peasant spares it. Its leaves are small, its powerful limbs spread wide in all directions; there is perpetual shade under them.

Once, as I was wandering about the fields after partridges with Yermolai, I saw some way off a deserted garden, and turned into it. I had hardly crossed its borders when a snipe rose up out of a bush with a clatter. I fired my gun, and at the same instant, a few paces from me, I heard a shriek; the frightened face of a young girl peeped out for a second from behind the trees, and instantly disappeared. Yermolai ran up to me: 'Why are you shooting here? there is a landowner living here.'

Before I had time to answer him, before my dog had had time to bring me, with dignified importance, the bird I had shot, swift footsteps were heard, and a tall man with moustaches came out of the thicket and stopped, with an air of displeasure, before me. I made my apologies as best I could, gave him my name, and offered him the bird that had been killed on his domains.

'Very well,' he said to me with a smile; 'I will take your game, but only on one condition: that you will stay and dine with us.'

I must confess I was not greatly delighted at his proposition, but it was impossible to refuse.

'I am a landowner here, and your neighbour, Radilov; perhaps you have heard of me?' continued my new acquaintance; 'to-day is Sunday, and we shall be sure to have a decent dinner, otherwise I would not have invited you.'

I made such a reply as one does make in such circumstances, and turned to follow him. A little path that had lately been cleared soon led us out of the grove of lime-trees; we came into the kitchen-garden. Between the old apple-trees and gooseberry bushes were rows of curly whitish-green cabbages; the hop twined its tendrils round high poles; there were thick ranks of brown twigs tangled over with dried peas; large flat pumpkins seemed rolling on the ground; cucumbers showed yellow under their dusty angular leaves; tall nettles were waving along the hedge; in two or three places grew clumps of tartar honeysuckle, elder, and wild rose--the remnants of former flower-beds. Near a small fish-pond, full of reddish and slimy water, we saw the well, surrounded by puddles. Ducks were busily splashing and waddling about these puddles; a dog blinking and twitching in every limb was gnawing a bone in the meadow, where a piebald cow was lazily chewing the grass, from time to time flicking its tail over its lean back. The little path turned to one side; from behind thick willows and birches we caught sight of a little grey old house, with a boarded roof and a winding flight of steps. Radilov stopped short.

'But,' he said, with a good-humoured and direct look in my face,' on second thoughts ... perhaps you don't care to come and see me, after all.... In that case--'

I did not allow him to finish, but assured him that, on the contrary, it would be a great pleasure to me to dine with him.

'Well, you know best.'

We went into the house. A young man in a long coat of stout blue cloth met us on the steps. Radilov at once told him to bring Yermolai some vodka; my huntsman made a respectful bow to the back of the munificent host. From the hall, which was decorated with various parti-coloured pictures and check curtains, we went into a small room--Radilov's study. I took off my hunting accoutrements, and put my gun in a corner; the young man in the long-skirted coat busily brushed me down.

'Well, now, let us go into the drawing-room.' said Radilov cordially. 'I will make you acquainted with my mother.'

I walked after him. In the drawing-room, in the sofa in the centre of the room, was sitting an old lady of medium height, in a cinnamon- coloured dress and a white cap, with a thinnish, kind old face, and a timid, mournful expression.

'Here, mother, let me introduce to you our neighbour....'

The old lady got up and made me a bow, not letting go out of her withered hands a fat worsted reticule that looked like a sack.

'Have you been long in our neighbourhood?' she asked, in a weak and gentle voice, blinking her eyes.

'No, not long.'

'Do you intend to remain here long?'

'Till the winter, I think.'

The old lady said no more.

'And here,' interposed Radilov, indicating to me a tall and thin man, whom I had not noticed on entering the drawing-room, 'is Fyodor Miheitch. ... Come, Fedya, give the visitor a specimen of your art. Why have you hidden yourself away in that corner?'

Fyodor Miheitch got up at once from his chair, fetched a wretched little fiddle from the window, took the bow--not by the end, as is usual, but by the middle--put the fiddle to his chest, shut his eyes, and fell to dancing, singing a song, and scraping on the strings. He looked about seventy; a thin nankin overcoat flapped pathetically about his dry and bony limbs. He danced, at times skipping boldly, and then dropping his little bald head with his scraggy neck stretched out as if he were dying, stamping his feet on the ground, and sometimes bending his knees with obvious difficulty. A voice cracked with age came from his toothless mouth.

Radilov must have guessed from the expression of my face that Fedya's 'art' did not give me much pleasure.

'Very good, old man, that's enough,' he said. 'You can go and refresh yourself.'

Fyodor Miheitch at once laid down the fiddle on the window-sill, bowed first to me as the guest, then to the old lady, then to Radilov, and went away.

'He too was a landowner,' my new friend continued, 'and a rich one too, but he ruined himself--so he lives now with me.... But in his day he was considered the most dashing fellow in the province; he eloped with two married ladies; he used to keep singers, and sang himself, and danced like a master.... But won't you take some vodka? dinner is just ready.'

A young girl, the same that I had caught a glimpse of in the garden, came into the room.

'And here is Olga!' observed Radilov, slightly turning his head; 'let me present you....
Well, let us go into dinner.'

We went in and sat down to the table. While we were coming out of the drawing-room and taking our seats, Fyodor Miheitch, whose eyes were bright and his nose rather red after his 'refreshment,' sang 'Raise the cry of Victory.' They laid a separate cover for him in a corner on a little table without a table-napkin. The poor old man could not boast of very nice habits, and so they always kept him at some distance from society. He crossed himself, sighed, and began to eat like a shark. The dinner was in reality not bad, and in honour of Sunday was accompanied, of course, with shaking jelly and Spanish puffs of pastry. At the table Radilov, who had served ten years in an infantry regiment and had been in Turkey, fell to telling anecdotes; I listened to him with attention, and secretly watched Olga. She was not very pretty; but the tranquil and resolute expression of her face, her broad, white brow, her thick hair, and especially her brown eyes--not large, but clear, sensible and lively--would have made an impression on anyone in my place. She seemed to be following every word Radilov uttered--not so much sympathy as passionate attention was expressed on her face. Radilov in years might have been her father; he called her by her Christian name, but I guessed at once that she was not his daughter. In the course of conversation he referred to his deceased wife--'her sister,' he added, indicating Olga. She blushed quickly and dropped her eyes. Radilov paused a moment and then changed the subject. The old lady did not utter a word during the whole of dinner; she ate scarcely anything herself, and did not press me to partake. Her features had an air of timorous and hopeless expectation, that melancholy of old age which it pierces one's heart to look upon. At the end of dinner Fyodor Miheitch was beginning to 'celebrate' the hosts and guests, but Radilov looked at me and asked him to be quiet; the old man passed his hand over his lips, began to blink, bowed, and sat down again, but only on the very edge of his chair. After dinner I returned with Radilov to his study.

In people who are constantly and intensely preoccupied with one idea, or one emotion, there is something in common, a kind of external resemblance in manner, however different may be their qualities, their abilities, their position in society, and their education. The more I watched Radilov, the more I felt that he belonged to the class of such people. He talked of husbandry, of the crops, of the war, of the gossip of the district and the approaching elections; he talked without constraint, and even with interest; but suddenly he would sigh and drop into a chair, and pass his hand over his face, like a man wearied out by a tedious task. His whole nature--a good and warm-hearted one too--seemed saturated through, steeped in some one feeling. I was amazed by the fact that I could not discover in him either a passion for eating, nor for wine, nor for sport, nor for Kursk nightingales, nor for epileptic pigeons, nor for Russian literature, nor for trotting-hacks, nor for Hungarian coats, nor for cards, nor billiards, nor for dances, nor trips to the provincial town or the capital, nor for paper- factories and beet-sugar refineries, nor for painted pavilions, nor for tea, nor for trace-horses trained to hold their heads askew, nor even for fat coachmen belted under their very armpits--those magnificent coachmen whose eyes, for some mysterious reason, seem rolling and starting out of their heads at every movement.... 'What sort of landowner is this, then?' I thought. At the same time he did not in the least pose as a gloomy man discontented with his destiny; on the contrary, he seemed full of indiscrimating good-will, cordial and even offensive readiness to become intimate with every one he came across. In reality you felt at the same time that he could not be friends, nor be really intimate with anyone, and that he could not be so, not because in general he was independent of other people, but because his whole being was for a time turned inwards upon himself. Looking at Radilov, I could never imagine him happy either now or at any time. He, too, was not handsome; but in his eyes, his smile, his whole being, there was a something, mysterious and extremely attractive--yes, mysterious is just what it was. So that you felt you would like to know him better, to get to love him. Of course, at times the landowner and the man of the steppes peeped out in him; but all the same he was a capital fellow.

We were beginning to talk about the new marshal of the district, when suddenly we heard Olga's voice at the door: 'Tea is ready.' We went into the drawing-room. Fyodor Miheitch was sitting as before in his corner between the little window and the door, his legs curled up under him. Radilov's mother was knitting a stocking. From the opened windows came a breath of autumn freshness and the scent of apples. Olga was busy pouring out tea. I looked at her now with more attention than at dinner. Like provincial girls as a rule, she spoke very little, but at any rate I did not notice in her any of their anxiety to say something fine, together with their painful consciousness of stupidity and helplessness; she did not sigh as though from the burden of unutterable emotions, nor cast up her eyes, nor smile vaguely and dreamily. Her look expressed tranquil self-possession, like a man who is taking breath after great happiness or great excitement. Her carriage and her movements were resolute and free. I liked her very much.

I fell again into conversation with Radilov. I don't recollect what brought us to the familiar observation that often the most insignificant things produce more effect on people than the most important.

'Yes,' Radilov agreed, 'I have experienced that in my own case. I, as you know, have been married. It was not for long--three years; my wife died in child-birth. I thought that I should not survive her; I was fearfully miserable, broken down, but I could not weep--I wandered about like one possessed. They decked her out, as they always do, and laid her on a table--in this very room. The priest came, the deacons came, began to sing, to pray, and to burn incense; I bowed to the ground, and hardly shed a tear. My heart seemed turned to stone--and my head too--I was heavy all over. So passed my first day. Would you believe it? I even slept in the night. The next morning I went in to look at my wife: it was summer-time, the sunshine fell upon her from head to foot, and it was so bright. Suddenly I saw ...' (here Radilov gave an involuntary shudder) 'what do you think? One of her eyes was not quite shut, and on this eye a fly was moving.... I fell down in a heap, and when I came to myself, I began to weep and weep ... I could not stop myself....'

Radilov was silent. I looked at him, then at Olga.... I can never forget the expression of her face. The old lady had laid the stocking down on her knees, and taken a handkerchief out of her reticule; she was stealthily wiping away her tears. Fyodor Miheitch suddenly got up, seized his fiddle, and in a wild and hoarse voice began to sing a song. He wanted doubtless to restore our spirits; but we all shuddered at his first note, and Radilov asked him to be quiet.

'Still what is past, is past,' he continued; 'we cannot recall the past, and in the end ... all is for the best in this world below, as I think Voltaire said,' he added hurriedly.

'Yes,' I replied, 'of course. Besides, every trouble can be endured, and there is no position so terrible that there is no escape from it.'

'Do you think so?' said Radilov. 'Well, perhaps you are right. I recollect I lay once in the hospital in Turkey half dead; I had typhus fever. Well, our quarters were nothing to boast of--of course, in time of war--and we had to thank God for what we had! Suddenly they bring in more sick--where are they to put them? The doctor goes here and there--there is no room left. So he comes up to me and asks the attendant, "Is he alive?" He answers, "He was alive this morning." The doctor bends down, listens; I am breathing.

The good man could not help saying, "Well, what an absurd constitution; the man's dying; he's certain to die, and he keeps hanging on, lingering, taking up space for nothing, and keeping out others." Well, I thought to myself, "So you are in a bad way, Mihal Mihalitch...." And, after all, I got well, and am alive till now, as you may see for yourself. You are right, to be sure.'

'In any case I am right,' I replied; 'even if you had died, you would just the same have escaped from your horrible position.'

'Of course, of course,' he added, with a violent blow of his fist on the table. 'One has only to come to a decision.... What is the use of being in a horrible position?... What is the good of delaying, lingering.'

Olga rose quickly and went out into the garden.

'Well, Fedya, a dance!' cried Radilov.

Fedya jumped up and walked about the room with that artificial and peculiar motion which is affected by the man who plays the part of a goat with a tame bear. He sang meanwhile, 'While at our Gates....'

The rattle of a racing droshky sounded in the drive, and in a few minutes a tall, broad-shouldered and stoutly made man, the peasant proprietor, Ovsyanikov, came into the room.

But Ovsyanikov is such a remarkable and original personage that, with the reader's permission, we will put off speaking about him till the next sketch. And now I will only add for myself that the next day I started off hunting at earliest dawn with Yermolai, and returned home after the day's sport was over ... that a week later I went again to Radilov's, but did not find him or Olga at home, and within a fortnight I learned that he had suddenly disappeared, left his mother, and gone away somewhere with his sister-in-law. The whole province was excited, and talked about this event, and I only then completely understood the expression of Olga's face while Radilov was telling us his story. It was breathing, not with sympathetic suffering only: it was burning with jealousy.

Before leaving the country I called on old Madame Radilov. I found her in the drawing-room; she was playing cards with Fyodor Miheitch.

'Have you news of your son?' I asked her at last.

The old lady began to weep. I made no more inquiries about Radilov.

VI   THE PEASANT PROPRIETOR OVSYANIKOV

Picture to yourselves, gentle readers, a stout, tall man of seventy, with a face reminding one somewhat of the face of Kriloff, clear and intelligent eyes under overhanging brows, dignified in bearing, slow in speech, and deliberate in movement: there you have Ovsyanikov. He wore an ample blue overcoat with long sleeves, buttoned all the way up, a lilac silk-handkerchief round his neck, brightly polished boots with tassels, and altogether resembled in appearance a well-to-do merchant. His hands were handsome, soft, and white; he often fumbled with the buttons of his coat as he talked.

With his dignity and his composure, his good sense and his indolence, his uprightness and his obstinacy, Ovsyanikov reminded me of the Russian boyars of the times before Peter the Great.... The national holiday dress would have suited him well. He was one of the last men left of the old time. All his neighbours had a great respect for him, and considered it an honour to be acquainted with him. His fellow peasant-proprietors almost worshipped him, and took off their hats to him from a distance: they were proud of him. Generally speaking, in these days, it is difficult to tell a peasant- proprietor from a peasant; his husbandry is almost worse than the peasant's; his calves are wretchedly small; his horses are only half alive; his harness is made of rope. Ovsyanikov was an exception to the general rule, though he did not pass for a wealthy man. He lived alone with his wife in a clean and comfortable little house, kept a few servants, whom he dressed in the Russian style and called his 'workmen.' They were employed also in ploughing his land. He did not attempt to pass for a nobleman, did not affect to be a landowner; never, as they say, forgot himself; he did not take a seat at the first invitation to do so, and he never failed to rise from his seat on the entrance of a new guest, but with such dignity, with such stately courtesy, that the guest involuntarily made him a more deferential bow. Ovsyanikov adhered to the antique usages, not from superstition (he was naturally rather independent in mind), but from habit. He did not, for instance, like carriages with springs, because he did not find them comfortable, and preferred to drive in a racing droshky, or in a pretty little trap with leather cushions, and he always drove his good bay himself (he kept none but bay horses). His coachman, a young, rosy- cheeked fellow, his hair cut round like a basin, in a dark blue coat with a strap round the waist, sat respectfully beside him. Ovsyanikov always had a nap after dinner and visited the bath-house on Saturdays; he read none but religious books and used gravely to fix his round silver spectacles on his nose when he did so; he got up, and went to bed early. He shaved his beard, however, and wore his hair in the German style. He always received visitors cordially and affably, but he did not bow down to the ground, nor fuss over them and press them to partake of every kind of dried and salted delicacy. 'Wife!' he would say deliberately, not getting up from his seat, but only turning his head a little in her direction, 'bring the gentleman a little of something to eat.' He regarded it as a sin to sell wheat: it was the gift of God. In the year '40, at the time of the general famine and terrible scarcity, he shared all his store with the surrounding landowners and peasants; the following year they gratefully repaid their debt to him in kind. The neighbours often had recourse to Ovsyanikov as arbitrator and mediator between them, and they almost always acquiesced in his decision, and listened to his advice. Thanks to his intervention, many had conclusively settled their boundaries.... But after two or three tussles with lady-landowners, he announced that he declined all mediation between persons of the feminine gender. He could not bear the flurry and excitement, the chatter of women and the 'fuss.' Once his house had somehow got on fire. A workman ran to him in headlong haste shrieking, 'Fire, fire!' 'Well, what are you screaming about?' said Ovsyanikov tranquilly, 'give me my cap and my stick.' He liked to break in his horses himself. Once a spirited horse he was training bolted with him down a hillside and over a precipice. 'Come, there, there, you young colt, you'll kill yourself!' said Ovsyanikov soothingly to him, and an instant later he flew over the precipice together with the racing droshky, the boy who was sitting behind, and the horse. Fortunately, the bottom of the ravine was covered with heaps of sand. No one was injured; only the horse sprained a leg. 'Well, you see,' continued Ovsyanikov in a calm voice as he got up from the ground, 'I told you so.' He had found a wife to match him. Tatyana Ilyinitchna Ovsyanikov was a tall woman, dignified and taciturn, always dressed in a cinnamon-coloured silk dress. She had a cold air, though none complained of her severity, but, on the contrary, many poor creatures called her their little mother and benefactress. Her regular features, her large dark eyes, and her delicately cut lips, bore witness even now to her once celebrated beauty. Ovsyanikov had no children.

I made his acquaintance, as the reader is already aware, at Radilov's, and two days later I went to see him. I found him at home. He was reading the lives of the Saints. A grey cat was purring on his shoulder. He received me, according to his habit, with stately cordiality. We fell into conversation.

'But tell me the truth, Luka Petrovitch,' I said to him, among other things; 'weren't things better of old, in your time?'

'In some ways, certainly, things were better, I should say,' replied Ovsyanikov; 'we lived more easily; there was a greater abundance of everything. ... All the same, things are better now, and they will be better still for your children, please God.'

'I had expected you, Luka Petrovitch, to praise the old times.'

'No, I have no special reason to praise old times. Here, for instance, though you are a landowner now, and just as much a landowner as your grandfather was, you have not the same power--and, indeed, you are not yourself the same kind of man. Even now, some noblemen oppress us; but, of course, it is impossible to help that altogether. Where there are mills grinding there will be flour. No; I don't see now what I have experienced myself in my youth.'

'What, for instance?'

'Well, for instance, I will tell you about your grandfather. He was an overbearing man; he oppressed us poorer folks. You know, perhaps-- indeed, you surely know your own estates--that bit of land that runs from Tchepligin to Malinina--you have it under oats now.... Well, you know, it is ours--it is all ours. Your grandfather took it away from us; he rode by on his horse, pointed to it with his hand, and said, "It's my property," and took possession of it. My father (God rest his soul!) was a just man; he was a hot-tempered man, too; he would not put up with it--indeed, who does like to lose his property?--and he laid a petition before the court. But he was alone: the others did not appear --they were afraid. So they reported to your grandfather that "Piotr Ovsyanikov is making a complaint against you that you were pleased to take away his land." Your grandfather at once sent his huntsman Baush with a detachment of men.... Well, they seized my father, and carried him to your estate. I was a little boy at that time; I ran after him barefoot. What happened? They brought him to your house, and flogged him right under your windows. And your grandfather stands on the balcony and looks on; and your grandmother sits at the window and looks on too. My father cries out, "Gracious lady, Marya Vasilyevna, intercede for me! have mercy on me!" But her only answer was to keep getting up to have a look at him. So they exacted a promise from my father to give up the land, and bade him be thankful they let him go alive. So it has remained with you. Go and ask your peasants--what do they call the land, indeed? It's called "The Cudgelled Land," because it was gained by the cudgel. So you see from that, we poor folks can't bewail the old order very much.'

I did not know what answer to make Ovsyanikov, and I had not the courage to look him in the face.

'We had another neighbour who settled amongst us in those days, Komov, Stepan Niktopolionitch. He used to worry my father out of his life; when it wasn't one thing, it was another. He was a drunken fellow, and fond of treating others; and when he was drunk he would say in French, " Say bon ," and "Take away the holy images!" He would go to all the neighbours to ask them to come to him. His horses stood always in readiness, and if you wouldn't go he would come after you himself at once!... And he was such a strange fellow! In his sober times he was not a liar; but when he was drunk he would begin to relate how he had three houses in Petersburg--one red, with one chimney; another yellow, with two chimneys; and a third blue, with no chimneys; and three sons (though he had never even been married), one in the infantry, another in the cavalry, and the third was his own master.... And he would say that in each house lived one of his sons; that admirals visited the eldest, and generals the second, and the third only Englishmen! Then he would get up and say, "To the health of my eldest son; he is the most dutiful!" and he would begin to weep. Woe to anyone who refused to drink the toast! "I will shoot him!" he would say; "and I won't let him be buried!" ... Then he would jump up and scream, "Dance, God's people, for your pleasure and my diversion!" Well, then, you must dance; if you had to die for it, you must dance. He thoroughly worried his serf-girls to death. Sometimes all night long till morning they would be singing in chorus, and the one who made the most noise would have a prize. If they began to be tired, he would lay his head down in his hands, and begins moaning: "Ah, poor forsaken orphan that I am! They abandon me, poor little dove!" And the stable-boys would wake the girls up at once. He took a liking to my father; what was he to do? He almost drove my father into his grave, and would actually have driven him into it, but (thank Heaven!) he died himself; in one of his drunken fits he fell off the pigeon-house. ... There, that's what our sweet little neighbours were like!'

'How the times have changed!' I observed.

'Yes, yes,' Ovsyanikov assented. 'And there is this to be said--in the old days the nobility lived more sumptuously. I'm not speaking of the real grandees now. I used to see them in Moscow. They say such people are scarce nowadays.'

'Have you been in Moscow?'

'I used to stay there long, very long ago. I am now in my seventy-third year; and I went to Moscow when I was sixteen.'

Ovsyanikov sighed.

'Whom did you see there?'

'I saw a great many grandees--and every one saw them; they kept open house for the wonder and admiration of all! Only no one came up to Count Alexey Grigoryevitch Orlov-Tchesmensky. I often saw Alexey Grigoryevitch; my uncle was a steward in his service. The count was pleased to live in Shabolovka, near the Kaluga Gate. He was a grand gentleman! Such stateliness, such gracious condescension you can't imagine! and it's impossible to describe it. His figure alone was worth something, and his strength, and the look in his eyes! Till you knew him, you did not dare come near him--you were afraid, overawed indeed; but directly you came near him he was like sunshine warming you up and making you quite cheerful. He allowed every man access to him in person, and he was devoted to every kind of sport. He drove himself in races and out-stripped every one, and he would never get in front at the start, so as not to offend his adversary; he would not cut it short, but would pass him at the finish; and he was so pleasant--he would soothe his adversary, praising his horse. He kept tumbler-pigeons of a first-rate kind. He would come out into the court, sit down in an arm-chair, and order them to let loose the pigeons; and his men would stand all round on the roofs with guns to keep off the hawks. A large silver basin of water used to be placed at the count's feet, and he looked at the pigeons reflected in the water. Beggars and poor people were fed in hundreds at his expense; and what a lot of money he used to give away!... When he got angry, it was like a clap of thunder. Everyone was in a great fright, but there was nothing to weep over; look round a minute after, and he was all smiles again! When he gave a banquet he made all Moscow drunk!-- and see what a clever man he was! you know he beat the Turk. He was fond of wrestling too; strong men used to come from Tula, from Harkoff, from Tamboff, and from everywhere to him. If he threw any one he would pay him a reward; but if any one threw him, he perfectly loaded him with presents, and kissed him on the lips.... And once, during my stay at Moscow, he arranged a hunting party such as had never been in Russia before; he sent invitations to all the sportsmen in the whole empire, and fixed a day for it, and gave them three months' notice. They brought with them dogs and grooms: well, it was an army of people--a regular army!

'First they had a banquet in the usual way, and then they set off into the open country. The people flocked there in thousands! And what do you think?... Your father's dog outran them all.'

'Wasn't that Milovidka?' I inquired.

'Milovidka, Milovidka!... So the count began to ask him, "Give me your dog," says he; "take what you like for her." "No, count," he said, "I am not a tradesman; I don't sell anything for filthy lucre; for your sake I am ready to part with my wife even, but not with Milovidka.... I would give myself into bondage first." And Alexey Grigoryevitch praised him for it. "I like you for it," he said. Your grandfather took her back in the coach with him, and when Milovidka died, he buried her in the garden with music at the burial--yes, a funeral for a dog--and put a stone with an inscription on it over the dog.'

'Then Alexey Grigoryevitch did not oppress anyone,' I observed.

'Yes, it is always like that; those who can only just keep themselves afloat are the ones to drag others under.'

'And what sort of a man was this Baush?' I asked after a short silence.

'Why, how comes it you have heard about Milovidka, and not about Baush? He was your grandfather's chief huntsman and whipper-in. Your grandfather was as fond of him as of Milovidka. He was a desperate fellow, and whatever order your grandfather gave him, he would carry it out in a minute--he'd have run on to a sword at his bidding.... And when he hallooed ... it was something like a tally-ho in the forest. And then he would suddenly turn nasty, get off his horse, and lie down on the ground ... and directly the dogs ceased to hear his voice, it was all over! They would give up the hottest scent, and wouldn't go on for anything. Ay, ay, your grandfather did get angry! "Damn me, if I don't hang the scoundrel! I'll turn him inside out, the antichrist! I'll stuff his heels down his gullet, the cut-throat!" And it ended by his going up to find out what he wanted; why he wouldn't halloo to the hounds? Usually, on such occasions, Baush asked for some vodka, drank it up, got on his horse, and began to halloo as lustily as ever again.'

'You seem to be fond of hunting too, Luka Petrovitch?'

'I should have been--certainly, not now; now my time is over--but in my young days.... But you know it was not an easy matter in my position. It's not suitable for people like us to go trailing after noblemen. Certainly you may find in our class some drinking, good-for-nothing fellow who associates with the gentry--but it's a queer sort of enjoyment.... He only brings shame on himself. They mount him on a wretched stumbling nag, keep knocking his hat off on to the ground and cut at him with a whip, pretending to whip the horse, and he must laugh at everything, and be a laughing-stock for the others.

No, I tell you, the lower your station, the more reserved must be your behaviour, or else you disgrace yourself directly.'

'Yes,' continued Ovsyanikov with a sigh, 'there's many a gallon of water has flowed down to the sea since I have been living in the world; times are different now. Especially I see a great change in the nobility. The smaller landowners have all either become officials, or at any rate do not stop here; as for the larger owners, there's no making them out. I have had experience of them--the larger landowners-- in cases of settling boundaries. And I must tell you; it does my heart good to see them: they are courteous and affable. Only this is what astonishes me; they have studied all the sciences, they speak so fluently that your heart is melted, but they don't understand the actual business in hand; they don't even perceive what's their own interest; some bailiff, a bondservant, drives them just where he pleases, as though they were in a yoke. There's Korolyov--Alexandr Vladimirovitch--for instance; you know him, perhaps--isn't he every inch a nobleman? He is handsome, rich, has studied at the 'versities, and travelled, I think, abroad; he speaks simply and easily, and shakes hands with us all. You know him?... Well, listen then. Last week we assembled at Beryozovka at the summons of the mediator, Nikifor Ilitch. And the mediator, Nikifor Ilitch, says to us: "Gentlemen, we must settle the boundaries; it's disgraceful; our district is behind all the others; we must get to work." Well, so we got to work. There followed discussions, disputes, as usual; our attorney began to make objections. But the first to make an uproar was Porfiry Ovtchinnikov.... And what had the fellow to make an uproar about?... He hasn't an acre of ground; he is acting as representative of his brother. He bawls: "No, you shall not impose on me! no, you shan't drive me to that! give the plans here! give me the surveyor's plans, the Judas's plans here!" "But what is your claim, then?" "Oh, you think I'm a fool! Indeed! do you suppose I am going to lay bare my claim to you offhand? No, let me have the plans here--that's what I want!" And he himself is banging his fist on the plans all the time. Then he mortally offended Marfa Dmitrievna. She shrieks out, "How dare you asperse my reputation?" "Your reputation," says he; "I shouldn't like my chestnut mare to have your reputation." They poured him out some Madeira at last, and so quieted him; then others begin to make a row. Alexandr Vladimirovitch Korolyov, the dear fellow, sat in a corner sucking the knob of his cane, and only shook his head. I felt ashamed; I could hardly sit it out. "What must he be thinking of us?" I said to myself. When, behold! Alexandr Vladimirovitch has got up, and shows signs of wanting to speak. The mediator exerts himself, says, "Gentlemen, gentlemen, Alexandr Vladimirovitch wishes to speak." And I must do them this credit; they were all silent at once. And so Alexandr Vladimirovitch began and said "that we seemed to have forgotten what we had come together for; that, indeed, the fixing of boundaries was indisputably advantageous for owners of land, but actually what was its object? To make things easier for the peasant, so that he could work and pay his dues more conveniently; that now the peasant hardly knows his own land, and often goes to work five miles away; and one can't expect too much of him." Then Alexandr Vladimirovitch said "that it was disgraceful in a landowner not to interest himself in the well-being of his peasants; that in the end, if you look at it rightly, their interests and our interests are inseparable; if they are well-off we are well-off, and if they do badly we do badly, and that, consequently, it was injudicious and wrong to disagree over trifles" ... and so on--and so on.... There, how he did speak! He seemed to go right to your heart.... All the gentry hung their heads; I myself, faith, it nearly brought me to tears. To tell the truth, you would not find sayings like that in the old books even.... But what was the end of it? He himself would not give up four acres of peat marsh, and wasn't willing to sell it. He said, "I am going to drain that marsh for my people, and set up a cloth-factory on it, with all the latest improvements. I have already," he said, "fixed on that place; I have thought out my plans on the subject." And if only that had been the truth, it would be all very well; but the simple fact is, Alexandr Vladimirovitch's neighbour, Anton Karasikov, had refused to buy over Korolyov's bailiff for a hundred roubles. And so we separated without having done anything. But Alexandr Vladimirovitch considers to this day that he is right, and still talks of the cloth-factory; but he does not start draining the marsh.'

'And how does he manage in his estate?'

'He is always introducing new ways. The peasants don't speak well of him--but it's useless to listen to them. Alexandr Vladimirovitch is doing right.'

'How's that, Luka Petrovitch? I thought you kept to the old ways.'

'I--that's another thing. You see I am not a nobleman or a landowner. What sort of management is mine?... Besides, I don't know how to do things differently. I try to act according to justice and the law, and leave the rest in God's hands! Young gentlemen don't like the old method; I think they are right.... It's the time to take in ideas. Only this is the pity of it; the young are too theoretical. They treat the peasant like a doll; they turn him this way and that way; twist him about and throw him away. And their bailiff, a serf, or some overseer from the German natives, gets the peasant under his thumb again. Now, if any one of the young gentlemen would set us an example, would show us, "See, this is how you ought to manage!" ... What will be the end of it? Can it be that I shall die without seeing the new methods?... What is the proverb?--the old is dead, but the young is not born!'

I did not know what reply to make to Ovsyanikov. He looked round, drew himself nearer to me, and went on in an undertone:

'Have you heard talk of Vassily Nikolaitch Lubozvonov?'

'No, I haven't.'

'Explain to me, please, what sort of strange creature he is. I can't make anything of it. His peasants have described him, but I can't make any sense of their tales. He is a young man, you know; it's not long since he received his heritage from his mother. Well, he arrived at his estate. The peasants were all collected to stare at their master. Vassily Nikolaitch came out to them. The peasants looked at him-- strange to relate! the master wore plush pantaloons like a coachman, and he had on boots with trimming at the top; he wore a red shirt and a coachman's long coat too; he had let his beard grow, and had such a strange hat and such a strange face--could he be drunk? No, he wasn't drunk, and yet he didn't seem quite right. "Good health to you, lads!" he says; "God keep you!" The peasants bow to the ground, but without speaking; they began to feel frightened, you know. And he too seemed timid. He began to make a speech to them: "I am a Russian," he says, "and you are Russians; I like everything Russian.... Russia," says he, "is my heart, and my blood too is Russian".... Then he suddenly gives the order: "Come, lads, sing a Russian national song!" The peasants' legs shook under them with fright; they were utterly stupefied. One bold spirit did begin to sing, but he sat down at once on the ground and hid himself behind the others.... And what is so surprising is this: we have had landowners like that, dare-devil gentlemen, regular rakes, of course: they dressed pretty much like coachmen, and danced themselves and played on the guitar, and sang and drank with their house-serfs and feasted with the peasants; but this Vassily Nikolaitch is like a girl; he is always reading books or writing, or else declaiming poetry aloud--he never addresses any one; he is shy, walks by himself in his garden; seems either bored or sad. The old bailiff at first was in a thorough scare; before Vassily Nikolaitch's arrival he was afraid to go near the peasants' houses; he bowed to all of them-- one could see the cat knew whose butter he had eaten! And the peasants were full of hope; they thought, 'Fiddlesticks, my friend!--now they'll make you answer for it, my dear; they'll lead you a dance now, you robber!' ... But instead of this it has turned out--how shall I explain it to you?--God Almighty could not account for how things have turned out! Vassily Nikolaitch summoned him to his presence and says, blushing himself and breathing quick, you know: "Be upright in my service; don't oppress any one--do you hear?" And since that day he has never asked to see him in person again! He lives on his own property like a stranger. Well, the bailiff's been enjoying himself, and the peasants don't dare to go to Vassily Nikolaitch; they are afraid. And do you see what's a matter for wonder again; the master even bows to them and looks graciously at them; but he seems to turn their stomachs with fright! 'What do you say to such a strange state of things, your honour? Either I have grown stupid in my old age, or something.... I can't understand it.'

I said to Ovsyanikov that Mr. Lubozvonov must certainly be ill.

'Ill, indeed! He's as broad as he's long, and a face like this--God bless him!--and bearded, though he is so young.... Well, God knows!' And Ovsyanikov gave a deep sigh.

'Come, putting the nobles aside,' I began, 'what have you to tell me about the peasant proprietors, Luka Petrovitch?'

'No, you must let me off that,' he said hurriedly. 'Truly.... I could tell you ... but what's the use!' (with a wave of his hand). 'We had better have some tea.... We are common peasants and nothing more; but when we come to think of it, what else could we be?'

He ceased talking. Tea was served. Tatyana Ilyinitchna rose from her place and sat down rather nearer to us. In the course of the evening she several times went noiselessly out and as quietly returned. Silence reigned in the room. Ovsyanikov drank cup after cup with gravity and deliberation.

'Mitya has been to see us to-day,' said Tatyana Ilyinitchna in a low voice.

Ovsyanikov frowned.

'What does he want?'

'He came to ask forgiveness.'

Ovsyanikov shook his head.

'Come, tell me,' he went on, turning to me, 'what is one to do with relations? And to abandon them altogether is impossible.... Here God has bestowed on me a nephew. He's a fellow with brains--a smart fellow --I don't dispute that; he has had a good education, but I don't expect much good to come of him. He went into a government office; threw up his position--didn't get on fast enough, if you please.... Does he suppose he's a noble? And even noblemen don't come to be generals all at once. So now he is living without an occupation.... And that, even, would not be such a great matter--except that he has taken to litigation! He gets up petitions for the peasants, writes memorials; he instructs the village delegates, drags the surveyors over the coals, frequents drinking houses, is seen in taverns with city tradesmen and inn-keepers. He's bound to come to ruin before long. The constables and police-captains have threatened him more than once already. But he luckily knows how to turn it off--he makes them laugh; but they will boil his kettle for him some day.... But, there, isn't he sitting in your little room?' he added, turning to his wife; 'I know you, you see; you're so soft-hearted--you will always take his part.'

Tatyana Ilyinitchna dropped her eyes, smiled, and blushed.

'Well, I see it is so,' continued Ovsyanikov. 'Fie! you spoil the boy! Well, tell him to come in.... So be it, then; for the sake of our good guest I will forgive the silly fellow.... Come, tell him, tell him.'

Tatyana Ilyinitchna went to the door, and cried 'Mitya!'

Mitya, a young man of twenty-eight, tall, well-made, and curly-headed, came into the room, and seeing me, stopped short in the doorway. His costume was in the German style, but the unnatural size of the puffs on his shoulders was enough alone to prove convincingly that the tailor who had cut it was a Russian of the Russians.

'Well, come in, come in,' began the old man; 'why are you bashful? You must thank your aunt--you're forgiven.... Here, your honour, I commend him to you,' he continued, pointing to Mitya; 'he's my own nephew, but I don't get on with him at all. The end of the world is coming!' (We bowed to one another.) 'Well, tell me what is this you have got mixed up in? What is the complaint they are making against you? Explain it to us.'

Mitya obviously did not care to explain matters and justify himself before me.

'Later on, uncle,' he muttered.

'No, not later--now,' pursued the old man.... 'You are ashamed, I see, before this gentleman; all the better--it's only what you deserve. Speak, speak; we are listening.'

'I have nothing to be ashamed of,' began Mitya spiritedly, with a toss of his head. 'Be so good as to judge for yourself, uncle. Some peasant proprietors of Reshetilovo came to me, and said, "Defend us, brother." "What is the matter?"' "This is it: our grain stores were in perfect order--in fact, they could not be better; all at once a government inspector came to us with orders to inspect the granaries. He inspected them, and said, 'Your granaries are in disorder--serious neglect; it's my duty to report it to the authorities.' 'But what does the neglect consist in?' 'That's my business,' he says.... We met together, and decided to tip the official in the usual way; but old Prohoritch prevented us. He said, 'No; that's only giving him a taste for more. Come; after all, haven't we the courts of justice?' We obeyed the old man, and the official got in a rage, and made a complaint, and wrote a report. So now we are called up to answer to his charges." "But are your granaries actually in order?" I asked. "God knows they are in order; and the legal quantity of corn is in them." "Well, then," say I, "you have nothing to fear"; and I drew up a document for them.... And it is not yet known in whose favour it is decided.... And as to the complaints they have made to you about me over that affair--it's very easy to understand that--every man's shirt is nearest to his own skin.

'Everyone's, indeed--but not yours seemingly,' said the old man in an undertone. 'But what plots have you been hatching with the Shutolomovsky peasants?'

'How do you know anything of it?'

'Never mind; I do know of it.'

'And there, too, I am right--judge for yourself again. A neighbouring landowner, Bezpandin, has ploughed over four acres of the Shutolomovsky peasants' land. "The land's mine," he says. The Shutolomovsky people are on the rent-system; their landowner has gone abroad--who is to stand up for them? Tell me yourself? But the land is theirs beyond dispute; they've been bound to it for ages and ages. So they came to me, and said, "Write us a petition." So I wrote one. And Bezpandin heard of it, and began to threaten me. "I'll break every bone in that Mitya's body, and knock his head off his shoulders...." We shall see how he will knock it off; it's still on, so far.'

'Come, don't boast; it's in a bad way, your head,' said the old man. 'You are a mad fellow altogether!'

'Why, uncle, what did you tell me yourself?'

'I know, I know what you will say,' Ovsyanikov interrupted him; 'of course a man ought to live uprightly, and he is bound to succour his neighbour. Sometimes one must not spare oneself.... But do you always behave in that way? Don't they take you to the tavern, eh? Don't they treat you; bow to you, eh? "Dmitri Alexyitch," they say, "help us, and we will prove our gratitude to you." And they slip a silver rouble or note into your hand. Eh? doesn't that happen? Tell me, doesn't that happen?'

'I am certainly to blame in that,' answered Mitya, rather confused; 'but I take nothing from the poor, and I don't act against my conscience.'

'You don't take from them now; but when you are badly off yourself, then you will. You don't act against your conscience--fie on you! Of course, they are all saints whom you defend!... Have you forgotten Borka Perohodov? Who was it looked after him? Who took him under his protection--eh?'

'Perohodov suffered through his own fault, certainly.'

'He appropriated the public moneys.... That was all!'

'But, consider, uncle: his poverty, his family.'

'Poverty, poverty.... He's a drunkard, a quarrelsome fellow; that's what it is!'

'He took to drink through trouble,' said Mitya, dropping his voice.

'Through trouble, indeed! Well, you might have helped him, if your heart was so warm to him, but there was no need for you to sit in taverns with the drunken fellow yourself. Though he did speak so finely ... a prodigy, to be sure!'

'He was a very good fellow.'

'Every one is good with you.... But did you send him?' ... pursued Ovsyanikov, turning to his wife; 'come; you know?'

Tatyana Ilyinitchna nodded.

'Where have you been lately?' the old man began again.

'I have been in the town.'

'You have been doing nothing but playing billiards, I wager, and drinking tea, and running to and fro about the government offices, drawing up petitions in little back rooms, flaunting about with merchants' sons? That's it, of course?... Tell us!'

'Perhaps that is about it,' said Mitya with a smile.... 'Ah! I had almost forgotten-- Funtikov, Anton Parfenitch asks you to dine with him next Sunday.'

'I shan't go to see that old tub. He gives you costly fish and puts rancid butter on it. God bless him!'

'And I met Fedosya Mihalovna.'

'What Fedosya is that?'

'She belongs to Garpentchenko, the landowner, who bought Mikulino by auction. Fedosya is from Mikulino. She lived in Moscow as a dress- maker, paying her service in money, and she paid her service-money accurately--a hundred and eighty two-roubles and a half a year.... And she knows her business; she got good orders in Moscow. But now Garpentchenko has written for her back, and he retains her here, but does not provide any duties for her. She would be prepared to buy her freedom, and has spoken to the master, but he will not give any decisive answer. You, uncle, are acquainted with Garpentchenko ... so couldn't you just say a word to him?... And Fedosya would give a good price for her freedom.'

'Not with your money I hope? Hey? Well, well, all right; I will speak to him, I will speak to him. But I don't know,' continued the old man with a troubled face; 'this Garpentchenko, God forgive him! is a shark; he buys up debts, lends money at interest, purchases estates at auctions.... And who brought him into our parts? Ugh, I can't bear these new-comers! One won't get an answer out of him very quickly.... However, we shall see.'

'Try to manage it, uncle.'

'Very well, I will see to it. Only you take care; take care of yourself! There, there, don't defend yourself.... God bless you! God bless you!... Only take care for the future, or else, Mitya, upon my word, it will go ill with you.... Upon my word, you will come to grief.... I can't always screen you ... and I myself am not a man of influence. There, go now, and God be with you!'

Mitya went away. Tatyana Ilyinitchna went out after him.

'Give him some tea, you soft-hearted creature,' cried Ovsyanikov after her. 'He's not a stupid fellow,' he continued, 'and he's a good heart, but I feel afraid for him.... But pardon me for having so long kept you occupied with such details.'

The door from the hall opened. A short grizzled little man came in, in a velvet coat.

'Ah, Frantz Ivanitch!' cried Ovsyanikov, 'good day to you. Is God merciful to you?'

Allow me, gentle reader, to introduce to you this gentleman.

Frantz Ivanitch Lejeune, my neighbour, and a landowner of Orel, had arrived at the respectable position of a Russian nobleman in a not quite ordinary way. He was born in Orleans of French parents, and had gone with Napoleon, on the invasion of Russia, in the capacity of a drummer. At first all went smoothly, and our Frenchman arrived in Moscow with his head held high. But on the return journey poor Monsieur Lejeune, half-frozen and without his drum, fell into the hands of some peasants of Smolensk. The peasants shut him up for the night in an empty cloth factory, and the next morning brought him to an ice-hole near the dyke, and began to beg the drummer ' de la Grrrrande Armee ' to oblige them; in other words, to swim under the ice. Monsieur Lejeune could not agree to their proposition, and in his turn began to try to persuade the Smolensk peasants, in the dialect of France, to let him go to Orleans. 'There, messieurs,' he said, ' my mother is living, une tendre mere ' But the peasants, doubtless through their ignorance of the geographical position of Orleans, continued to offer him a journey under water along the course of the meandering river Gniloterka, and had already begun to encourage him with slight blows on the vertebrae of the neck and back, when suddenly, to the indescribable delight of Lejeune, the sound of bells was heard, and there came along the dyke a huge sledge with a striped rug over its excessively high dickey, harnessed with three roan horses. In the sledge sat a stout and red-faced landowner in a wolfskin pelisse.

'What is it you are doing there?' he asked the peasants.

'We are drowning a Frenchman, your honour.'

'Ah!' replied the landowner indifferently, and he turned away.

'Monsieur! Monsieur!' shrieked the poor fellow.

'Ah, ah!' observed the wolfskin pelisse reproachfully, 'you came with twenty nations into Russia, burnt Moscow, tore down, you damned heathen! the cross from Ivan the Great, and now--mossoo, mossoo, indeed! now you turn tail! You are paying the penalty of your sins!... Go on, Filka!'

The horses were starting.

'Stop, though!' added the landowner. 'Eh? you mossoo, do you know anything of music?'

' Sauvez-moi, sauvez-moi, mon bon monsieur! ' repeated Lejeune.

'There, see what a wretched people they are! Not one of them knows Russian! Muzeek, muzeek, savey muzeek voo? savey? Well, speak, do! Compreny? savey muzeek voo? on the piano, savey zhooey?'

Lejeune comprehended at last what the landowner meant, and persistently nodded his head.

' Oui, monsieur, oui, oui, je suis musicien; je joue tous les instruments possibles! Oui, monsieur.... Sauvez-moi, monsieur! '

'Well, thank your lucky star!' replied the landowner. 'Lads, let him go: here's a twenty-copeck piece for vodka.'

'Thank you, your honour, thank you. Take him, your honour.'

They sat Lejeune in the sledge. He was gasping with delight, weeping, shivering, bowing, thanking the landowner, the coachman, the peasants. He had nothing on but a green jacket with pink ribbons, and it was freezing very hard. The landowner looked at his blue and benumbed shoulders in silence, wrapped the unlucky fellow in his own pelisse, and took him home. The household ran out. They soon thawed the Frenchman, fed him, and clothed him. The landowner conducted him to his daughters.

'Here, children!' he said to them, 'a teacher is found for you. You were always entreating me to have you taught music and the French jargon; here you have a Frenchman, and he plays on the piano.... Come, mossoo,' he went on, pointing to a wretched little instrument he had bought five years before of a Jew, whose special line was eau de Cologne, 'give us an example of your art; zhooey!'

Lejeune, with a sinking heart, sat down on the music-stool; he had never touched a piano in his life.

'Zhooey, zhooey!' repeated the landowner.

In desperation, the unhappy man beat on the keys as though on a drum, and played at hazard. 'I quite expected,' he used to tell afterwards, 'that my deliverer would seize me by the collar, and throw me out of the house.' But, to the utmost amazement of the unwilling improvisor, the landowner, after waiting a little, patted him good-humouredly on the shoulder.

'Good, good,' he said; 'I see your attainments; go now, and rest yourself.'

Within a fortnight Lejeune had gone from this landowner's to stay with another, a rich and cultivated man. He gained his friendship by his bright and gentle disposition, was married to a ward of his, went into a government office, rose to the nobility, married his daughter to Lobizanyev, a landowner of Orel, and a retired dragoon and poet, and settled himself on an estate in Orel.

It was this same Lejeune, or rather, as he is called now, Frantz Ivanitch, who, when I was there, came in to see Ovsyanikov, with whom he was on friendly terms....

But perhaps the reader is already weary of sitting with me at the Ovsyanikovs', and so I will become eloquently silent.

VII   LGOV

'Let us go to Lgov,' Yermolai, whom the reader knows already, said to me one day; 'there we can shoot ducks to our heart's content.'

Although wild duck offers no special attraction for a genuine sportsman, still, through lack of other game at the time (it was the beginning of September; snipe were not on the wing yet, and I was tired of running across the fields after partridges), I listened to my huntsman's suggestion, and we went to Lgov.

Lgov is a large village of the steppes, with a very old stone church with a single cupola, and two mills on the swampy little river Rossota. Five miles from Lgov, this river becomes a wide swampy pond, overgrown at the edges, and in places also in the centre, with thick reeds. Here, in the creeks or rather pools between the reeds, live and breed a countless multitude of ducks of all possible kinds--quackers, half- quackers, pintails, teals, divers, etc. Small flocks are for ever flitting about and swimming on the water, and at a gunshot, they rise in such clouds that the sportsman involuntarily clutches his hat with one hand and utters a prolonged Pshaw! I walked with Yermolai along beside the pond; but, in the first place, the duck is a wary bird, and is not to be met quite close to the bank; and secondly, even when some straggling and inexperienced teal exposed itself to our shots and lost its life, our dogs were not able to get it out of the thick reeds; in spite of their most devoted efforts they could neither swim nor tread on the bottom, and only cut their precious noses on the sharp reeds for nothing.

'No,' was Yermolai's comment at last, 'it won't do; we must get a boat.... Let us go back to Lgov.'

We went back. We had only gone a few paces when a rather wretched- looking setter-dog ran out from behind a bushy willow to meet us, and behind him appeared a man of middle height, in a blue and much-worn greatcoat, a yellow waistcoat, and pantaloons of a nondescript grey colour, hastily tucked into high boots full of holes, with a red handkerchief round his neck, and a single-barrelled gun on his shoulder. While our dogs, with the ordinary Chinese ceremonies peculiar to their species, were sniffing at their new acquaintance, who was obviously ill at ease, held his tail between his legs, dropped his ears back, and kept turning round and round showing his teeth--the stranger approached us, and bowed with extreme civility. He appeared to be about twenty-five; his long dark hair, perfectly saturated with kvas, stood up in stiff tufts, his small brown eyes twinkled genially; his face was bound up in a black handkerchief, as though for toothache; his countenance was all smiles and amiability.

'Allow me to introduce myself,' he began in a soft and insinuating voice; 'I am a sportsman of these parts--Vladimir.... Having heard of your presence, and having learnt that you proposed to visit the shores of our pond, I resolved, if it were not displeasing to you, to offer you my services.'

The sportsman, Vladimir, uttered those words for all the world like a young provincial actor in the role of leading lover. I agreed to his proposition, and before we had reached Lgov I had succeeded in learning his whole history. He was a freed house-serf; in his tender youth had been taught music, then served as valet, could read and write, had read--so much I could discover--some few trashy books, and existed now, as many do exist in Russia, without a farthing of ready money; without any regular occupation; fed by manna from heaven, or something hardly less precarious. He expressed himself with extraordinary elegance, and obviously plumed himself on his manners; he must have been devoted to the fair sex too, and in all probability popular with them: Russian girls love fine talking. Among other things, he gave me to understand that he sometimes visited the neighbouring landowners, and went to stay with friends in the town, where he played preference, and that he was acquainted with people in the metropolis. His smile was masterly and exceedingly varied; what specially suited him was a modest, contained smile which played on his lips as he listened to any other man's conversation. He was attentive to you; he agreed with you completely, but still he did not lose sight of his own dignity, and seemed to wish to give you to understand that he could, if occasion arose, express convictions of his own. Yermolai, not being very refined, and quite devoid of 'subtlety,' began to address him with coarse familiarity. The fine irony with which Vladimir used 'Sir' in his reply was worth seeing.

'Why is your face tied up?' I inquired; 'have you toothache?'

'No,' he answered; 'it was a most disastrous consequence of carelessness. I had a friend, a good fellow, but not a bit of a sportsman, as sometimes occurs. Well, one day he said to me, "My dear friend, take me out shooting; I am curious to learn what this diversion consists in." I did not like, of course, to refuse a comrade; I got him a gun and took him out shooting. Well, we shot a little in the ordinary way; at last we thought we would rest I sat down under a tree; but he began instead to play with his gun, pointing it at me meantime. I asked him to leave off, but in his inexperience he did not attend to my words, the gun went off, and I lost half my chin, and the first finger of my right hand.'

We reached Lgov. Vladimir and Yermolai had both decided that we could not shoot without a boat.

'Sutchok (i.e. the twig) has a punt,' observed Vladimir, 'but I don't know where he has hidden it. We must go to him.'

'To whom?' I asked.

'The man lives here; Sutchok is his nickname.'

Vladimir went with Yermolai to Sutchok's. I told them I would wait for them at the church. While I was looking at the tombstones in the churchyard, I stumbled upon a blackened, four-cornered urn with the following inscription, on one side in French: 'Ci-git Theophile-Henri, Vicomte de Blangy'; on the next; 'Under this stone is laid the body of a French subject, Count Blangy; born 1737, died 1799, in the 62nd year of his age': on the third, 'Peace to his ashes': and on the fourth:--

'Under this stone there lies from France an emigrant.
Of high descent was he, and also of talent.
A wife and kindred murdered he bewailed,
And left his land by tyrants cruel assailed;
The friendly shores of Russia he attained,
And hospitable shelter here he gained;
Children he taught; their parents' cares allayed:
Here, by God's will, in peace he has been laid.'

The approach of Yermolai with Vladimir and the man with the strange nickname, Sutchok, broke in on my meditations.

Barelegged, ragged and dishevelled, Sutchok looked like a discharged stray house-serf of sixty years old.

'Have you a boat?' I asked him.

'I have a boat,' he answered in a hoarse, cracked voice; 'but it's a very poor one.'

'How so?'

'Its boards are split apart, and the rivets have come off the cracks.'

'That's no great disaster!' interposed Yermolai; 'we can stuff them up with tow.'

'Of course you can,' Sutchok assented.

'And who are you?'

'I am the fisherman of the manor.'

'How is it, when you're a fisherman, your boat is in such bad condition?'

'There are no fish in our river.'

'Fish don't like slimy marshes,' observed my huntsman, with the air of an authority.

'Come,' I said to Yermolai, 'go and get some tow, and make the boat right for us as soon as you can.'

Yermolai went off.

'Well, in this way we may very likely go to the bottom,' I said to Vladimir. 'God is merciful,' he answered. 'Anyway, we must suppose that the pond is not deep.'

'No, it is not deep,' observed Sutchok, who spoke in a strange, far-away voice, as though he were in a dream, 'and there's sedge and mud at the bottom, and it's all overgrown with sedge. But there are deep holes too.'

'But if the sedge is so thick,' said Vladimir, 'it will be impossible to row.'

'Who thinks of rowing in a punt? One has to punt it. I will go with you; my pole is there--or else one can use a wooden spade.'

'With a spade it won't be easy; you won't touch the bottom perhaps in some places,' said Vladimir.

'It's true; it won't be easy.'

I sat down on a tomb-stone to wait for Yermolai. Vladimir moved a little to one side out of respect to me, and also sat down. Sutchok remained standing in the same place, his head bent and his hands clasped behind his back, according to the old habit of house-serfs.

'Tell me, please,' I began, 'have you been the fisherman here long?' 'It is seven years now,' he replied, rousing himself with a start.

'And what was your occupation before?'

'I was coachman before.'

'Who dismissed you from being coachman?'

'The new mistress.'

'What mistress?'

'Oh, that bought us. Your honour does not know her; Alyona Timofyevna; she is so fat ... not young.'

'Why did she decide to make you a fisherman?'

'God knows. She came to us from her estate in Tamboff, gave orders for all the household to come together, and came out to us. We first kissed her hand, and she said nothing; she was not angry.... Then she began to question us in order; "How are you employed? what duties have you?" She came to me in my turn; so she asked: "What have you been?" I say, "Coachman." "Coachman? Well, a fine coachman you are; only look at you! You're not fit for a coachman, but be my fisherman, and shave your beard. On the occasions of my visits provide fish for the table; do you hear?" ... So since then I have been enrolled as a fisherman. "And mind you keep my pond in order." But how is one to keep it in order?'

'Whom did you belong to before?'

'To Sergai Sergiitch Pehterev. We came to him by inheritance. But he did not own us long; only six years altogether. I was his coachman ... but not in town, he had others there--only in the country.'

'And were you always a coachman from your youth up?'

'Always a coachman? Oh, no! I became a coachman in Sergai Sergiitch's time, but before that I was a cook--but not town-cook; only a cook in the country.'

'Whose cook were you, then?'

'Oh, my former master's, Afanasy Nefeditch, Sergai Sergiitch's uncle. Lgov was bought by him, by Afanasy Nefeditch, but it came to Sergai Sergiitch by inheritance from him.'

'Whom did he buy it from?'

'From Tatyana Vassilyevna.'

'What Tatyana Vassilyevna was that?'

'Why, that died last year in Bolhov ... that is, at Karatchev, an old maid.... She had never married. Don't you know her? We came to her from her father, Vassily Semenitch. She owned us a goodish while ... twenty years.'

'Then were you cook to her?'

'At first, to be sure, I was cook, and then I was coffee-bearer.'

'What were you?'

'Coffee-bearer.'

'What sort of duty is that?'

'I don't know, your honour. I stood at the sideboard, and was called Anton instead of Kuzma. The mistress ordered that I should be called so.'

'Your real name, then, is Kuzma?'

'Yes.'

'And were you coffee-bearer all the time?'

'No, not all the time; I was an actor too.'

'Really?'

'Yes, I was.... I played in the theatre. Our mistress set up a theatre of her own.'

'What kind of parts did you take?'

'What did you please to say?'

'What did you do in the theatre?'

'Don't you know? Why, they take me and dress me up; and I walk about dressed up, or stand or sit down there as it happens, and they say, "See, this is what you must say," and I say it. Once I represented a blind man.... They laid little peas under each eyelid.... Yes, indeed.'

'And what were you afterwards?'

'Afterwards I became a cook again.'

'Why did they degrade you to being a cook again?'

'My brother ran away.'

'Well, and what were you under the father of your first mistress?'

'I had different duties; at first I found myself a page; I have been a postilion, a gardener, and a whipper-in.'

'A whipper-in?... And did you ride out with the hounds?'

'Yes, I rode with the hounds, and was nearly killed; I fell off my horse, and the horse was injured. Our old master was very severe; he ordered them to flog me, and to send me to learn a trade to Moscow, to a shoemaker.'

'To learn a trade? But you weren't a child, I suppose, when you were a whipper-in?'

'I was twenty and over then.'

'But could you learn a trade at twenty?'

'I suppose one could, some way, since the master ordered it. But he luckily died soon after, and they sent me back to the country.'

'And when were you taught to cook?'

Sutchok lifted his thin yellowish little old face and grinned.

'Is that a thing to be taught?... Old women can cook.'

'Well,' I commented, 'you have seen many things, Kuzma, in your time! What do you do now as a fisherman, seeing there are no fish?'

'Oh, your honour, I don't complain. And, thank God, they made me a fisherman. Why another old man like me--Andrey Pupir--the mistress ordered to be put into the paper factory, as a ladler. "It's a sin," she said, "to eat bread in idleness." And Pupir had even hoped for favour; his cousin's son was clerk in the mistress's counting-house: he had promised to send his name up to the mistress, to remember him: a fine way he remembered him!... And Pupir fell at his cousin's knees before my eyes.'

'Have you a family? Have you married?'

'No, your honour, I have never been married. Tatyana Vassilyevna--God rest her soul!--did not allow anyone to marry. "God forbid!" she said sometimes, "here am I living single: what indulgence! What are they thinking of!"'

'What do you live on now? Do you get wages?'

'Wages, your honour!... Victuals are given me, and thanks be to Thee, Lord! I am very contented. May God give our lady long life!'

Yermolai returned.

'The boat is repaired,' he announced churlishly. 'Go after your pole-- you there!'

Sutchok ran to get his pole. During the whole time of my conversation with the poor old man, the sportsman Vladimir had been staring at him with a contemptuous smile.

'A stupid fellow,' was his comment, when the latter had gone off; 'an absolutely uneducated fellow; a peasant, nothing more. One cannot even call him a house-serf, and he was boasting all the time. How could he be an actor, be pleased to judge for yourself! You were pleased to trouble yourself for no good in talking to him.'

A quarter of an hour later we were sitting in Sutchok's punt. The dogs we left in a hut in charge of my coachman. We were not very comfortable, but sportsmen are not a fastidious race. At the rear end, which was flattened and straight, stood Sutchok, punting; I sat with Vladimir on the planks laid across the boat, and Yermolai ensconced himself in front, in the very beak. In spite of the tow, the water soon made its appearance under our feet. Fortunately, the weather was calm and the pond seemed slumbering.

We floated along rather slowly. The old man had difficulty in drawing his long pole out of the sticky mud; it came up all tangled in green threads of water-sedge; the flat round leaves of the water-lily also hindered the progress of our boat last we got up to the reeds, and then the fun began. Ducks flew up noisily from the pond, scared by our unexpected appearance in their domains, shots sounded at once after them; it was a pleasant sight to see these short-tailed game turning somersaults in the air, splashing heavily into the water. We could not, of course, get at all the ducks that were shot; those who were slightly wounded swam away; some which had been quite killed fell into such thick reeds that even Yermolai's little lynx eyes could not discover them, yet our boat was nevertheless filled to the brim with game for dinner.

Vladimir, to Yermolai's great satisfaction, did not shoot at all well; he seemed surprised after each unsuccessful shot, looked at his gun and blew down it, seemed puzzled, and at last explained to us the reason why he had missed his aim. Yermolai, as always, shot triumphantly; I-- rather badly, after my custom. Sutchok looked on at us with the eyes of a man who has been the servant of others from his youth up; now and then he cried out: 'There, there, there's another little duck'; and he constantly rubbed his back, not with his hands, but by a peculiar movement of the shoulder-blades. The weather kept magnificent; curly white clouds moved calmly high above our heads, and were reflected clearly in the water; the reeds were whispering around us; here and there the pond sparkled in the sunshine like steel. We were preparing to return to the village, when suddenly a rather unpleasant adventure befel us.

For a long time we had been aware that the water was gradually filling our punt. Vladimir was entrusted with the task of baling it out by means of a ladle, which my thoughtful huntsman had stolen to be ready for any emergency from a peasant woman who was staring away in another direction. All went well so long as Vladimir did not neglect his duty. But just at the end the ducks, as if to take leave of us, rose in such flocks that we scarcely had time to load our guns. In the heat of the sport we did not pay attention to the state of our punt--when suddenly, Yermolai, in trying to reach a wounded duck, leaned his whole weight on the boat's-edge; at his over-eager movement our old tub veered on one side, began to fill, and majestically sank to the bottom, fortunately not in a deep place. We cried out, but it was too late; in an instant we were standing in the water up to our necks, surrounded by the floating bodies of the slaughtered ducks. I cannot help laughing now when I recollect the scared white faces of my companions (probably my own face was not particularly rosy at that moment), but I must confess at the time it did not enter my head to feel amused. Each of us kept his gun above his head, and Sutchok, no doubt from the habit of imitating his masters, lifted his pole above him. The first to break the silence was Yermolai.

'Tfoo! curse it!' he muttered, spitting into the water; 'here's a go. It's all you, you old devil!' he added, turning wrathfully to Sutchok; 'you've such a boat!'

'It's my fault,' stammered the old man.

'Yes; and you're a nice one,' continued my huntsman, turning his head in Vladimir's direction; 'what were you thinking of? Why weren't you baling out?--you, you?'

But Vladimir was not equal to a reply; he was shaking like a leaf, his teeth were chattering, and his smile was utterly meaningless. What had become of his fine language, his feeling of fine distinctions, and of his own dignity!

The cursed punt rocked feebly under our feet... At the instant of our ducking the water seemed terribly cold to us, but we soon got hardened to it, when the first shock had passed off. I looked round me; the reeds rose up in a circle ten paces from us; in the distance above their tops the bank could be seen. 'It looks bad,' I thought.

'What are we to do?' I asked Yermolai.

'Well, we'll take a look round; we can't spend the night here,' he answered. 'Here, you, take my gun,' he said to Vladimir.

Vladimir obeyed submissively.

'I will go and find the ford,' continued Yermolai, as though there must infallibly be a ford in every pond: he took the pole from Sutchok, and went off in the direction of the bank, warily sounding the depth as he walked.

'Can you swim?' I asked him.

'No, I can't,' his voice sounded from behind the reeds.

'Then he'll be drowned,' remarked Sutchok indifferently. He had been terrified at first, not by the danger, but through fear of our anger, and now, completely reassured, he drew a long breath from time to time, and seemed not to be aware of any necessity for moving from his present position.

'And he will perish without doing any good,' added Vladimir piteously.

Yermolai did not return for more than an hour. That hour seemed an eternity to us. At first we kept calling to him very energetically; then his answering shouts grew less frequent; at last he was completely silent. The bells in the village began ringing for evening service. There was not much conversation between us; indeed, we tried not to look at one another. The ducks hovered over our heads; some seemed disposed to settle near us, but suddenly rose up into the air and flew away quacking. We began to grow numb. Sutchok shut his eyes as though he were disposing himself to sleep.

At last, to our indescribable delight, Yermolai returned.

'Well?'

'I have been to the bank; I have found the ford.... Let us go.'

We wanted to set off at once; but he first brought some string out of his pocket out of the water, tied the slaughtered ducks together by their legs, took both ends in his teeth, and moved slowly forward; Vladimir came behind him, and I behind Vladimir, and Sutchok brought up the rear. It was about two hundred paces to the bank. Yermolai walked boldly and without stopping (so well had he noted the track), only occasionally crying out: 'More to the left--there's a hole here to the right!' or 'Keep to the right--you'll sink in there to the left....' Sometimes the water was up to our necks, and twice poor Sutchok, who was shorter than all the rest of us, got a mouthful and spluttered. 'Come, come, come!' Yermolai shouted roughly to him--and Sutchok, scrambling, hopping and skipping, managed to reach a shallower place, but even in his greatest extremity was never so bold as to clutch at the skirt of my coat. Worn out, muddy and wet, we at last reached the bank.

Two hours later we were all sitting, as dry as circumstances would allow, in a large hay barn, preparing for supper. The coachman Yehudiil, an exceedingly deliberate man, heavy in gait, cautious and sleepy, stood at the entrance, zealously plying Sutchok with snuff (I have noticed that coachmen in Russia very quickly make friends); Sutchok was taking snuff with frenzied energy, in quantities to make him ill; he was spitting, sneezing, and apparently enjoying himself greatly. Vladimir had assumed an air of languor; he leaned his head on one side, and spoke little. Yermolai was cleaning our guns. The dogs were wagging their tails at a great rate in the expectation of porridge; the horses were stamping and neighing in the out-house.... The sun had set; its last rays were broken up into broad tracts of purple; golden clouds were drawn out over the heavens into finer and ever finer threads, like a fleece washed and combed out. ... There was the sound of singing in the village.

VIII   BYEZHIN PRAIRIE

It was a glorious July day, one of those days which only come after many days of fine weather. From earliest morning the sky is clear; the sunrise does not glow with fire; it is suffused with a soft roseate flush. The sun, not fiery, not red-hot as in time of stifling drought, not dull purple as before a storm, but with a bright and genial radiance, rises peacefully behind a long and narrow cloud, shines out freshly, and plunges again into its lilac mist. The delicate upper edge of the strip of cloud flashes in little gleaming snakes; their brilliance is like polished silver. But, lo! the dancing rays flash forth again, and in solemn joy, as though flying upward, rises the mighty orb. About mid-day there is wont to be, high up in the sky, a multitude of rounded clouds, golden-grey, with soft white edges. Like islands scattered over an overflowing river, that bathes them in its unbroken reaches of deep transparent blue, they scarcely stir; farther down the heavens they are in movement, packing closer; now there is no blue to be seen between them, but they are themselves almost as blue as the sky, filled full with light and heat. The colour of the horizon, a faint pale lilac, does not change all day, and is the same all round; nowhere is there storm gathering and darkening; only somewhere rays of bluish colour stretch down from the sky; it is a sprinkling of scarce- perceptible rain. In the evening these clouds disappear; the last of them, blackish and undefined as smoke, lie streaked with pink, facing the setting sun; in the place where it has gone down, as calmly as it rose, a crimson glow lingers long over the darkening earth, and, softly flashing like a candle carried carelessly, the evening star flickers in the sky. On such days all the colours are softened, bright but not glaring; everything is suffused with a kind of touching tenderness. On such days the heat is sometimes very great; often it is even 'steaming' on the slopes of the fields, but a wind dispels this growing sultriness, and whirling eddies of dust--sure sign of settled, fine weather--move along the roads and across the fields in high white columns. In the pure dry air there is a scent of wormwood, rye in blossom, and buckwheat; even an hour before nightfall there is no moisture in the air. It is for such weather that the farmer longs, for harvesting his wheat....

On just such a day I was once out grouse-shooting in the Tchern district of the province of Tula. I started and shot a fair amount of game; my full game-bag cut my shoulder mercilessly; but already the evening glow had faded, and the cool shades of twilight were beginning to grow thicker, and to spread across the sky, which was still bright, though no longer lighted up by the rays of the setting sun, when I at last decided to turn back homewards. With swift steps I passed through the long 'square' of underwoods, clambered up a hill, and instead of the familiar plain I expected to see, with the oakwood on the right and the little white church in the distance, I saw before me a scene completely different, and quite new to me. A narrow valley lay at my feet, and directly facing me a dense wood of aspen-trees rose up like a thick wall. I stood still in perplexity, looked round me.... 'Aha!' I thought, 'I have somehow come wrong; I kept too much to the right,' and surprised at my own mistake, I rapidly descended the hill. I was at once plunged into a disagreeable clinging mist, exactly as though I had gone down into a cellar; the thick high grass at the bottom of the valley, all drenched with dew, was white like a smooth tablecloth; one felt afraid somehow to walk on it. I made haste to get on the other side, and walked along beside the aspenwood, bearing to the left. Bats were already hovering over its slumbering tree-tops, mysteriously flitting and quivering across the clear obscure of the sky; a young belated hawk flew in swift, straight course upwards, hastening to its nest. 'Here, directly I get to this corner,' I thought to myself, 'I shall find the road at once; but I have come a mile out of my way!'

I did at last reach the end of the wood, but there was no road of any sort there; some kind of low bushes overgrown with long grass extended far and wide before me; behind them in the far, far distance could be discerned a tract of waste land. I stopped again. 'Well? Where am I?' I began ransacking my brain to recall how and where I had been walking during the day.... 'Ah! but these are the bushes at Parahin,' I cried at last; 'of course! then this must be Sindyev wood. But how did I get here? So far?... Strange! Now I must bear to the right again.'

I went to the right through the bushes. Meantime the night had crept close and grown up like a storm-cloud; it seemed as though, with the mists of evening, darkness was rising up on all sides and flowing down from overhead. I had come upon some sort of little, untrodden, overgrown path; I walked along it, gazing intently before me. Soon all was blackness and silence around--only the quail's cry was heard from time to time. Some small night-bird, flitting noiselessly near the ground on its soft wings, almost flapped against me and skurried away in alarm. I came out on the further side of the bushes, and made my way along a field by the hedge. By now I could hardly make out distant objects; the field showed dimly white around; beyond it rose up a sullen darkness, which seemed moving up closer in huge masses every instant. My steps gave a muffled sound in the air, that grew colder and colder. The pale sky began again to grow blue--but it was the blue of night. The tiny stars glimmered and twinkled in it.

What I had been taking for a wood turned out to be a dark round hillock. 'But where am I, then?' I repeated again aloud, standing still for the third time and looking inquiringly at my spot and tan English dog, Dianka by name, certainly the most intelligent of four-footed creatures. But the most intelligent of four-footed creatures only wagged her tail, blinked her weary eyes dejectedly, and gave me no sensible advice. I felt myself disgraced in her eyes and pushed desperately forward, as though I had suddenly guessed which way I ought to go; I scaled the hill, and found myself in a hollow of no great depth, ploughed round.

A strange sensation came over me at once. This hollow had the form of an almost perfect cauldron, with sloping sides; at the bottom of it were some great white stones standing upright--it seemed as though they had crept there for some secret council--and it was so still and dark in it, so dreary and weird seemed the sky, overhanging it, that my heart sank. Some little animal was whining feebly and piteously among the stones. I made haste to get out again on to the hillock. Till then I had not quite given up all hope of finding the way home; but at this point I finally decided that I was utterly lost, and without any further attempt to make out the surrounding objects, which were almost completely plunged in darkness, I walked straight forward, by the aid of the stars, at random.... For about half-an-hour I walked on in this way, though I could hardly move one leg before the other. It seemed as if I had never been in such a deserted country in my life; nowhere was there the glimmer of a fire, nowhere a sound to be heard. One sloping hillside followed another; fields stretched endlessly upon fields; bushes seemed to spring up out of the earth under my very nose. I kept walking and was just making up my mind to lie down somewhere till morning, when suddenly I found myself on the edge of a horrible precipice.

I quickly drew back my lifted foot, and through the almost opaque darkness I saw far below me a vast plain. A long river skirted it in a semi-circle, turned away from me; its course was marked by the steely reflection of the water still faintly glimmering here and there. The hill on which I found myself terminated abruptly in an almost overhanging precipice, whose gigantic profile stood out black against the dark-blue waste of sky, and directly below me, in the corner formed by this precipice and the plain near the river, which was there a dark, motionless mirror, under the lee of the hill, two fires side by side were smoking and throwing up red flames. People were stirring round them, shadows hovered, and sometimes the front of a little curly head was lighted up by the glow.

I found out at last where I had got to. This plain was well known in our parts under the name of Byezhin Prairie.... But there was no possibility of returning home, especially at night; my legs were sinking under me from weariness. I decided to get down to the fires and to wait for the dawn in the company of these men, whom I took for drovers. I got down successfully, but I had hardly let go of the last branch I had grasped, when suddenly two large shaggy white dogs rushed angrily barking upon me. The sound of ringing boyish voices came from round the fires; two or three boys quickly got up from the ground. I called back in response to their shouts of inquiry. They ran up to me, and at once called off the dogs, who were specially struck by the appearance of my Dianka. I came down to them.

I had been mistaken in taking the figures sitting round the fires for drovers. They were simply peasant boys from a neighbouring village, who were in charge of a drove of horses. In hot summer weather with us they drive the horses out at night to graze in the open country: the flies and gnats would give them no peace in the daytime; they drive out the drove towards evening, and drive them back in the early morning: it's a great treat for the peasant boys. Bare-headed, in old fur-capes, they bestride the most spirited nags, and scurry along with merry cries and hooting and ringing laughter, swinging their arms and legs, and leaping into the air. The fine dust is stirred up in yellow clouds and moves along the road; the tramp of hoofs in unison resounds afar; the horses race along, pricking up their ears; in front of all, with his tail in the air and thistles in his tangled mane, prances some shaggy chestnut, constantly shifting his paces as he goes.

I told the boys I had lost my way, and sat down with them. They asked me where I came from, and then were silent for a little and turned away. Then we talked a little again. I lay down under a bush, whose shoots had been nibbled off, and began to look round. It was a marvellous picture; about the fire a red ring of light quivered and seemed to swoon away in the embrace of a background of darkness; the flame flaring up from time to time cast swift flashes of light beyond the boundary of this circle; a fine tongue of light licked the dry twigs and died away at once; long thin shadows, in their turn breaking in for an instant, danced right up to the very fires; darkness was struggling with light. Sometimes, when the fire burnt low and the circle of light shrank together, suddenly out of the encroaching darkness a horse's head was thrust in, bay, with striped markings or all white, stared with intent blank eyes upon us, nipped hastily the long grass, and drawing back again, vanished instantly. One could only hear it still munching and snorting. From the circle of light it was hard to make out what was going on in the darkness; everything close at hand seemed shut off by an almost black curtain; but farther away hills and forests were dimly visible in long blurs upon the horizon.

The dark unclouded sky stood, inconceivably immense, triumphant, above us in all its mysterious majesty. One felt a sweet oppression at one's heart, breathing in that peculiar, overpowering, yet fresh fragrance-- the fragrance of a summer night in Russia. Scarcely a sound was to be heard around.... Only at times, in the river near, the sudden splash of a big fish leaping, and the faint rustle of a reed on the bank, swaying lightly as the ripples reached it ... the fires alone kept up a subdued crackling.

The boys sat round them: there too sat the two dogs, who had been so eager to devour me. They could not for long after reconcile themselves to my presence, and, drowsily blinking and staring into the fire, they growled now and then with an unwonted sense of their own dignity; first they growled, and then whined a little, as though deploring the impossibility of carrying out their desires. There were altogether five boys: Fedya, Pavlusha, Ilyusha, Kostya and Vanya. (From their talk I learnt their names, and I intend now to introduce them to the reader.)

The first and eldest of all, Fedya, one would take to be about fourteen. He was a well-made boy, with good-looking, delicate, rather small features, curly fair hair, bright eyes, and a perpetual half- merry, half-careless smile. He belonged, by all appearances, to a well- to-do family, and had ridden out to the prairie, not through necessity, but for amusement. He wore a gay print shirt, with a yellow border; a short new overcoat slung round his neck was almost slipping off his narrow shoulders; a comb hung from his blue belt. His boots, coming a little way up the leg, were certainly his own--not his father's. The second boy, Pavlusha, had tangled black hair, grey eyes, broad cheek- bones, a pale face pitted with small-pox, a large but well-cut mouth; his head altogether was large--'a beer-barrel head,' as they say--and his figure was square and clumsy. He was not a good-looking boy-- there's no denying it!--and yet I liked him; he looked very sensible and straightforward, and there was a vigorous ring in his voice. He had nothing to boast of in his attire; it consisted simply of a homespun shirt and patched trousers. The face of the third, Ilyusha, was rather uninteresting; it was a long face, with short-sighted eyes and a hook nose; it expressed a kind of dull, fretful uneasiness; his tightly- drawn lips seemed rigid; his contracted brow never relaxed; he seemed continually blinking from the firelight. His flaxen--almost white--hair hung out in thin wisps under his low felt hat, which he kept pulling down with both hands over his ears. He had on new bast-shoes and leggings; a thick string, wound three times round his figure, carefully held together his neat black smock. Neither he nor Pavlusha looked more than twelve years old. The fourth, Kostya, a boy of ten, aroused my curiosity by his thoughtful and sorrowful look. His whole face was small, thin, freckled, pointed at the chin like a squirrel's; his lips were barely perceptible; but his great black eyes, that shone with liquid brilliance, produced a strange impression; they seemed trying to express something for which the tongue--his tongue, at least--had no words. He was undersized and weakly, and dressed rather poorly. The remaining boy, Vanya, I had not noticed at first; he was lying on the ground, peacefully curled up under a square rug, and only occasionally thrust his curly brown head out from under it: this boy was seven years old at the most.

So I lay under the bush at one side and looked at the boys. A small pot was hanging over one of the fires; in it potatoes were cooking. Pavlusha was looking after them, and on his knees he was trying them by poking a splinter of wood into the boiling water. Fedya was lying leaning on his elbow, and smoothing out the skirts of his coat. Ilyusha was sitting beside Kostya, and still kept blinking constrainedly. Kostya's head drooped despondently, and he looked away into the distance. Vanya did not stir under his rug. I pretended to be asleep. Little by little, the boys began talking again.

At first they gossiped of one thing and another, the work of to-morrow, the horses; but suddenly Fedya turned to Ilyusha, and, as though taking up again an interrupted conversation, asked him:

'Come then, so you've seen the domovoy?'

'No, I didn't see him, and no one ever can see him,' answered Ilyusha, in a weak hoarse voice, the sound of which was wonderfully in keeping with the expression of his face; 'I heard him.... Yes, and not I alone.'

'Where does he live--in your place?' asked Pavlusha.

'In the old paper-mill.'

'Why, do you go to the factory?'

'Of course we do. My brother Avdushka and I, we are paper-glazers.'

'I say--factory-hands!'

'Well, how did you hear it, then?' asked Fedya.

'It was like this. It happened that I and my brother Avdushka, with Fyodor of Mihyevska, and Ivashka the Squint-eyed, and the other Ivashka who comes from the Red Hills, and Ivashka of Suhorukov too--and there were some other boys there as well--there were ten of us boys there altogether--the whole shift, that is--it happened that we spent the night at the paper-mill; that's to say, it didn't happen, but Nazarov, the overseer, kept us. 'Why,' said he, "should you waste time going home, boys; there's a lot of work to-morrow, so don't go home, boys." So we stopped, and were all lying down together, and Avdushka had just begun to say, "I say, boys, suppose the domovoy were to come?" And before he'd finished saying so, some one suddenly began walking over our heads; we were lying down below, and he began walking upstairs overhead, where the wheel is. We listened: he walked; the boards seemed to be bending under him, they creaked so; then he crossed over, above our heads; all of a sudden the water began to drip and drip over the wheel; the wheel rattled and rattled and again began to turn, though the sluices of the conduit above had been let down. We wondered who could have lifted them up so that the water could run; any way, the wheel turned and turned a little, and then stopped. Then he went to the door overhead and began coming down-stairs, and came down like this, not hurrying himself; the stairs seemed to groan under him too.... Well, he came right down to our door, and waited and waited ... and all of a sudden the door simply flew open. We were in a fright; we looked-- there was nothing.... Suddenly what if the net on one of the vats didn't begin moving; it got up, and went rising and ducking and moving in the air as though some one were stirring with it, and then it was in its place again. Then, at another vat, a hook came off its nail, and then was on its nail again; and then it seemed as if some one came to the door, and suddenly coughed and choked like a sheep, but so loudly!... We all fell down in a heap and huddled against one another.... Just weren't we in a fright that night!'

'I say!' murmured Pavel, 'what did he cough for?'

'I don't know; perhaps it was the damp.'

All were silent for a little.

'Well,' inquired Fedya, 'are the potatoes done?'

Pavlusha tried them.

'No, they are raw.... My, what a splash!' he added, turning his face in the direction of the river; 'that must be a pike.... And there's a star falling.'

'I say, I can tell you something, brothers,' began Kostya, in a shrill little voice; 'listen what my dad told me the other day.'

'Well, we are listening,' said Fedya with a patronising air.

'You know Gavrila, I suppose, the carpenter up in the big village?'

'Yes, we know him.'

'And do you know why he is so sorrowful always, never speaks? do you know? I'll tell you why he's so sorrowful; he went one day, daddy said, he went, brothers, into the forest nutting. So he went nutting into the forest and lost his way; he went on--God only can tell where he got to. So he went on and on, brothers--but 'twas no good!--he could not find the way; and so night came on out of doors. So he sat down under a tree. "I'll wait till morning," thought he. He sat down and began to drop asleep. So as he was falling asleep, suddenly he heard some one call him. He looked up; there was no one. He fell asleep again; again he was called. He looked and looked again; and in front of him there sat a russalka on a branch, swinging herself and calling him to her, and simply dying with laughing; she laughed so.... And the moon was shining bright, so bright, the moon shone so clear--everything could be seen plain, brothers. So she called him, and she herself was as bright and as white sitting on the branch as some dace or a roach, or like some little carp so white and silvery.... Gavrila the carpenter almost fainted, brothers, but she laughed without stopping, and kept beckoning him to her like this. Then Gavrila was just getting up; he was just going to yield to the russalka, brothers, but--the Lord put it into his heart, doubtless--he crossed himself like this.... And it was so hard for him to make that cross, brothers; he said, "My hand was simply like a stone; it would not move." ... Ugh! the horrid witch.... So when he made the cross, brothers, the russalka, she left off laughing, and all at once how she did cry.... She cried, brothers, and wiped her eyes with her hair, and her hair was green as any hemp. So Gavrila looked and looked at her, and at last he fell to questioning her. "Why are you weeping, wild thing of the woods?" And the russalka began to speak to him like this: "If you had not crossed yourself, man," she says, "you should have lived with me in gladness of heart to the end of your days; and I weep, I am grieved at heart because you crossed yourself; but I will not grieve alone; you too shall grieve at heart to the end of your days." Then she vanished, brothers, and at once it was plain to Gavrila how to get out of the forest.... Only since then he goes always sorrowful, as you see.'

'Ugh!' said Fedya after a brief silence; 'but how can such an evil thing of the woods ruin a Christian soul--he did not listen to her?'

'And I say!' said Kostya. 'Gavrila said that her voice was as shrill and plaintive as a toad's.'

'Did your father tell you that himself?' Fedya went on.

'Yes. I was lying in the loft; I heard it all.'

'It's a strange thing. Why should he be sorrowful?... But I suppose she liked him, since she called him.'

'Ay, she liked him!' put in Ilyusha. 'Yes, indeed! she wanted to tickle him to death, that's what she wanted. That's what they do, those russalkas.'

'There ought to be russalkas here too, I suppose,' observed Fedya.

'No,' answered Kostya, 'this is a holy open place. There's one thing, though: the river's near.'

All were silent. Suddenly from out of the distance came a prolonged, resonant, almost wailing sound, one of those inexplicable sounds of the night, which break upon a profound stillness, rise upon the air, linger, and slowly die away at last. You listen: it is as though there were nothing, yet it echoes still. It is as though some one had uttered a long, long cry upon the very horizon, as though some other had answered him with shrill harsh laughter in the forest, and a faint, hoarse hissing hovers over the river. The boys looked round about shivering....

'Christ's aid be with us!' whispered Ilyusha.

'Ah, you craven crows!' cried Pavel, 'what are you frightened of? Look, the potatoes are done.' (They all came up to the pot and began to eat the smoking potatoes; only Vanya did not stir.) 'Well, aren't you coming?' said Pavel.

But he did not creep out from under his rug. The pot was soon completely emptied.

'Have you heard, boys,' began Ilyusha, 'what happened with us at Varnavitsi?'

'Near the dam?' asked Fedya.

'Yes, yes, near the dam, the broken-down dam. That is a haunted place, such a haunted place, and so lonely. All round there are pits and quarries, and there are always snakes in pits.'

'Well, what did happen? Tell us.'

'Well, this is what happened. You don't know, perhaps, Fedya, but there a drowned man was buried; he was drowned long, long ago, when the water was still deep; only his grave can still be seen, though it can only just be seen ... like this--a little mound.... So one day the bailiff called the huntsman Yermil, and says to him, "Go to the post, Yermil." Yermil always goes to the post for us; he has let all his dogs die; they never will live with him, for some reason, and they have never lived with him, though he's a good huntsman, and everyone liked him. So Yermil went to the post, and he stayed a bit in the town, and when he rode back, he was a little tipsy. It was night, a fine night; the moon was shining.... So Yermil rode across the dam; his way lay there. So, as he rode along, he saw, on the drowned man's grave, a little lamb, so white and curly and pretty, running about. So Yermil thought, "I will take him," and he got down and took him in his arms. But the little lamb didn't take any notice. So Yermil goes back to his horse, and the horse stares at him, and snorts and shakes his head; however, he said "wo" to him and sat on him with the lamb, and rode on again; he held the lamb in front of him. He looks at him, and the lamb looks him straight in the face, like this. Yermil the huntsman felt upset. "I don't remember," he said, "that lambs ever look at any one like that"; however, he began to stroke it like this on its wool, and to say, "Chucky! chucky!" And the lamb suddenly showed its teeth and said too, "Chucky! chucky!"'

The boy who was telling the story had hardly uttered this last word, when suddenly both dogs got up at once, and, barking convulsively, rushed away from the fire and disappeared in the darkness. All the boys were alarmed. Vanya jumped up from under his rug. Pavlusha ran shouting after the dogs. Their barking quickly grew fainter in the distance.... There was the noise of the uneasy tramp of the frightened drove of horses. Pavlusha shouted aloud: 'Hey Grey! Beetle!' ... In a few minutes the barking ceased; Pavel's voice sounded still in the distance.... A little time more passed; the boys kept looking about in perplexity, as though expecting something to happen.... Suddenly the tramp of a galloping horse was heard; it stopped short at the pile of wood, and, hanging on to the mane, Pavel sprang nimbly off it. Both the dogs also leaped into the circle of light and at once sat down, their red tongues hanging out.

'What was it? what was it?' asked the boys.

'Nothing,' answered Pavel, waving his hand to his horse; 'I suppose the dogs scented something. I thought it was a wolf,' he added, calmly drawing deep breaths into his chest.

I could not help admiring Pavel. He was very fine at that moment. His ugly face, animated by his swift ride, glowed with hardihood and determination. Without even a switch in his hand, he had, without the slightest hesitation, rushed out into the night alone to face a wolf.... 'What a splendid fellow!' I thought, looking at him.

'Have you seen any wolves, then?' asked the trembling Kostya.

'There are always a good many of them here,' answered Pavel; 'but they are only troublesome in the winter.'

He crouched down again before the fire. As he sat down on the ground, he laid his hand on the shaggy head of one of the dogs. For a long while the flattered brute did not turn his head, gazing sidewise with grateful pride at Pavlusha.

Vanya lay down under his rug again.

'What dreadful things you were telling us, Ilyusha!' began Fedya, whose part it was, as the son of a well-to-do peasant, to lead the conversation. (He spoke little himself, apparently afraid of lowering his dignity.) 'And then some evil spirit set the dogs barking.... Certainly I have heard that place was haunted.'

'Varnavitsi?... I should think it was haunted! More than once, they say, they have seen the old master there--the late master. He wears, they say, a long skirted coat, and keeps groaning like this, and looking for something on the ground. Once grandfather Trofimitch met him. "What," says he, "your honour, Ivan Ivanitch, are you pleased to look for on the ground?"'

'He asked him?' put in Fedya in amazement.

'Yes, he asked him.'

'Well, I call Trofimitch a brave fellow after that.... Well, what did he say?'

'"I am looking for the herb that cleaves all things," says he. But he speaks so thickly, so thickly. "And what, your honour, Ivan Ivanitch, do you want with the herb that cleaves all things?" "The tomb weighs on me; it weighs on me, Trofimitch: I want to get away--away."'

'My word!' observed Fedya, 'he didn't enjoy his life enough, I suppose.'

'What a marvel!' said Kosyta. 'I thought one could only see the departed on All Hallows' day.'

'One can see the departed any time,' Ilyusha interposed with conviction. From what I could observe, I judged he knew the village superstitions better than the others.... 'But on All Hallows' day you can see the living too; those, that is, whose turn it is to die that year. You need only sit in the church porch, and keep looking at the road. They will come by you along the road; those, that is, who will die that year. Last year old Ulyana went to the porch.'

'Well, did she see anyone?' asked Kostya inquisitively.

'To be sure she did. At first she sat a long, long while, and saw no one and heard nothing ... only it seemed as if some dog kept whining and whining like this somewhere.... Suddenly she looks up: a boy comes along the road with only a shirt on. She looked at him. It was Ivashka Fedosyev.'

'He who died in the spring?' put in Fedya.

'Yes, he. He came along and never lifted up his head. But Ulyana knew him. And then she looks again: a woman came along. She stared and stared at her.... Ah, God Almighty! ... it was herself coming along the road; Ulyana herself.'

'Could it be herself?' asked Fedya.

'Yes, by God, herself.'

'Well, but she is not dead yet, you know?' 'But the year is not over yet. And only look at her; her life hangs on a thread.'

All were still again. Pavel threw a handful of dry twigs on to the fire. They were soon charred by the suddenly leaping flame; they cracked and smoked, and began to contract, curling up their burning ends. Gleams of light in broken flashes glanced in all directions, especially upwards. Suddenly a white dove flew straight into the bright light, fluttered round and round in terror, bathed in the red glow, and disappeared with a whirr of its wings.

'It's lost its home, I suppose,' remarked Pavel. 'Now it will fly till it gets somewhere, where it can rest till dawn.'

'Why, Pavlusha,' said Kostya, 'might it not be a just soul flying to heaven?'

Pavel threw another handful of twigs on to the fire.

'Perhaps,' he said at last.

'But tell us, please, Pavlusha,' began Fedya, 'what was seen in your parts at Shalamovy at the heavenly portent?'

[Footnote: This is what the peasants call an eclipse.-- Author's Note .]

'When the sun could not be seen? Yes, indeed.'

'Were you frightened then?'

'Yes; and we weren't the only ones. Our master, though he talked to us beforehand, and said there would be a heavenly portent, yet when it got dark, they say he himself was frightened out of his wits. And in the house-serfs' cottage the old woman, directly it grew dark, broke all the dishes in the oven with the poker. 'Who will eat now?' she said; 'the last day has come.' So the soup was all running about the place. And in the village there were such tales about among us: that white wolves would run over the earth, and would eat men, that a bird of prey would pounce down on us, and that they would even see Trishka.'

[Footnote: The popular belief in Trishka is probably derived from some tradition of Antichrist.-- Author's Note .]

'What is Trishka?' asked Kostya.

'Why, don't you know?' interrupted Ilyusha warmly. 'Why, brother, where have you been brought up, not to know Trishka? You're a stay-at-home, one-eyed lot in your village, really! Trishka will be a marvellous man, who will come one day, and he will be such a marvellous man that they will never be able to catch him, and never be able to do anything with him; he will be such a marvellous man. The people will try to take him; for example, they will come after him with sticks, they will surround him, but he will blind their eyes so that they fall upon one another. They will put him in prison, for example; he will ask for a little water to drink in a bowl; they will bring him the bowl, and he will plunge into it and vanish from their sight. They will put chains on him, but he will only clap his hands--they will fall off him. So this Trishka will go through villages and towns; and this Trishka will be a wily man; he will lead astray Christ's people ... and they will be able to do nothing to him.... He will be such a marvellous, wily man.'

'Well, then,' continued Pavel, in his deliberate voice, 'that's what he 's like. And so they expected him in our parts. The old men declared that directly the heavenly portent began, Trishka would come. So the heavenly portent began. All the people were scattered over the street, in the fields, waiting to see what would happen. Our place, you know, is open country. They look; and suddenly down the mountain-side from the big village comes a man of some sort; such a strange man, with such a wonderful head ... that all scream: "Oy, Trishka is coming! Oy, Trishka is coming!" and all run in all directions! Our elder crawled into a ditch; his wife stumbled on the door-board and screamed with all her might; she terrified her yard-dog, so that he broke away from his chain and over the hedge and into the forest; and Kuzka's father, Dorofyitch, ran into the oats, lay down there, and began to cry like a quail. 'Perhaps' says he, 'the Enemy, the Destroyer of Souls, will spare the birds, at least.' So they were all in such a scare! But he that was coming was our cooper Vavila; he had bought himself a new pitcher, and had put the empty pitcher over his head.'

All the boys laughed; and again there was a silence for a while, as often happens when people are talking in the open air. I looked out into the solemn, majestic stillness of the night; the dewy freshness of late evening had been succeeded by the dry heat of midnight; the darkness still had long to lie in a soft curtain over the slumbering fields; there was still a long while left before the first whisperings, the first dewdrops of dawn. There was no moon in the heavens; it rose late at that time. Countless golden stars, twinkling in rivalry, seemed all running softly towards the Milky Way, and truly, looking at them, you were almost conscious of the whirling, never--resting motion of the earth.... A strange, harsh, painful cry, sounded twice together over the river, and a few moments later, was repeated farther down....

Kostya shuddered. 'What was that?'

'That was a heron's cry,' replied Pavel tranquilly.

'A heron,' repeated Kostya.... 'And what was it, Pavlusha, I heard yesterday evening,' he added, after a short pause; 'you perhaps will know.'

'What did you hear?'

'I will tell you what I heard. I was going from Stony Ridge to Shashkino; I went first through our walnut wood, and then passed by a little pool--you know where there's a sharp turn down to the ravine-- there is a water-pit there, you know; it is quite overgrown with reeds; so I went near this pit, brothers, and suddenly from this came a sound of some one groaning, and piteously, so piteously; oo-oo, oo-oo! I was in such a fright, my brothers; it was late, and the voice was so miserable. I felt as if I should cry myself.... What could that have been, eh?'

'It was in that pit the thieves drowned Akim the forester, last summer,' observed Pavel; 'so perhaps it was his soul lamenting.'

'Oh, dear, really, brothers,' replied Kostya, opening wide his eyes, which were round enough before, 'I did not know they had drowned Akim in that pit. Shouldn't I have been frightened if I'd known!'

'But they say there are little, tiny frogs,' continued Pavel, 'who cry piteously like that.'

'Frogs? Oh, no, it was not frogs, certainly not. (A heron again uttered a cry above the river.) Ugh, there it is!' Kostya cried involuntarily; 'it is just like a wood-spirit shrieking.'

'The wood-spirit does not shriek; it is dumb,' put in Ilyusha; 'it only claps its hands and rattles.'

'And have you seen it then, the wood-spirit?' Fedya asked him ironically.

'No, I have not seen it, and God preserve me from seeing it; but others have seen it. Why, one day it misled a peasant in our parts, and led him through the woods and all in a circle in one field.... He scarcely got home till daylight.'

'Well, and did he see it?'

'Yes. He says it was a big, big creature, dark, wrapped up, just like a tree; you could not make it out well; it seemed to hide away from the moon, and kept staring and staring with its great eyes, and winking and winking with them....'

'Ugh!' exclaimed Fedya with a slight shiver, and a shrug of the shoulders; 'pfoo.'

'And how does such an unclean brood come to exist in the world?' said Pavel; 'it's a wonder.'

'Don't speak ill of it; take care, it will hear you,' said Ilyusha.

Again there was a silence.

'Look, look, brothers,' suddenly came Vanya's childish voice; 'look at God's little stars; they are swarming like bees!'

He put his fresh little face out from under his rug, leaned on his little fist, and slowly lifted up his large soft eyes. The eyes of all the boys were raised to the sky, and they were not lowered quickly.

'Well, Vanya,' began Fedya caressingly, 'is your sister Anyutka well?'

'Yes, she is very well,' replied Vanya with a slight lisp.

'You ask her, why doesn't she come to see us?'

'I don't know.'

'You tell her to come.'

'Very well.'

'Tell her I have a present for her.'

'And a present for me too?'

'Yes, you too.'

Vanya sighed.

'No; I don't want one. Better give it to her; she is so kind to us at home.'

And Vanya laid his head down again on the ground. Pavel got up and took the empty pot in his hand.

'Where are you going?' Fedya asked him.

'To the river, to get water; I want some water to drink.'

The dogs got up and followed him.

'Take care you don't fall into the river!' Ilyusha cried after him.

'Why should he fall in?' said Fedya. 'He will be careful.'

'Yes, he will be careful. But all kinds of things happen; he will stoop over, perhaps, to draw the water, and the water-spirit will clutch him by the hand, and drag him to him. Then they will say, "The boy fell into the water." ... Fell in, indeed! ... "There, he has crept in among the reeds," he added, listening.

The reeds certainly 'shished,' as they call it among us, as they were parted.

'But is it true,' asked Kostya, 'that crazy Akulina has been mad ever since she fell into the water?'

'Yes, ever since.... How dreadful she is now! But they say she was a beauty before then. The water-spirit bewitched her. I suppose he did not expect they would get her out so soon. So down there at the bottom he bewitched her.'

(I had met this Akulina more than once. Covered with rags, fearfully thin, with face as black as a coal, blear-eyed and for ever grinning, she would stay whole hours in one place in the road, stamping with her feet, pressing her fleshless hands to her breast, and slowly shifting from one leg to the other, like a wild beast in a cage. She understood nothing that was said to her, and only chuckled spasmodically from time to time.)

'But they say,' continued Kostya, 'that Akulina threw herself into the river because her lover had deceived her.'

'Yes, that was it.'

'And do you remember Vasya?' added Kostya, mournfully.

'What Vasya?' asked Fedya.

'Why, the one who was drowned,' replied Kostya,' in this very river. Ah, what a boy he was! What a boy he was! His mother, Feklista, how she loved him, her Vasya! And she seemed to have a foreboding, Feklista did, that harm would come to him from the water. Sometimes, when Vasya went with us boys in the summer to bathe in the river, she used to be trembling all over. The other women did not mind; they passed by with the pails, and went on, but Feklista put her pail down on the ground, and set to calling him, 'Come back, come back, my little joy; come back, my darling!' And no one knows how he was drowned. He was playing on the bank, and his mother was there haymaking; suddenly she hears, as though some one was blowing bubbles through the water, and behold! there was only Vasya's little cap to be seen swimming on the water. You know since then Feklista has not been right in her mind: she goes and lies down at the place where he was drowned; she lies down, brothers, and sings a song--you remember Vasya was always singing a song like that--so she sings it too, and weeps and weeps, and bitterly rails against God.'

'Here is Pavlusha coming,' said Fedya.

Pavel came up to the fire with a full pot in his hand.

'Boys,' he began, after a short silence, 'something bad happened.'

'Oh, what?' asked Kostya hurriedly.

'I heard Vasya's voice.'

They all seemed to shudder.

'What do you mean? what do you mean?' stammered Kostya.

'I don't know. Only I went to stoop down to the water; suddenly I hear my name called in Vasya's voice, as though it came from below water: "Pavlusha, Pavlusha, come here." I came away. But I fetched the water, though.'

'Ah, God have mercy upon us!' said the boys, crossing themselves.

'It was the water-spirit calling you, Pavel,' said Fedya; 'we were just talking of Vasya.'

'Ah, it's a bad omen,' said Ilyusha, deliberately.

'Well, never mind, don't bother about it,' Pavel declared stoutly, and he sat down again; 'no one can escape his fate.'

The boys were still. It was clear that Pavel's words had produced a strong impression on them. They began to lie down before the fire as though preparing to go to sleep.

'What is that?' asked Kostya, suddenly lifting his head.

Pavel listened.

'It's the curlews flying and whistling.'

'Where are they flying to?'

'To a land where, they say, there is no winter.'

'But is there such a land?'

'Yes.'

'Is it far away?'

'Far, far away, beyond the warm seas.'

Kostya sighed and shut his eyes.

More than three hours had passed since I first came across the boys. The moon at last had risen; I did not notice it at first; it was such a tiny crescent. This moonless night was as solemn and hushed as it had been at first.... But already many stars, that not long before had been high up in the heavens, were setting over the earth's dark rim; everything around was perfectly still, as it is only still towards morning; all was sleeping the deep unbroken sleep that comes before daybreak. Already the fragrance in the air was fainter; once more a dew seemed falling.... How short are nights in summer!... The boys' talk died down when the fires did. The dogs even were dozing; the horses, so far as I could make out, in the hardly-perceptible, faintly shining light of the stars, were asleep with downcast heads.... I fell into a state of weary unconsciousness, which passed into sleep.

A fresh breeze passed over my face. I opened my eyes; the morning was beginning. The dawn had not yet flushed the sky, but already it was growing light in the east. Everything had become visible, though dimly visible, around. The pale grey sky was growing light and cold and bluish; the stars twinkled with a dimmer light, or disappeared; the earth was wet, the leaves covered with dew, and from the distance came sounds of life and voices, and a light morning breeze went fluttering over the earth. My body responded to it with a faint shudder of delight. I got up quickly and went to the boys. They were all sleeping as though they were tired out round the smouldering fire; only Pavel half rose and gazed intently at me.

I nodded to him, and walked homewards beside the misty river. Before I had walked two miles, already all around me, over the wide dew-drenched prairie, and in front from forest to forest, where the hills were growing green again, and behind, over the long dusty road and the sparkling bushes, flushed with the red glow, and the river faintly blue now under the lifting mist, flowed fresh streams of burning light, first pink, then red and golden.... All things began to stir, to awaken, to sing, to flutter, to speak. On all sides thick drops of dew sparkled in glittering diamonds; to welcome me, pure and clear as though bathed in the freshness of morning, came the notes of a bell, and suddenly there rushed by me, driven by the boys I had parted from, the drove of horses, refreshed and rested....

Sad to say, I must add that in that year Pavel met his end. He was not drowned; he was killed by a fall from his horse. Pity! he was a splendid fellow!

IX KASSYAN OF FAIR SPRINGS

I was returning from hunting in a jolting little trap, and overcome by the stifling heat of a cloudy summer day (it is well known that the heat is often more insupportable on such days than in bright days, especially when there is no wind), I dozed and was shaken about, resigning myself with sullen fortitude to being persecuted by the fine white dust which was incessantly raised from the beaten road by the warped and creaking wheels, when suddenly my attention was aroused by the extraordinary uneasiness and agitated movements of my coachman, who had till that instant been more soundly dozing than I. He began tugging at the reins, moved uneasily on the box, and started shouting to the horses, staring all the while in one direction. I looked round. We were driving through a wide ploughed plain; low hills, also ploughed over, ran in gently sloping, swelling waves over it; the eye took in some five miles of deserted country; in the distance the round-scolloped tree-tops of some small birch-copses were the only objects to break the almost straight line of the horizon. Narrow paths ran over the fields, disappeared into the hollows, and wound round the hillocks. On one of these paths, which happened to run into our road five hundred paces ahead of us, I made out a kind of procession. At this my coachman was looking.

It was a funeral. In front, in a little cart harnessed with one horse, and advancing at a walking pace, came the priest; beside him sat the deacon driving; behind the cart four peasants, bareheaded, carried the coffin, covered with a white cloth; two women followed the coffin. The shrill wailing voice of one of them suddenly reached my ears; I listened; she was intoning a dirge. Very dismal sounded this chanted, monotonous, hopelessly-sorrowful lament among the empty fields. The coachman whipped up the horses; he wanted to get in front of this procession. To meet a corpse on the road is a bad omen. And he did succeed in galloping ahead beyond this path before the funeral had had time to turn out of it into the high-road; but we had hardly got a hundred paces beyond this point, when suddenly our trap jolted violently, heeled on one side, and all but overturned. The coachman pulled up the galloping horses, and spat with a gesture of his hand.

'What is it?' I asked.

My coachman got down without speaking or hurrying himself.

'But what is it?'

'The axle is broken ... it caught fire,' he replied gloomily, and he suddenly arranged the collar on the off-side horse with such indignation that it was almost pushed over, but it stood its ground, snorted, shook itself, and tranquilly began to scratch its foreleg below the knee with its teeth.

I got out and stood for some time on the road, a prey to a vague and unpleasant feeling of helplessness. The right wheel was almost completely bent in under the trap, and it seemed to turn its centre- piece upwards in dumb despair.

'What are we to do now?' I said at last.

'That's what's the cause of it!' said my coachman, pointing with his whip to the funeral procession, which had just turned into the highroad and was approaching us. 'I have always noticed that,' he went on; 'it's a true saying--"Meet a corpse"--yes, indeed.'

And again he began worrying the off-side horse, who, seeing his ill- humour, resolved to remain perfectly quiet, and contented itself with discreetly switching its tail now and then. I walked up and down a little while, and then stopped again before the wheel.

Meanwhile the funeral had come up to us. Quietly turning off the road on to the grass, the mournful procession moved slowly past us. My coachman and I took off our caps, saluted the priest, and exchanged glances with the bearers. They moved with difficulty under their burden, their broad chests standing out under the strain. Of the two women who followed the coffin, one was very old and pale; her set face, terribly distorted as it was by grief, still kept an expression of grave and severe dignity. She walked in silence, from time to time lifting her wasted hand to her thin drawn lips. The other, a young woman of five-and-twenty, had her eyes red and moist and her whole face swollen with weeping; as she passed us she ceased wailing, and hid her face in her sleeve.... But when the funeral had got round us and turned again into the road, her piteous, heart-piercing lament began again. My coachman followed the measured swaying of the coffin with his eyes in silence. Then he turned to me.

'It's Martin, the carpenter, they're burying,' he said; 'Martin of Ryaby.'

'How do you know?'

'I know by the women. The old one is his mother, and the young one's his wife.'

'Has he been ill, then?'

'Yes ... fever. The day before yesterday the overseer sent for the doctor, but they did not find the doctor at home. He was a good carpenter; he drank a bit, but he was a good carpenter. See how upset his good woman is.... But, there; women's tears don't cost much, we know. Women's tears are only water ... yes, indeed.'

And he bent down, crept under the side-horse's trace, and seized the wooden yoke that passes over the horses' heads with both hands.

'Any way,' I observed, 'what are we going to do?'

My coachman just supported himself with his knees on the shaft-horse's shoulder, twice gave the back-strap a shake, and straightened the pad; then he crept out of the side-horse's trace again, and giving it a blow on the nose as he passed, went up to the wheel. He went up to it, and, never taking his eyes off it, slowly took out of the skirts of his coat a box, slowly pulled open its lid by a strap, slowly thrust into it his two fat fingers (which pretty well filled it up), rolled and rolled up some snuff, and creasing up his nose in anticipation, helped himself to it several times in succession, accompanying the snuff-taking every time by a prolonged sneezing. Then, his streaming eyes blinking faintly, he relapsed into profound meditation.

'Well?' I said at last.

My coachman thrust his box carefully into his pocket, brought his hat forward on to his brows without the aid of his hand by a movement of his head, and gloomily got up on the box.

'What are you doing?' I asked him, somewhat bewildered.

'Pray be seated,' he replied calmly, picking up the reins.

'But how can we go on?'

'We will go on now.'

'But the axle.'

'Pray be seated.'

'But the axle is broken.'

'It is broken; but we will get to the settlement ... at a walking pace, of course. Over here, beyond the copse, on the right, is a settlement; they call it Yudino.'

'And do you think we can get there?'

My coachman did not vouchsafe me a reply.

'I had better walk,' I said.

'As you like....' And he nourished his whip. The horses started.

We did succeed in getting to the settlement, though the right front wheel was almost off, and turned in a very strange way. On one hillock it almost flew off, but my coachman shouted in a voice of exasperation, and we descended it in safety.

Yudino settlement consisted of six little low-pitched huts, the walls of which had already begun to warp out of the perpendicular, though they had certainly not been long built; the back-yards of some of the huts were not even fenced in with a hedge. As we drove into this settlement we did not meet a single living soul; there were no hens even to be seen in the street, and no dogs, but one black crop-tailed cur, which at our approach leaped hurriedly out of a perfectly dry and empty trough, to which it must have been driven by thirst, and at once, without barking, rushed headlong under a gate. I went up to the first hut, opened the door into the outer room, and called for the master of the house. No one answered me. I called once more; the hungry mewing of a cat sounded behind the other door. I pushed it open with my foot; a thin cat ran up and down near me, her green eyes glittering in the dark. I put my head into the room and looked round; it was empty, dark, and smoky. I returned to the yard, and there was no one there either.... A calf lowed behind the paling; a lame grey goose waddled a little away. I passed on to the second hut. Not a soul in the second hut either. I went into the yard....

In the very middle of the yard, in the glaring sunlight, there lay, with his face on the ground and a cloak thrown over his head, a boy, as it seemed to me. In a thatched shed a few paces from him a thin little nag with broken harness was standing near a wretched little cart. The sunshine falling in streaks through the narrow cracks in the dilapidated roof, striped his shaggy, reddish-brown coat in small bands of light. Above, in the high bird-house, starlings were chattering and looking down inquisitively from their airy home. I went up to the sleeping figure and began to awaken him.

He lifted his head, saw me, and at once jumped up on to his feet.... 'What? what do you want? what is it?' he muttered, half asleep.

I did not answer him at once; I was so much impressed by his appearance.

Picture to yourself a little creature of fifty years old, with a little round wrinkled face, a sharp nose, little, scarcely visible, brown eyes, and thick curly black hair, which stood out on his tiny head like the cap on the top of a mushroom. His whole person was excessively thin and weakly, and it is absolutely impossible to translate into words the extraordinary strangeness of his expression.

'What do you want?' he asked me again. I explained to him what was the matter; he listened, slowly blinking, without taking his eyes off me.

'So cannot we get a new axle?' I said finally; 'I will gladly pay for it.'

'But who are you? Hunters, eh?' he asked, scanning me from head to foot.

'Hunters.'

'You shoot the fowls of heaven, I suppose?... the wild things of the woods?... And is it not a sin to kill God's birds, to shed the innocent blood?'

The strange old man spoke in a very drawling tone. The sound of his voice also astonished me. There was none of the weakness of age to be heard in it; it was marvellously sweet, young and almost feminine in its softness.

'I have no axle,' he added after a brief silence. 'That thing will not suit you.' He pointed to his cart. 'You have, I expect, a large trap.'

'But can I get one in the village?'

'Not much of a village here!... No one has an axle here.... And there is no one at home either; they are all at work. You must go on,' he announced suddenly; and he lay down again on the ground.

I had not at all expected this conclusion.

'Listen, old man,' I said, touching him on the shoulder; 'do me a kindness, help me.'

'Go on, in God's name! I am tired; I have driven into the town,' he said, and drew his cloak over his head.

'But pray do me a kindness,' I said. 'I ... I will pay for it.' 'I don't want your money.'

'But please, old man.'

He half raised himself and sat up, crossing his little legs.

'I could take you perhaps to the clearing. Some merchants have bought the forest here--God be their judge! They are cutting down the forest, and they have built a counting-house there--God be their judge! You might order an axle of them there, or buy one ready made.'

'Splendid!' I cried delighted; 'splendid! let us go.'

'An oak axle, a good one,' he continued, not getting up from his place.

'And is it far to this clearing?'

'Three miles.'

'Come, then! we can drive there in your trap.'

'Oh, no....'

'Come, let us go,' I said; 'let us go, old man! The coachman is waiting for us in the road.'

The old man rose unwillingly and followed me into the street. We found my coachman in an irritable frame of mind; he had tried to water his horses, but the water in the well, it appeared, was scanty in quantity and bad in taste, and water is the first consideration with coachmen.... However, he grinned at the sight of the old man, nodded his head and cried: 'Hallo! Kassyanushka! good health to you!'

'Good health to you, Erofay, upright man!' replied Kassyan in a dejected voice.

I at once made known his suggestion to the coachman; Erofay expressed his approval of it and drove into the yard. While he was busy deliberately unharnessing the horses, the old man stood leaning with his shoulders against the gate, and looking disconsolately first at him and then at me. He seemed in some uncertainty of mind; he was not very pleased, as it seemed to me, at our sudden visit.

'So they have transported you too?' Erofay asked him suddenly, lifting the wooden arch of the harness.

'Yes.'

'Ugh!' said my coachman between his teeth. 'You know Martin the carpenter.... Of course, you know Martin of Ryaby?'

'Yes.'

'Well, he is dead. We have just met his coffin.'

Kassyan shuddered.

'Dead?' he said, and his head sank dejectedly.

'Yes, he is dead. Why didn't you cure him, eh? You know they say you cure folks; you're a doctor.'

My coachman was apparently laughing and jeering at the old man.

'And is this your trap, pray?' he added, with a shrug of his shoulders in its direction.

'Yes.'

'Well, a trap ... a fine trap!' he repeated, and taking it by the shafts almost turned it completely upside down. 'A trap!... But what will you drive in it to the clearing?... You can't harness our horses in these shafts; our horses are all too big.'

'I don't know,' replied Kassyan, 'what you are going to drive; that beast perhaps,' he added with a sigh.

'That?' broke in Erofay, and going up to Kassyan's nag, he tapped it disparagingly on the back with the third finger of his right hand. 'See,' he added contemptuously, 'it's asleep, the scare-crow!'

I asked Erofay to harness it as quickly as he could. I wanted to drive myself with Kassyan to the clearing; grouse are fond of such places. When the little cart was quite ready, and I, together with my dog, had been installed in the warped wicker body of it, and Kassyan huddled up into a little ball, with still the same dejected expression on his face, had taken his seat in front, Erofay came up to me and whispered with an air of mystery:

'You did well, your honour, to drive with him. He is such a queer fellow; he's cracked, you know, and his nickname is the Flea. I don't know how you managed to make him out....'

I tried to say to Erofay that so far Kassyan had seemed to me a very sensible man; but my coachman continued at once in the same voice:

'But you keep a look-out where he is driving you to. And, your honour, be pleased to choose the axle yourself; be pleased to choose a sound one.... Well, Flea,' he added aloud, 'could I get a bit of bread in your house?'

'Look about; you may find some,' answered Kassyan. He pulled the reins and we rolled away.

His little horse, to my genuine astonishment, did not go badly. Kassyan preserved an obstinate silence the whole way, and made abrupt and unwilling answers to my questions. We quickly reached the clearing, and then made our way to the counting-house, a lofty cottage, standing by itself over a small gully, which had been dammed up and converted into a pool. In this counting-house I found two young merchants' clerks, with snow-white teeth, sweet and soft eyes, sweet and subtle words, and sweet and wily smiles. I bought an axle of them and returned to the clearing. I thought that Kassyan would stay with the horse and await my return; but he suddenly came up to me. 'Are you going to shoot birds, eh?' he said.

'Yes, if I come across any.'

'I will come with you.... Can I?'

'Certainly, certainly.'

So we went together. The land cleared was about a mile in length. I must confess I watched Kassyan more than my dogs. He had been aptly called 'Flea.' His little black uncovered head (though his hair, indeed, was as good a covering as any cap) seemed to flash hither and thither among the bushes. He walked extraordinarily swiftly, and seemed always hopping up and down as he moved; he was for ever stooping down to pick herbs of some kind, thrusting them into his bosom, muttering to himself, and constantly looking at me and my dog with such a strange searching gaze. Among low bushes and in clearings there are often little grey birds which constantly flit from tree to tree, and which whistle as they dart away. Kassyan mimicked them, answered their calls; a young quail flew from between his feet, chirruping, and he chirruped in imitation of him; a lark began to fly down above him, moving his wings and singing melodiously: Kassyan joined in his song. He did not speak to me at all....

The weather was glorious, even more so than before; but the heat was no less. Over the clear sky the high thin clouds were hardly stirred, yellowish-white, like snow lying late in spring, flat and drawn out like rolled-up sails. Slowly but perceptibly their fringed edges, soft and fluffy as cotton-wool, changed at every moment; they were melting away, even these clouds, and no shadow fell from them. I strolled about the clearing for a long while with Kassyan. Young shoots, which had not yet had time to grow more than a yard high, surrounded the low blackened stumps with their smooth slender stems; and spongy funguses with grey edges--the same of which they make tinder--clung to these; strawberry plants flung their rosy tendrils over them; mushrooms squatted close in groups. The feet were constantly caught and entangled in the long grass, that was parched in the scorching sun; the eyes were dazzled on all sides by the glaring metallic glitter on the young reddish leaves of the trees; on all sides were the variegated blue clusters of vetch, the golden cups of bloodwort, and the half-lilac, half-yellow blossoms of the heart's-ease. In some places near the disused paths, on which the tracks of wheels were marked by streaks on the fine bright grass, rose piles of wood, blackened by wind and rain, laid in yard-lengths; there was a faint shadow cast from them in slanting oblongs; there was no other shade anywhere. A light breeze rose, then sank again; suddenly it would blow straight in the face and seem to be rising; everything would begin to rustle merrily, to nod, to shake around one; the supple tops of the ferns bow down gracefully, and one rejoices in it, but at once it dies away again, and all is at rest once more. Only the grasshoppers chirrup in chorus with frenzied energy, and wearisome is this unceasing, sharp dry sound. It is in keeping with the persistent heat of mid-day; it seems akin to it, as though evoked by it out of the glowing earth.

Without having started one single covey we at last reached another clearing. There the aspen-trees had only lately been felled, and lay stretched mournfully on the ground, crushing the grass and small undergrowth below them: on some the leaves were still green, though they were already dead, and hung limply from the motionless branches; on others they were crumpled and dried up. Fresh golden-white chips lay in heaps round the stumps that were covered with bright drops; a peculiar, very pleasant, pungent odour rose from them. Farther away, nearer the wood, sounded the dull blows of the axe, and from time to time, bowing and spreading wide its arms, a bushy tree fell slowly and majestically to the ground.

For a long time I did not come upon a single bird; at last a corncrake flew out of a thick clump of young oak across the wormwood springing up round it. I fired; it turned over in the air and fell. At the sound of the shot, Kassyan quickly covered his eyes with his hand, and he did not stir till I had reloaded the gun and picked up the bird. When I had moved farther on, he went up to the place where the wounded bird had fallen, bent down to the grass, on which some drops of blood were sprinkled, shook his head, and looked in dismay at me.... I heard him afterwards whispering: 'A sin!... Ah, yes, it's a sin!'

The heat forced us at last to go into the wood. I flung myself down under a high nut-bush, over which a slender young maple gracefully stretched its light branches. Kassyan sat down on the thick trunk of a felled birch-tree. I looked at him. The leaves faintly stirred overhead, and their thin greenish shadows crept softly to and fro over his feeble body, muffled in a dark coat, and over his little face. He did not lift his head. Bored by his silence, I lay on my back and began to admire the tranquil play of the tangled foliage on the background of the bright, far away sky. A marvellously sweet occupation it is to lie on one's back in a wood and gaze upwards! You may fancy you are looking into a bottomless sea; that it stretches wide below you; that the trees are not rising out of the earth, but, like the roots of gigantic weeds, are dropping--falling straight down into those glassy, limpid depths; the leaves on the trees are at one moment transparent as emeralds, the next, they condense into golden, almost black green. Somewhere, afar off, at the end of a slender twig, a single leaf hangs motionless against the blue patch of transparent sky, and beside it another trembles with the motion of a fish on the line, as though moving of its own will, not shaken by the wind. Round white clouds float calmly across, and calmly pass away like submarine islands; and suddenly, all this ocean, this shining ether, these branches and leaves steeped in sunlight--all is rippling, quivering in fleeting brilliance, and a fresh trembling whisper awakens like the tiny, incessant plash of suddenly stirred eddies.

One does not move--one looks, and no word can tell what peace, what joy, what sweetness reigns in the heart. One looks: the deep, pure blue stirs on one's lips a smile, innocent as itself; like the clouds over the sky, and, as it were, with them, happy memories pass in slow procession over the soul, and still one fancies one's gaze goes deeper and deeper, and draws one with it up into that peaceful, shining immensity, and that one cannot be brought back from that height, that depth....

'Master, master!' cried Kassyan suddenly in his musical voice.

I raised myself in surprise: up till then he had scarcely replied to my questions, and now he suddenly addressed me of himself.

'What is it?' I asked.

'What did you kill the bird for?' he began, looking me straight in the face.

'What for? Corncrake is game; one can eat it.'

'That was not what you killed it for, master, as though you were going to eat it! You killed it for amusement.'

'Well, you yourself, I suppose, eat geese or chickens?'

'Those birds are provided by God for man, but the corncrake is a wild bird of the woods: and not he alone; many they are, the wild things of the woods and the fields, and the wild things of the rivers and marshes and moors, flying on high or creeping below; and a sin it is to slay them: let them live their allotted life upon the earth. But for man another food has been provided; his food is other, and other his sustenance: bread, the good gift of God, and the water of heaven, and the tame beasts that have come down to us from our fathers of old.'

I looked in astonishment at Kassyan. His words flowed freely; he did not hesitate for a word; he spoke with quiet inspiration and gentle dignity, sometimes closing his eyes.

'So is it sinful, then, to kill fish, according to you?' I asked.

'Fishes have cold blood,' he replied with conviction. 'The fish is a dumb creature; it knows neither fear nor rejoicing. The fish is a voiceless creature. The fish does not feel; the blood in it is not living.... Blood,' he continued, after a pause, 'blood is a holy thing! God's sun does not look upon blood; it is hidden away from the light ... it is a great sin to bring blood into the light of day; a great sin and horror.... Ah, a great sin!'

He sighed, and his head drooped forward. I looked, I confess, in absolute amazement at the strange old man. His language did not sound like the language of a peasant; the common people do not speak like that, nor those who aim at fine speaking. His speech was meditative, grave, and curious.... I had never heard anything like it.

'Tell me, please, Kassyan,' I began, without taking my eyes off his slightly flushed face, 'what is your occupation?'

He did not answer my question at once. His eyes strayed uneasily for an instant.

'I live as the Lord commands,' he brought out at last; 'and as for occupation--no, I have no occupation. I've never been very clever from a child: I work when I can: I'm not much of a workman--how should I be? I have no health; my hands are awkward. In the spring I catch nightingales.'

'You catch nightingales?... But didn't you tell me that we must not touch any of the wild things of the woods and the fields, and so on?'

'We must not kill them, of a certainty; death will take its own without that. Look at Martin the carpenter; Martin lived, and his life was not long, but he died; his wife now grieves for her husband, for her little children.... Neither for man nor beast is there any charm against death. Death does not hasten, nor is there any escaping it; but we must not aid death.... And I do not kill nightingales--God forbid! I do not catch them to harm them, to spoil their lives, but for the pleasure of men, for their comfort and delight.'

'Do you go to Kursk to catch them?'

'Yes, I go to Kursk, and farther too, at times. I pass nights in the marshes, or at the edge of the forests; I am alone at night in the fields, in the thickets; there the curlews call and the hares squeak and the wild ducks lift up their voices.... I note them at evening; at morning I give ear to them; at daybreak I cast my net over the bushes.... There are nightingales that sing so pitifully sweet ... yea, pitifully.'

'And do you sell them?'

'I give them to good people.'

'And what are you doing now?'

'What am I doing?'

'Yes, how are you employed?'

The old man was silent for a little.

'I am not employed at all.... I am a poor workman. But I can read and write.'

'You can read?'

'Yes, I can read and write. I learnt, by the help of God and good people.'

'Have you a family?'

'No, not a family.'

'How so?... Are they dead, then?'

'No, but ... I have never been lucky in life. But all that is in God's hands; we are all in God's hands; and a man should be righteous--that is all! Upright before God, that is it.'

'And you have no kindred?'

'Yes ... well....'

The old man was confused.

'Tell me, please,' I began: 'I heard my coachman ask you why you did not cure Martin? You cure disease?'

'Your coachman is a righteous man,' Kassyan answered thoughtfully. 'I too am not without sin. They call me a doctor.... Me a doctor, indeed! And who can heal the sick? That is all a gift from God. But there are ... yes, there are herbs, and there are flowers; they are of use, of a certainty. There is plantain, for instance, a herb good for man; there is bud-marigold too; it is not sinful to speak of them: they are holy herbs of God. Then there are others not so; and they may be of use, but it's a sin; and to speak of them is a sin. Still, with prayer, may be.... And doubtless there are such words.... But who has faith, shall be saved,' he added, dropping his voice.

'You did not give Martin anything?' I asked.

'I heard of it too late,' replied the old man. 'But what of it! Each man's destiny is written from his birth. The carpenter Martin was not to live; he was not to live upon the earth: that was what it was. No, when a man is not to live on the earth, him the sunshine does not warm like another, and him the bread does not nourish and make strong; it is as though something is drawing him away.... Yes: God rest his soul!'

'Have you been settled long amongst us?' I asked him after a short pause.

Kassyan started.

'No, not long; four years. In the old master's time we always lived in our old houses, but the trustees transported us. Our old master was a kind heart, a man of peace--the Kingdom of Heaven be his! The trustees doubtless judged righteously.'

'And where did you live before?'

'At Fair Springs.'

'Is it far from here?'

'A hundred miles.'

'Well, were you better off there?'

'Yes ... yes, there there was open country, with rivers; it was our home: here we are cramped and parched up.... Here we are strangers. There at home, at Fair Springs, you could get up on to a hill--and ah, my God, what a sight you could see! Streams and plains and forests, and there was a church, and then came plains beyond. You could see far, very far. Yes, how far you could look--you could look and look, ah, yes! Here, doubtless, the soil is better; it is clay--good fat clay, as the peasants say; for me the corn grows well enough everywhere.'

'Confess then, old man; you would like to visit your birth-place again?'

'Yes, I should like to see it. Still, all places are good. I am a man without kin, without neighbours. And, after all, do you gain much, pray, by staying at home? But, behold! as you walk, and as you walk,' he went on, raising his voice, 'the heart grows lighter, of a truth. And the sun shines upon you, and you are in the sight of God, and the singing comes more tunefully. Here, you look--what herb is growing; you look on it--you pick it. Here water runs, perhaps--spring water, a source of pure holy water; so you drink of it-- you look on it too. The birds of heaven sing.... And beyond Kursk come the steppes, that steppes-country: ah, what a marvel, what a delight for man! what freedom, what a blessing of God! And they go on, folks tell, even to the warm seas where dwells the sweet-voiced bird, the Hamayune, and from the trees the leaves fall not, neither in autumn nor in winter, and apples grow of gold, on silver branches, and every man lives in uprightness and content. And I would go even there.... Have I journeyed so little already! I have been to Romyon and to Simbirsk the fair city, and even to Moscow of the golden domes; I have been to Oka the good nurse, and to Tsna the dove, and to our mother Volga, and many folks, good Christians have I seen, and noble cities I have visited.... Well, I would go thither ... yes ... and more too ... and I am not the only one, I a poor sinner ... many other Christians go in bast-shoes, roaming over the world, seeking truth, yea!... For what is there at home? No righteousness in man--it's that.'

These last words Kassyan uttered quickly, almost unintelligibly; then he said something more which I could not catch at all, and such a strange expression passed over his face that I involuntarily recalled the epithet 'cracked.' He looked down, cleared his throat, and seemed to come to himself again. 'What sunshine!' he murmured in a low voice. 'It is a blessing, oh, Lord! What warmth in the woods!'

He gave a movement of the shoulders and fell into silence. With a vague look round him he began softly to sing. I could not catch all the words of his slow chant; I heard the following:

> 'They call me Kassyan,
> But my nickname's the Flea.'

'Oh!' I thought, 'so he improvises.' Suddenly he started and ceased singing, looking intently at a thick part of the wood. I turned and saw a little peasant girl, about seven years old, in a blue frock, with a checked handkerchief over her head, and a woven bark-basket in her little bare sunburnt hand. She had certainly not expected to meet us; she had, as they say, 'stumbled upon' us, and she stood motionless in a shady recess among the thick foliage of the nut-trees, looking dismayed at me with her black eyes. I had scarcely time to catch a glimpse of her; she dived behind a tree.

'Annushka! Annushka! come here, don't be afraid!' cried the old man caressingly.

'I'm afraid,' came her shrill voice.

'Don't be afraid, don't be afraid; come to me.'

Annushka left her hiding place in silence, walked softly round--her little childish feet scarcely sounded on the thick grass--and came out of the bushes near the old man. She was not a child of seven, as I had fancied at first, from her diminutive stature, but a girl of thirteen or fourteen. Her whole person was small and thin, but very neat and graceful, and her pretty little face was strikingly like Kassyan's own, though he was certainly not handsome. There were the same thin features, and the same strange expression, shy and confiding, melancholy and shrewd, and her gestures were the same.... Kassyan kept his eyes fixed on her; she took her stand at his side.

'Well, have you picked any mushrooms?' he asked.

'Yes,' she answered with a shy smile.

'Did you find many?'

'Yes.' (She stole a swift look at him and smiled again.)

'Are they white ones?'

'Yes.'

'Show me, show me.... (She slipped the basket off her arm and half- lifted the big burdock leaf which covered up the mushrooms.) 'Ah!' said Kassyan, bending down over the basket; 'what splendid ones! Well done, Annushka!'

'She's your daughter, Kassyan, isn't she?' I asked. (Annushka's face flushed faintly.)

'No, well, a relative,' replied Kassyan with affected indifference. 'Come, Annushka, run along,' he added at once, 'run along, and God be with you! And take care.'

'But why should she go on foot?' I interrupted. 'We could take her with us.'

Annushka blushed like a poppy, grasped the handle of her basket with both hands, and looked in trepidation at the old man.

'No, she will get there all right,' he answered in the same languid and indifferent voice. 'Why not?... She will get there.... Run along.'

Annushka went rapidly away into the forest. Kassyan looked after her, then looked down and smiled to himself. In this prolonged smile, in the few words he had spoken to Annushka, and in the very sound of his voice when he spoke to her, there was an intense, indescribable love and tenderness. He looked again in the direction she had gone, again smiled to himself, and, passing his hand across his face, he nodded his head several times.

'Why did you send her away so soon?' I asked him. 'I would have bought her mushrooms.'

'Well, you can buy them there at home just the same, sir, if you like,' he answered, for the first time using the formal 'sir' in addressing me.

'She's very pretty, your girl.'

'No ... only so-so,' he answered, with seeming reluctance, and from that instant he relapsed into the same uncommunicative mood as at first.

Seeing that all my efforts to make him talk again were fruitless, I went off into the clearing. Meantime the heat had somewhat abated; but my ill-success, or, as they say among us, my 'ill-luck,' continued, and I returned to the settlement with nothing but one corncrake and the new axle. Just as we were driving into the yard, Kassyan suddenly turned to me.

'Master, master,' he began, 'do you know I have done you a wrong; it was I cast a spell to keep all the game off.'

'How so?'

'Oh, I can do that. Here you have a well-trained dog and a good one, but he could do nothing. When you think of it, what are men? what are they? Here's a beast; what have they made of him?'

It would have been useless for me to try to convince Kassyan of the impossibility of 'casting a spell' on game, and so I made him no reply. Meantime we had turned into the yard.

Annushka was not in the hut: she had had time to get there before us, and to leave her basket of mushrooms. Erofay fitted in the new axle, first exposing it to a severe and most unjust criticism; and an hour later I set off, leaving a small sum of money with Kassyan, which at first he was unwilling to accept, but afterwards, after a moment's thought, holding it in his hand, he put it in his bosom. In the course of this hour he had scarcely uttered a single word; he stood as before, leaning against the gate. He made no reply to the reproaches of my coachman, and took leave very coldly of me.

Directly I turned round, I could see that my worthy Erofay was in a gloomy frame of mind.... To be sure, he had found nothing to eat in the country; the only water for his horses was bad. We drove off. With dissatisfaction expressed even in the back of his head, he sat on the box, burning to begin to talk to me. While waiting for me to begin by some question, he confined himself to a low muttering in an undertone, and some rather caustic instructions to the horses. 'A village,' he muttered; 'call that a village? You ask for a drop of kvas--not a drop of kvas even.... Ah, Lord!... And the water--simply filth!' (He spat loudly.) 'Not a cucumber, nor kvas, nor nothing.... Now, then!' he added aloud, turning to the right trace-horse; 'I know you, you humbug.' (And he gave him a cut with the whip.)

'That horse has learnt to shirk his work entirely, and yet he was a willing beast once. Now, then--look alive!'

'Tell me, please, Erofay,' I began, 'what sort of a man is Kassyan?'

Erofay did not answer me at once: he was, in general, a reflective and deliberate fellow; but I could see directly that my question was soothing and cheering to him.

'The Flea?' he said at last, gathering up the reins; 'he's a queer fellow; yes, a crazy chap; such a queer fellow, you wouldn't find another like him in a hurry. You know, for example, he's for all the world like our roan horse here; he gets out of everything--out of work, that's to say. But, then, what sort of workman could he be?... He's hardly body enough to keep his soul in ... but still, of course.... He's been like that from a child up, you know. At first he followed his uncle's business as a carrier--there were three of them in the business; but then he got tired of it, you know--he threw it up. He began to live at home, but he could not keep at home long; he's so restless--a regular flea, in fact. He happened, by good luck, to have a good master--he didn't worry him. Well, so ever since he has been wandering about like a lost sheep. And then, he's so strange; there's no understanding him. Sometimes he'll be as silent as a post, and then he'll begin talking, and God knows what he'll say! Is that good manners, pray? He's an absurd fellow, that he is. But he sings well, for all that.'

'And does he cure people, really?'

'Cure people!... Well, how should he? A fine sort of doctor! Though he did cure me of the king's evil, I must own.... But how can he? He's a stupid fellow, that's what he is,' he added, after a moment's pause.

'Have you known him long?' 'A long while. I was his neighbour at Sitchovka up at Fair Springs.'

'And what of that girl--who met us in the wood, Annushka--what relation is she to him?'

Erofay looked at me over his shoulder, and grinned all over his face.

'He, he!... yes, they are relations. She is an orphan; she has no mother, and it's not even known who her mother was. But she must be a relation; she's too much like him.... Anyway, she lives with him. She's a smart girl, there's no denying; a good girl; and as for the old man, she's simply the apple of his eye; she's a good girl. And, do you know, you wouldn't believe it, but do you know, he's managed to teach Annushka to read? Well, well! that's quite like him; he's such an extraordinary fellow, such a changeable fellow; there's no reckoning on him, really.... Eh! eh! eh!' My coachman suddenly interrupted himself, and stopping the horses, he bent over on one side and began sniffing. 'Isn't there a smell of burning? Yes! Why, that new axle, I do declare!... I thought I'd greased it.... We must get on to some water; why, here is a puddle, just right.'

And Erofay slowly got off his seat, untied the pail, went to the pool, and coming back, listened with a certain satisfaction to the hissing of the box of the wheel as the water suddenly touched it.... Six times during some eight miles he had to pour water on the smouldering axle, and it was quite evening when we got home at last.

X THE AGENT

Twelve miles from my place lives an acquaintance of mine, a landowner and a retired officer in the Guards--Arkady Pavlitch Pyenotchkin. He has a great deal of game on his estate, a house built after the design of a French architect, and servants dressed after the English fashion; he gives capital dinners, and a cordial reception to visitors, and, with all that, one goes to see him reluctantly. He is a sensible and practical man, has received the excellent education now usual, has been in the service, mixed in the highest society, and is now devoting himself to his estate with great success. Arkady Pavlitch is, to judge by his own words, severe but just; he looks after the good of the peasants under his control and punishes them--for their good. 'One has to treat them like children,' he says on such occasions; 'their ignorance, mon cher; il faut prendre cela en consideration .' When this so-called painful necessity arises, he eschews all sharp or violent gestures, and prefers not to raise his voice, but with a straight blow in the culprit's face, says calmly, 'I believe I asked you to do something, my friend?' or 'What is the matter, my boy? what are you thinking about?' while he sets his teeth a little, and the corners of his mouth are drawn. He is not tall, but has an elegant figure, and is very good-looking; his hands and nails are kept perfectly exquisite; his rosy cheeks and lips are simply the picture of health. He has a ringing, light-hearted laugh, and there is sometimes a very genial twinkle in his clear brown eyes. He dresses in excellent taste; he orders French books, prints, and papers, though he's no great lover of reading himself: he has hardly as much as waded through the Wandering Jew . He plays cards in masterly style. Altogether, Arkady Pavlitch is reckoned one of the most cultivated gentlemen and most eligible matches in our province; the ladies are perfectly wild over him, and especially admire his manners. He is wonderfully well conducted, wary as a cat, and has never from his cradle been mixed up in any scandal, though he is fond of making his power felt, intimidating or snubbing a nervous man, when he gets a chance. He has a positive distaste for doubtful society--he is afraid of compromising himself; in his lighter moments, however, he will avow himself a follower of Epicurus, though as a rule he speaks slightingly of philosophy, calling it the foggy food fit for German brains, or at times, simply, rot. He is fond of music too; at the card-table he is given to humming through his teeth, but with feeling; he knows by heart some snatches from Lucia and Somnambula , but he is always apt to sing everything a little sharp. The winters he spends in Petersburg. His house is kept in extraordinarily good order; the very grooms feel his influence, and every day not only rub the harness and brush their coats, but even wash their faces. Arkady Pavlitch's house-serfs have, it is true, something of a hang-dog look; but among us Russians there's no knowing what is sullenness and what is sleepiness. Arkady Pavlitch speaks in a soft, agreeable voice, with emphasis and, as it were, with satisfaction; he brings out each word through his handsome perfumed moustaches; he uses a good many French expressions too, such as: Mais c'est impayable! Mais comment donc ? and so so. For all that, I, for one, am never over-eager to visit him, and if it were not for the grouse and the partridges, I should probably have dropped his acquaintance altogether. One is possessed by a strange sort of uneasiness in his house; the very comfort is distasteful to one, and every evening when a befrizzed valet makes his appearance in a blue livery with heraldic buttons, and begins, with cringing servility, drawing off one's boots, one feels that if his pale, lean figure could suddenly be replaced by the amazingly broad cheeks and incredibly thick nose of a stalwart young labourer fresh from the plough, who has yet had time in his ten months of service to tear his new nankin coat open at every seam, one would be unutterably overjoyed, and would gladly run the risk of having one's whole leg pulled off with the boot....

In spite of my aversion for Arkady Pavlitch, I once happened to pass a night in his house. The next day I ordered my carriage to be ready early in the morning, but he would not let me start without a regular breakfast in the English style, and conducted me into his study. With our tea they served us cutlets, boiled eggs, butter, honey, cheese, and so on. Two footmen in clean white gloves swiftly and silently anticipated our faintest desires. We sat on a Persian divan. Arkady Pavlitch was arrayed in loose silk trousers, a black velvet smoking jacket, a red fez with a blue tassel, and yellow Chinese slippers without heels. He drank his tea, laughed, scrutinised his finger-nails, propped himself up with cushions, and was altogether in an excellent humour. After making a hearty breakfast with obvious satisfaction, Arkady Pavlitch poured himself out a glass of red wine, lifted it to his lips, and suddenly frowned.

'Why was not the wine warmed?' he asked rather sharply of one of the footmen.

The footman stood stock-still in confusion, and turned white.

'Didn't I ask you a question, my friend?' Arkady Pavlitch resumed tranquilly, never taking his eyes off the man.

The luckless footman fidgeted in his place, twisted the napkin, and uttered not a word.

Arkady Pavlitch dropped his head and looked up at him thoughtfully from under his eyelids.

' Pardon, mon cher ', he observed, patting my knee amicably, and again he stared at the footman. 'You can go,' he added, after a short silence, raising his eyebrows, and he rang the bell.

A stout, swarthy, black-haired man, with a low forehead, and eyes positively lost in fat, came into the room.

'About Fyodor ... make the necessary arrangements,' said Arkady Pavlitch in an undertone, and with complete composure.

'Yes, sir,' answered the fat man, and he went out.

' Voila, mon cher, les desagrements de la campagne ,' Arkady Pavlitch remarked gaily. 'But where are you off to? Stop, you must stay a little.'

'No,' I answered; 'it's time I was off.'

'Nothing but sport! Oh, you sportsmen! And where are you going to shoot just now?'

'Thirty-five miles from here, at Ryabovo.'

'Ryabovo? By Jove! now in that case I will come with you. Ryabovo's only four miles from my village Shipilovka, and it's a long while since I've been over to Shipilovka; I've never been able to get the time. Well, this is a piece of luck; you can spend the day shooting in Ryabovo and come on in the evening to me. We'll have supper together-- we'll take the cook with us, and you'll stay the night with me. Capital! capital!' he added without waiting for my answer.

' C'est arrange .... Hey, you there! Have the carriage brought out, and look sharp. You have never been in Shipilovka? I should be ashamed to suggest your putting up for the night in my agent's cottage, but you're not particular, I know, and at Ryabovo you'd have slept in some hayloft.... We will go, we will go!'

And Arkady Pavlitch hummed some French song.

'You don't know, I dare say,' he pursued, swaying from side to side; 'I've some peasants there who pay rent. It's the custom of the place-- what was I to do? They pay their rent very punctually, though. I should, I'll own, have put them back to payment in labour, but there's so little land. I really wonder how they manage to make both ends meet. However, c'est leur affaire . My agent there's a fine fellow, une forte tete , a man of real administrative power! You shall see.... Really, how luckily things have turned out!'

There was no help for it. Instead of nine o'clock in the morning, we started at two in the afternoon. Sportsmen will sympathise with my impatience. Arkady Pavlitch liked, as he expressed it, to be comfortable when he had the chance, and he took with him such a supply of linen, dainties, wearing apparel, perfumes, pillows, and dressing- cases of all sorts, that a careful and self-denying German would have found enough to last him for a year. Every time we went down a steep hill, Arkady Pavlitch addressed some brief but powerful remarks to the coachman, from which I was able to deduce that my worthy friend was a thorough coward. The journey was, however, performed in safety, except that, in crossing a lately-repaired bridge, the trap with the cook in it broke down, and he got squeezed in the stomach against the hind- wheel.

Arkady Pavlitch was alarmed in earnest at the sight of the fall of Karem, his home-made professor of the culinary art, and he sent at once to inquire whether his hands were injured. On receiving a reassuring reply to this query, his mind was set at rest immediately. With all this, we were rather a long time on the road; I was in the same carriage as Arkady Pavlitch, and towards the end of the journey I was a prey to deadly boredom, especially as in a few hours my companion ran perfectly dry of subjects of conversation, and even fell to expressing his liberal views on politics. At last we did arrive--not at Ryabovo, but at Shipilovka; it happened so somehow. I could have got no shooting now that day in any case, and so, raging inwardly, I submitted to my fate.

The cook had arrived a few minutes before us, and apparently had had time to arrange things and prepare those whom it concerned, for on our very entrance within the village boundaries we were met by the village bailiff (the agent's son), a stalwart, red-haired peasant of seven feet; he was on horseback, bareheaded, and wearing a new overcoat, not buttoned up. 'And where's Sofron?' Arkady Pavlitch asked him. The bailiff first jumped nimbly off his horse, bowed to his master till he was bent double, and said: 'Good health to you, Arkady Pavlitch, sir!' then raised his head, shook himself, and announced that Sofron had gone to Perov, but they had sent after him.

'Well, come along after us,' said Arkady Pavlitch. The bailiff deferentially led his horse to one side, clambered on to it, and followed the carriage at a trot, his cap in his hand. We drove through the village. A few peasants in empty carts happened to meet us; they were driving from the threshing-floor and singing songs, swaying backwards and forwards, and swinging their legs in the air; but at the sight of our carriage and the bailiff they were suddenly silent, took off their winter caps (it was summer-time) and got up as though waiting for orders. Arkady Pavlitch nodded to them graciously. A flutter of excitement had obviously spread through the hamlet. Peasant women in check petticoats flung splinters of wood at indiscreet or over-zealous dogs; an old lame man with a beard that began just under his eyes pulled a horse away from the well before it had drunk, gave it, for some obscure reason, a blow on the side, and fell to bowing low. Boys in long smocks ran with a howl to the huts, flung themselves on their bellies on the high door-sills, with their heads down and legs in the air, rolled over with the utmost haste into the dark outer rooms, from which they did not reappear again. Even the hens sped in a hurried scuttle to the turning; one bold cock with a black throat like a satin waistcoat and a red tail, rumpled up to his very comb, stood his ground in the road, and even prepared for a crow, then suddenly took fright and scuttled off too. The agent's cottage stood apart from the rest in the middle of a thick green patch of hemp. We stopped at the gates. Mr. Pyenotchkin got up, flung off his cloak with a picturesque motion, and got out of the carriage, looking affably about him. The agent's wife met us with low curtseys, and came up to kiss the master's hand. Arkady Pavlitch let her kiss it to her heart's content, and mounted the steps. In the outer room, in a dark corner, stood the bailiff's wife, and she too curtsied, but did not venture to approach his hand. In the cold hut, as it is called--to the right of the outer room--two other women were still busily at work; they were carrying out all the rubbish, empty tubs, sheepskins stiff as boards, greasy pots, a cradle with a heap of dish-clouts and a baby covered with spots, and sweeping out the dirt with bathbrooms. Arkady Pavlitch sent them away, and installed himself on a bench under the holy pictures. The coachmen began bringing in the trunks, bags, and other conveniences, trying each time to subdue the noise of their heavy boots.

Meantime Arkady Pavlitch began questioning the bailiff about the crops, the sowing, and other agricultural subjects. The bailiff gave satisfactory answers, but spoke with a sort of heavy awkwardness, as though he were buttoning up his coat with benumbed fingers. He stood at the door and kept looking round on the watch to make way for the nimble footman. Behind his powerful shoulders I managed to get a glimpse of the agent's wife in the outer room surreptitiously belabouring some other peasant woman. Suddenly a cart rumbled up and stopped at the steps; the agent came in.

This man, as Arkady Pavlitch said, of real administrative power, was short, broad-shouldered, grey, and thick-set, with a red nose, little blue eyes, and a beard of the shape of a fan. We may observe, by the way, that ever since Russia has existed, there has never yet been an instance of a man who has grown rich and prosperous without a big, bushy beard; sometimes a man may have had a thin, wedge-shape beard all his life; but then he begins to get one all at once, it is all round his face like a halo--one wonders where the hair has come from! The agent must have been making merry at Perov: his face was unmistakably flushed, and there was a smell of spirits about him.

'Ah, our father, our gracious benefactor!' he began in a sing-song voice, and with a face of such deep feeling that it seemed every minute as if he would burst into tears; 'at last you have graciously deigned to come to us ... your hand, your honour's hand,' he added, his lips protruded in anticipation. Arkady Pavlitch gratified his desire. 'Well, brother Sofron, how are things going with you?' he asked in a friendly voice.

'Ah, you, our father!' cried Sofron; 'how should they go ill? how should things go ill, now that you, our father, our benefactor, graciously deign to lighten our poor village with your presence, to make us happy till the day of our death? Thank the Lord for thee, Arkady Pavlitch! thank the Lord for thee! All is right by your gracious favour.'

At this point Sofron paused, gazed upon his master, and, as though carried away by a rush of feeling (tipsiness had its share in it too), begged once more for his hand, and whined more than before.

'Ah, you, our father, benefactor ... and ... There, God bless me! I'm a regular fool with delight.... God bless me! I look and can't believe my eyes! Ah, our father!'

Arkady Pavlitch glanced at me, smiled, and asked: ' N'est-ce pas que c'est touchant? '

'But, Arkady Pavlitch, your honour,' resumed the indefatigable agent; 'what are you going to do? You'll break my heart, your honour; your honour didn't graciously let me know of your visit. Where are you to put up for the night? You see here it's dirty, nasty.'

'Nonsense, Sofron, nonsense!' Arkady Pavlitch responded, with a smile; 'it's all right here.'

'But, our father, all right--for whom? For peasants like us it's all right; but for you ... oh, our father, our gracious protector! oh, you ... our father!... Pardon an old fool like me; I'm off my head, bless me! I'm gone clean crazy.'

Meanwhile supper was served; Arkady Pavlitch began to eat. The old man packed his son off, saying he smelt too strong.

'Well, settled the division of land, old chap, hey?' enquired Mr. Pyenotchkin, obviously trying to imitate the peasant speech, with a wink to me.

'We've settled the land shares, your honour; all by your gracious favour. Day before yesterday the list was made out. The Hlinovsky folks made themselves disagreeable about it at first ... they were disagreeable about it, certainly. They wanted this ... and they wanted that ... and God knows what they didn't want! but they're a set of fools, your honour!--an ignorant lot. But we, your honour, graciously please you, gave an earnest of our gratitude, and satisfied Nikolai Nikolaitch, the mediator; we acted in everything according to your orders, your honour; as you graciously ordered, so we did, and nothing did we do unbeknown to Yegor Dmitritch.'

'Yegor reported to me,' Arkady Pavlitch remarked with dignity.

'To be sure, your honour, Yegor Dmitritch, to be sure.'

'Well, then, now I suppose you 're satisfied.'

Sofron had only been waiting for this.

'Ah, you are our father, our benefactor!' he began, in the same sing- song as before. 'Indeed, now, your honour ... why, for you, our father, we pray day and night to God Almighty.... There's too little land, of course....'

Pyenotchkin cut him short.

'There, that'll do, that'll do, Sofron; I know you're eager in my service.... Well, and how goes the threshing?'

Sofron sighed.

'Well, our father, the threshing's none too good. But there, your honour, Arkady Pavlitch, let me tell you about a little matter that came to pass.' (Here he came closer to Mr. Pyenotchkin, with his arms apart, bent down, and screwed up one eye.) 'There was a dead body found on our land.'

'How was that?'

'I can't think myself, your honour; it seems like the doing of the evil one. But, luckily, it was found near the boundary; on our side of it, to tell the truth. I ordered them to drag it on to the neighbour's strip of land at once, while it was still possible, and set a watch there, and sent word round to our folks. "Mum's the word," says I. But I explained how it was to the police officer in case of the worst. "You see how it was," says I; and of course I had to treat him and slip some notes into his hand.... Well, what do you say, your honour? We shifted the burden on to other shoulders; you see a dead body's a matter of two hundred roubles, as sure as ninepence.'

Mr. Pyenotchkin laughed heartily at his agent's cunning, and said several times to me, indicating him with a nod, ' Quel gaillard , eh!'

Meantime it was quite dark out of doors; Arkady Pavlitch ordered the table to be cleared, and hay to be brought in. The valet spread out sheets for us, and arranged pillows; we lay down. Sofron retired after receiving his instructions for the next day. Arkady Pavlitch, before falling asleep, talked a little more about the first-rate qualities of the Russian peasant, and at that point made the observation that since Sofron had had the management of the place, the Shipilovka peasants had never been one farthing in arrears.... The watchman struck his board; a baby, who apparently had not yet had time to be imbued with a sentiment of dutiful self-abnegation, began crying somewhere in the cottage ... we fell asleep.

The next morning we got up rather early; I was getting ready to start for Ryabovo, but Arkady Pavlitch was anxious to show me his estate, and begged me to remain. I was not averse myself to seeing more of the first-rate qualities of that man of administrative power--Sofron--in their practical working. The agent made his appearance. He wore a blue loose coat, tied round the waist with a red handkerchief. He talked much less than on the previous evening, kept an alert, intent eye on his master's face, and gave connected and sensible answers. We set off with him to the threshing-floor. Sofron's son, the seven-foot bailiff, by every external sign a very slow-witted fellow, walked after us also, and we were joined farther on by the village constable, Fedosyitch, a retired soldier, with immense moustaches, and an extraordinary expression of face; he looked as though he had had some startling shock of astonishment a very long while ago, and had never quite got over it. We took a look at the threshing-floor, the barn, the corn-stacks, the outhouses, the windmill, the cattle-shed, the vegetables, and the hempfields; everything was, as a fact, in excellent order; only the dejected faces of the peasants rather puzzled me. Sofron had had an eye to the ornamental as well as the useful; he had planted all the ditches with willows, between the stacks he had made little paths to the threshing-floor and strewn them with fine sand; on the windmill he had constructed a weathercock of the shape of a bear with his jaws open and a red tongue sticking out; he had attached to the brick cattle-shed something of the nature of a Greek facade, and on it inscribed in white letters: 'Construt in the village Shipilovky 1 thousand eight Hunderd farthieth year. This cattle-shed.' Arkady Pavlitch was quite touched, and fell to expatiating in French to me upon the advantages of the system of rent-payment, adding, however, that labour-dues came more profitable to the owner--'but, after all, that wasn't everything.' He began giving the agent advice how to plant his potatoes, how to prepare cattle-food, and so on. Sofron heard his master's remarks out with attention, sometimes replied, but did not now address Arkady Pavlitch as his father, or his benefactor, and kept insisting that there was too little land; that it would be a good thing to buy more. 'Well, buy some then,' said Arkady Pavlitch; 'I've no objection; in my name, of course.' To this Sofron made no reply; he merely stroked his beard. 'And now it would be as well to ride down to the copse,' observed Mr. Pyenotchkin. Saddle-horses were led out to us at once; we went off to the copse, or, as they call it about us, the 'enclosure.' In this 'enclosure' we found thick undergrowth and abundance of wild game, for which Arkady Pavlitch applauded Sofron and clapped him on the shoulder. In regard to forestry, Arkady Pavlitch clung to the Russian ideas, and told me on that subject an amusing--in his words--anecdote, of how a jocose landowner had given his forester a good lesson by pulling out nearly half his beard, by way of a proof that growth is none the thicker for being cut back. In other matters, however, neither Sofron nor Arkady Pavlitch objected to innovations. On our return to the village, the agent took us to look at a winnowing machine he had recently ordered from Moscow. The winnowing machine did certainly work beautifully, but if Sofron had known what a disagreeable incident was in store for him and his master on this last excursion, he would doubtless have stopped at home with us.

This was what happened. As we came out of the barn the following spectacle confronted us. A few paces from the door, near a filthy pool, in which three ducks were splashing unconcernedly, there stood two peasants--one an old man of sixty, the other, a lad of twenty--both in patched homespun shirts, barefoot, and with cord tied round their waists for belts. The village constable Fedosyitch was busily engaged with them, and would probably have succeeded in inducing them to retire if we had lingered a little longer in the barn, but catching sight of us, he grew stiff all over, and seemed bereft of all sensation on the spot. Close by stood the bailiff gaping, his fists hanging irresolute. Arkady Pavlitch frowned, bit his lip, and went up to the suppliants. They both prostrated themselves at his feet in silence.

'What do you want? What are you asking about?' he inquired in a stern voice, a little through his nose. (The peasants glanced at one another, and did not utter a syllable, only blinked a little as if the sun were in their faces, and their breathing came quicker.)

'Well, what is it?' Arkady Pavlitch said again; and turning at once to Sofron, 'Of what family?'

'The Tobolyev family,' the agent answered slowly.

'Well, what do you want?' Mr. Pyenotchkin said again; 'have you lost your tongues, or what? Tell me, you, what is it you want?' he added, with a nod at the old man. 'And don't be afraid, stupid.'

The old man craned forward his dark brown, wrinkled neck, opened his bluish twitching lips, and in a hoarse voice uttered the words, 'Protect us, lord!' and again he bent his forehead to the earth. The young peasant prostrated himself too. Arkady Pavlitch looked at their bent necks with an air of dignity, threw back his head, and stood with his legs rather wide apart. 'What is it? Whom do you complain of?'

'Have mercy, lord! Let us breathe.... We are crushed, worried, tormented to death quite. (The old man spoke with difficulty.)

'Who worries you?'

'Sofron Yakovlitch, your honour.'

Arkady Pavlitch was silent a minute.

'What's your name?'

'Antip, your honour.'

'And who's this?'

'My boy, your honour.'

Arkady Pavlitch was silent again; he pulled his moustaches.

'Well! and how has he tormented you?' he began again, looking over his moustaches at the old man.

'Your honour, he has ruined us utterly. Two sons, your honour, he's sent for recruits out of turn, and now he is taking the third also. Yesterday, your honour, our last cow was taken from the yard, and my old wife was beaten by his worship here: that is all the pity he has for us!' (He pointed to the bailiff.)

'Hm!' commented Arkady Pavlitch.

'Let him not destroy us to the end, gracious protector!'

Mr. Pyenotchkin scowled, 'What's the meaning of this?' he asked the agent, in a low voice, with an air of displeasure.

'He's a drunken fellow, sir,' answered the agent, for the first time using this deferential address, 'and lazy too. He's never been out of arrears this five years back, sir.'

'Sofron Yakovlitch paid the arrears for me, your honour,' the old man went on; 'it's the fifth year's come that he's paid it, he's paid it-- and he's brought me into slavery to him, your honour, and here--'

'And why did you get into arrears?' Mr. Pyenotchkin asked threateningly. (The old man's head sank.) 'You're fond of drinking, hanging about the taverns, I dare say.' (The old man opened his mouth to speak.) 'I know you,' Arkady Pavlitch went on emphatically; 'you think you've nothing to do but drink, and lie on the stove, and let steady peasants answer for you.'

'And he's an impudent fellow, too,' the agent threw in.

'That's sure to be so; it's always the way; I've noticed it more than once. The whole year round, he's drinking and abusive, and then he falls at one's feet.'

'Your honour, Arkady Pavlitch,' the old man began despairingly, 'have pity, protect us; when have I been impudent? Before God Almighty, I swear it was beyond my strength. Sofron Yakovlitch has taken a dislike to me; for some reason he dislikes me-- God be his judge! He will ruin me utterly, your honour.... The last ... here ... the last boy ... and him he....' (A tear glistened in the old man's wrinkled yellow eyes). 'Have pity, gracious lord, defend us!'

'And it's not us only,' the young peasant began....

Arkady Pavlitch flew into a rage at once.

'And who asked your opinion, hey? Till you're spoken to, hold your tongue.... What's the meaning of it? Silence, I tell you, silence!... Why, upon my word, this is simply mutiny! No, my friend, I don't advise you to mutiny on my domain ... on my ... (Arkady Pavlitch stepped forward, but probably recollected my presence, turned round, and put his hands in his pockets ...) ' Je vous demande bien pardon, mon cher ,' he said, with a forced smile, dropping his voice significantly. ' C'est le mauvais cote de la medaille ... There, that'll do, that'll do,' he went on, not looking at the peasants: 'I say ... that'll do, you can go.' (The peasants did not rise.) 'Well, haven't I told you ... that'll do. You can go, I tell you.'

Arkady Pavlitch turned his back on them. 'Nothing but vexation,' he muttered between his teeth, and strode with long steps homewards. Sofron followed him. The village constable opened his eyes wide, looking as if he were just about to take a tremendous leap into space. The bailiff drove a duck away from the puddle. The suppliants remained as they were a little, then looked at each other, and, without turning their heads, went on their way.

Two hours later I was at Ryabovo, and making ready to begin shooting, accompanied by Anpadist, a peasant I knew well. Pyenotchkin had been out of humour with Sofron up to the time I left. I began talking to Anpadist about the Shipilovka peasants, and Mr. Pyenotchkin, and asked him whether he knew the agent there.

'Sofron Yakovlitch? ... ugh!' 'What sort of man is he?'

'He's not a man; he's a dog; you couldn't find another brute like him between here and Kursk.'

'Really?'

'Why, Shipilovka's hardly reckoned as--what's his name?--Mr. Pyenotchkin's at all; he's not the master there; Sofron's the master.'

'You don't say so!'

'He's master, just as if it were his own. The peasants all about are in debt to him; they work for him like slaves; he'll send one off with the waggons; another, another way.... He harries them out of their lives.'

'They haven't much land, I suppose?'

'Not much land! He rents two hundred acres from the Hlinovsky peasants alone, and two hundred and eighty from our folks; there's more than three hundred and seventy-five acres he's got. And he doesn't only traffic in land; he does a trade in horses and stock, and pitch, and butter, and hemp, and one thing and the other.... He's sharp, awfully sharp, and rich too, the beast! But what's bad--he beats them. He's a brute, not a man; a dog, I tell you; a cur, a regular cur; that's what he is!'

'How is it they don't make complaints of him?'

'I dare say, the master'd be pleased! There's no arrears; so what does he care? Yes, you'd better,' he added, after a brief pause; 'I should advise you to complain! No, he'd let you know ... yes, you'd better try it on.... No, he'd let you know....'

I thought of Antip, and told him what I had seen.

'There,' commented Anpadist, 'he will eat him up now; he'll simply eat the man up. The bailiff will beat him now. Such a poor, unlucky chap, come to think of it! And what's his offence?... He had some wrangle in meeting with him, the agent, and he lost all patience, I suppose, and of course he wouldn't stand it.... A great matter, truly, to make so much of! So he began pecking at him, Antip. Now he'll eat him up altogether. You see, he's such a dog. Such a cur--God forgive my transgressions!--he knows whom to fall upon. The old men that are a bit richer, or've more children, he doesn't touch, the red-headed devil! but there's all the difference here! Why he's sent Antip's sons for recruits out of turn, the heartless ruffian, the cur! God forgive my transgressions!'

We went on our way.

XI   THE COUNTING-HOUSE

It was autumn. For some hours I had been strolling across country with my gun, and should probably not have returned till evening to the tavern on the Kursk high-road where my three-horse trap was awaiting me, had not an exceedingly fine and persistent rain, which had worried me all day with the obstinacy and ruthlessness of some old maiden lady, driven me at last to seek at least a temporary shelter somewhere in the neighbourhood. While I was still deliberating in which direction to go, my eye suddenly fell on a low shanty near a field sown with peas. I went up to the shanty, glanced under the thatched roof, and saw an old man so infirm that he reminded me at once of the dying goat Robinson Crusoe found in some cave on his island. The old man was squatting on his heels, his little dim eyes half-closed, while hurriedly, but carefully, like a hare (the poor fellow had not a single tooth), he munched a dry, hard pea, incessantly rolling it from side to side. He was so absorbed in this occupation that he did not notice my entrance.

'Grandfather! hey, grandfather!' said I. He ceased munching, lifted his eyebrows high, and with an effort opened his eyes.

'What?' he mumbled in a broken voice.

'Where is there a village near?' I asked.

The old man fell to munching again. He had not heard me. I repeated my question louder than before.

'A village?... But what do you want?'

'Why, shelter from the rain.'

'What?'

'Shelter from the rain.'

'Ah!' (He scratched his sunburnt neck.) 'Well, now, you go,' he said suddenly, waving his hands indefinitely, 'so ... as you go by the copse--see, as you go--there'll be a road; you pass it by, and keep right on to the right; keep right on, keep right on, keep right on.... Well, there will be Ananyevo. Or else you'd go to Sitovka.'

I followed the old man with difficulty. His moustaches muffled his voice, and his tongue too did not obey him readily.

'Where are you from?' I asked him.

'What?'

'Where are you from?'

'Ananyevo.'

'What are you doing here?'

'I'm watchman.'

'Why, what are you watching?'

'The peas.'

I could not help smiling.

'Really!--how old are you?'

'God knows.'

'Your sight's failing, I expect.'

'What?'

'Your sight's failing, I daresay?'

'Yes, it's failing. At times I can hear nothing.'

'Then how can you be a watchman, eh?'

'Oh, my elders know about that.'

'Elders!' I thought, and I gazed not without compassion at the poor old man. He fumbled about, pulled out of his bosom a bit of coarse bread, and began sucking it like a child, with difficulty moving his sunken cheeks.

I walked in the direction of the copse, turned to the right, kept on, kept right on as the old man had advised me, and at last got to a large village with a stone church in the new style, i.e. with columns, and a spacious manor-house, also with columns. While still some way off I noticed through the fine network of falling rain a cottage with a deal roof, and two chimneys, higher than the others, in all probability the dwelling of the village elder; and towards it I bent my steps in the hope of finding, in this cottage, a samovar, tea, sugar, and some not absolutely sour cream. Escorted by my half-frozen dog, I went up the steps into the outer room, opened the door, and instead of the usual appurtenances of a cottage, I saw several tables, heaped up with papers, two red cupboards, bespattered inkstands, pewter boxes of blotting sand weighing half a hundred-weight, long penholders, and so on. At one of the tables was sitting a young man of twenty with a swollen, sickly face, diminutive eyes, a greasy-looking forehead, and long straggling locks of hair. He was dressed, as one would expect, in a grey nankin coat, shiny with wear at the waist and the collar.

'What do you want?' he asked me, flinging his head up like a horse taken unexpectedly by the nose.

'Does the bailiff live here... or--'

'This is the principal office of the manor,' he interrupted. 'I'm the clerk on duty.... Didn't you see the sign-board? That's what it was put up for.'

'Where could I dry my clothes here? Is there a samovar anywhere in the village?'

'Samovars, of course,' replied the young man in the grey coat with dignity; 'go to Father Timofey's, or to the servants' cottage, or else to Nazar Tarasitch, or to Agrafena, the poultry-woman.'

'Who are you talking to, you blockhead? Can't you let me sleep, dummy!' shouted a voice from the next room.

'Here's a gentleman's come in to ask where he can dry himself.'

'What sort of a gentleman?'

'I don't know. With a dog and a gun.'

A bedstead creaked in the next room. The door opened, and there came in a stout, short man of fifty, with a bull neck, goggle-eyes, extraordinarily round cheeks, and his whole face positively shining with sleekness.

'What is it you wish?' he asked me.

'To dry my things.'

'There's no place here.'

'I didn't know this was the counting-house; I am willing, though, to pay...'

'Well, perhaps it could be managed here,' rejoined the fat man; 'won't you come inside here?' (He led me into another room, but not the one he had come from.) 'Would this do for you?'

'Very well.... And could I have tea and milk?'

'Certainly, at once. If you'll meantime take off your things and rest, the tea shall be got ready this minute.'

'Whose property is this?'

'Madame Losnyakov's, Elena Nikolaevna.'

He went out I looked round: against the partition separating my room from the office stood a huge leather sofa; two high-backed chairs, also covered in leather, were placed on both sides of the solitary window which looked out on the village street. On the walls, covered with a green paper with pink patterns on it, hung three immense oil paintings. One depicted a setter-dog with a blue collar, bearing the inscription: 'This is my consolation'; at the dog's feet flowed a river; on the opposite bank of the river a hare of quite disproportionate size with ears cocked up was sitting under a pine tree. In another picture two old men were eating a melon; behind the melon was visible in the distance a Greek temple with the inscription: 'The Temple of Satisfaction.' The third picture represented the half-nude figure of a woman in a recumbent position, much fore-shortened, with red knees and very big heels. My dog had, with superhuman efforts, crouched under the sofa, and apparently found a great deal of dust there, as he kept sneezing violently. I went to the window. Boards had been laid across the street in a slanting direction from the manor-house to the counting-house--a very useful precaution, as, thanks to our rich black soil and the persistent rain, the mud was terrible. In the grounds of the manor-house, which stood with its back to the street, there was the constant going and coming there always is about manor-houses: maids in faded chintz gowns flitted to and fro; house-serfs sauntered through the mud, stood still and scratched their spines meditatively; the constable's horse, tied up to a post, lashed his tail lazily, and with his nose high up, gnawed at the hedge; hens were clucking; sickly turkeys kept up an incessant gobble-gobble. On the steps of a dark crumbling out-house, probably the bath-house, sat a stalwart lad with a guitar, singing with some spirit the well-known ballad:

'I'm leaving this enchanting spot
To go into the desert.'
The fat man came into the room.
'They're bringing you in your tea,' he told me, with an affable smile.

The young man in the grey coat, the clerk on duty, laid on the old card-table a samovar, a teapot, a tumbler on a broken saucer, a jug of cream, and a bunch of Bolhovo biscuit rings. The fat man went out.

'What is he?' I asked the clerk; 'the steward?'

'No, sir; he was the chief cashier, but now he has been promoted to be head-clerk.'

'Haven't you got a steward, then?'

'No, sir. There's an agent, Mihal Vikulov, but no steward.'

'Is there a manager, then?'

'Yes; a German, Lindamandol, Karlo Karlitch; only he does not manage the estate.'

'Who does manage it, then?'

'Our mistress herself.'

'You don't say so. And are there many of you in the office?'

The young man reflected.

'There are six of us.'

'Who are they?' I inquired.

'Well, first there's Vassily Nikolaevitch, the head cashier; then Piotr, one clerk; Piotr's brother, Ivan, another clerk; the other Ivan, a clerk; Konstantin Narkizer, another clerk; and me here--there's a lot of us, you can't count all of them.'

'I suppose your mistress has a great many serfs in her house?'

'No, not to say a great many.'

'How many, then?'

'I dare say it runs up to about a hundred and fifty.'

We were both silent for a little.

'I suppose you write a good hand, eh?' I began again.

The young man grinned from ear to ear, went into the office and brought in a sheet covered with writing.

'This is my writing,' he announced, still with the same smile on his face.

I looked at it; on the square sheet of greyish paper there was written, in a good bold hand, the following document:--

ORDER
From the Chief Office of the Manor of Ananyevo to the Agent, Mihal Vikulov.
No. 209.
'Whereas some person unknown entered the garden at Ananyevo last night in an intoxicated condition, and with unseemly songs waked the French governess, Madame Engene, and disturbed her; and whether the watchmen saw anything, and who were on watch in the garden and permitted such disorderliness: as regards all the above-written matters, your orders are to investigate in detail, and report immediately to the Office.'
' Head-Clerk , NIKOLAI HVOSTOV.'

A huge heraldic seal was attached to the order, with the inscription: 'Seal of the chief office of the manor of Ananyevo'; and below stood the signature: 'To be executed exactly, Elena Losnyakov.'

'Your lady signed it herself, eh?' I queried.

'To be sure; she always signs herself. Without that the order would be of no effect.'

'Well, and now shall you send this order to the agent?'

'No, sir. He'll come himself and read it. That's to say, it'll be read to him; you see, he's no scholar.' (The clerk on duty was silent again for a while.) 'But what do you say?' he added, simpering; 'is it well written?'

'Very well written.'

'It wasn't composed, I must confess, by me. Konstantin is the great one for that.'

'What?... Do you mean the orders have first to be composed among you?'

'Why, how else could we do? Couldn't write them off straight without making a fair copy.'

'And what salary do you get?' I inquired.

'Thirty-five roubles, and five roubles for boots.'

'And are you satisfied?'

'Of course I am satisfied. It's not everyone can get into an office like ours. It was God's will, in my case, to be sure; I'd an uncle who was in service as a butler.'

'And you're well-off?'

'Yes, sir. Though, to tell the truth,' he went on, with a sigh, 'a place at a merchant's, for instance, is better for the likes of us. At a merchant's they're very well off. Yesterday evening a merchant came to us from Venev, and his man got talking to me.... Yes, that's a good place, no doubt about it; a very good place.'

'Why? Do the merchants pay more wages?'

'Lord preserve us! Why, a merchant would soon give you the sack if you asked him for wages. No, at a merchant's you must live on trust and on fear. He'll give you food, and drink, and clothes, and all. If you give him satisfaction, he'll do more.... Talk of wages, indeed! You don't need them.... And a merchant, too, lives in plain Russian style, like ourselves; you go with him on a journey--he has tea, and you have it; what he eats, you eat. A merchant ... one can put up with; a merchant's a very different thing from what a gentleman is; a merchant's not whimsical; if he's out of temper, he'll give you a blow, and there it ends. He doesn't nag nor sneer.... But with a gentleman it's a woeful business! Nothing's as he likes it--this is not right, and that he can't fancy. You hand him a glass of water or something to eat: "Ugh, the water stinks! positively stinks!" You take it out, stay a minute outside the door, and bring it back: "Come, now, that's good; this doesn't stink now." And as for the ladies, I tell you, the ladies are something beyond everything!... and the young ladies above all!...'

'Fedyushka!' came the fat man's voice from the office.

The clerk went out quickly. I drank a glass of tea, lay down on the sofa, and fell asleep. I slept for two hours.

When I woke, I meant to get up, but I was overcome by laziness; I closed my eyes, but did not fall asleep again. On the other side of the partition, in the office, they were talking in subdued voices. Unconsciously I began to listen.

'Quite so, quite so, Nikolai Eremyitch,' one voice was saying; 'quite so. One can't but take that into account; yes, certainly!... Hm!' (The speaker coughed.)

'You may believe me, Gavrila Antonitch,' replied the fat man's voice: 'don't I know how things are done here? Judge for yourself.'

'Who does, if you don't, Nikolai Eremyitch? you're, one may say, the first person here. Well, then, how's it to be?' pursued the voice I did not recognise; 'what decision are we to come to, Nikolai Eremyitch? Allow me to put the question.'

'What decision, Gavrila Antonitch? The thing depends, so to say, on you; you don't seem over anxious.'

'Upon my word, Nikolai Eremyitch, what do you mean? Our business is trading, buying; it's our business to buy. That's what we live by, Nikolai Eremyitch, one may say.'

'Eight roubles a measure,' said the fat man emphatically.

A sigh was audible.

'Nikolai Eremyitch, sir, you ask a heavy price.' 'Impossible, Gavrila Antonitch, to do otherwise; I speak as before God Almighty; impossible.'

Silence followed.

I got up softly and looked through a crack in the partition. The fat man was sitting with his back to me. Facing him sat a merchant, a man about forty, lean and pale, who looked as if he had been rubbed with oil. He was incessantly fingering his beard, and very rapidly blinking and twitching his lips.

'Wonderful the young green crops this year, one may say,' he began again; 'I've been going about everywhere admiring them. All the way from Voronezh they've come up wonderfully, first-class, one may say.'

'The crops are pretty fair, certainly,' answered the head-clerk; 'but you know the saying, Gavrila Antonitch, autumn bids fair, but spring may be foul.'

'That's so, indeed, Nikolai Eremyitch; all is in God's hands; it's the absolute truth what you've just remarked, sir.... But perhaps your visitor's awake now.'

The fat man turned round ... listened....

'No, he's asleep. He may, though....'

He went to the door.

'No, he's asleep,' he repeated and went back to his place.

'Well, so what are we to say, Nikolai Eremyitch?' the merchant began again; 'we must bring our little business to a conclusion.... Let it be so, Nikolai Eremyitch, let it be so,' he went on, blinking incessantly; 'two grey notes and a white for your favour, and there' (he nodded in the direction of the house), 'six and a half. Done, eh?'

'Four grey notes,' answered the clerk.

'Come, three, then.'

'Four greys, and no white.'

'Three, Nikolai Eremyitch.'

'Three and a half, and not a farthing less.'

'Three, Nikolai Eremyitch.'

'You're not talking sense, Gavrila Antonitch.'

'My, what a pig-headed fellow!' muttered the merchant. 'Then I'd better arrange it with the lady herself.'

'That's as you like,' answered the fat man; 'far better, I should say. Why should you worry yourself, after all?... Much better, indeed!'

'Well, well! Nikolai Eremyitch. I lost my temper for a minute! That was nothing but talk.'

'No, really, why?...'

'Nonsense, I tell you.... I tell you I was joking. Well, take your three and a half; there's no doing anything with you.'

'I ought to have got four, but I was in too great a hurry--like an ass!' muttered the fat man.

'Then up there at the house, six and a half, Nikolai Eremyitch; the corn will be sold for six and a half?'

'Six and a half, as we said already.'

'Well, your hand on that then, Nikolai Eremyitch' (the merchant clapped his outstretched fingers into the clerk's palm). 'And good-bye, in God's name!' (The merchant got up.) 'So then, Nikolai Eremyitch, sir, I'll go now to your lady, and bid them send up my name, and so I'll say to her, "Nikolai Eremyitch," I'll say, "has made a bargain with me for six and a half."'

'That's what you must say, Gavrila Antonitch.'

'And now, allow me.'

The merchant handed the manager a small roll of notes, bowed, shook his head, picked up his hat with two fingers, shrugged his shoulders, and, with a sort of undulating motion, went out, his boots creaking after the approved fashion. Nikolai Eremyitch went to the wall, and, as far as I could make out, began sorting the notes handed him by the merchant. A red head, adorned with thick whiskers, was thrust in at the door.

'Well?' asked the head; 'all as it should be?'

'Yes.'

'How much?'

The fat man made an angry gesture with his hand, and pointed to my room.

'Ah, all right!' responded the head, and vanished.

The fat man went up to the table, sat down, opened a book, took out a reckoning frame, and began shifting the beads to and fro as he counted, using not the forefinger but the third finger of his right hand, which has a much more showy effect.

The clerk on duty came in.

'What is it?'

'Sidor is here from Goloplek.'

'Oh! ask him in. Wait a bit, wait a bit.... First go and look whether the strange gentleman's still asleep, or whether he has waked up.'

The clerk on duty came cautiously into my room. I laid my head on my game-bag, which served me as a pillow, and closed my eyes.

'He's asleep,' whispered the clerk on duty, returning to the counting-house.

The fat man muttered something.

'Well, send Sidor in,' he said at last.

I got up again. A peasant of about thirty, of huge stature, came in--a red-cheeked, vigorous-looking fellow, with brown hair, and a short curly beard. He crossed himself, praying to the holy image, bowed to the head-clerk, held his hat before him in both hands, and stood erect.

'Good day, Sidor,' said the fat man, tapping with the reckoning beads.

'Good-day to you, Nikolai Eremyitch.'

'Well, what are the roads like?'

'Pretty fair, Nikolai Eremyitch. A bit muddy.' (The peasant spoke slowly and not loud.)

'Wife quite well?'

'She's all right!'

The peasant gave a sigh and shifted one leg forward. Nikolai Eremyitch put his pen behind his ear, and blew his nose.

'Well, what have you come about?' he proceeded to inquire, putting his check handkerchief into his pocket.

'Why, they do say, Nikolai Eremyitch, they're asking for carpenters from us.'

'Well, aren't there any among you, hey?'

'To be sure there are, Nikolai Eremyitch; our place is right in the woods; our earnings are all from the wood, to be sure. But it's the busy time, Nikolai Eremyitch. Where's the time to come from?'

'The time to come from! Busy time! I dare say, you're so eager to work for outsiders, and don't care to work for your mistress.... It's all the same!'

'The work's all the same, certainly, Nikolai Eremyitch ... but....'

'Well?'

'The pay's ... very....'

'What next! You've been spoiled; that's what it is. Get along with you!'

'And what's more, Nikolai Eremyitch, there'll be only a week's work, but they'll keep us hanging on a month. One time there's not material enough, and another time they'll send us into the garden to weed the path.'

'What of it? Our lady herself is pleased to give the order, so it's useless you and me talking about it.'

Sidor was silent; he began shifting from one leg to the other.

Nikolai Eremyitch put his head on one side, and began busily playing with the reckoning beads.

'Our ... peasants ... Nikolai Eremyitch....' Sidor began at last, hesitating over each word; 'sent word to your honour ... there is ... see here....' (He thrust his big hand into the bosom of his coat, and began to pull out a folded linen kerchief with a red border.)

'What are you thinking of? Goodness, idiot, are you out of your senses?' the fat man interposed hurriedly. 'Go on; go to my cottage,' he continued, almost shoving the bewildered peasant out; 'ask for my wife there ... she'll give you some tea; I'll be round directly; go on. For goodness' sake, I tell you, go on.'

Sidor went away.

'Ugh!... what a bear!' the head clerk muttered after him, shaking his head, and set to work again on his reckoning frame.

Suddenly shouts of 'Kuprya! Kuprya! there's no knocking down Kuprya!' were heard in the street and on the steps, and a little later there came into the counting-house a small man of sickly appearance, with an extraordinarily long nose and large staring eyes, who carried himself with a great air of superiority. He was dressed in a ragged little old surtout, with a plush collar and diminutive buttons. He carried a bundle of firewood on his shoulder. Five house-serfs were crowding round him, all shouting, 'Kuprya! there's no suppressing Kuprya! Kuprya's been turned stoker; Kuprya's turned a stoker!' But the man in the coat with the plush collar did not pay the slightest attention to the uproar made by his companions, and was not in the least out of countenance. With measured steps he went up to the stove, flung down his load, straightened himself, took out of his tail-pocket a snuff- box, and with round eyes began helping himself to a pinch of dry trefoil mixed with ashes. At the entrance of this noisy party the fat man had at first knitted his brows and risen from his seat, but, seeing what it was, he smiled, and only told them not to shout. 'There's a sportsman,' said he, 'asleep in the next room.' 'What sort of sportsman?' two of them asked with one voice.

'A gentleman.'

'Ah!'

'Let them make a row,' said the man with the plush collar, waving his arms; 'what do I care, so long as they don't touch me? They've turned me into a stoker....'

'A stoker! a stoker!' the others put in gleefully.

'It's the mistress's orders,' he went on, with a shrug of his shoulders; 'but just you wait a bit ... they'll turn you into swineherds yet. But I've been a tailor, and a good tailor too, learnt my trade in the best house in Moscow, and worked for generals ... and nobody can take that from me. And what have you to boast of?... What? you're a pack of idlers, not worth your salt; that's what you are! Turn me off! I shan't die of hunger; I shall be all right; give me a passport. I'd send a good rent home, and satisfy the masters. But what would you do? You'd die off like flies, that's what you'd do!'

'That's a nice lie!' interposed a pock-marked lad with white eyelashes, a red cravat, and ragged elbows. 'You went off with a passport sharp enough, but never a halfpenny of rent did the masters see from you, and you never earned a farthing for yourself, you just managed to crawl home again and you've never had a new rag on you since.'

'Ah, well, what could one do! Konstantin Narkizitch,' responded Kuprya; 'a man falls in love--a man's ruined and done for! You go through what I have, Konstantin Narkizitch, before you blame me!'

'And you picked out a nice one to fall in love with!--a regular fright.'

'No, you must not say that, Konstantin Narkizitch.'

'Who's going to believe that? I've seen her, you know; I saw her with my own eyes last year in Moscow.'

'Last year she had gone off a little certainly,' observed Kuprya.

'No, gentlemen, I tell you what,' a tall, thin man, with a face spotted with pimples, a valet probably, from his frizzed and pomatumed head, remarked in a careless and disdainful voice; 'let Kuprya Afanasyitch sing us his song. Come on, now; begin, Kuprya Afanasyitch.

'Yes! yes!' put in the others. 'Hoorah for Alexandra! That's one for Kuprya; 'pon my soul ... Sing away, Kuprya!... You're a regular brick, Alexandra!' (Serfs often use feminine terminations in referring to a man as an expression of endearment.) 'Sing away!'

'This is not the place to sing,' Kuprya replied firmly; 'this is the manor counting-house.'

'And what's that to do with you? you've got your eye on a place as clerk, eh?' answered Konstantin with a coarse laugh. 'That's what it is!'

'Everything rests with the mistress,' observed the poor wretch.

'There, that's what he's got his eye on! a fellow like him! oo! oo! a!'

And they all roared; some rolled about with merriment. Louder than all laughed a lad of fifteen, probably the son of an aristocrat among the house-serfs; he wore a waistcoat with bronze buttons, and a cravat of lilac colour, and had already had time to fill out his waistcoat.

'Come tell us, confess now, Kuprya,' Nikolai Eremyitch began complacently, obviously tickled and diverted himself; 'is it bad being stoker? Is it an easy job, eh?'

'Nikolai Eremyitch,' began Kuprya, 'you're head-clerk among us now, certainly; there's no disputing that, no; but you know you have been in disgrace yourself, and you too have lived in a peasant's hut.'

'You'd better look out and not forget yourself in my place,' the fat man interrupted emphatically; 'people joke with a fool like you; you ought, you fool, to have sense, and be grateful to them for taking notice of a fool like you.'

'It was a slip of the tongue, Nikolai Eremyitch; I beg your pardon....'

'Yes, indeed, a slip of the tongue.'

The door opened and a little page ran in.

'Nikolai Eremyitch, mistress wants you.'

'Who's with the mistress?' he asked the page.

'Aksinya Nikitishna, and a merchant from Venev.'

'I'll be there this minute. And you, mates,' he continued in a persuasive voice, 'better move off out of here with the newly-appointed stoker; if the German pops in, he'll make a complaint for certain.'

The fat man smoothed his hair, coughed into his hand, which was almost completely hidden in his coat-sleeve, buttoned himself, and set off with rapid strides to see the lady of the manor. In a little while the whole party trailed out after him, together with Kuprya. My old friend, the clerk-on duty, was left alone. He set to work mending the pens, and dropped asleep in his chair. A few flies promptly seized the opportunity and settled on his mouth. A mosquito alighted on his forehead, and, stretching its legs out with a regular motion, slowly buried its sting into his flabby flesh. The same red head with whiskers showed itself again at the door, looked in, looked again, and then came into the office, together with the rather ugly body belonging to it.

'Fedyushka! eh, Fedyushka! always asleep,' said the head.

The clerk on duty opened his eyes and got up from his seat.

'Nikolai Eremyitch has gone to the mistress?'

'Yes, Vassily Nikolaevitch.'

'Ah! ah!' thought I; 'this is he, the head cashier.'

The head cashier began walking about the room. He really slunk rather than walked, and altogether resembled a cat. An old black frock-coat with very narrow skirts hung about his shoulders; he kept one hand in his bosom, while the other was for ever fumbling about his high, narrow horse-hair collar, and he turned his head with a certain effort. He wore noiseless kid boots, and trod very softly.

'The landowner, Yagushkin, was asking for you to-day,' added the clerk on duty.

'Hm, asking for me? What did he say?'

'Said he'd go to Tyutyurov this evening and would wait for you. "I want to discuss some business with Vassily Nikolaevitch," said he, but what the business was he didn't say; "Vassily Nikolaevitch will know," says he.'

'Hm!' replied the head cashier, and he went up to the window.

'Is Nikolai Eremyitch in the counting-house?' a loud voice was heard asking in the outer room, and a tall man, apparently angry, with an irregular but bold and expressive face, and rather clean in his dress, stepped over the threshold.

'Isn't he here?' he inquired, looking rapidly round.

'Nikolai Eremyitch is with the mistress,' responded the cashier. 'Tell me what you want, Pavel Andreitch; you can tell me.... What is it you want?'

'What do I want? You want to know what I want?' (The cashier gave a sickly nod.) 'I want to give him a lesson, the fat, greasy villain, the scoundrelly tell-tale!... I'll give him a tale to tell!'

Pavel flung himself into a chair.

'What are you saying, Pavel Andreitch! Calm yourself.... Aren't you ashamed? Don't forget whom you're talking about, Pavel Andreitch!' lisped the cashier.

'Forget whom I'm talking about? What do I care for his being made head- clerk? A fine person they've found to promote, there's no denying that! They've let the goat loose in the kitchen garden, you may say!'

'Hush, hush, Pavel Andreitch, hush! drop that ... what rubbish are you talking?'

'So Master Fox is beginning to fawn? I will wait for him,' Pavel said with passion, and he struck a blow on the table. 'Ah, here he's coming!' he added with a look at the window; 'speak of the devil. With your kind permission!' (He, got up.)

Nikolai Eremyitch came into the counting-house. His face was shining with satisfaction, but he was rather taken aback at seeing Pavel Andreitch.

'Good day to you, Nikolai Eremyitch,' said Pavel in a significant tone, advancing deliberately to meet him.

The head-clerk made no reply. The face of the merchant showed itself in the doorway.

'What, won't you deign to answer me?' pursued Pavel. 'But no ... no,' he added; 'that's not it; there's no getting anything by shouting and abuse. No, you'd better tell me in a friendly way, Nikolai Eremyitch; what do you persecute me for? what do you want to ruin me for? Come, speak, speak.'

'This is no fit place to come to an understanding with you,' the head- clerk answered in some agitation, 'and no fit time. But I must say I wonder at one thing: what makes you suppose I want to ruin you, or that I'm persecuting you? And if you come to that, how can I persecute you? You're not in my counting-house.'

'I should hope not,' answered Pavel; 'that would be the last straw! But why are you hum-bugging, Nikolai Eremyitch?... You understand me, you know.'

'No, I don't understand.'

'No, you do understand.'

'No, by God, I don't understand!'

'Swearing too! Well, tell us, since it's come to that: have you no fear of God? Why can't you let the poor girl live in peace? What do you want of her?'

'Whom are you talking of?' the fat man asked with feigned amazement.

'Ugh! doesn't know; what next? I'm talking of Tatyana. Have some fear of God-- what do you want to revenge yourself for? You ought to be ashamed: a married man like you, with children as big as I am; it's a very different thing with me.... I mean marriage: I'm acting straight- forwardly.'

'How am I to blame in that, Pavel Andreitch? The mistress won't permit you to marry; it's her seignorial will! What have I to do with it?'

'Why, haven't you been plotting with that old hag, the housekeeper, eh? Haven't you been telling tales, eh? Tell me, aren't you bringing all sorts of stories up against the defenceless girl? I suppose it's not your doing that she's been degraded from laundrymaid to washing dishes in the scullery? And it's not your doing that she's beaten and dressed in sackcloth?... You ought to be ashamed, you ought to be ashamed--an old man like you! You know there's a paralytic stroke always hanging over you.... You will have to answer to God.'

'You're abusive, Pavel Andreitch, you're abusive.... You shan't have a chance to be insolent much longer.'

Pavel fired up.

'What? You dare to threaten me?' he said passionately. 'You think I'm afraid of you. No, my man, I'm not come to that! What have I to be afraid of?... I can make my bread everywhere. For you, now, it's another thing! It's only here you can live and tell tales, and filch....'

'Fancy the conceit of the fellow!' interrupted the clerk, who was also beginning to lose patience; 'an apothecary's assistant, simply an apothecary's assistant, a wretched leech; and listen to him--fie upon you! you're a high and mighty personage!'

'Yes, an apothecary's assistant, and except for this apothecary's assistant you'd have been rotting in the graveyard by now.... It was some devil drove me to cure him,' he added between his teeth.

'You cured me?... No, you tried to poison me; you dosed me with aloes,' the clerk put in.

'What was I to do if nothing but aloes had any effect on you?'

'The use of aloes is forbidden by the Board of Health,' pursued Nikolai. 'I'll lodge a complaint against you yet.... You tried to compass my death--that was what you did! But the Lord suffered it not.'

'Hush, now, that's enough, gentlemen,' the cashier was beginning....

'Stand off!' bawled the clerk. 'He tried to poison me! Do you understand that?'

'That's very likely.... Listen, Nikolai Eremyitch,' Pavel began in despairing accents. 'For the last time, I beg you.... You force me to it--can't stand it any longer. Let us alone, do you hear? or else, by God, it'll go ill with one or other of us--I mean with you!'

The fat man flew into a rage.

'I'm not afraid of you!' he shouted; 'do you hear, milksop? I got the better of your father; I broke his horns--a warning to you; take care!'

'Don't talk of my father, Nikolai Eremyitch.'

'Get away! who are you to give me orders?'

'I tell you, don't talk of him!'

'And I tell you, don't forget yourself.... However necessary you think yourself, if our lady has a choice between us, it's not you'll be kept, my dear! None's allowed to mutiny, mind!' (Pavel was shaking with fury.) 'As for the wench, Tatyana, she deserves ... wait a bit, she'll get something worse!'

Pavel dashed forward with uplifted fists, and the clerk rolled heavily on the floor.

'Handcuff him, handcuff him,' groaned Nikolai Eremyitch....

I won't take upon myself to describe the end of this scene; I fear I have wounded the reader's delicate susceptibilities as it is.

The same day I returned home. A week later I heard that Madame Losnyakov had kept both Pavel and Nikolai in her service, but had sent away the girl Tatyana; it appeared she was not wanted.

XII   BIRYUK

I was coming back from hunting one evening alone in a racing droshky. I was six miles from home; my good trotting mare galloped bravely along the dusty road, pricking up her ears with an occasional snort; my weary dog stuck close to the hind-wheels, as though he were fastened there. A tempest was coming on. In front, a huge, purplish storm-cloud slowly rose from behind the forest; long grey rain-clouds flew over my head and to meet me; the willows stirred and whispered restlessly. The suffocating heat changed suddenly to a damp chilliness; the darkness rapidly thickened. I gave the horse a lash with the reins, descended a steep slope, pushed across a dry water-course overgrown with brushwood, mounted the hill, and drove into the forest. The road ran before me, bending between thick hazel bushes, now enveloped in darkness; I advanced with difficulty. The droshky jumped up and down over the hard roots of the ancient oaks and limes, which were continually intersected by deep ruts--the tracks of cart wheels; my horse began to stumble. A violent wind suddenly began to roar overhead; the trees blustered; big drops of rain fell with slow tap and splash on the leaves; there came a flash of lightning and a clap of thunder. The rain fell in torrents. I went on a step or so, and soon was forced to stop; my horse foundered; I could not see an inch before me. I managed to take refuge somehow in a spreading bush. Crouching down and covering my face, I waited patiently for the storm to blow over, when suddenly, in a flash of lightning, I saw a tall figure on the road. I began to stare intently in that direction--the figure seemed to have sprung out of the ground near my droshky.

'Who's that?' inquired a ringing voice.

'Why, who are you?'

'I'm the forester here.'

I mentioned my name.

'Oh, I know! Are you on your way home?'

'Yes. But, you see, in such a storm....'

'Yes, there is a storm,' replied the voice.

A pale flash of lightning lit up the forester from head to foot; a brief crashing clap of thunder followed at once upon it. The rain lashed with redoubled force.

'It won't be over just directly,' the forester went on.

'What's to be done?'

'I'll take you to my hut, if you like,' he said abruptly.

'That would be a service.'

'Please to take your seat'

He went up to the mare's head, took her by the bit, and pulled her up. We set off. I held on to the cushion of the droshky, which rocked 'like a boat on the sea,' and called my dog. My poor mare splashed with difficulty through the mud, slipped and stumbled; the forester hovered before the shafts to right and to left like a ghost. We drove rather a long while; at last my guide stopped. 'Here we are home, sir,' he observed in a quiet voice. The gate creaked; some puppies barked a welcome. I raised my head, and in a flash of lightning I made out a small hut in the middle of a large yard, fenced in with hurdles. From the one little window there was a dim light. The forester led his horse up to the steps and knocked at the door. 'Coming, coming!' we heard in a little shrill voice; there was the patter of bare feet, the bolt creaked, and a girl of twelve, in a little old smock tied round the waist with list, appeared in the doorway with a lantern in her hand.

'Show the gentleman a light,' he said to her 'and I will put your droshky in the shed.'

The little girl glanced at me, and went into the hut. I followed her.

The forester's hut consisted of one room, smoky, low-pitched, and empty, without curtains or partition. A tattered sheepskin hung on the wall. On the bench lay a single-barrelled gun; in the corner lay a heap of rags; two great pots stood near the oven. A pine splinter was burning on the table flickering up and dying down mournfully. In the very middle of the hut hung a cradle, suspended from the end of a long horizontal pole. The little girl put out the lantern, sat down on a tiny stool, and with her right hand began swinging the cradle, while with her left she attended to the smouldering pine splinter. I looked round--my heart sank within me: it's not cheering to go into a peasant's hut at night. The baby in the cradle breathed hard and fast.

'Are you all alone here?' I asked the little girl.

'Yes,' she uttered, hardly audibly.

'You're the forester's daughter?'

'Yes,' she whispered.

The door creaked, and the forester, bending his head, stepped across the threshold. He lifted the lantern from the floor, went up to the table, and lighted a candle.

'I dare say you're not used to the splinter light?' said he, and he shook back his curls.

I looked at him. Rarely has it been my fortune to behold such a comely creature. He was tall, broad-shouldered, and in marvellous proportion. His powerful muscles stood out in strong relief under his wet homespun shirt. A curly, black beard hid half of his stern and manly face; small brown eyes looked out boldly from under broad eyebrows which met in the middle. He stood before me, his arms held lightly akimbo.

I thanked him, and asked his name.

'My name's Foma,' he answered, 'and my nickname's Biryuk' (i.e. wolf). [Footnote: The name Biryuk is used in the Orel province to denote a solitary, misanthropic man.-- Author's Note .]

'Oh, you're Biryuk.'

I looked with redoubled curiosity at him. From my Yermolai and others I had often heard stories about the forester Biryuk, whom all the peasants of the surrounding districts feared as they feared fire. According to them there had never been such a master of his business in the world before. 'He won't let you carry off a handful of brushwood; he'll drop upon you like a fall of snow, whatever time it may be, even in the middle of the night, and you needn't think of resisting him-- he's strong, and cunning as the devil.... And there's no getting at him anyhow; neither by brandy nor by money; there's no snare he'll walk into. More than once good folks have planned to put him out of the world, but no-- it's never come off.'

That was how the neighbouring peasants spoke of Biryuk.

'So you're Biryuk,' I repeated; 'I've heard talk of you, brother. They say you show no mercy to anyone.'

'I do my duty,' he answered grimly; 'it's not right to eat the master's bread for nothing.'

He took an axe from his girdle and began splitting splinters.

'Have you no wife?' I asked him.

'No,' he answered, with a vigorous sweep of the axe.

'She's dead, I suppose?'

'No ... yes ... she's dead,' he added, and turned away. I was silent; he raised his eyes and looked at me.

'She ran away with a travelling pedlar,' he brought out with a bitter smile. The little girl hung her head; the baby waked up and began crying; the little girl went to the cradle. 'There, give it him,' said Biryuk, thrusting a dirty feeding-bottle into her hand. 'Him, too, she abandoned,' he went on in an undertone, pointing to the baby. He went up to the door, stopped, and turned round.

'A gentleman like you,' he began, 'wouldn't care for our bread, I dare say, and except bread, I've--'

'I'm not hungry.'

'Well, that's for you to say. I would have heated the samovar, but I've no tea.... I'll go and see how your horse is getting on.'

He went out and slammed the door. I looked round again, the hut struck me as more melancholy than ever. The bitter smell of stale smoke choked my breathing unpleasantly. The little girl did not stir from her place, and did not raise her eyes; from time to time she jogged the cradle, and timidly pulled her slipping smock up on to shoulder; her bare legs hung motionless.

'What's your name?' I asked her.

'Ulita,' she said, her mournful little face drooping more than ever.

The forester came in and sat down on the bench.

'The storm 's passing over,' he observed, after a brief silence; 'if you wish it, I will guide you out of the forest.'

I got up; Biryuk took his gun and examined the firepan.

'What's that for?' I inquired.

'There's mischief in the forest.... They're cutting a tree down on Mares' Ravine,' he added, in reply to my look of inquiry.

'Could you hear it from here?'

'I can hear it outside.'

We went out together. The rain had ceased. Heavy masses of storm-cloud were still huddled in the distance; from time to time there were long flashes of lightning; but here and there overhead the dark blue sky was already visible; stars twinkled through the swiftly flying clouds. The outline of the trees, drenched with rain, and stirred by the wind, began to stand out in the darkness. We listened. The forester took off his cap and bent his head.... 'Th ... there!' he said suddenly, and he stretched out his hand: 'see what a night he's pitched on.' I had heard nothing but the rustle of the leaves. Biryuk led the mare out of the shed. 'But, perhaps,' he added aloud, 'this way I shall miss him.' 'I'll go with you ... if you like?' 'Certainly,' he answered, and he backed the horse in again; 'we'll catch him in a trice, and then I'll take you. Let's be off.' We started, Biryuk in front, I following him. Heaven only knows how he found out his way, but he only stopped once or twice, and then merely to listen to the strokes of the axe. 'There,' he muttered, 'do you hear? do you hear?' 'Why, where?' Biryuk shrugged his shoulders. We went down into the ravine; the wind was still for an instant; the rhythmical strokes reached my hearing distinctly. Biryuk glanced at me and shook his head. We went farther through the wet bracken and nettles. A slow muffled crash was heard....

'He's felled it,' muttered Biryuk. Meantime the sky had grown clearer and clearer; there was a faint light in the forest. We clambered at last out of the ravine.

'Wait here a little,' the forester whispered to me. He bent down, and raising his gun above his head, vanished among the bushes. I began listening with strained attention. Across the continual roar of the wind faint sounds from close by reached me; there was a cautious blow of an axe on the brushwood, the crash of wheels, the snort of a horse....

'Where are you off to? Stop!' the iron voice of Biryuk thundered suddenly. Another voice was heard in a pitiful shriek, like a trapped hare.... A struggle was beginning.

'No, no, you've made a mistake,' Biryuk declared panting; 'you're not going to get off....' I rushed in the direction of the noise, and ran up to the scene of the conflict, stumbling at every step. A felled tree lay on the ground, and near it Biryuk was busily engaged holding the thief down and binding his hands behind his back with a kerchief. I came closer. Biryuk got up and set him on his feet. I saw a peasant drenched with rain, in tatters, and with a long dishevelled beard. A sorry little nag, half covered with a stiff mat, was standing by, together with a rough cart. The forester did not utter a word; the peasant too was silent; his head was shaking.

'Let him go,' I whispered in Biryuk's ears; 'I'll pay for the tree.'

Without a word Biryuk took the horse by the mane with his left hand; in his right he held the thief by the belt. 'Now turn round, you rat!' he said grimly.

'The bit of an axe there, take it,' muttered the peasant.

'No reason to lose it, certainly,' said the forester, and he picked up the axe. We started. I walked behind.... The rain began sprinkling again, and soon fell in torrents. With difficulty we made our way to the hut. Biryuk pushed the captured horse into the middle of the yard, led the peasant into the room, loosened the knot in the kerchief, and made him sit down in a corner. The little girl, who had fallen asleep near the oven, jumped up and began staring at us in silent terror. I sat down on the locker.

'Ugh, what a downpour!' remarked the forester; 'you will have to wait till it's over. Won't you lie down?'

'Thanks.'

'I would have shut him in the store loft, on your honour's account,' he went on, indicating the peasant; 'but you see the bolt--'

'Leave him here; don't touch him,' I interrupted.

The peasant stole a glance at me from under his brows. I vowed inwardly to set the poor wretch free, come what might. He sat without stirring on the locker. By the light of the lantern I could make out his worn, wrinkled face, his overhanging yellow eyebrows, his restless eyes, his thin limbs.... The little girl lay down on the floor, just at his feet, and again dropped asleep. Biryuk sat at the table, his head in his hands. A cricket chirped in the corner ... the rain pattered on the roof and streamed down the windows; we were all silent.

'Foma Kuzmitch,' said the peasant suddenly in a thick, broken voice; 'Foma Kuzmitch!'

'What is it?'

'Let me go.'

Biryuk made no answer.

'Let me go ... hunger drove me to it; let me go.'

'I know you,' retorted the forester severely; 'your set's all alike-- all thieves.'

'Let me go,' repeated the peasant. 'Our manager ... we 're ruined, that's what it is--let me go!'

'Ruined, indeed!... Nobody need steal.'

'Let me go, Foma Kuzmitch.... Don't destroy me. Your manager, you know yourself, will have no mercy on me; that's what it is.'

Biryuk turned away. The peasant was shivering as though he were in the throes of fever. His head was shaking, and his breathing came in broken gasps.

'Let me go,' he repeated with mournful desperation. 'Let me go; by God, let me go! I'll pay; see, by God, I will! By God, it was through hunger!... the little ones are crying, you know yourself. It's hard for us, see.'

'You needn't go stealing, for all that.'

'My little horse,' the peasant went on, 'my poor little horse, at least ... our only beast ... let it go.'

'I tell you I can't. I'm not a free man; I'm made responsible. You oughtn't to be spoilt, either.'

'Let me go! It's through want, Foma Kuzmitch, want--and nothing else-- let me go!'

'I know you!'

'Oh, let me go!'

'Ugh, what's the use of talking to you! sit quiet, or else you'll catch it. Don't you see the gentleman, hey?'

The poor wretch hung his head.... Biryuk yawned and laid his head on the table. The rain still persisted. I was waiting to see what would happen.

Suddenly the peasant stood erect. His eyes were glittering, and his face flushed dark red. 'Come, then, here; strike yourself, here,' he began, his eyes puckering up and the corners of his mouth dropping; 'come, cursed destroyer of men's souls! drink Christian blood, drink.'

The forester turned round.

'I'm speaking to you, Asiatic, blood-sucker, you!'

'Are you drunk or what, to set to being abusive?' began the forester, puzzled. 'Are you out of your senses, hey?'

'Drunk! not at your expense, cursed destroyer of souls--brute, brute, brute!'

'Ah, you----I'll show you!'

'What's that to me? It's all one; I'm done for; what can I do without a home? Kill me--it's the same in the end; whether it's through hunger or like this--it's all one. Ruin us all--wife, children ... kill us all at once. But, wait a bit, we'll get at you!'

Biryuk got up.

'Kill me, kill me,' the peasant went on in savage tones; 'kill me; come, come, kill me....' (The little girl jumped up hastily from the ground and stared at him.) 'Kill me, kill me!'

'Silence!' thundered the forester, and he took two steps forward.

'Stop, Foma, stop,' I shouted; 'let him go.... Peace be with him.'

'I won't be silent,' the luckless wretch went on. 'It's all the same-- ruin anyway--you destroyer of souls, you brute; you've not come to ruin yet.... But wait a bit; you won't have long to boast of; they'll wring your neck; wait a bit!'

Biryuk clutched him by the shoulder. I rushed to help the peasant....

'Don't touch him, master!' the forester shouted to me.

I should not have feared his threats, and already had my fist in the air; but to my intense amazement, with one pull he tugged the kerchief off the peasant's elbows, took him by the scruff of the neck, thrust his cap over his eyes, opened the door, and shoved him out.

'Go to the devil with your horse!' he shouted after him; 'but mind, next time....'

He came back into the hut and began rummaging in the corner.

'Well, Biryuk,' I said at last, 'you've astonished me; I see you're a splendid fellow.'

'Oh, stop that, master,' he cut me short with an air of vexation; 'please don't speak of it. But I'd better see you on your way now,' he added; 'I suppose you won't wait for this little rain....'

In the yard there was the rattle of the wheels of the peasant's cart.

'He's off, then!' he muttered; 'but next time!'

Half-an-hour later he parted from me at the edge of the wood.

XIII   TWO COUNTRY GENTLEMEN

I have already had the honour, kind readers, of introducing to you several of my neighbours; let me now seize a favourable opportunity (it is always a favourable opportunity with us writers) to make known to you two more gentlemen, on whose lands I often used to go shooting-- very worthy, well-intentioned persons, who enjoy universal esteem in several districts.

First I will describe to you the retired General-major Vyatcheslav Ilarionovitch Hvalinsky. Picture to yourselves a tall and once slender man, now inclined to corpulence, but not in the least decrepit or even elderly, a man of ripe age; in his very prime, as they say. It is true the once regular and even now rather pleasing features of his face have undergone some change; his cheeks are flabby; there are close wrinkles like rays about his eyes; a few teeth are not, as Saadi, according to Pushkin, used to say; his light brown hair-- at least, all that is left of it--has assumed a purplish hue, thanks to a composition bought at the Romyon horse-fair of a Jew who gave himself out as an Armenian; but Vyatcheslav Ilarionovitch has a smart walk and a ringing laugh, jingles his spurs and curls his moustaches, and finally speaks of himself as an old cavalry man, whereas we all know that really old men never talk of being old. He usually wears a frock-coat buttoned up to the top, a high cravat, starched collars, and grey sprigged trousers of a military cut; he wears his hat tilted over his forehead, leaving all the back of his head exposed. He is a good-natured man, but of rather curious notions and principles. For instance, he can never treat noblemen of no wealth or standing as equals. When he talks to them, he usually looks sideways at them, his cheek pressed hard against his stiff white collar, and suddenly he turns and silently fixes them with a clear stony stare, while he moves the whole skin of his head under his hair; he even has a way of his own in pronouncing many words; he never says, for instance: 'Thank you, Pavel Vasilyitch,' or 'This way, if you please, Mihalo Ivanitch,' but always 'Fanks, Pa'l 'Asilitch,' or "Is wy, please, Mil' 'Vanitch.' With persons of the lower grades of society, his behaviour is still more quaint; he never looks at them at all, and before making known his desires to them, or giving an order, he repeats several times in succession, with a puzzled, far-away air: 'What's your name?... what, what's your name?' with extraordinary sharp emphasis on the first word, which gives the phrase a rather close resemblance to the call of a quail. He is very fussy and terribly close-fisted, but manages his land badly; he had chosen as overseer on his estate a retired quartermaster, a Little Russian, and a man of really exceptional stupidity. None of us, though, in the management of land, has ever surpassed a certain great Petersburg dignitary, who, having perceived from the reports of his steward that the cornkilns in which the corn was dried on his estate were often liable to catch fire, whereby he lost a great deal of grain, gave the strictest orders that for the future they should not put the sheaves in till the fire had been completely put out! This same great personage conceived the brilliant idea of sowing his fields with poppies, as the result of an apparently simple calculation; poppy being dearer than rye, he argued, it is consequently more profitable to sow poppy. He it was, too, who ordered his women serfs to wear tiaras after a pattern bespoken from Moscow; and to this day the peasant women on his lands do actually wear the tiaras, only they wear them over their skull-caps.... But let us return to Vyatcheslav Ilarionovitch. Vyatcheslav Ilarionovitch is a devoted admirer of the fair sex, and directly he catches sight of a pretty woman in the promenade of his district town, he is promptly off in pursuit, but falls at once into a sort of limping gait--that is the remarkable feature of the case. He is fond of playing cards, but only with people of a lower standing; they toady him with 'Your Excellency' in every sentence, while he can scold them and find fault to his heart's content. When he chances to play with the governor or any official personage, a marvellous change comes over him; he is all nods and smiles; he looks them in the face; he seems positively flowing with honey.... He even loses without grumbling. Vyatcheslav Ilarionovitch does not read much; when he is reading he incessantly works his moustaches and eyebrows up and down, as if a wave were passing from below upwards over his face. This undulatory motion in Vyatcheslav Ilarionovitch's face is especially marked when (before company, of course) he happens to be reading the columns of the Journal des Debats . In the assemblies of nobility he plays a rather important part, but on grounds of economy he declines the honourable dignity of marshal. 'Gentlemen,' he usually says to the noblemen who press that office upon him, and he speaks in a voice filled with condescension and self-sufficiency: 'much indebted for the honour; but I have made up my mind to consecrate my leisure to solitude.' And, as he utters these words, he turns his head several times to right and to left, and then, with a dignified air, adjusts his chin and his cheek over his cravat. In his young days he served as adjutant to some very important person, whom he never speaks of except by his Christian name and patronymic; they do say he fulfilled other functions than those of an adjutant; that, for instance, in full parade get-up, buttoned up to the chin, he had to lather his chief in his bath--but one can't believe everything one hears. General Hvalinsky is not, however, fond of talking himself about his career in the army, which is certainly rather curious; it seems that he had never seen active service. General Hvalinsky lives in a small house alone; he has never known the joys of married life, and consequently he still regards himself as a possible match, and indeed a very eligible one. But he has a house-keeper, a dark-eyed, dark-browed, plump, fresh-looking woman of five-and-thirty with a moustache; she wears starched dresses even on week-days, and on Sundays puts on muslin sleeves as well. Vyatcheslav Ilarionovitch is at his best at the large invitation dinners given by gentlemen of the neighbourhood in honour of the governor and other dignitaries: then he is, one may say, in his natural element. On these occasions he usually sits, if not on the governor's right hand, at least at no great distance from him; at the beginning of dinner he is more disposed to nurse his sense of personal dignity, and, sitting back in his chair, he loftily scans the necks and stand-up collars of the guests, without turning his head, but towards the end of the meal he unbends, begins smiling in all directions (he had been all smiles for the governor from the first), and sometimes even proposes the toast in honour of the fair sex, the ornament of our planet, as he says. General Hvalinsky shows to advantage too at all solemn public functions, inspections, assemblies, and exhibitions; no one in church goes up for the benediction with such style. Vyatcheslav Ilarionovitch's servants are never noisy and clamorous on the breaking up of assemblies or in crowded thoroughfares; as they make a way for him through the crowd or call his carriage, they say in an agreeable guttural baritone: 'By your leave, by your leave allow General Hvalinsky to pass,' or 'Call for General Hvalinsky's carriage.' ... Hvalinsky's carriage is, it must be admitted, of a rather queer design, and the footmen's liveries are rather threadbare (that they are grey, with red facings, it is hardly necessary to remark); his horses too have seen a good deal of hard service in their time; but Vyatcheslav Ilarionovitch has no pretensions to splendour, and goes so far as to think it beneath his rank to make an ostentation of wealth. Hvalinsky has no special gift of eloquence, or possibly has no opportunity of displaying his rhetorical powers, as he has a particular aversion, not only for disputing, but for discussion in general, and assiduously avoids long conversation of all sorts, especially with young people. This was certainly judicious on his part; the worst of having to do with the younger generation is that they are so ready to forget the proper respect and submission due to their superiors. In the presence of persons of high rank Hvalinsky is for the most part silent, while with persons of a lower rank, whom to judge by appearances he despises, though he constantly associates with them, his remarks are sharp and abrupt, expressions such as the following occurring incessantly: 'That's a piece of folly, what you're saying now,' or 'I feel myself compelled, sir, to remind you,' or 'You ought to realise with whom you are dealing,' and so on. He is peculiarly dreaded by post-masters, officers of the local boards, and superintendents of posting stations. He never entertains any one in his house, and lives, as the rumour goes, like a screw. For all that, he's an excellent country gentleman, 'An old soldier, a disinterested fellow, a man of principle, vieux grognard ,' his neighbours say of him. The provincial prosecutor alone permits himself to smile when General Hvalinsky's excellent and solid qualities are referred to before him--but what will not envy drive men to!...

However, we will pass now to another landed proprietor.

Mardary Apollonitch Stegunov has no sort of resemblance to Hvalinsky; I hardly think he has ever served under government in any capacity, and he has never been reckoned handsome. Mardary Apollonitch is a little, fattish, bald old man of a respectable corpulence, with a double chin and little soft hands. He is very hospitable and jovial; lives, as the saying is, for his comfort; summer and winter alike, he wears a striped wadded dressing-gown. There's only one thing in which he is like General Hvalinsky; he too is a bachelor. He owns five hundred souls. Mardary Apollonitch's interest in his estate is of a rather superficial description; not to be behind the age, he ordered a threshing-machine from Butenop's in Moscow, locked it up in a barn, and then felt his mind at rest on the subject. Sometimes on a fine summer day he would have out his racing droshky, and drive off to his fields, to look at the crops and gather corn-flowers. Mardary Apollonitch's existence is carried on in quite the old style. His house is of an old-fashioned construction; in the hall there is, of course, a smell of kvas, tallow candles, and leather; close at hand, on the right, there is a sideboard with pipes and towels; in the dining-room, family portraits, flies, a great pot of geraniums, and a squeaky piano; in the drawing-room, three sofas, three tables, two looking-glasses, and a wheezy clock of tarnished enamel with engraved bronze hands; in the study, a table piled up with papers, and a bluish-coloured screen covered with pictures cut out of various works of last century; a bookcase full of musty books, spiders, and black dust; a puffy armchair; an Italian window; a sealed-up door into the garden.... Everything, in short, just as it always is. Mardary Apollonitch has a multitude of servants, all dressed in the old-fashioned style; in long blue full coats, with high collars, shortish pantaloons of a muddy hue, and yellow waistcoats. They address visitors as 'father.' His estate is under the superintendence of an agent, a peasant with a beard that covers the whole of his sheepskin; his household is managed by a stingy, wrinkled old woman, whose face is always tied up in a cinnamon-coloured handkerchief. In Mardary Apollonitch's stable there are thirty horses of various kinds; he drives out in a coach built on the estate, that weighs four tons. He receives visitors very cordially, and entertains them sumptuously; in other words, thanks to the stupefying powers of our national cookery, he deprives them of all capacity for doing anything but playing preference. For his part, he never does anything, and has even given up reading the Dream-book . But there are a good many of our landed gentry in Russia exactly like this. It will be asked: 'What is my object in talking about him?...' Well, by way of answering that question, let me describe to you one of my visits at Mardary Apollonitch's.

I arrived one summer evening at seven o'clock. An evening service was only just over; the priest, a young man, apparently very timid, and only lately come from the seminary, was sitting in the drawing-room near the door, on the extreme edge of a chair. Mardary Apollonitch received me as usual, very cordially; he was genuinely delighted to see any visitor, and indeed he was the most good-natured of men altogether. The priest got up and took his hat.

'Wait a bit, wait a bit, father,' said Mardary Apollonitch, not yet leaving go of my hand; 'don't go ... I have sent for some vodka for you.'

'I never drink it, sir,' the priest muttered in confusion, blushing up to his ears.

'What nonsense!' answered Mardary Apollonitch; 'Mishka! Yushka! vodka for the father!'

Yushka, a tall, thin old man of eighty, came in with a glass of vodka on a dark-coloured tray, with a few patches of flesh-colour on it, all that was left of the original enamel.

The priest began to decline.

'Come, drink it up, father, no ceremony; it's too bad of you,' observed the landowner reproachfully.

The poor young man had to obey.

'There, now, father, you may go.'

The priest took leave.

'There, there, that'll do, get along with you....'

'A capital fellow,' pursued Mardary Apollonitch, looking after him, 'I like him very much; there's only one thing--he's young yet. But how are you, my dear sir?... What have you been doing? How are you? Let's come out on to the balcony--such a lovely evening.'

We went out on the balcony, sat down, and began to talk. Mardary Apollonitch glanced below, and suddenly fell into a state of tremendous excitement.

'Whose hens are those? whose hens are those?' he shouted: 'Whose are those hens roaming about in the garden?... Whose are those hens? How many times I've forbidden it! How many times I've spoken about it!'

Yushka ran out.

'What disorder!' protested Mardary Apollonitch; 'it's horrible!'

The unlucky hens, two speckled and one white with a topknot, as I still remember, went on stalking tranquilly about under the apple-trees, occasionally giving vent to their feelings in a prolonged clucking, when suddenly Yushka, bareheaded and stick in hand, with three other house-serfs of mature years, flew at them simultaneously. Then the fun began. The hens clucked, flapped their wings, hopped, raised a deafening cackle; the house-serfs ran, tripping up and tumbling over; their master shouted from the balcony like one possessed: 'Catch 'em, catch 'em, catch 'em, catch 'em, catch 'em, catch 'em, catch 'em!'

At last one servant succeeded in catching the hen with the topknot, tumbling upon her, and at the very same moment a little girl of eleven, with dishevelled hair, and a dry branch in her hand, jumped over the garden-fence from the village street.

'Ah, we see now whose hens!' cried the landowner in triumph. 'They're Yermil, the coachman's, hens! he's sent his Natalka to chase them out.... He didn't send his Parasha, no fear!' the landowner added in a low voice with a significant snigger. 'Hey, Yushka! let the hens alone; catch Natalka for me.'

But before the panting Yushka had time to reach the terrified little girl the house-keeper suddenly appeared, snatched her by the arm, and slapped her several times on the back....

'That's it! that's it!' cried the master, 'tut-tut-tut!... And carry off the hens, Avdotya,' he added in a loud voice, and he turned with a beaming face to me; 'that was a fine chase, my dear sir, hey?--I'm in a regular perspiration: look.'

And Mardary Apollonitch went off into a series of chuckles.

We remained on the balcony. The evening was really exceptionally fine.

Tea was served us.

'Tell me,' I began, 'Mardary Apollonitch: are those your peasants' huts, out there on the highroad, above the ravine?'

'Yes ... why do you ask?'

'I wonder at you, Mardary Apollonitch? It's really sinful. The huts allotted to the peasants there are wretched cramped little hovels; there isn't a tree to be seen near them; there's not a pond even; there's only one well, and that's no good. Could you really find no other place to settle them?... And they say you're taking away the old hemp-grounds, too?'

'And what is one to do with this new division of the lands?' Mardary Apollonitch made answer. 'Do you know I've this re-division quite on my mind, and I foresee no sort of good from it. And as for my having taken away the hemp-ground, and their not having dug any ponds, or what not-- as to that, my dear sir, I know my own business. I'm a plain man--I go on the old system. To my ideas, when a man's master--he's master; and when he's peasant--he's peasant. ... That's what I think about it.'

To an argument so clear and convincing there was of course no answer.

'And besides,' he went on, 'those peasants are a wretched lot; they're in disgrace. Particularly two families there; why, my late father--God rest his soul--couldn't bear them; positively couldn't bear them. And you know my precept is: where the father's a thief, the son's a thief; say what you like.... Blood, blood--oh, that's the great thing!'

Meanwhile there was a perfect stillness in the air. Only rarely there came a gust of wind, which, as it sank for the last time near the house, brought to our ears the sound of rhythmically repeated blows, seeming to come from the stable. Mardary Apollonitch was in the act of lifting a saucer full of tea to his lips, and was just inflating his nostrils to sniff its fragrance--no true-born Russian, as we all know, can drink his tea without this preliminary--but he stopped short, listened, nodded his head, sipped his tea, and laying the saucer on the table, with the most good-natured smile imaginable, he murmured as though involuntarily accompanying the blows: 'Tchuki-tchuki-tchuk! Tchuki-tchuk!'

'What is it?' I asked puzzled. 'Oh, by my order, they're punishing a scamp of a fellow.... Do you happen to remember Vasya, who waits at the sideboard?'

'Which Vasya?'

'Why, that waited on us at dinner just now. He with the long whiskers.'

The fiercest indignation could not have stood against the clear mild gaze of Mardary Apollonitch.

'What are you after, young man? what is it?' he said, shaking his head. 'Am I a criminal or something, that you stare at me like that? "Whom he loveth he chasteneth"; you know that.'

A quarter of an hour later I had taken leave of Mardary Apollonitch. As I was driving through the village I caught sight of Vasya. He was walking down the village street, cracking nuts. I told the coachman to stop the horses and called him up.

'Well, my boy, so they've been punishing you to-day?' I said to him.

'How did you know?' answered Vasya.

'Your master told me.'

'The master himself?'

'What did he order you to be punished for?'

'Oh, I deserved it, father; I deserved it. They don't punish for trifles among us; that's not the way with us--no, no. Our master's not like that; our master ... you won't find another master like him in all the province.'

'Drive on!' I said to the coachman.' There you have it, old Russia!' I mused on my homeward way.

XIV   LEBEDYAN

One of the principal advantages of hunting, my dear readers, consists in its forcing you to be constantly moving from place to place, which is highly agreeable for a man of no occupation. It is true that sometimes, especially in wet weather, it's not over pleasant to roam over by-roads, to cut 'across country,' to stop every peasant you meet with the question, 'Hey! my good man! how are we to get to Mordovka?' and at Mordovka to try to extract from a half-witted peasant woman (the working population are all in the fields) whether it is far to an inn on the high-road, and how to get to it--and then when you have gone on eight miles farther, instead of an inn, to come upon the deserted village of Hudobubnova, to the great amazement of a whole herd of pigs, who have been wallowing up to their ears in the black mud in the middle of the village street, without the slightest anticipation of ever being disturbed. There is no great joy either in having to cross planks that dance under your feet; to drop down into ravines; to wade across boggy streams: it is not over-pleasant to tramp twenty-four hours on end through the sea of green that covers the highroads or (which God forbid!) stay for hours stuck in the mud before a striped milestone with the figures 22 on one side and 23 on the other; it is not wholly pleasant to live for weeks together on eggs, milk, and the rye-bread patriots affect to be so fond of.... But there is ample compensation for all these inconveniences and discomforts in pleasures and advantages of another sort. Let us come, though, to our story.

After all I have said above, there is no need to explain to the reader how I happened five years ago to be at Lebedyan just in the very thick of the horse-fair. We sportsmen may often set off on a fine morning from our more or less ancestral roof, in the full intention of returning there the following evening, and little by little, still in pursuit of snipe, may get at last to the blessed banks of Petchora. Besides, every lover of the gun and the dog is a passionate admirer of the noblest animal in the world, the horse. And so I turned up at Lebedyan, stopped at the hotel, changed my clothes, and went out to the fair. (The waiter, a thin lanky youth of twenty, had already informed me in a sweet nasal tenor that his Excellency Prince N----, who purchases the chargers of the--regiment, was staying at their house; that many other gentlemen had arrived; that some gypsies were to sing in the evenings, and there was to be a performance of Pan Tvardovsky at the theatre; that the horses were fetching good prices; and that there was a fine show of them.)

In the market square there were endless rows of carts drawn up, and behind the carts, horses of every possible kind: racers, stud-horses, dray horses, cart-horses, posting-hacks, and simple peasants' nags. Some fat and sleek, assorted by colours, covered with striped horse- cloths, and tied up short to high racks, turned furtive glances backward at the too familiar whips of their owners, the horse-dealers; private owners' horses, sent by noblemen of the steppes a hundred or two hundred miles away, in charge of some decrepit old coachman and two or three headstrong stable-boys, shook their long necks, stamped with ennui, and gnawed at the fences; roan horses, from Vyatka, huddled close to one another; race-horses, dapple-grey, raven, and sorrel, with large hindquarters, flowing tails, and shaggy legs, stood in majestic immobility like lions. Connoisseurs stopped respectfully before them. The avenues formed by the rows of carts were thronged with people of every class, age, and appearance; horse-dealers in long blue coats and high caps, with sly faces, were on the look-out for purchasers; gypsies, with staring eyes and curly heads, strolled up and down, like uneasy spirits, looking into the horses' mouths, lifting up a hoof or a tail, shouting, swearing, acting as go-betweens, casting lots, or hanging about some army horse-contracter in a foraging-cap and military cloak, with beaver collar. A stalwart Cossack rode up and down on a lanky gelding with the neck of a stag, offering it for sale 'in one lot,' that is, saddle, bridle, and all. Peasants, in sheepskins torn at the arm-pits, were forcing their way despairingly through the crowd, or packing themselves by dozens into a cart harnessed to a horse, which was to be 'put to the test,' or somewhere on one side, with the aid of a wily gypsy, they were bargaining till they were exhausted, clasping each other's hands a hundred times over, each still sticking to his price, while the subject of their dispute, a wretched little jade covered with a shrunken mat, was blinking quite unmoved, as though it was no concern of hers.... And, after all, what difference did it make to her who was to have the beating of her? Broad-browed landowners, with dyed moustaches and an expression of dignity on their faces, in Polish hats and cotton overcoats pulled half-on, were talking condescendingly with fat merchants in felt hats and green gloves. Officers of different regiments were crowding everywhere; an extraordinarily lanky cuirassier of German extraction was languidly inquiring of a lame horse-dealer 'what he expected to get for that chestnut.' A fair-haired young hussar, a boy of nineteen, was choosing a trace-horse to match a lean carriage-horse; a post-boy in a low-crowned hat, with a peacock's feather twisted round it, in a brown coat and long leather gloves tied round the arm with narrow, greenish bands, was looking for a shaft-horse. Coachmen were plaiting the horses' tails, wetting their manes, and giving respectful advice to their masters. Those who had completed a stroke of business were hurrying to hotel or to tavern, according to their class.... And all the crowd were moving, shouting, bustling, quarrelling and making it up again, swearing and laughing, all up to their knees in the mud. I wanted to buy a set of three horses for my covered trap; mine had begun to show signs of breaking down. I had found two, but had not yet succeeded in picking up a third. After a hotel dinner, which I cannot bring myself to describe (even Aeneas had discovered how painful it is to dwell on sorrows past), I repaired to a cafe so-called, which was the evening resort of the purchasers of cavalry mounts, horse-breeders, and other persons. In the billiard-room, which was plunged in grey floods of tobacco smoke, there were about twenty men. Here were free-and-easy young landowners in embroidered jackets and grey trousers, with long curling hair and little waxed moustaches, staring about them with gentlemanly insolence; other noblemen in Cossack dress, with extraordinarily short necks, and eyes lost in layers of fat, were snorting with distressing distinctness; merchants sat a little apart on the qui-vive , as it is called; officers were chatting freely among themselves. At the billiard-table was Prince N----a young man of two- and-twenty, with a lively and rather contemptuous face, in a coat hanging open, a red silk shirt, and loose velvet pantaloons; he was playing with the ex-lieutenant, Viktor Hlopakov.

The ex-lieutenant, Viktor Hlopakov, a little, thinnish, dark man of thirty, with black hair, brown eyes, and a thick snub nose, is a diligent frequenter of elections and horse-fairs. He walks with a skip and a hop, waves his fat hands with a jovial swagger, cocks his cap on one side, and tucks up the sleeves of his military coat, showing the blue-black cotton lining. Mr. Hlopakov knows how to gain the favour of rich scapegraces from Petersburg; smokes, drinks, and plays cards with them; calls them by their Christian names. What they find to like in him it is rather hard to comprehend. He is not clever; he is not amusing; he is not even a buffoon. It is true they treat him with friendly casualness, as a good-natured fellow, but rather a fool; they chum with him for two or three weeks, and then all of a sudden do not recognise him in the street, and he on his side, too, does not recognise them. The chief peculiarity of Lieutenant Hlopakov consists in his continually for a year, sometimes two at a time, using in season and out of season one expression, which, though not in the least humorous, for some reason or other makes everyone laugh. Eight years ago he used on every occasion to say, "'Umble respecks and duty," and his patrons of that date used always to fall into fits of laughter and make him repeat "Umble respecks and duty'; then he began to adopt a more complicated expression: 'No, that's too, too k'essk'say,' and with the same brilliant success; two years later he had invented a fresh saying: ' Ne voo excite voo self pa , man of sin, sewn in a sheepskin,' and so on. And strange to say! these, as you see, not overwhelmingly witty phrases, keep him in food and drink and clothes. (He has run through his property ages ago, and lives solely upon his friends.) There is, observe, absolutely no other attraction about him; he can, it is true, smoke a hundred pipes of Zhukov tobacco in a day, and when he plays billiards, throws his right leg higher than his head, and while taking aim shakes his cue affectedly; but, after all, not everyone has a fancy for these accomplishments. He can drink, too ... but in Russia it is hard to gain distinction as a drinker. In short, his success is a complete riddle to me.... There is one thing, perhaps; he is discreet; he has no taste for washing dirty linen away from home, never speaks a word against anyone.

'Well,' I thought, on seeing Hlopakov, 'I wonder what his catchword is now?'

The prince hit the white.

'Thirty love,' whined a consumptive marker, with a dark face and blue rings under his eyes.

The prince sent the yellow with a crash into the farthest pocket.

'Ah!' a stoutish merchant, sitting in the corner at a tottering little one-legged table, boomed approvingly from the depths of his chest, and immediately was overcome by confusion at his own presumption. But luckily no one noticed him. He drew a long breath, and stroked his beard.

'Thirty-six love!' the marker shouted in a nasal voice.

'Well, what do you say to that, old man?' the prince asked Hlopakov.

'What! rrrakaliooon, of course, simply rrrakaliooooon!'

The prince roared with laughter.

'What? what? Say it again.'

'Rrrrrakaliooon!' repeated the ex-lieutenant complacently.

'So that's the catchword!' thought I.

The prince sent the red into the pocket.

'Oh! that's not the way, prince, that's not the way,' lisped a fair- haired young officer with red eyes, a tiny nose, and a babyish, sleepy face. 'You shouldn't play like that ... you ought ... not that way!'

'Eh?' the prince queried over his shoulder.

'You ought to have done it ... in a triplet.'

'Oh, really?' muttered the prince.

'What do you say, prince? Shall we go this evening to hear the gypsies?' the young man hurriedly went on in confusion. 'Styoshka will sing ... Ilyushka....'

The prince vouchsafed no reply.

'Rrrrrakaliooon, old boy,' said Hlopakov, with a sly wink of his left eye.

And the prince exploded.

'Thirty-nine to love,' sang out the marker.

'Love ... just look, I'll do the trick with that yellow.' ... Hlopakov, fidgeting his cue in his hand, took aim, and missed.

'Eh, rrrakalioon,' he cried with vexation.

The prince laughed again.

'What, what, what?'

'Your honour made a miss,' observed the marker. 'Allow me to chalk the cue.... Forty love.'

'Yes, gentlemen,' said the prince, addressing the whole company, and not looking at any one in particular; 'you know, Verzhembitskaya must be called before the curtain to-night.'

'To be sure, to be sure, of course,' several voices cried in rivalry, amazingly flattered at the chance of answering the prince's speech; 'Verzhembitskaya, to be sure....'

'Verzhembitskaya's an excellent actress, far superior to Sopnyakova,' whined an ugly little man in the corner with moustaches and spectacles. Luckless wretch! he was secretly sighing at Sopnyakova's feet, and the prince did not even vouchsafe him a look.

'Wai-ter, hey, a pipe!' a tall gentleman, with regular features and a most majestic manner--in fact, with all the external symptoms of a card-sharper--muttered into his cravat.

A waiter ran for a pipe, and when he came back, announced to his excellency that the groom Baklaga was asking for him.

'Ah! tell him to wait a minute and take him some vodka.'

'Yes, sir.'

Baklaga, as I was told afterwards, was the name of a youthful, handsome, and excessively depraved groom; the prince loved him, made him presents of horses, went out hunting with him, spent whole nights with him.... Now you would not know this same prince, who was once a rake and a scapegrace.... In what good odour he is now; how straight- laced, how supercilious! How devoted to the government--and, above all, so prudent and judicious!

However, the tobacco smoke had begun to make my eyes smart. After hearing Hlopakov's exclamation and the prince's chuckle one last time more, I went off to my room, where, on a narrow, hair-stuffed sofa pressed into hollows, with a high, curved back, my man had already made me up a bed.

The next day I went out to look at the horses in the stables, and began with the famous horsedealer Sitnikov's. I went through a gate into a yard strewn with sand. Before a wide open stable-door stood the horsedealer himself--a tall, stout man no longer young, in a hareskin coat, with a raised turnover collar. Catching sight of me, he moved slowly to meet me, held his cap in both hands above his head, and in a sing-song voice brought out:

'Ah, our respects to you. You'd like to have a look at the horses, may be?'

'Yes; I've come to look at the horses.'

'And what sort of horses, precisely, I make bold to ask?'

'Show me what you have.'

'With pleasure.'

We went into the stable. Some white pug-dogs got up from the hay and ran up to us, wagging their tails, and a long-bearded old goat walked away with an air of dissatisfaction; three stable-boys, in strong but greasy sheepskins, bowed to us without speaking. To right and to left, in horse-boxes raised above the ground, stood nearly thirty horses, groomed to perfection. Pigeons fluttered cooing about the rafters.

'What, now, do you want a horse for? for driving or for breeding?' Sitnikov inquired of me.

'Oh, I'll see both sorts.'

'To be sure, to be sure,' the horsedealer commented, dwelling on each syllable. 'Petya, show the gentleman Ermine.'

We came out into the yard.

'But won't you let them bring you a bench out of the hut?... You don't want to sit down.... As you please.'

There was the thud of hoofs on the boards, the crack of a whip, and Petya, a swarthy fellow of forty, marked by small-pox, popped out of the stable with a rather well-shaped grey stallion, made it rear, ran twice round the yard with it, and adroitly pulled it up at the right place. Ermine stretched himself, snorted, raised his tail, shook his head, and looked sideways at me.

'A clever beast,' I thought.

'Give him his head, give him his head,' said Sitniker, and he stared at me.

'What may you think of him?' he inquired at last.

'The horse's not bad--the hind legs aren't quite sound.'

'His legs are first-rate!' Sitnikov rejoined, with an air of conviction;' and his hind-quarters ... just look, sir ... broad as an oven--you could sleep up there.' 'His pasterns are long.'

'Long! mercy on us! Start him, Petya, start him, but at a trot, a trot ... don't let him gallop.'

Again Petya ran round the yard with Ermine. None of us spoke for a little.

'There, lead him back,' said Sitnikov,' and show us Falcon.'

Falcon, a gaunt beast of Dutch extraction with sloping hind-quarters, as black as a beetle, turned out to be little better than Ermine. He was one of those beasts of whom fanciers will tell you that 'they go chopping and mincing and dancing about,' meaning thereby that they prance and throw out their fore-legs to right and to left without making much headway. Middle-aged merchants have a great fancy for such horses; their action recalls the swaggering gait of a smart waiter; they do well in single harness for an after-dinner drive; with mincing paces and curved neck they zealously draw a clumsy droshky laden with an overfed coachman, a depressed, dyspeptic merchant, and his lymphatic wife, in a blue silk mantle, with a lilac handkerchief over her head. Falcon too I declined. Sitnikov showed me several horses.... One at last, a dapple-grey beast of Voyakov breed, took my fancy. I could not restrain my satisfaction, and patted him on the withers. Sitnikov at once feigned absolute indifference.

"Well, does he go well in harness?" I inquired. (They never speak of a trotting horse as "being driven.")

"Oh, yes," answered the horsedealer carelessly.

"Can I see him?"

"If you like, certainly. Hi, Kuzya, put Pursuer into the droshky!"

Kuzya, the jockey, a real master of horsemanship, drove three times past us up and down the street. The horse went well, without changing its pace, nor shambling; it had a free action, held its tail high, and covered the ground well.

"And what are you asking for him?"

Sitnikov asked an impossible price. We began bargaining on the spot in the street, when suddenly a splendidly-matched team of three posting- horses flew noisily round the corner and drew up sharply at the gates before Sitnikov's house. In the smart little sportsman's trap sat Prince N----; beside him Hlopakov. Baklaga was driving ... and how he drove! He could have driven them through an earring, the rascal! The bay trace-horses, little, keen, black-eyed, black-legged beasts, were all impatience; they kept rearing--a whistle, and off they would have bolted! The dark-bay shaft-horse stood firmly, its neck arched like a swan's, its breast forward, its legs like arrows, shaking its head and proudly blinking.... They were splendid! No one could desire a finer turn out for an Easter procession!

'Your excellency, please to come in!' cried Sitnikov.

The prince leaped out of the trap. Hlopakov slowly descended on the other side.

'Good morning, friend ... any horses.'

'You may be sure we've horses for your excellency! Pray walk in.... Petya, bring out Peacock! and let them get Favourite ready too. And with you, sir,' he went on, turning to me, 'we'll settle matters another time.... Fomka, a bench for his excellency.'

From a special stable which I had not at first observed they led out Peacock. A powerful dark sorrel horse seemed to fly across the yard with all its legs in the air. Sitnikov even turned away his head and winked.

'Oh, rrakalion!' piped Hlopakov; 'Zhaymsah (j'aime ca .)'

The prince laughed.

Peacock was stopped with difficulty; he dragged the stable-boy about the yard; at last he was pushed against the wall. He snorted, started and reared, while Sitnikov still teased him, brandishing a whip at him.

'What are you looking at? there! oo!' said the horsedealer with caressing menace, unable to refrain from admiring his horse himself.

'How much?' asked the prince.

'For your excellency, five thousand.'

'Three.'

'Impossible, your excellency, upon my word.'

'I tell you three, rrakalion,' put in Hlopakov.

I went away without staying to see the end of the bargaining. At the farthest corner of the street I noticed a large sheet of paper fixed on the gate of a little grey house. At the top there was a pen-and-ink sketch of a horse with a tail of the shape of a pipe and an endless neck, and below his hoofs were the following words, written in an old-fashioned hand:

'Here are for sale horses of various colours, brought to the Lebedyan fair from the celebrated steppes stud of Anastasei Ivanitch Tchornobai, landowner of Tambov. These horses are of excellent sort; broken in to perfection, and free from vice. Purchasers will kindly ask for Anastasei Ivanitch himself: should Anastasei Ivanitch be absent, then ask for Nazar Kubishkin, the coachman. Gentlemen about to purchase, kindly honour an old man.'

I stopped. 'Come,' I thought, 'let's have a look at the horses of the celebrated steppes breeder, Mr. Tchornobai.'

I was about to go in at the gate, but found that, contrary to the common usage, it was locked. I knocked.

'Who's there?... A customer?' whined a woman's voice.

'Yes.'

'Coming, sir, coming.'

The gate was opened. I beheld a peasant-woman of fifty, bareheaded, in boots, and a sheepskin worn open.

'Please to come in, kind sir, and I'll go at once, and tell Anastasei Ivanitch ... Nazar, hey, Nazar!'

'What?' mumbled an old man's voice from the stable.

'Get a horse ready; here's a customer.'

The old woman ran into the house.

'A customer, a customer,' Nazar grumbled in response; 'I've not washed all their tails yet.'

'Oh, Arcadia!' thought I.

'Good day, sir, pleased to see you,' I heard a rich, pleasant voice saying behind my back. I looked round; before me, in a long-skirted blue coat, stood an old man of medium height, with white hair, a friendly smile, and fine blue eyes.

'You want a little horse? By all means, my dear sir, by all means.... But won't you step in and drink just a cup of tea with me first?'

I declined and thanked him.

'Well, well, as you please. You must excuse me, my dear sir; you see I'm old-fashioned.' (Mr. Tchornobai spoke with deliberation, and in a broad Doric.) 'Everything with me is done in a plain way, you know.... Nazar, hey, Nazar!' he added, not raising his voice, but prolonging each syllable. Nazar, a wrinkled old man with a little hawk nose and a wedge-shaped beard, showed himself at the stable door.

'What sort of horses is it you're wanting, my dear sir?' resumed Mr. Tchornobai.

'Not too expensive; for driving in my covered gig.'

'To be sure ... we have got them to suit you, to be sure.... Nazar, Nazar, show the gentleman the grey gelding, you know, that stands at the farthest corner, and the sorrel with the star, or else the other sorrel--foal of Beauty, you know.'

Nazar went back to the stable.

'And bring them out by their halters just as they are,' Mr. Tchornobai shouted after him. 'You won't find things with me, my good sir,' he went on, with a clear mild gaze into my face, 'as they are with the horse-dealers; confound their tricks! There are drugs of all sorts go in there, salt and malted grains; God forgive them! But with me, you will see, sir, everything's above-board; no underhandedness.'

The horses were led in; I did not care for them.

'Well, well, take them back, in God's name,' said Anastasei Ivanitch. 'Show us the others.'

Others were shown. At last I picked out one, rather a cheap one. We began to haggle over the price. Mr. Tchornobai did not get excited; he spoke so reasonably, with such dignity, that I could not help 'honouring' the old man; I gave him the earnest-money.

'Well, now,' observed Anastasei Ivanitch, 'allow me to give over the horse to you from hand to hand, after the old fashion.... You will thank me for him ... as sound as a nut, see ... fresh ... a true child of the steppes! Goes well in any harness.'

He crossed himself, laid the skirt of his coat over his hand, took the halter, and handed me the horse.

'You're his master now, with God's blessing.... And you still won't take a cup of tea?'

'No, I thank you heartily; it's time I was going home.'

'That's as you think best.... And shall my coachman lead the horse after you?'

'Yes, now, if you please.'

'By all means, my dear sir, by all means.... Vassily, hey, Vassily! step along with the gentleman, lead the horse, and take the money for him. Well, good-bye, my good sir; God bless you.'

'Good-bye, Anastasei Ivanitch.'

They led the horse home for me. The next day he turned out to be broken-winded and lame. I tried having him put in harness; the horse backed, and if one gave him a flick with the whip he jibbed, kicked, and positively lay down. I set off at once to Mr. Tchornobai's. I inquired: 'At home?'

'Yes.'

'What's the meaning of this?' said I; 'here you've sold me a broken- winded horse.'

'Broken-winded?... God forbid!'

'Yes, and he's lame too, and vicious besides.'

'Lame! I know nothing about it: your coachman must have ill-treated him somehow.... But before God, I--'

'Look here, Anastasei Ivanitch, as things stand, you ought to take him back.'

'No, my good sir, don't put yourself in a passion; once gone out of the yard, is done with. You should have looked before, sir.'

I understood what that meant, accepted my fate, laughed, and walked off. Luckily, I had not paid very dear for the lesson.

Two days later I left, and in a week I was again at Lebedyan on my way home again. In the cafe I found almost the same persons, and again I came upon Prince N----at billiards. But the usual change in the fortunes of Mr. Hlopakov had taken place in this interval: the fair- haired young officer had supplanted him in the prince's favours. The poor ex-lieutenant once more tried letting off his catchword in my presence, on the chance it might succeed as before; but, far from smiling, the prince positively scowled and shrugged his shoulders. Mr. Hlopakov looked downcast, shrank into a corner, and began furtively filling himself a pipe....

XV   TATYANA BORISSOVNA AND HER NEPHEW

Give me your hand, gentle reader, and come along with me. It is glorious weather; there is a tender blue in the May sky; the smooth young leaves of the willows glisten as though they had been polished; the wide even road is all covered with that delicate grass with the little reddish stalk that the sheep are so fond of nibbling; to right and to left, over the long sloping hillsides, the green rye is softly waving; the shadows of small clouds glide in thin long streaks over it. In the distance is the dark mass of forests, the glitter of ponds, yellow patches of village; larks in hundreds are soaring, singing, falling headlong with outstretched necks, hopping about the clods; the crows on the highroad stand still, look at you, peck at the earth, let you drive close up, and with two hops lazily move aside. On a hill beyond a ravine a peasant is ploughing; a piebald colt, with a cropped tail and ruffled mane, is running on unsteady legs after its mother; its shrill whinnying reaches us. We drive on into the birch wood, and drink in the strong, sweet, fresh fragrance. Here we are at the boundaries. The coachman gets down; the horses snort; the trace-horses look round; the centre horse in the shafts switches his tail, and turns his head up towards the wooden yoke above it... the great gate opens creaking; the coachman seats himself.... Drive on! the village is before us. Passing five homesteads, and turning off to the right, we drop down into a hollow and drive along a dyke, the farther side of a small pond; behind the round tops of the lilacs and apple-trees a wooden roof, once red, with two chimneys, comes into sight; the coachman keeps along the hedge to the left, and to the spasmodic and drowsy baying of three pug dogs he drives through the wide open gates, whisks smartly round the broad courtyard past the stable and the barn, gallantly salutes the old housekeeper, who is stepping sideways over the high lintel in the open doorway of the storehouse, and pulls up at last before the steps of a dark house with light windows.... We are at Tatyana Borissovna's. And here she is herself opening the window and nodding at us.... 'Good day, ma'am!'

Tatyana Borissovna is a woman of fifty, with large, prominent grey eyes, a rather broad nose, rosy cheeks and a double chin. Her face is brimming over with friendliness and kindness. She was once married, but was soon left a widow. Tatyana Borissovna is a very remarkable woman. She lives on her little property, never leaving it, mixes very little with her neighbours, sees and likes none but young people. She was the daughter of very poor landowners, and received no education; in other words, she does not know French; she has never been in Moscow--and in spite of all these defects, she is so good and simple in her manners, so broad in her sympathies and ideas, so little infected with the ordinary prejudices of country ladies of small means, that one positively cannot help marvelling at her.... Indeed, a woman who lives all the year round in the country and does not talk scandal, nor whine, nor curtsey, is never flurried, nor depressed, nor in a flutter of curiosity, is a real marvel! She usually wears a grey taffetas gown and a white cap with lilac streamers; she is fond of good cheer, but not to excess; all the preserving, pickling, and salting she leaves to her housekeeper. 'What does she do all day long?' you will ask.... 'Does she read?' No, she doesn't read, and, to tell the truth, books are not written for her.... If there are no visitors with her, Tatyana Borissovna sits by herself at the window knitting a stocking in winter; in summer time she is in the garden, planting and watering her flowers, playing for hours together with her cats, or feeding her doves.... She does not take much part in the management of her estate. But if a visitor pays her a call--some young neighbour whom she likes--Tatyana Borissovna is all life directly; she makes him sit down, pours him out some tea, listens to his chat, laughs, sometimes pats his cheek, but says little herself; in trouble or sorrow she comforts and gives good advice. How many people have confided their family secrets and the griefs of their hearts to her, and have wept over her hands! At times she sits opposite her visitor, leaning lightly on her elbow, and looks with such sympathy into his face, smiles so affectionately, that he cannot help feeling: 'What a dear, good woman you are, Tatyana Borissovna! Let me tell you what is in my heart.' One feels happy and warm in her small, snug rooms; in her house it is always, so to speak, fine weather. Tatyana Borissovna is a wonderful woman, but no one wonders at her; her sound good sense, her breadth and firmness, her warm sympathy in the joys and sorrows of others--in a word, all her qualities are so innate in her; they are no trouble, no effort to her.... One cannot fancy her otherwise, and so one feels no need to thank her. She is particularly fond of watching the pranks and follies of young people; she folds her hands over her bosom, throws back her head, puckers up her eyes, and sits smiling at them, then all of a sudden she heaves a sigh, and says, 'Ah, my children, my children!'... Sometimes one longs to go up to her, take hold of her hands and say: 'Let me tell you, Tatyana Borissovna, you don't know your own value; for all your simplicity and lack of learning, you're an extraordinary creature!' Her very name has a sweet familiar ring; one is glad to utter it; it calls up a kindly smile at once. How often, for instance, have I chanced to ask a peasant: 'Tell me, my friend, how am I to get to Gratchevka?' let us say. 'Well, sir, you go on first to Vyazovoe, and from there to Tatyana Borissovna's, and from Tatyana Borissovna's any one will show you the way.' And at the name of Tatyana Borissovna the peasant wags his head in quite a special way. Her household is small, in accordance with her means. The house, the laundry, the stores and the kitchen, are in the charge of the housekeeper, Agafya, once her nurse, a good-natured, tearful, toothless creature; she has under her two stalwart girls with stout crimson cheeks like Antonovsky apples. The duties of valet, steward, and waiter are filled by Policarp, an extraordinary old man of seventy, a queer fellow, full of erudition, once a violinist and worshipper of Viotti, with a personal hostility to Napoleon, or, as he calls him, Bonaparty, and a passion for nightingales. He always keeps five or six of the latter in his room; in early spring he will sit for whole days together by the cage, waiting for the first trill, and when he hears it, he covers his face with his hands, and moans, 'Oh, piteous, piteous!' and sheds tears in floods. Policarp has, to help him, his grandson Vasya, a curly-headed, sharp-eyed boy of twelve; Policarp adores him, and grumbles at him from morning till night. He undertakes his education too. 'Vasya,' he says, 'say Bonaparty was a scoundrel.' 'And what'll you give me, granddad?' 'What'll I give you?... I'll give you nothing.... Why, what are you? Aren't you a Russian?' 'I'm a Mtchanin, granddad; I was born in Mtchensk.' 'Oh, silly dunce! but where is Mtchensk?' 'How can I tell?' 'Mtchensk's in Russia, silly!' 'Well, what then, if it is in Russia?' 'What then? Why, his Highness the late Prince Mihalo Ilarionovitch Golenishtchev-Kutuzov-Smolensky, with God's aid, graciously drove Bonaparty out of the Russian territories. It's on that event the song was composed: "Bonaparty's in no mood to dance, He's lost the garters he brought from France."'... Do you understand? he liberated your fatherland.' 'And what's that to do with me?' 'Ah! you silly boy! Why, if his Highness Prince Mihalo Ilarionovitch hadn't driven out Bonaparty, some mounseer would have been beating you about the head with a stick this minute. He'd come up to you like this, and say: "Koman voo porty voo?" and then a box on the ear!' 'But I'd give him one in the belly with my fist' 'But he'd go on: "Bonzhur, bonzhur, veny ici," and then a cuff on the head.' 'And I'd give him one in his legs, his bandy legs.' 'You're quite right, their legs are bandy.... Well, but suppose he tied your hands?' 'I wouldn't let him; I'd call Mihay the coachman to help me.' 'But, Vasya, suppose you weren't a match for the Frenchy even with Mihay?' 'Not a match for him! See how strong Mihay is!' 'Well, and what would you do with him?' 'We'd get him on his back, we would.' 'And he'd shout, "Pardon, pardon, seevooplay!"' 'We'd tell him, "None of your seevooplays, you old Frenchy!"' 'Bravo, Vasya!... Well, now then, shout, "Bonaparty's a scoundrel!"' 'But you must give me some sugar!' 'You scamp!' Of the neighbouring ladies Tatyana Borissovna sees very little; they do not care about going to see her, and she does not know how to amuse them; the sound of their chatter sends her to sleep; she starts, tries to keep her eyes open, and drops off again. Tatyana Borissovna is not fond of women as a rule. One of her friends, a good, harmless young man, had a sister, an old maid of thirty-eight and a half, a good-natured creature, but exaggerated, affected, and enthusiastic. Her brother had often talked to her of their neighbour. One fine morning our old maid has her horse saddled, and, without a word to any one, sallies off to Tatyana Borissovna's. In her long habit, a hat on her head, a green veil and floating curls, she went into the hall, and passing by the panic-stricken Vasya, who took her for a wood-witch, ran into the drawing-room. Tatyana Borissovna, scared, tried to rise, but her legs sank under her. 'Tatyana Borissovna,' began the visitor in a supplicating voice, 'forgive my temerity; I am the sister of your friend, Alexy Nikolaevitch K----, and I have heard so much about you from him that I resolved to make your acquaintance.' 'Greatly honoured,' muttered the bewildered lady. The sister flung off her hat, shook her curls, seated herself near Tatyana Borissovna; took her by the hand... 'So this is she,' she began in a pensive voice fraught with feeling: 'this is that sweet, clear, noble, holy being! This is she! that woman at once so simple and so deep! How glad I am! how glad I am! How we shall love each other! I can breathe easily at last... I always fancied her just so,' she added in a whisper, her eyes riveted on the eyes of Tatyana Borissovna. 'You won't be angry with me, will you, my dear kind friend?' 'Really, I'm delighted!... Won't you have some tea?' The lady smiled patronisingly: 'Wie wahr, wie unreflectiert' , she murmured, as it were to herself. 'Let me embrace you, my dear one!'

The old maid stayed three hours at Tatyana Borissovna's, never ceasing talking an instant. She tried to explain to her new acquaintance all her own significance. Directly after the unexpected visitor had departed, the poor lady took a bath, drank some lime-flower water, and took to her bed. But the next day the old maid came back, stayed four hours, and left, promising to come to see Tatyana Borissovna every day. Her idea, please to observe, was to develop, to complete the education of so rich a nature, to use her own expression, and she would probably have really been the death of her, if she had not, in the first place, been utterly disillusioned as regards her brother's friend within a fortnight, and secondly, fallen in love with a young student on a visit in the neighbourhood, with whom she at once rushed into a fervid and active correspondence; in her missives she consecrated him, as the manner of such is, to a noble, holy life, offered herself wholly a sacrifice, asked only for the name of sister, launched into endless descriptions of nature, made allusions to Goethe, Schiller, Bettina and German philosophy, and drove the luckless young man at last to the blackest desperation. But youth asserted itself: one fine morning he woke up with such a furious hatred for 'his sister and best of friends' that he almost killed his valet in his passion, and was snappish for a long while after at the slightest allusion to elevated and disinterested passion. But from that time forth Tatyana Borissovna began to avoid all intimacy with ladies of the neighbourhood more than ever.

Alas! nothing is lasting on this earth. All I have related as to the way of life of my kind-hearted neighbour is a thing of the past; the peace that used to reign in her house has been destroyed for ever. For more than a year now there has been living with her a nephew, an artist from Petersburg. This is how it came about.

Eight years ago, there was living with Tatyana Borissovna a boy of twelve, an orphan, the son of her brother, Andryusha. Andryusha had large, clear, humid eyes, a tiny little mouth, a regular nose, and a fine lofty brow. He spoke in a low, sweet voice, was attentive and coaxing with visitors, kissed his auntie's hand with an orphan's sensibility; and one hardly had time to show oneself before he had put a chair for one. He had no mischievous tricks; he was never noisy; he would sit by himself in a corner with a book, and with such sedateness and propriety, never even leaning back in his chair. When a visitor came in, Andryusha would get up, with a decorous smile and a flush; when the visitor went away he would sit down again, pull out of his pocket a brush and a looking-glass, and brush his hair. From his earliest years he had shown a taste for drawing. Whenever he got hold of a piece of paper, he would ask Agafya the housekeeper for a pair of scissors at once, carefully cut a square piece out of the paper, trace a border round it and set to work; he would draw an eye with an immense pupil, or a Grecian nose, or a house with a chimney and smoke coming out of it in the shape of a corkscrew, a dog, en face , looking rather like a bench, or a tree with two pigeons on it, and would sign it: 'Drawn by Andrei Byelovzorov, such a day in such a year, in the village of Maliya-Briki.' He used to toil with special industry for a fortnight before Tatyana Borissovna's birthday; he was the first to present his congratulations and offer her a roll of paper tied up with a pink ribbon. Tatyana Borissovna would kiss her nephew and undo the knot; the roll was unfolded and presented to the inquisitive gaze of the spectator, a round, boldly sketched temple in sepia, with columns and an altar in the centre; on the altar lay a burning heart and a wreath, while above, on a curling scroll, was inscribed in legible characters: 'To my aunt and benefactress, Tatyana Borissovna Bogdanov, from her dutiful and loving nephew, as a token of his deepest affection.' Tatyana Borissovna would kiss him again and give him a silver rouble. She did not, though, feel any very warm affection for him; Andryusha's fawning ways were not quite to her taste. Meanwhile, Andryusha was growing up; Tatyana Borissovna began to be anxious about his future. An unexpected incident solved the difficulty to her.

One day eight years ago she received a visit from a certain Mr. Benevolensky, Piotr Mihalitch, a college councillor with a decoration. Mr. Benevolensky had at one time held an official post in the nearest district town, and had been assiduous in his visits to Tatyana Borissovna; then he had moved to Petersburg, got into the ministry, and attained a rather important position, and on one of the numerous journeys he took in the discharge of his official duties, he remembered his old friend, and came back to see her, with the intention of taking a rest for two days from his official labours 'in the bosom of the peace of nature.' Tatyana Borissovna greeted him with her usual cordiality, and Mr. Benevolensky.... But before we proceed with the rest of the story, gentle reader, let us introduce you to this new personage.

Mr. Benevolensky was a stoutish man, of middle height and mild appearance, with little short legs and little fat hands; he wore a roomy and excessively spruce frock-coat, a high broad cravat, snow-white linen, a gold chain on his silk waistcoat, a gem-ring on his forefinger, and a white wig on his head; he spoke softly and persuasively, trod noiselessly, and had an amiable smile, an amiable look in his eyes, and an amiable way of settling his chin in his cravat; he was, in fact, an amiable person altogether. God had given him a heart, too, of the softest; he was easily moved to tears and to transports; moreover, he was all aglow with disinterested passion for art: disinterested it certainly was, for Mr. Benevolensky, if the truth must be told, knew absolutely nothing about art. One is set wondering, indeed, whence, by virtue of what mysterious uncomprehended forces, this passion had come upon him. He was, to all appearance, a practical, even prosaic person... however, we have a good many people of the same sort among us in Russia.

Their devotion to art and artists produces in these people an inexpressible mawkishness; it is distressing to have to do with them and to talk to them; they are perfect logs smeared with honey. They never, for instance, call Raphael, Raphael, or Correggio, Correggio; 'the divine Sanzio, the incomparable di Allegri,' they murmur, and always with the broadest vowels. Every pretentious, conceited, home-bred mediocrity they hail as a genius: 'the blue sky of Italy,' 'the lemons of the South,' 'the balmy breezes of the banks of the Brenta,' are for ever on their lips. 'Ah, Vasya, Vasya,' or 'Oh, Sasha, Sasha,' they say to one another with deep feeling, 'we must away to the South... we are Greeks in soul--ancient Greeks.' One may observe them at exhibitions before the works of some Russian painters (these gentlemen, it should be noted, are, for the most part, passionate patriots). First they step back a couple of paces, and throw back their heads; then they go up to the picture again; their eyes are suffused with an oily moisture.... 'There you have it, my God!' they say at last, in voices broken with emotion; 'there's soul, soul! Ah! what feeling, what feeling! Ah, what soul he has put into it! what a mass of soul!... And how he has thought it out! thought it out like a master!' And, oh! the pictures in their own drawing-rooms! Oh, the artists that come to them in the evenings, drink tea, and listen to their conversation! And the views in perspective they make them of their own rooms, with a broom in the foreground, a little heap of dust on the polished floor, a yellow samovar on a table near the window, and the master of the house himself in skull-cap and dressing-gown, with a brilliant streak of sunlight falling on his cheek! Oh, the long-haired nurslings of the Muse, wearing spasmodic and contemptuous smiles, that cluster about them! Oh, the young ladies, with faces of greenish pallor, who squeal; over their pianos! For that is the established rule with us in Russia; a man cannot be devoted to one art alone--he must have them all. And so it is not to be wondered at that these gentlemen extend their powerful patronage to Russian literature also, especially to dramatic literature.... The Jacob Sannazars are written for them; the struggle of unappreciated talent against the whole world, depicted a thousand times over, still moves them profoundly....

The day after Mr. Benevolensky's arrival, Tatyana Borissovna told her nephew at tea-time to show their guest his drawings. 'Why, does he draw?' said Mr. Benevolensky, with some surprise, and he turned with interest to Andryusha. 'Yes, he draws,' said Tatyana Borissovna; 'he's so fond of it! and he does it all alone, without a master.' 'Ah! show me, show me,' cried Mr. Benevolensky. Andryusha, blushing and smiling, brought the visitor his sketch-book. Mr. Benevolensky began turning it over with the air of a connoisseur. 'Good, young man,' he pronounced at last; 'good, very good.' And he patted Andryusha on the head. Andryusha intercepted his hand and kissed it 'Fancy, now, a talent like that!... I congratulate you, Tatyana Borissovna.' 'But what am I to do, Piotr Mihalitch? I can't get him a teacher here. To have one from the town is a great expense; our neighbours, the Artamonovs, have a drawing-master, and they say an excellent one, but his mistress forbids his giving lessons to outsiders.' 'Hm,' pronounced Mr. Benevolensky; he pondered and looked askance at Andryusha. 'Well, we will talk it over,' he added suddenly, rubbing his hands. The same day he begged Tatyana Borissovna's permission for an interview with her alone. They shut themselves up together. In half-an-hour they called Andryusha--Andryusha went in. Mr. Benevolensky was standing at the window with a slight flush on his face and a beaming expression. Tatyana Borissovna was sitting in a corner wiping her eyes. 'Come, Andryusha,' she said at last, 'you must thank Piotr Mihalitch; he will take you under his protection; he will take you to Petersburg.' Andryusha almost fainted on the spot. 'Tell me candidly,' began Mr. Benevolensky, in a voice filled with dignity and patronising indulgence; 'do you want to be an artist, young man? Do you feel yourself consecrated to the holy service of Art?' 'I want to be an artist, Piotr Mihalitch,' Andryusha declared in a trembling voice. 'I am delighted, if so it be. It will, of course,' continued Mr. Benevolensky, 'be hard for you to part from your revered aunt; you must feel the liveliest gratitude to her.' 'I adore my auntie,' Andryusha interrupted, blinking. 'Of course, of course, that's readily understood, and does you great credit; but, on the other hand, consider the pleasure that in the future... your success....' 'Kiss me, Andryusha,' muttered the kind-hearted lady. Andryusha flung himself on her neck. 'There, now, thank your benefactor.' Andryusha embraced Mr. Benevolensky's stomach, and stretching on tiptoe, reached his hand and imprinted a kiss, which his benefactor, though with some show of reluctance, accepted.... He had, to be sure, to pacify the child, and, after all, might reflect that he deserved it. Two days later, Mr. Benevolensky departed, taking with him his new protege .

During the first three years of Andryusha's absence he wrote pretty often, sometimes enclosing drawings in his letters. From time to time Mr. Benevolensky added a few words, for the most part of approbation; then the letters began to be less and less frequent, and at last ceased altogether. A whole year passed without a word from her nephew; and Tatyana Borissovna was beginning to be uneasy when suddenly she got the following note:--

'DEAREST AUNTIE,--Piotr Mihalitch, my patron, died three days ago. A severe paralytic stroke has deprived me of my sole support. To be sure, I am now twenty. I have made considerable progress during the last seven years; I have the greatest confidence in my talent, and can make my living by means of it; I do not despair; but all the same send me, if you can, as soon as convenient, 250 roubles. I kiss your hand and remain...' etc.

Tatyana Borissovna sent her nephew 250 roubles. Two months later he asked for more; she got together every penny she had and sent it him. Not six weeks after the second donation he was asking a third time for help, ostensibly to buy colours for a portrait bespoken by Princess Tertereshenev. Tatyana Borissovna refused. 'Under these circumstances,' he wrote to her, 'I propose coming to you to regain my health in the country.' And in the May of the same year Andryusha did, in fact, return to Maliya-Briki.

Tatyana Borissovna did not recognise him for the first minute. From his letter she had expected to see a wasted invalid, and she beheld a stout, broad-shouldered fellow, with a big red face and greasy, curly hair. The pale, slender little Andryusha had turned into the stalwart Andrei Ivanovitch Byelovzorov. And it was not only his exterior that was transformed. The modest spruceness, the sedateness and tidiness of his earlier years, was replaced by a careless swagger and slovenliness quite insufferable; he rolled from side to side as he walked, lolled in easy-chairs, put his elbows on the table, stretched and yawned, and behaved rudely to his aunt and the servants. 'I'm an artist,' he would say; 'a free Cossack! That's our sort!' Sometimes he did not touch a brush for whole days together; then the inspiration, as he called it, would come upon him; then he would swagger about as if he were drunk, clumsy, awkward, and noisy; his cheeks were flushed with a coarse colour, his eyes dull; he would launch into discourses upon his talent, his success, his development, the advance he was making.... It turned out in actual fact that he had barely talent enough to produce passable portraits. He was a perfect ignoramus, had read nothing; why should an artist read, indeed? Nature, freedom, poetry were his fitting elements; he need do nothing but shake his curls, talk, and suck away at his eternal cigarette! Russian audacity is a fine thing, but it doesn't suit every one; and Polezhaevs at second-hand, without the genius, are insufferable beings. Andrei Ivanovitch went on living at his aunt's; he did not seem to find the bread of charity bitter, notwithstanding the proverb. Visitors to the house found him a mortal nuisance. He would sit at the piano (a piano, too, had been installed at Tatyana Borissovna's) and begin strumming 'The Swift Sledge' with one finger; he would strike some chords, tap on the keys, and for hours together he would howl Varlamov's songs, 'The Solitary Pine,' or 'No, doctor, no, don't come to me,' in the most distressing manner, and his eyes seemed to disappear altogether, his cheeks were so puffed out and tense as drums.... Then he would suddenly strike up: 'Be still, distracting passion's tempest!'... Tatyana Borissovna positively shuddered.

'It's a strange thing,' she observed to me one day, 'the songs they compose nowadays; there's something desperate about them; in my day they were very different. We had mournful songs, too, but it was always a pleasure to hear them.... For instance:--

"'Come, come to me in the meadow,
Where I am awaiting thee;
Come, come to me in the meadow,
Where I'm shedding tears for thee...
Alas! thou'rt coming to the meadow,
But too late, dear love, for me!'"

Tatyana Borissovna smiled slyly.

'I agon-ise, I agon-ise!' yelled her nephew in the next room.

'Be quiet, Andryusha!'

'My soul's consumed apart from thee!' the indefatigable singer continued.

Tatyana Borissovna shook her head.

'Ah, these artists! these artists!'....

A year has gone by since then. Byelovzorov is still living at his aunt's, and still talking of going back to Petersburg. He has grown as broad as he is long in the country. His aunt--who could have imagined such a thing?--idolises him, and the young girls of the neighbourhood are falling in love with him....

Many of her old friends have given up going to Tatyana Borissovna's.

XVI   DEATH

I have a neighbour, a young landowner and a young sportsman. One fine July morning I rode over to him with a proposition that we should go out grouse-shooting together. He agreed. 'Only let's go,' he said, 'to my underwoods at Zusha; I can seize the opportunity to have a look at Tchapligino; you know my oakwood; they're felling timber there.' 'By all means.' He ordered his horse to be saddled, put on a green coat with bronze buttons, stamped with a boar's head, a game-bag embroidered in crewels, and a silver flask, slung a new-fangled French gun over his shoulder, turned himself about with some satisfaction before the looking-glass, and called his dog, Hope, a gift from his cousin, an old maid with an excellent heart, but no hair on her head. We started. My neighbour took with him the village constable, Arhip, a stout, squat peasant with a square face and jaws of antediluvian proportions, and an overseer he had recently hired from the Baltic provinces, a youth of nineteen, thin, flaxen-haired, and short-sighted, with sloping shoulders and a long neck, Herr Gottlieb von der Kock. My neighbour had himself only recently come into the property. It had come to him by inheritance from an aunt, the widow of a councillor of state, Madame Kardon-Kataev, an excessively stout woman, who did nothing but lie in her bed, sighing and groaning. We reached the underwoods. 'You wait for me here at the clearing,' said Ardalion Mihalitch (my neighbour) addressing his companions. The German bowed, got off his horse, pulled a book out of his pocket--a novel of Johanna Schopenhauer's, I fancy--and sat down under a bush; Arhip remained in the sun without stirring a muscle for an hour. We beat about among the bushes, but did not come on a single covey. Ardalion Mihalitch announced his intention of going on to the wood. I myself had no faith, somehow, in our luck that day; I, too, sauntered after him. We got back to the clearing. The German noted the page, got up, put the book in his pocket, and with some difficulty mounted his bob-tailed, broken-winded mare, who neighed and kicked at the slightest touch; Arhip shook himself, gave a tug at both reins at once, swung his legs, and at last succeeded in starting his torpid and dejected nag. We set off.

I had been familiar with Ardalion Mihalitch's wood from my childhood. I had often strolled in Tchapligino with my French tutor, Monsieur Desire Fleury, the kindest of men (who had, however, almost ruined my constitution for life by dosing me with Leroux's mixture every evening). The whole wood consisted of some two or three hundred immense oaks and ash-trees. Their stately, powerful trunks were magnificently black against the transparent golden green of the nut bushes and mountain-ashes; higher up, their wide knotted branches stood out in graceful lines against the clear blue sky, unfolding into a tent overhead; hawks, honey-buzzards and kestrels flew whizzing under the motionless tree-tops; variegated wood-peckers tapped loudly on the stout bark; the blackbird's bell-like trill was heard suddenly in the thick foliage, following on the ever-changing note of the gold-hammer; in the bushes below was the chirp and twitter of hedge-warblers, siskins, and peewits; finches ran swiftly along the paths; a hare would steal along the edge of the wood, halting cautiously as he ran; a squirrel would hop sporting from tree to tree, then suddenly sit still, with its tail over its head. In the grass among the high ant-hills under the delicate shade of the lovely, feathery, deep-indented bracken, were violets and lilies of the valley, and funguses, russet, yellow, brown, red and crimson; in the patches of grass among the spreading bushes red strawberries were to be found.... And oh, the shade in the wood! In the most stifling heat, at mid-day, it was like night in the wood: such peace, such fragrance, such freshness.... I had spent happy times in Tchapligino, and so, I must own, it was with melancholy feelings I entered the wood I knew so well. The ruinous, snowless winter of 1840 had not spared my old friends, the oaks and the ashes; withered, naked, covered here and there with sickly foliage, they struggled mournfully up above the young growth which 'took their place, but could never replace them.' [Footnote: In 1840 there were severe frosts, and no snow fell up to the very end of December; all the wintercorn was frozen, and many splendid oak-forests were destroyed by that merciless winter. It will be hard to replace them; the productive force of the land is apparently diminishing; in the 'interdicted' wastelands (visited by processions with holy images, and so not to be touched), instead of the noble trees of former days, birches and aspens grow of themselves; and, indeed, they have no idea among us of planting woods at all.-- Author's Note .]

Some trees, still covered with leaves below, fling their lifeless, ruined branches upwards, as it were, in reproach and despair; in others, stout, dead, dry branches are thrust out of the midst of foliage still thick, though with none of the luxuriant abundance of old; others have fallen altogether, and lie rotting like corpses on the ground. And--who could have dreamed of this in former days?--there was no shade--no shade to be found anywhere in Tchapligino! 'Ah,' I thought, looking at the dying trees: 'isn't it shameful and bitter for you?'... Koltsov's lines recurred to me:

'What has become
Of the mighty voices,
The haughty strength,
The royal pomp?
Where now is the
Wealth of green?...

'How is it, Ardalion Mihalitch,' I began, 'that they didn't fell these trees the very next year? You see they won't give for them now a tenth of what they would have done before.'

He merely shrugged his shoulders.

'You should have asked my aunt that; the timber merchants came, offered money down, pressed the matter, in fact.'

' Mein Gott! mein Gott! ' Von der Kock cried at every step. 'Vat a bity, vat a bity!'

'What's a bity!' observed my neighbour with a smile.

'That is; how bitiful, I meant to say.'

What particularly aroused his regrets were the oaks lying on the ground--and, indeed, many a miller would have given a good sum for them. But the constable Arhip preserved an unruffled composure, and did not indulge in any lamentations; on the contrary, he seemed even to jump over them and crack his whip on them with a certain satisfaction.

We were getting near the place where they were cutting down the trees, when suddenly a shout and hurried talk was heard, following on the crash of a falling tree, and a few instants after a young peasant, pale and dishevelled, dashed out of the thicket towards us.

'What is it? where are you running?' Ardalion Mihalitch asked him.

He stopped at once.

'Ah, Ardalion Mihalitch, sir, an accident!'

'What is it?'

'Maksim, sir, crushed by a tree.'

'How did it happen?... Maksim the foreman?'

'The foreman, sir. We'd started cutting an ash-tree, and he was standing looking on.... He stood there a bit, and then off he went to the well for some water--wanted a drink, seemingly--when suddenly the ash-tree began creaking and coming straight towards him. We shout to him: 'Run, run, run!'.... He should have rushed to one side, but he up and ran straight before him.... He was scared, to be sure. The ash-tree covered him with its top branches. But why it fell so soon, the Lord only knows!... Perhaps it was rotten at the core.'

'And so it crushed Maksim?'

'Yes, sir.'

'To death?'

'No, sir, he's still alive--but as good as dead; his arms and legs are crushed. I was running for Seliverstitch, for the doctor.'

Ardalion Mihalitch told the constable to gallop to the village for Seliverstitch, while he himself pushed on at a quick trot to the clearing.... I followed him.

We found poor Maksim on the ground. The peasants were standing about him. We got off our horses. He hardly moaned at all; from time to time he opened his eyes wide, looked round, as it were, in astonishment, and bit his lips, fast turning blue.... The lower part of his face was twitching; his hair was matted on his brow; his breast heaved irregularly: he was dying. The light shade of a young lime-tree glided softly over his face.

We bent down to him. He recognised Ardalion Mihalitch.

'Please sir,' he said to him, hardly articulately, 'send... for the priest... tell... the Lord... has punished me... arms, legs, all smashed... to-day's... Sunday... and I... I... see... didn't let the lads off... work.'

He ceased, out of breath.

'And my money... for my wife... after deducting.... Onesim here knows... whom I... what I owe.'

'We've sent for the doctor, Maksim,' said my neighbour; 'perhaps you may not die yet.'

He tried to open his eyes, and with an effort raised the lids.

'No, I'm dying. Here... here it is coming... here it.... Forgive me, lads, if in any way....'

'God will forgive you, Maksim Andreitch,' said the peasants thickly with one voice, and they took off their caps; 'do you forgive us!'

He suddenly shook his head despairingly, his breast heaved with a painful effort, and he fell back again.

'We can't let him lie here and die, though,' cried Ardalion Mihalitch; 'lads, give us the mat from the cart, and carry him to the hospital.'

Two men ran to the cart.

'I bought a horse... yesterday,' faltered the dying man, 'off Efim... Sitchovsky... paid earnest money... so the horse is mine.... Give it... to my wife....'

They began to move him on to the mat.... He trembled all over, like a wounded bird, and stiffened....

'He is dead,' muttered the peasants.

We mounted our horses in silence and rode away.

The death of poor Maksim set me musing. How wonderfully indeed the Russian peasant dies! The temper in which he meets his end cannot be called indifference or stolidity; he dies as though he were performing a solemn rite, coolly and simply.

A few years ago a peasant belonging to another neighbour of mine in the country got burnt in the drying shed, where the corn is put. (He would have remained there, but a passing pedlar pulled him out half-dead; he plunged into a tub of water, and with a run broke down the door of the burning outhouse.) I went to his hut to see him. It was dark, smoky, stifling, in the hut. I asked, 'Where is the sick man?' 'There, sir, on the stove,' the sorrowing peasant woman answered me in a sing-song voice. I went up; the peasant was lying covered with a sheepskin, breathing heavily. 'Well, how do you feel?' The injured man stirred on the stove; all over burns, within sight of death as he was, tried to rise. 'Lie still, lie still, lie still.... Well, how are you?' 'In a bad way, surely,' said he. 'Are you in pain?' No answer. 'Is there anything you want?'--No answer. 'Shouldn't I send you some tea, or anything.' 'There's no need.' I moved away from him and sat down on the bench. I sat there a quarter of an hour; I sat there half an hour--the silence of the tomb in the hut. In the corner behind the table under the holy pictures crouched a little girl of twelve years old, eating a piece of bread. Her mother threatened her every now and then. In the outer room there was coming and going, noise and talk: the brother's wife was chopping cabbage. 'Hey, Aksinya,' said the injured man at last. 'What?' 'Some kvas.' Aksinya gave him some kvas. Silence again. I asked in a whisper, 'Have they given him the sacrament?' 'Yes.' So, then, everything was in order: he was waiting for death, that was all. I could not bear it, and went away....

Again, I recall how I went one day to the hospital in the village of Krasnogorye to see the surgeon Kapiton, a friend of mine, and an enthusiastic sportsman.

This hospital consisted of what had once been the lodge of the manor-house; the lady of the manor had founded it herself; in other words, she ordered a blue board to be nailed up above the door with an inscription in white letters: 'Krasnogorye Hospital,' and had herself handed to Kapiton a red album to record the names of the patients in. On the first page of this album one of the toadying parasites of this Lady Bountiful had inscribed the following lines:

'Dans ces beaux lieux, ou regne l'allegresse
Ce temple fut ouvert par la Beaute;
De vos seigneurs admirez la tendresse
Bons habitants de Krasnogorie!'

while another gentleman had written below:

'Et moi aussi j'aime la nature!

JEAN KOBYLIATNIKOFF.'

The surgeon bought six beds at his own expense, and had set to work in a thankful spirit to heal God's people. Besides him, the staff consisted of two persons; an engraver, Pavel, liable to attacks of insanity, and a one-armed peasant woman, Melikitrisa, who performed the duties of cook. Both of them mixed the medicines and dried and infused herbs; they, too, controlled the patients when they were delirious. The insane engraver was sullen in appearance and sparing of words; at night he would sing a song about 'lovely Venus,' and would besiege every one he met with a request for permission to marry a girl called Malanya, who had long been dead. The one-armed peasant woman used to beat him and set him to look after the turkeys. Well, one day I was at Kapiton's. We had begun talking over our last day's shooting, when suddenly a cart drove into the yard, drawn by an exceptionally stout horse, such as are only found belonging to millers. In the cart sat a thick-set peasant, in a new greatcoat, with a beard streaked with grey. 'Hullo, Vassily Dmitritch,' Kapiton shouted from the window; 'please come in.... The miller of Liobovshin,' he whispered to me. The peasant climbed groaning out of the cart, came into the surgeon's room, and after looking for the holy pictures, crossed himself, bowing to them. 'Well, Vassily Dmitritch, any news?... But you must be ill; you don't look well.' 'Yes, Kapiton Timofeitch, there's something not right.' 'What's wrong with you?' 'Well, it was like this, Kapiton Timofeitch. Not long ago I bought some mill-stones in the town, so I took them home, and as I went to lift them out of the cart, I strained myself, or something; I'd a sort of rick in the loins, as though something had been torn away, and ever since I've been out of sorts. To-day I feel worse than ever.' 'Hm,' commented Kapiton, and he took a pinch of snuff; 'that's a rupture, no doubt. But is it long since this happened?' 'It's ten days now.' 'Ten days?' (The surgeon drew a long inward breath and shook his head.) 'Let me examine you.' 'Well, Vassily Dmitritch,' he pronounced at last, 'I am sorry for you, heartily sorry, but things aren't right with you at all; you're seriously ill; stay here with me; I will do everything I can, for my part, though I can't answer for anything.' 'So bad as that?' muttered the astounded peasant. 'Yes, Vassily Dmitritch, it is bad; if you'd come to me a day or two sooner, it would have been nothing much; I could have cured you in a trice; but now inflammation has set in; before we know where we are, there'll be mortification.' 'But it can't be, Kapiton Timofeitch.' 'I tell you it is so.' 'But how comes it?' (The surgeon shrugged his shoulders.) 'And I must die for a trifle like that?' 'I don't say that... only you must stop here.' The peasant pondered and pondered, his eyes fixed on the floor, then he glanced up at us, scratched his head, and picked up his cap. 'Where are you off to, Vassily Dmitritch?' 'Where? why, home to be sure, if it's so bad. I must put things to rights, if it's like that.' 'But you'll do yourself harm, Vassily Dmitritch; you will, really; I'm surprised how you managed to get here; you must stop.' 'No, brother, Kapiton Timofeitch, if I must die, I'll die at home; why die here? I've got a home, and the Lord knows how it will end.' 'No one can tell yet, Vassily Dmitritch, how it will end.... Of course, there is danger, considerable danger; there's no disputing that... but for that reason you ought to stay here.' (The peasant shook his head.) 'No, Kapiton

Timofeitch, I won't stay... but perhaps you will prescribe me a medicine.' 'Medicine alone will be no good.' 'I won't stay, I tell you.' 'Well, as you like.... Mind you don't blame me for it afterwards.'

The surgeon tore a page out of the album, and, writing out a prescription, gave him some advice as to what he could do besides. The peasant took the sheet of paper, gave Kapiton half-a-rouble, went out of the room, and took his seat in the cart. 'Well, good-bye, Kapiton Timofeitch, don't remember evil against me, and remember my orphans, if anything....' 'Oh, do stay, Vassily!' The peasant simply shook his head, struck the horse with the reins, and drove out of the yard. The road was muddy and full of holes; the miller drove cautiously, without hurry, guiding his horse skilfully, and nodding to the acquaintances he met. Three days later he was dead.

The Russians, in general, meet death in a marvellous way. Many of the dead come back now to my memory. I recall you, my old friend, who left the university with no degree, Avenir Sorokoumov, noblest, best of men! I see once again your sickly, consumptive face, your lank brown tresses, your gentle smile, your ecstatic glance, your long limbs; I can hear your weak, caressing voice. You lived at a Great Russian landowner's, called Gur Krupyanikov, taught his children, Fofa and Zyozya, Russian grammar, geography, and history, patiently bore all the ponderous jokes of the said Gur, the coarse familiarities of the steward, the vulgar pranks of the spiteful urchins; with a bitter smile, but without repining, you complied with the caprices of their bored and exacting mother; but to make up for it all, what bliss, what peace was yours in the evening, after supper, when, free at last of all duties, you sat at the window pensively smoking a pipe, or greedily turned the pages of a greasy and mutilated number of some solid magazine, brought you from the town by the land-surveyor--just such another poor, homeless devil as yourself! How delighted you were then with any sort of poem or novel; how readily the tears started into your eyes; with what pleasure you laughed; what genuine love for others, what generous sympathy for everything good and noble, filled your pure youthful soul! One must tell the truth: you were not distinguished by excessive sharpness of wit; Nature had endowed you with neither memory nor industry; at the university you were regarded as one of the least promising students; at lectures you slumbered, at examinations you preserved a solemn silence; but who was beaming with delight and breathless with excitement at a friend's success, a friend's triumphs?... Avenir!... Who had a blind faith in the lofty destiny of his friends? who extolled them with pride? who championed them with angry vehemence? who was innocent of envy as of vanity? who was ready for the most disinterested self-sacrifice? who eagerly gave way to men who were not worthy to untie his latchet?... That was you, all you, our good Avenir! I remember how broken-heartedly you parted from your comrades, when you were going away to be a tutor in the country; you were haunted by presentiment of evil.... And, indeed, your lot was a sad one in the country; you had no one there to listen to with veneration, no one to admire, no one to love.... The neighbours--rude sons of the steppes, and polished gentlemen alike--treated you as a tutor: some, with rudeness and neglect, others carelessly. Besides, you were not pre-possessing in person; you were shy, given to blushing, getting hot and stammering.... Even your health was no better for the country air: you wasted like a candle, poor fellow! It is true your room looked out into the garden; wild cherries, apple-trees, and limes strewed their delicate blossoms on your table, your ink-stand, your books; on the wall hung a blue silk watch-pocket, a parting present from a kind-hearted, sentimental German governess with flaxen curls and little blue eyes; and sometimes an old friend from Moscow would come out to you and throw you into ecstasies with new poetry, often even with his own. But, oh, the loneliness, the insufferable slavery of a tutor's lot! the impossibility of escape, the endless autumns and winters, the ever-advancing disease!... Poor, poor Avenir!

I paid Sorokoumov a visit not long before his death. He was then hardly able to walk. The landowner, Gur Krupyanikov, had not turned him out of the house, but had given up paying him a salary, and had taken another tutor for Zyozya.... Fofa had been sent to a school of cadets. Avenir was sitting near the window in an old easy-chair. It was exquisite weather. The clear autumn sky was a bright blue above the dark-brown line of bare limes; here and there a few last leaves of lurid gold rustled and whispered about them. The earth had been covered with frost, now melting into dewdrops in the sun, whose ruddy rays fell aslant across the pale grass; there was a faint crisp resonance in the air; the voices of the labourers in the garden reached us clearly and distinctly. Avenir wore an old Bokhara dressing-gown; a green neckerchief threw a deathly hue over his terribly sunken face. He was greatly delighted to see me, held out his hand, began talking and coughing at once. I made him be quiet, and sat down by him.... On Avenir's knee lay a manuscript book of Koltsov's poems, carefully copied out; he patted it with a smile. 'That's a poet,' he stammered, with an effort repressing his cough; and he fell to declaiming in a voice scarcely audible:

'Can the eagle's wings
Be chained and fettered?
Can the pathways of heaven
Be closed against him?'

I stopped him: the doctor had forbidden him to talk. I knew what would please him. Sorokoumov never, as they say, 'kept up' with the science of the day; but he was always anxious to know what results the leading intellects had reached. Sometimes he would get an old friend into a corner and begin questioning him; he would listen and wonder, take every word on trust, and even repeat it all after him. He took a special interest in German philosophy. I began discoursing to him about Hegel (this all happened long ago, as you may gather). Avenir nodded his head approvingly, raised his eyebrows, smiled, and whispered: 'I see! I see! ah, that's splendid! splendid!'... The childish curiosity of this poor, dying, homeless outcast, moved me, I confess, to tears. It must be noted that Avenir, unlike the general run of consumptives, did not deceive himself in regard to his disease.... But what of that?--he did not sigh, nor grieve; he did not even once refer to his position....

Rallying his strength, he began talking of Moscow, of old friends, of Pushkin, of the drama, of Russian literature; he recalled our little suppers, the heated debates of our circle; with regret he uttered the names of two or three friends who were dead....

'Do you remember Dasha?' he went on. 'Ah, there was a heart of pure gold! What a heart! and how she loved me!... What has become of her now? Wasted and fallen away, poor dear, I daresay!'

I had not the courage to disillusion the sick man; and, indeed, why should he know that his Dasha was now broader than she was long, and that she was living under the protection of some merchants, the brothers Kondatchkov, that she used powder and paint, and was for ever swearing and scolding?

'But can't we,' I thought, looking at his wasted face, 'get him away from here? Perhaps there may still be a chance of curing him.' But Avenir cut short my suggestion.

'No, brother, thanks,' he said; 'it makes no difference where one dies. I shan't live till the winter, you see.... Why give trouble for nothing? I'm used to this house. It's true the people...'

'They're unkind, eh?' I put in.

'No, not unkind! but wooden-headed creatures. However, I can't complain of them. There are neighbours: there's a Mr. Kasatkin's daughter, a cultivated, kind, charming girl... not proud...'

Sorokoumov began coughing again.

'I shouldn't mind anything,' he went on, after taking breath, 'if they'd only let me smoke my pipe.... But I'll have my pipe, if I die for it!' he added, with a sly wink. 'Thank God, I have had life enough! I have known so many fine people.

'But you should, at least, write to your relations,' I interrupted.

'Why write to them? They can't be any help; when I die they'll hear of it. But, why talk about it... I'd rather you'd tell me what you saw abroad.'

I began to tell him my experiences. He seemed positively to gloat over my story. Towards evening I left, and ten days later I received the following letter from Mr. Krupyanikov:

> 'I have the honour to inform you, my dear sir, that your friend, the student, living in my house, Mr. Avenir Sorokoumov, died at two o'clock in the afternoon, three days ago, and was buried to-day, at my expense, in the parish church. He asked me to forward you the books and manuscripts enclosed herewith. He was found to have twenty-two roubles and a half, which, with the rest of his belongings, pass into the possession of his relatives. Your friend died fully conscious, and, I may say, with so little sensibility that he showed no signs of regret even when the whole family of us took a last farewell of him. My wife, Kleopatra Aleksandrovna, sends you her regards. The death of your friend has, of course, affected her nerves; as regards myself, I am, thank God, in good health, and have the honour to remain, your humble servant,'

> 'G. KRUPYANIKOV.'

Many more examples recur to me, but one cannot relate everything. I will confine myself to one.

I was present at an old lady's death-bed; the priest had begun reading the prayers for the dying over her, but, suddenly noticing that the patient seemed to be actually dying, he made haste to give her the cross to kiss. The lady turned away with an air of displeasure. 'You're in too great a hurry, father,' she said, in a voice almost inarticulate; 'in too great a hurry.'... She kissed the cross, put her hand under the pillow and expired. Under the pillow was a silver rouble; she had meant to pay the priest for the service at her own death....

Yes, the Russians die in a wonderful way.

XVII   THE SINGERS

The small village of Kolotovka once belonged to a lady known in the neighbourhood by the nickname of Skin-flint, in illusion to her keen business habits (her real name is lost in oblivion), but has of late years been the property of a German from Petersburg. The village lies on the slope of a barren hill, which is cut in half from top to bottom by a tremendous ravine. It is a yawning chasm, with shelving sides hollowed out by the action of rain and snow, and it winds along the very centre of the village street; it separates the two sides of the unlucky hamlet far more than a river would do, for a river could, at least, be crossed by a bridge. A few gaunt willows creep timorously down its sandy sides; at the very bottom, which is dry and yellow as copper, lie huge slabs of argillaceous rock. A cheerless position, there's no denying, yet all the surrounding inhabitants know the road to Kolotovka well; they go there often, and are always glad to go.

At the very summit of the ravine, a few paces from the point where it starts as a narrow fissure in the earth, there stands a small square hut. It stands alone, apart from all the others. It is thatched, and has a chimney; one window keeps watch like a sharp eye over the ravine, and on winter evenings when it is lighted from within, it is seen far away in the dim frosty fog, and its twinkling light is the guiding star of many a peasant on his road. A blue board is nailed up above the door; this hut is a tavern, called the 'Welcome Resort.' Spirits are sold here probably no cheaper than the usual price, but it is far more frequented than any other establishment of the same sort in the neighbourhood. The explanation of this is to be found in the tavern-keeper, Nikolai Ivanitch.

Nikolai Ivanitch--once a slender, curly-headed and rosy-cheeked young fellow, now an excessively stout, grizzled man with a fat face, sly and good-natured little eyes, and a shiny forehead, with wrinkles like lines drawn all over it--has lived for more than twenty years in Kolotovka. Nikolai Ivanitch is a shrewd, acute fellow, like the majority of tavern-keepers. Though he makes no conspicuous effort to please or to talk to people, he has the art of attracting and keeping customers, who find it particularly pleasant to sit at his bar under the placid and genial, though alert eye, of the phlegmatic host. He has a great deal of common sense; he thoroughly understands the landowner's conditions of life, the peasant's, and the tradesman's. He could give sensible advice on difficult points, but, like a cautious man and an egoist, prefers to stand aloof, and at most--and that only in the case of his favourite customers--by remote hints, dropped, as it were, unintentionally, to lead them into the true way. He is an authority on everything that is of interest or importance to a Russian; on horses and cattle, on timber, bricks, and crockery, on woollen stuffs and on leather, on songs and dances. When he has no customers he is usually sitting like a sack on the ground before the door of his hut, his thin legs tucked under him, exchanging a friendly greeting with every passer-by. He has seen a great deal in his time; many a score of petty landowners, who used to come to him for spirits, he has seen pass away before him; he knows everything that is done for eighty miles round, and never gossips, never gives a sign of knowing what is unsuspected by the most keen-sighted police-officer. He keeps his own counsel, laughs, and makes his glasses ring. His neighbours respect him; the civilian general Shtcherpetenko, the landowner highest in rank in the district, gives him a condescending nod whenever he drives past his little house. Nikolai Ivanitch is a man of influence; he made a notorious horse-stealer return a horse he had taken from the stable of one of his friends; he brought the peasants of a neighbouring village to their senses when they refused to accept a new overseer, and so on. It must not be imagined, though, that he does this from love of justice, from devotion to his neighbour--no! he simply tries to prevent anything that might, in any way, interfere with his ease and comfort. Nikolai

Ivanitch is married, and has children. His wife, a smart, sharp-nosed and keen-eyed woman of the tradesman class, has grown somewhat stout of late years, like her husband. He relies on her in everything, and she keeps the key of the cash-box. Drunken brawlers are afraid of her; she does not like them; they bring little profit and make a great deal of noise: those who are taciturn and surly in their cups are more to her taste. Nikolai Ivanitch's children are still small; the first four all died, but those that are left take after their parents: it is a pleasure to look at their intelligent, healthy little faces.

It was an insufferably hot day in July when, slowly dragging my feet along, I went up alongside the Kolotovka ravine with my dog towards the Welcome Resort. The sun blazed, as it were, fiercely in the sky, baking the parched earth relentlessly; the air was thick with stifling dust. Glossy crows and ravens with gaping beaks looked plaintively at the passers-by, as though asking for sympathy; only the sparrows did not droop, but, pluming their feathers, twittered more vigorously than ever as they quarrelled among the hedges, or flew up all together from the dusty road, and hovered in grey clouds over the green hempfields. I was tormented by thirst. There was no water near: in Kolotovka, as in many other villages of the steppes, the peasants, having no spring or well, drink a sort of thin mud out of the pond.... For no one could call that repulsive beverage water. I wanted to ask for a glass of beer or kvas at Nikolai Ivanitch's.

It must be confessed that at no time of the year does Kolotovka present a very cheering spectacle; but it has a particularly depressing effect when the relentless rays of a dazzling July sun pour down full upon the brown, tumble-down roofs of the houses and the deep ravine, and the parched, dusty common over which the thin, long-legged hens are straying hopelessly, and the remains of the old manor-house, now a hollow, grey framework of aspenwood, with holes instead of windows, overgrown with nettles, wormwood, and rank grass, and the pond black, as though charred and covered with goose feathers, with its edge of half-dried mud, and its broken-down dyke, near which, on the finely trodden, ash-like earth, sheep, breathless and gasping with the heat, huddle dejectedly together, their heads drooping with weary patience, as though waiting for this insufferable heat to pass at last. With weary steps I drew near Nikolai Ivanitch's dwelling, arousing in the village children the usual wonder manifested in a concentrated, meaningless stare, and in the dogs an indignation expressed in such hoarse and furious barking that it seemed as if it were tearing their very entrails, and left them breathless and choking, when suddenly in the tavern doorway there appeared a tall peasant without a cap, in a frieze cloak, girt about below his waist with a blue handkerchief. He looked like a house-serf; thick grey hair stood up in disorder above his withered and wrinkled face. He was calling to some one hurriedly, waving his arms, which obviously were not quite under his control. It could be seen that he had been drinking already.

'Come, come along!' he stammered, raising his shaggy eyebrows with an effort. 'Come, Blinkard, come along! Ah, brother, how you creep along, 'pon my word! It's too bad, brother. They're waiting for you within, and here you crawl along.... Come.'

'Well, I'm coming, I'm coming!' called a jarring voice, and from behind a hut a little, short, fat, lame man came into sight. He wore a rather tidy cloth coat, pulled half on, and a high pointed cap right over his brows, which gave his round plump face a sly and comic expression. His little yellow eyes moved restlessly about, his thin lips wore a continual forced smile, while his sharp, long nose peered forward saucily in front like a rudder. 'I'm coming, my dear fellow.' He went hobbling towards the tavern. 'What are you calling me for?... Who's waiting for me?'

'What am I calling you for?' repeated the man in the frieze coat reproachfully.' You're a queer fish, Blinkard: we call you to come to the tavern, and you ask what for? Here are honest folks all waiting for you: Yashka the Turk, and the Wild Master, and the booth-keeper from Zhizdry. Yashka's got a bet on with the booth-keeper: the stake's a pot of beer--for the one that does best, sings the best, I mean... do you see?'

'Is Yashka going to sing?' said the man addressed as Blinkard, with lively interest. 'But isn't it your humbug, Gabbler?'

'I'm not humbugging,' answered the Gabbler, with dignity; 'it's you are crazy. I should think he would sing since he's got a bet on it, you precious innocent, you noodle, Blinkard!'

'Well, come in, simpleton!' retorted the Blinkard.

'Then give us a kiss at least, lovey,' stammered the Gabbler, opening wide his arms.

'Get out, you great softy!' responded the Blinkard contemptuously, giving him a poke with his elbow, and both, stooping, entered the low doorway.

The conversation I had overheard roused my curiosity exceedingly. More than once rumours had reached me of Yashka the Turk as the best singer in the vicinity, and here was an opportunity all at once of hearing him in competition with another master of the art. I quickened my steps and went into the house.

Few of my readers have probably had an opportunity of getting a good view of any village taverns, but we sportsmen go everywhere. They are constructed on an exceedingly simple plan. They usually consist of a dark outer-shed, and an inner room with a chimney, divided in two by a partition, behind which none of the customers have a right to go. In this partition there is a wide opening cut above a broad oak table. At this table or bar the spirits are served. Sealed up bottles of various sizes stand on the shelves, right opposite the opening. In the front part of the room, devoted to customers, there are benches, two or three empty barrels, and a corner table. Village taverns are for the most part rather dark, and you hardly ever see on their wainscotted walls any of the glaring cheap prints which few huts are without.

When I went into the Welcome Resort, a fairly large party were already assembled there.

In his usual place behind the bar, almost filling up the entire opening in the partition, stood Nikolai Ivanitch in a striped print shirt; with a lazy smile on his full face, he poured out with his plump white hand two glasses of spirits for the Blinkard and the Gabbler as they came in; behind him, in a corner near the window, could be seen his sharp-eyed wife. In the middle of the room was standing Yashka the Turk, a thin, graceful fellow of three-and-twenty, dressed in a long skirted coat of blue nankin. He looked a smart factory hand, and could not, to judge by his appearance, boast of very good health. His hollow cheeks, his large, restless grey eyes, his straight nose, with its delicate mobile nostrils, his pale brown curls brushed back over the sloping white brow, his full but beautiful, expressive lips, and his whole face betrayed a passionate and sensitive nature. He was in a state of great excitement; he blinked, his breathing was hurried, his hands shook, as though in fever, and he was really in a fever--that sudden fever of excitement which is so well-known to all who have to speak and sing before an audience. Near him stood a man of about forty, with broad shoulders and broad jaws, with a low forehead, narrow Tartar eyes, a short flat nose, a square chin, and shining black hair coarse as bristles. The expression of his face--a swarthy face, with a sort of leaden hue in it--and especially of his pale lips, might almost have been called savage, if it had not been so still and dreamy. He hardly stirred a muscle; he only looked slowly about him like a bull under the yoke. He was dressed in a sort of surtout, not over new, with smooth brass buttons; an old black silk handkerchief was twisted round his immense neck. He was called the Wild Master. Right opposite him, on a bench under the holy pictures, was sitting Yashka's rival, the booth-keeper from Zhizdry; he was a short, stoutly-built man about thirty, pock-marked, and curly-headed, with a blunt, turn-up nose, lively brown eyes, and a scanty beard. He looked keenly about him, and, sitting with his hands under him, he kept carelessly swinging his legs and tapping with his feet, which were encased in stylish top-boots with a coloured edging. He wore a new thin coat of grey cloth, with a plush collar, in sharp contrast with the crimson shirt below, buttoned close across the chest. In the opposite corner, to the right of the door, a peasant sat at the table in a narrow, shabby smock-frock, with a huge rent on the shoulder. The sunlight fell in a narrow, yellowish streak through the dusty panes of the two small windows, but it seemed as if it struggled in vain with the habitual darkness of the room; all the objects in it were dimly, as it were, patchily lighted up. On the other hand, it was almost cool in the room, and the sense of stifling heat dropped off me like a weary load directly I crossed the threshold.

My entrance, I could see, was at first somewhat disconcerting to Nikolai Ivanitch's customers; but observing that he greeted me as a friend, they were reassured, and took no more notice of me. I asked for some beer and sat down in the corner, near the peasant in the ragged smock.

'Well, well,' piped the Gabbler, suddenly draining a glass of spirits at one gulp, and accompanying his exclamation with the strange gesticulations, without which he seemed unable to utter a single word; 'what are we waiting for? If we're going to begin, then begin. Hey, Yasha?'

'Begin, begin,' chimed in Nikolai Ivanitch approvingly.

'Let's begin, by all means,' observed the booth-keeper coolly, with a self-confident smile; 'I'm ready.'

'And I'm ready,' Yakov pronounced in a voice thrilled with excitement.

'Well, begin, lads,' whined the Blinkard. But, in spite of the unanimously expressed desire, neither began; the booth-keeper did not even get up from the bench--they all seemed to be waiting for something.

'Begin!' said the Wild Master sharply and sullenly. Yashka started. The booth-keeper pulled down his girdle and cleared his throat.

'But who's to begin?' he inquired in a slightly changed voice of the Wild Master, who still stood motionless in the middle of the room, his stalwart legs wide apart and his powerful arms thrust up to the elbow into his breeches pockets.

'You, you, booth-keeper,' stammered the Gabbler; 'you, to be sure, brother.'

The Wild Master looked at him from under his brows. The Gabbler gave a faint squeak, in confusion looked away at the ceiling, twitched his shoulder, and said no more.

'Cast lots,' the Wild Master pronounced emphatically; 'and the pot on the table.'

Nikolai Ivanitch bent down, and with a gasp picked up the pot of beer from the floor and set it on the table.

The Wild Master glanced at Yakov, and said 'Come!'

Yakov fumbled in his pockets, took out a halfpenny, and marked it with his teeth. The booth-keeper pulled from under the skirts of his long coat a new leather purse, deliberately untied the string, and shaking out a quantity of small change into his hand, picked out a new halfpenny. The Gabbler held out his dirty cap, with its broken peak hanging loose; Yakov dropped his halfpenny in, and the booth-keeper his.

'You must pick out one,' said the Wild Master, turning to the Blinkard.

The Blinkard smiled complacently, took the cap in both hands, and began shaking it.

For an instant a profound silence reigned; the halfpennies clinked faintly, jingling against each other. I looked round attentively; every face wore an expression of intense expectation; the Wild Master himself showed signs of uneasiness; my neighbour, even, the peasant in the tattered smock, craned his neck inquisitively. The Blinkard put his hand into the cap and took out the booth-keeper's halfpenny; every one drew a long breath. Yakov flushed, and the booth-keeper passed his hand over his hair.

'There, I said you'd begin,' cried the Gabbler; 'didn't I say so?'

'There, there, don't cluck,' remarked the Wild Master contemptuously. 'Begin,' he went on, with a nod to the booth-keeper.

'What song am I to sing?' asked the booth-keeper, beginning to be nervous.

'What you choose,' answered the Blinkard; 'sing what you think best.'

'What you choose, to be sure,' Nikolai Ivanitch chimed in, slowly smoothing his hand on his breast, 'you're quite at liberty about that. Sing what you like; only sing well; and we'll give a fair decision afterwards.'

'A fair decision, of course,' put in the Gabbler, licking the edge of his empty glass.

'Let me clear my throat a bit, mates,' said the booth-keeper, fingering the collar of his coat.

'Come, come, no nonsense--begin!' protested the Wild Master, and he looked down.

The booth-keeper thought a minute, shook his head, and stepped forward. Yakov's eyes were riveted upon him.

But before I enter upon a description of the contest itself, I think it will not be amiss to say a few words about each of the personages taking part in my story. The lives of some of them were known to me already when I met them in the Welcome Resort; I collected some facts about the others later on.

Let us begin with the Gabbler. This man's real name was Evgraf Ivanovitch; but no one in the whole neighbourhood knew him as anything but the Gabbler, and he himself referred to himself by that nickname; so well did it fit him. Indeed, nothing could have been more appropriate to his insignificant, ever-restless features. He was a dissipated, unmarried house-serf, whose own masters had long ago got rid of him, and who, without any employment, without earning a halfpenny, found means to get drunk every day at other people's expense. He had a great number of acquaintances who treated him to drinks of spirits and tea, though they could not have said why they did so themselves; for, far from being entertaining in company, he bored every one with his meaningless chatter, his insufferable familiarity, his spasmodic gestures and incessant, unnatural laugh. He could neither sing nor dance; he had never said a clever, or even a sensible thing in his life; he chattered away, telling lies about everything--a regular Gabbler! And yet not a single drinking party for thirty miles around took place without his lank figure turning up among the guests; so that they were used to him by now, and put up with his presence as a necessary evil. They all, it is true, treated him with contempt; but the Wild Master was the only one who knew how to keep his foolish sallies in check.

The Blinkard was not in the least like the Gabbler. His nickname, too, suited him, though he was no more given to blinking than other people; it is a well-known fact, that the Russian peasants have a talent for finding good nicknames. In spite of my endeavours to get more detailed information about this man's past, many passages in his life have remained spots of darkness to me, and probably to many other people; episodes, buried, as the bookmen say, in the darkness of oblivion. I could only find out that he was once a coachman in the service of an old childless lady; that he had run away with three horses he was in charge of; had been lost for a whole year, and no doubt, convinced by experience of the drawbacks and hardships of a wandering life, he had gone back, a cripple, and flung himself at his mistress's feet. He succeeded in a few years in smoothing over his offence by his exemplary conduct, and, gradually getting higher in her favour, at last gained her complete confidence, was made a bailiff, and on his mistress's death, turned out--in what way was never known--to have received his freedom. He got admitted into the class of tradesmen; rented patches of market garden from the neighbours; grew rich, and now was living in ease and comfort. He was a man of experience, who knew on which side his bread was buttered; was more actuated by prudence than by either good or ill-nature; had knocked about, understood men, and knew how to turn them to his own advantage. He was cautious, and at the same time enterprising, like a fox; though he was as fond of gossip as an old woman, he never let out his own affairs, while he made everyone else talk freely of theirs. He did not affect to be a simpleton, though, as so many crafty men of his sort do; indeed it would have been difficult for him to take any one in, in that way; I have never seen a sharper, keener pair of eyes than his tiny cunning little 'peepers,' as they call them in Orel. They were never simply looking about; they were always looking one up and down and through and through. The Blinkard would sometimes ponder for weeks together over some apparently simple undertaking, and again he would suddenly decide on a desperately bold line of action, which one would fancy would bring him to ruin.... But it would be sure to turn out all right; everything would go smoothly. He was lucky, and believed in his own luck, and believed in omens. He was exceedingly superstitious in general. He was not liked, because he would have nothing much to do with anyone, but he was respected. His whole family consisted of one little son, whom he idolised, and who, brought up by such a father, is likely to get on in the world. 'Little Blinkard'll be his father over again,' is said of him already, in undertones by the old men, as they sit on their mud walls gossiping on summer evenings, and every one knows what that means; there is no need to say more.

As to Yashka the Turk and the booth-keeper, there is no need to say much about them. Yakov, called the Turk because he actually was descended from a Turkish woman, a prisoner from the war, was by nature an artist in every sense of the word, and by calling, a ladler in a paper factory belonging to a merchant. As for the booth-keeper, his career, I must own, I know nothing of; he struck me as being a smart townsman of the tradesman class, ready to turn his hand to anything. But the Wild Master calls for a more detailed account.

The first impression the sight of this man produced on you was a sense of coarse, heavy, irresistible power. He was clumsily built, a 'shambler,' as they say about us, but there was an air of triumphant vigour about him, and--strange to say--his bear-like figure was not without a certain grace of its own, proceeding, perhaps, from his absolutely placid confidence in his own strength. It was hard to decide at first to what class this Hercules belonged: he did not look like a house-serf, nor a tradesman, nor an impoverished clerk out of work, nor a small ruined landowner, such as takes to being a huntsman or a fighting man; he was, in fact, quite individual. No one knew where he came from or what brought him into our district; it was said that he came of free peasant-proprietor stock, and had once been in the government service somewhere, but nothing positive was known about this; and indeed there was no one from whom one could learn--certainly not from him; he was the most silent and morose of men. So much so that no one knew for certain what he lived on; he followed no trade, visited no one, associated with scarcely anyone; yet he had money to spend; little enough, it is true, still he had some. In his behaviour he was not exactly retiring--retiring was not a word that could be applied to him: he lived as though he noticed no one about him, and cared for no one. The Wild Master (that was the nickname they had given him; his real name was Perevlyesov) enjoyed an immense influence in the whole district; he was obeyed with eager promptitude, though he had no kind of right to give orders to anyone, and did not himself evince the slightest pretension to authority over the people with whom he came into casual contact He spoke--they obeyed: strength always has an influence of its own. He scarcely drank at all, had nothing to do with women, and was passionately fond of singing. There was much that was mysterious about this man; it seemed as though vast forces sullenly reposed within him, knowing, as it were, that once roused, once bursting free, they were bound to crush him and everything they came in contact with; and I am greatly mistaken if, in this man's life, there had not been some such outbreak; if it was not owing to the lessons of experience, to a narrow escape from ruin, that he now kept himself so tightly in hand. What especially struck me in him was the combination of a sort of inborn natural ferocity, with an equally inborn generosity--a combination I have never met in any other man.

And so the booth-keeper stepped forward, and, half shutting his eyes, began singing in high falsetto. He had a fairly sweet and pleasant voice, though rather hoarse: he played with his voice like a woodlark, twisting and turning it in incessant roulades and trills up and down the scale, continually returning to the highest notes, which he held and prolonged with special care. Then he would break off, and again suddenly take up the first motive with a sort of go-ahead daring. His modulations were at times rather bold, at times rather comical; they would have given a connoisseur great satisfaction, and have made a German furiously indignant. He was a Russian tenore di grazia, tenor leger . He sang a song to a lively dance-tune, the words of which, all that I could catch through the endless maze of variations, ejaculations and repetitions, were as follows:

'A tiny patch of land, young lass,
I'll plough for thee,
And tiny crimson flowers, young lass,
I'll sow for thee.'

He sang; all listened to him with great attention. He seemed to feel that he had to do with really musical people, and therefore was exerting himself to do his best. And they really are musical in our part of the country; the village of Sergievskoe on the Orel highroad is deservedly noted throughout Russia for its harmonious chorus-singing. The booth-keeper sang for a long while without evoking much enthusiasm in his audience; he lacked the support of a chorus; but at last, after one particularly bold flourish, which set even the Wild Master smiling, the Gabbler could not refrain from a shout of delight.

Everyone was roused. The Gabbler and the Blinkard began joining in in an undertone, and exclaiming: 'Bravely done!... Take it, you rogue!... Sing it out, you serpent! Hold it! That shake again, you dog you!... May Herod confound your soul!' and so on. Nikolai Ivanitch behind the bar was nodding his head from side to side approvingly. The Gabbler at last was swinging his legs, tapping with his feet and twitching his shoulder, while Yashka's eyes fairly glowed like coal, and he trembled all over like a leaf, and smiled nervously. The Wild Master alone did not change countenance, and stood motionless as before; but his eyes, fastened on the booth-keeper, looked somewhat softened, though the expression of his lips was still scornful. Emboldened by the signs of general approbation, the booth-keeper went off in a whirl of flourishes, and began to round off such trills, to turn such shakes off his tongue, and to make such furious play with his throat, that when at last, pale, exhausted, and bathed in hot perspiration, he uttered the last dying note, his whole body flung back, a general united shout greeted him in a violent outburst. The Gabbler threw himself on his neck and began strangling him in his long, bony arms; a flush came out on Nikolai Ivanitch's oily face, and he seemed to have grown younger; Yashka shouted like mad: 'Capital, capital!'--even my neighbour, the peasant in the torn smock, could not restrain himself, and with a blow of his fist on the table he cried: 'Aha! well done, damn my soul, well done!' And he spat on one side with an air of decision.

'Well, brother, you've given us a treat!' bawled the Gabbler, not releasing the exhausted booth-keeper from his embraces; 'you've given us a treat, there's no denying! You've won, brother, you've won! I congratulate you--the quart's yours! Yashka's miles behind you... I tell you: miles... take my word for it.' (And again he hugged the booth-keeper to his breast.)

'There, let him alone, let him alone; there's no being rid of you'... said the Blinkard with vexation; 'let him sit down on the bench; he's tired, see... You're a ninny, brother, a perfect ninny! What are you sticking to him like a wet leaf for...'

'Well, then, let him sit down, and I'll drink to his health,' said the Gabbler, and he went up to the bar. 'At your expense, brother,' he added, addressing the booth-keeper.

The latter nodded, sat down on the bench, pulled a piece of cloth out of his cap, and began wiping his face, while the Gabbler, with greedy haste, emptied his glass, and, with a grunt, assumed, after the manner of confirmed drinkers, an expression of careworn melancholy.

'You sing beautifully, brother, beautifully,' Nikolai Ivanitch observed caressingly. 'And now it's your turn, Yasha; mind, now, don't be afraid. We shall see who's who; we shall see. The booth-keeper sings beautifully, though; 'pon my soul, he does.'

'Very beautifully,' observed Nikolai Ivanitch's wife, and she looked with a smile at Yakov.

'Beautifully, ha!' repeated my neighbour in an undertone.

'Ah, a wild man of the woods!' the Gabbler vociferated suddenly, and going up to the peasant with the rent on his shoulder, he pointed at him with his finger, while he pranced about and went off into an insulting guffaw. 'Ha! ha! get along! wild man of the woods! Here's a ragamuffin from Woodland village! What brought you here?' he bawled amidst laughter.

The poor peasant was abashed, and was just about to get up and make off as fast as he could, when suddenly the Wild Master's iron voice was heard:

'What does the insufferable brute mean?' he articulated, grinding his teeth.

'I wasn't doing nothing,' muttered the Gabbler. 'I didn't... I only....'

'There, all right, shut up!' retorted the Wild Master. 'Yakov, begin!'

Yakov took himself by his throat:

'Well, really, brothers,... something.... Hm, I don't know, on my word, what....'

'Come, that's enough; don't be timid. For shame!... why go back?... Sing the best you can, by God's gift.'

And the Wild Master looked down expectant. Yakov was silent for a minute; he glanced round, and covered his face with his hand. All had their eyes simply fastened upon him, especially the booth-keeper, on whose face a faint, involuntary uneasiness could be seen through his habitual expression of self-confidence and the triumph of his success. He leant back against the wall, and again put both hands under him, but did not swing his legs as before. When at last Yakov uncovered his face it was pale as a dead man's; his eyes gleamed faintly under their drooping lashes. He gave a deep sigh, and began to sing.... The first sound of his voice was faint and unequal, and seemed not to come from his chest, but to be wafted from somewhere afar off, as though it had floated by chance into the room. A strange effect was produced on all of us by this trembling, resonant note; we glanced at one another, and Nikolai Ivanitch's wife seemed to draw herself up. This first note was followed by another, bolder and prolonged, but still obviously quivering, like a harpstring when suddenly struck by a stray finger it throbs in a last, swiftly-dying tremble; the second was followed by a third, and, gradually gaining fire and breadth, the strains swelled into a pathetic melody. 'Not one little path ran into the field,' he sang, and sweet and mournful it was in our ears. I have seldom, I must confess, heard a voice like it; it was slightly hoarse, and not perfectly true; there was even something morbid about it at first; but it had genuine depth of passion, and youth and sweetness and a sort of fascinating, careless, pathetic melancholy. A spirit of truth and fire, a Russian spirit, was sounding and breathing in that voice, and it seemed to go straight to your heart, to go straight to all that was Russian in it. The song swelled and flowed. Yakov was clearly carried away by enthusiasm; he was not timid now; he surrendered himself wholly to the rapture of his art; his voice no longer trembled; it quivered, but with the scarce perceptible inward quiver of passion, which pierces like an arrow to the very soul of the listeners; and he steadily gained strength and firmness and breadth. I remember I once saw at sunset on a flat sandy shore, when the tide was low and the sea's roar came weighty and menacing from the distance, a great white sea-gull; it sat motionless, its silky bosom facing the crimson glow of the setting sun, and only now and then opening wide its great wings to greet the well-known sea, to greet the sinking lurid sun: I recalled it, as I heard Yakov. He sang, utterly forgetful of his rival and all of us; he seemed supported, as a bold swimmer by the waves, by our silent, passionate sympathy. He sang, and in every sound of his voice one seemed to feel something dear and akin to us, something of breadth and space, as though the familiar steppes were unfolding before our eyes and stretching away into endless distance. I felt the tears gathering in my bosom and rising to my eyes; suddenly I was struck by dull, smothered sobs.... I looked round--the innkeeper's wife was weeping, her bosom pressed close to the window. Yakov threw a quick glance at her, and he sang more sweetly, more melodiously than ever; Nikolai Ivanitch looked down; the Blinkard turned away; the Gabbler, quite touched, stood, his gaping mouth stupidly open; the humble peasant was sobbing softly in the corner, and shaking his head with a plaintive murmur; and on the iron visage of the Wild Master, from under his overhanging brows there slowly rolled a heavy tear; the booth-keeper raised his clenched fist to his brow, and did not stir.... I don't know how the general emotion would have ended, if Yakov had not suddenly come to a full stop on a high, exceptionally shrill note--as though his voice had broken. No one called out, or even stirred; every one seemed to be waiting to see whether he was not going to sing more; but he opened his eyes as though wondering at our silence, looked round at all of us with a face of inquiry, and saw that the victory was his....

'Yasha,' said the Wild Master, laying his hand on his shoulder, and he could say no more.

We all stood, as it were, petrified. The booth-keeper softly rose and went up to Yakov.

'You... yours... you've won,' he articulated at last with an effort, and rushed out of the room. His rapid, decided action, as it were, broke the spell; we all suddenly fell into noisy, delighted talk. The Gabbler bounded up and down, stammered and brandished his arms like mill-sails; the Blinkard limped up to Yakov and began kissing him; Nikolai Ivanitch got up and solemnly announced that he would add a second pot of beer from himself. The Wild Master laughed a sort of kind, simple laugh, which I should never have expected to see on his face; the humble peasant as he wiped his eyes, cheeks, nose, and beard on his sleeves, kept repeating in his corner: 'Ah, beautiful it was, by God! blast me for the son of a dog, but it was fine!' while Nikolai Ivanitch's wife, her face red with weeping, got up quickly and went away, Yakov was enjoying his triumph like a child; his whole face was tranformed, his eyes especially fairly glowed with happiness. They dragged him to the bar; he beckoned the weeping peasant up to it, and sent the innkeeper's little son to look after the booth-keeper, who was not found, however; and the festivities began. 'You'll sing to us again; you're going to sing to us till evening,' the Gabbler declared, flourishing his hands in the air.

I took one more look at Yakov and went out. I did not want to stay--I was afraid of spoiling the impression I had received. But the heat was as insupportable as before. It seemed hanging in a thick, heavy layer right over the earth; over the dark blue sky, tiny bright fires seemed whisking through the finest, almost black dust. Everything was still; and there was something hopeless and oppressive in this profound hush of exhausted nature. I made my way to a hay-loft, and lay down on the fresh-cut, but already almost dry grass. For a long while I could not go to sleep; for a long while Yakov's irresistible voice was ringing in my ears.... At last the heat and fatigue regained their sway, however, and I fell into a dead sleep. When I waked up, everything was in darkness; the hay scattered around smelt strong and was slightly damp; through the slender rafters of the half-open roof pale stars were faintly twinkling. I went out. The glow of sunset had long died away, and its last trace showed in a faint light on the horizon; but above the freshness of the night there was still a feeling of heat in the atmosphere, lately baked through by the sun, and the breast still craved for a draught of cool air. There was no wind, nor were there any clouds; the sky all round was clear, and transparently dark, softly glimmering with innumerable, but scarcely visible stars. There were lights twinkling about the village; from the flaring tavern close by rose a confused, discordant din, amid which I fancied I recognised the voice of Yakov. Violent laughter came from there in an outburst at times. I went up to the little window and pressed my face against the pane. I saw a cheerless, though varied and animated scene; all were drunk--all from Yakov upwards. With breast bared, he sat on a bench, and singing in a thick voice a street song to a dance-tune, he lazily fingered and strummed on the strings of a guitar. His moist hair hung in tufts over his fearfully pale face. In the middle of the room, the Gabbler, completely 'screwed' and without his coat, was hopping about in a dance before the peasant in the grey smock; the peasant, on his side, was with difficulty stamping and scraping with his feet, and grinning meaninglessly over his dishevelled beard; he waved one hand from time to time, as much as to say, 'Here goes!' Nothing could be more ludicrous than his face; however much he twitched up his eyebrows, his heavy lids would hardly rise, but seemed lying upon his scarcely visible, dim, and mawkish eyes. He was in that amiable frame of mind of a perfectly intoxicated man, when every passer-by, directly he looks him in the face, is sure to say, 'Bless you, brother, bless you!' The Blinkard, as red as a lobster, and his nostrils dilated wide, was laughing malignantly in a corner; only Nikolai Ivanitch, as befits a good tavern-keeper, preserved his composure unchanged. The room was thronged with many new faces; but the Wild Master I did not see in it.

I turned away with rapid steps and began descending the hill on which Kolotovka lies. At the foot of this hill stretches a wide plain; plunged in the misty waves of the evening haze, it seemed more immense, and was, as it were, merged in the darkening sky. I walked with long strides along the road by the ravine, when all at once from somewhere far away in the plain came a boy's clear voice: 'Antropka! Antropka-a-a!...' He shouted in obstinate and tearful desperation, with long, long drawing out of the last syllable.

He was silent for a few instants, and started shouting again. His voice rang out clear in the still, lightly slumbering air. Thirty times at least he had called the name, Antropka. When suddenly, from the farthest end of the plain, as though from another world, there floated a scarcely audible reply:

'Wha-a-t?'

The boy's voice shouted back at once with gleeful exasperation:

'Come here, devil! woo-od imp!'

'What fo-or?' replied the other, after a long interval.

'Because dad wants to thrash you!' the first voice shouted back hurriedly.

The second voice did not call back again, and the boy fell to shouting Antropka once more. His cries, fainter and less and less frequent, still floated up to my ears, when it had grown completely dark, and I had turned the corner of the wood which skirts my village and lies over three miles from Kolotovka.... 'Antropka-a-a!' was still audible in the air, filled with the shadows of night.

XVIII   PIOTR PETROVITCH KARATAEV

One autumn five years ago, I chanced, when on the road from Moscow to Tula, to spend almost a whole day at a posting station for want of horses. I was on the way back from a shooting expedition, and had been so incautious as to send my three horses on in front of me. The man in charge of the station, a surly, elderly man, with hair hanging over his brows to his very nose, with little sleepy eyes, answered all my complaints and requests with disconnected grumbling, slammed the door angrily, as though he were cursing his calling in life, and going out on the steps abused the postilions who were sauntering in a leisurely way through the mud with the weighty wooden yokes on their arms, or sat yawning and scratching themselves on a bench, and paid no special attention to the wrathful exclamations of their superior. I had already sat myself down three times to tea, had several times tried in vain to sleep, and had read all the inscriptions on the walls and windows; I was overpowered by fearful boredom. In chill and helpless despair I was staring at the upturned shafts of my carriage, when suddenly I heard the tinkling of a bell, and a small trap, drawn by three jaded horses, drew up at the steps. The new arrival leaped out of the trap, and shouting 'Horses! and look sharp!' he went into the room. While he was listening with the strange wonder customary in such cases to the overseer's answer that there were no horses, I had time to scan my new companion from top to toe with all the greedy curiosity of a man bored to death. He appeared to be nearly thirty. Small-pox had left indelible traces on his face, which was dry and yellowish, with an unpleasant coppery tinge; his long blue-black hair fell in ringlets on his collar behind, and was twisted into jaunty curls in front; his small swollen eyes were quite expressionless; a few hairs sprouted on his upper lip. He was dressed like a dissipated country gentleman, given to frequenting horse-fairs, in a rather greasy striped Caucasian jacket, a faded lilac silk-tie, a waistcoat with copper buttons, and grey trousers shaped like huge funnels, from under which the toes of unbrushed shoes could just be discerned. He smelt strongly of tobacco and spirits; on his fat, red hands, almost hidden in his sleeves, could be seen silver and Tula rings. Such figures are met in Russia not by dozens, but by hundreds; an acquaintance with them is not, to tell the truth, productive of any particular pleasure; but in spite of the prejudice with which I looked at the new-comer, I could not fail to notice the recklessly good-natured and passionate expression of his face.

'This gentleman's been waiting more than an hour here too,' observed the overseer indicating me.

More than an hour! The rascal was making fun of me.

'But perhaps he doesn't need them as I do,' answered the new comer.

'I know nothing about that,' said the overseer sulkily.

'Then is it really impossible? Are there positively no horses?'

'Impossible. There's not a single horse.'

'Well, tell them to bring me a samovar. I'll wait a little; there's nothing else to be done.'

The new comer sat down on the bench, flung his cap on the table, and passed his hand over his hair.

'Have you had tea already?' he inquired of me.

'Yes.'

'But won't you have a little more for company.'

I consented. The stout red samovar made its appearance for the fourth time on the table. I brought out a bottle of rum. I was not wrong in taking my new acquaintance for a country gentleman of small property. His name was Piotr Petrovitch Karataev.

We got into conversation. In less than half-an-hour after his arrival, he was telling me his whole life with the most simple-hearted openness.

'I'm on my way to Moscow now,' he told me as he sipped his fourth glass; 'there's nothing for me to do now in the country.'

'How so?'

'Well, it's come to that. My property's in disorder; I've ruined my peasants, I must confess; there have been bad years: bad harvests, and all sorts of ill-luck, you know.... Though, indeed,' he added, looking away dejectedly; 'how could I manage an estate!'

'Why's that?'

'But, no,' he interrupted me? 'there are people like me who make good managers! You see,' he went on, screwing his head on one side and sucking his pipe assiduously, 'looking at me, I dare say you think I'm not much... but you, see, I must confess, I've had a very middling education; I wasn't well off. I beg your pardon; I'm an open man, and if you come to that....'

He did not complete his sentence, but broke off with a wave of the hand. I began to assure him that he was mistaken, that I was highly delighted to meet him, and so on, and then observed that I should have thought a very thorough education was not indispensable for the good management of property.

'Agreed,' he responded; 'I agree with you. But still, a special sort of disposition's essential! There are some may do anything they like, and it's all right! but I.... Allow me to ask, are you from Petersburg or from Moscow?'

'I'm from Petersburg.'

He blew a long coil of smoke from his nostrils.

'And I'm going in to Moscow to be an official.'

'What department do you mean to enter?'

'I don't know; that's as it happens. I'll own to you, I'm afraid of official life; one's under responsibility at once. I've always lived in the country; I'm used to it, you know... but now, there's no help for it... it's through poverty! Oh, poverty, how I hate it!'

'But then you will be living in the capital.'

'In the capital.... Well, I don't know what there is that's pleasant in the capital. We shall see; may be, it's pleasant too.... Though nothing, I fancy, could be better than the country.'

'Then is it really impossible for you to live at your country place?'

He gave a sigh.

'Quite impossible. It's, so to say, not my own now.'

'Why, how so?'

'Well, a good fellow there--a neighbour--is in possession... a bill of exchange.'

Poor Piotr Petrovitch passed his hand over his face, thought a minute, and shook his head.

'Well?'... I must own, though,' he added after a brief silence, 'I can't blame anybody; it's my own fault. I was fond of cutting a dash, I am fond of cutting a dash, damn my soul!'

'You had a jolly life in the country?' I asked him.

'I had, sir,' he responded emphatically, looking me straight in the face, 'twelve harriers--harriers, I can tell you, such as you don't very often see.' (The last words he uttered in a drawl with great significance.) 'A grey hare they'd double upon in no time.

After the red fox--they were devils, regular serpents. And I could boast of my greyhounds too. It's all a thing of the past now, I've no reason to lie. I used to go out shooting too. I had a dog called the Countess, a wonderful setter, with a first-rate scent--she took everything. Sometimes I'd go to a marsh and call "Seek." If she refused, you might go with a dozen dogs, and you'd find nothing. But when she was after anything, it was a sight to see her. And in the house so well-bred. If you gave her bread with your left hand and said, "A Jew's tasted it," she wouldn't touch it; but give it with your right and say, "The young lady's had some," and she'd take it and eat it at once. I had a pup of hers--capital pup he was, and I meant to bring him with me to Moscow, but a friend asked me for him, together with a gun; he said, "In Moscow you'll have other things to think of." I gave him the pup and the gun; and so, you know, it stayed there.'

'But you might go shooting in Moscow.'

'No, what would be the use? I didn't know when to pull myself up, so now I must grin and bear it.

But there, kindly tell me rather about the living in Moscow--is it dear?'

'No, not very.'

'Not very.... And tell me, please, are there any gypsies in Moscow?'

'What sort of gypsies?'

'Why, such as hang about fairs?'

'Yes, there are in Moscow....'

'Well, that's good news. I like gypsies, damn my soul! I like 'em....'

And there was a gleam of reckless merriment in Piotr Petrovitch's eyes. But suddenly he turned round on the bench, then seemed to ponder, dropped his eyes, and held out his empty glass to me.

'Give me some of your rum,' he said.'

'But the tea's all finished.'

'Never mind, as it is, without tea... Ah--h!' Karataev laid his head in his hands and leaned his elbows on the table. I looked at him without speaking, and although I was expecting the sentimental exclamations, possibly even the tears of which the inebriate are so lavish, yet when he raised his head, I was, I must own, impressed by the profoundly mournful expression of his face.

'What's wrong with you?'

'Nothing.... I was thinking of old times. An anecdote that... I would tell it you, but I am ashamed to trouble you....'

'What nonsense!'

'Yes,' he went on with a sigh:--'there are cases... like mine, for instance. Well, if you like, I will tell you. Though really I don't know....'

'Do tell me, dear Piotr Petrovitch.'

'Very well, though it's a... Well, do you see,' he began; 'but, upon my word, I don't know.'

'Come, that's enough, dear Piotr Petrovitch.'

'All right. This, then, was what befel me, so to say. I used to live in the country... All of a sudden, I took a fancy to a girl. Ah, what a girl she was!... handsome, clever, and so good and sweet! Her name was Matrona. But she wasn't a lady--that is, you understand, she was a serf, simply a serf-girl. And not my girl; she belonged to someone else--that was the trouble. Well, so I loved her--it's really an incident that one can hardly... well, and she loved me, too. And so Matrona began begging me to buy her off from her mistress; and, indeed, the thought had crossed my mind too.... But her mistress was a rich, dreadful old body; she lived about twelve miles from me. Well, so one fine day, as the saying is, I ordered my team of three horses to be harnessed abreast to the droshky--in the centre I'd a first-rate goer, an extraordinary Asiatic horse, for that reason called Lampurdos--I dressed myself in my best, and went off to Matrona's mistress. I arrived; it was a big house with wings and a garden.... Matrona was waiting for me at the bend of the road; she tried to say a word to me, but she could only kiss her hand and turn away. Well, so I went into the hall and asked if the mistress were at home?... And a tall footman says to me: "What name shall I say?" I answered, "Say, brother, Squire Karataev has called on a matter of business." The footman walked away; I waited by myself and thought, "I wonder how it'll be? I daresay the old beast'll screw out a fearful price, for all she's so rich. Five hundred roubles she'll ask, I shouldn't be surprised." Well, at last the footman returned, saying, "If you please, walk up." I followed him into the drawing-room. A little yellowish old woman sat in an armchair blinking. "What do you want?" To begin with, you know, I thought it necessary to say how glad I was to make her acquaintance.... "You are making a mistake; I am not the mistress here; I'm a relation of hers.... What do you want?" I remarked upon that, "I had to speak to the mistress herself." "Marya Ilyinishna is not receiving to-day; she is unwell.... What do you want?" There's nothing for it, I thought to myself; so I explained my position to her. The old lady heard me out. "Matrona! what Matrona?"

'"Matrona Fedorovna, Kulik's daughter."

'"Fedor Kulik's daughter.... But how did you come to know her?" "By chance." "And is she aware of your intention?" "Yes." The old lady was silent for a minute. Then, "Ah, I'll let her know it, the worthless hussy!" she said. I was astounded, I must confess. "What ever for? upon my word!... I'm ready to pay a good sum, if you will be so good as to name it."'

'The old hag positively hissed at me. "A surprising idea you've concocted there; as though we needed your money!... I'll teach her, I'll show her!... I'll beat the folly out of her!" The old lady choked with spitefulness. "Wasn't she well off with us, pray?... Ah, she's a little devil! God forgive my transgressions!" I fired up, I'll confess. "What are you threatening the poor girl for? How is she to blame?" The old lady crossed herself. "Ah, Lord have mercy on me, do you suppose I'd..." "But she's not yours, you know!" "Well, Marya Ilyinishna knows best about that; it's not your business, my good sir; but I'll show that chit of a Matrona whose serf she is." I'll confess, I almost fell on the damned old woman, but I thought of Matrona, and my hands dropped. I was more frightened than I can tell you; I began entreating the old lady. "Take what you like," I said. "But what use is she to you?" "I like her, good ma'am; put yourself in my position.... Allow me to kiss your little hand." And I positively kissed the wretch's hand! "Well," mumbled the old witch, "I'll tell Marya Ilyinishna--it's for her to decide; you come back in a couple of days." I went home in great uneasiness. I began to suspect that I'd managed the thing badly; that I'd been wrong in letting her notice my state of mind, but I thought of that too late. Two days after, I went to see the mistress. I was shown into a boudoir. There were heaps of flowers and splendid furniture; the lady herself was sitting in a wonderful easy-chair, with her head lolling back on a cushion; and the same relation was sitting there too, and some young lady, with white eyebrows and a mouth all awry, in a green gown--a companion, most likely. The old lady said through her nose, "Please be seated." I sat down. She began questioning me as to how old I was, and where I'd been in the service, and what I meant to do, and all that very condescendingly and solemnly. I answered minutely. The old lady took a handkerchief off the table, flourished it, fanning herself.... "Katerina Karpovna informed me," says she, "of your scheme; she informed me of it; but I make it my rule," says she, "not to allow my people to leave my service. It is improper, and quite unsuitable in a well-ordered house; it is not good order. I have already given my orders," says she. "There will be no need for you to trouble yourself further," says she. "Oh, no trouble, really.... But can it be, Matrona Fedorovna is so necessary to you?" "No," says she, "she is not necessary." "Then why won't you part with her to me?" "Because I don't choose to; I don't choose--and that's all about it. I've already," says she, "given my orders: she is being sent to a village in the steppes." I was thunderstruck. The old lady said a couple of words in French to the young lady in green; she went out. "I am," says she, "a woman of strict principles, and my health is delicate; I can't stand being worried. You are still young, and I'm an old woman, and entitled to give you advice. Wouldn't it be better for you to settle down, get married; to look out a good match; wealthy brides are few, but a poor girl, of the highest moral character, could be found." I stared, do you know, at the old lady, and didn't understand what she was driving at; I could hear she was talking about marriage, but the village in the steppes was ringing in my ears all the while. Get married!... what the devil!...'

Here he suddenly stopped in his story and looked at me.

'You're not married, I suppose?'

'No.'

'There, of course, I could see it. I couldn't stand it. "But, upon my word, ma'am, what on earth are you talking about? How does marriage come in? I simply want to know from you whether you will part with your serf-girl Matrona or not?" The old lady began sighing and groaning. "Ah, he's worrying me! ah, send him away! ah!" The relation flew to her, and began scolding me, while the lady kept on moaning: "What have I done to deserve it?... I suppose I'm not mistress in my own house? Ah! ah!" I snatched my hat, and ran out of the house like a madman.

'Perhaps,' he continued, 'you will blame me for being so warmly attached to a girl of low position; I don't mean to justify myself exactly, either... but so it came to pass!... Would you believe it, I had no rest by day or by night.... I was in torment! Besides, I thought, "I have ruined the poor girl!" At times I thought that she was herding geese in a smock, and being ill-treated by her mistress's orders, and the bailiff, a peasant in tarred boots, reviling her with foul abuse. I positively fell into a cold sweat. Well, I could not stand it. I found out what village she had been sent to, mounted my horse, and set off. I only got there the evening of the next day. Evidently they hadn't expected such a proceeding on my part, and had given no order in regard to me. I went straight to the bailiff as though I were a neighbour; I go into the yard and look around; there was Matrona sitting on the steps leaning on her elbow. She was on the point of crying out, but I held up my finger and pointed outside, towards the open country. I went into the hut; I chatted away a bit to the bailiff, told him ten thousand lies, seized the right moment, and went out to Matrona. She, poor girl, fairly hung round my neck. She was pale and thin, my poor darling! I kept saying to her, do you know: "There, it's all right, Matrona; it's all right, don't cry," and my own tears simply flowed and flowed.... Well, at last though, I was ashamed, I said to her: "Matrona, tears are no help in trouble, but we must act, as they say, resolutely; you must run away with me; that's how we must act." Matrona fairly swooned away.... "How can it be! I shall be ruined; they will be the death of me altogether." "You silly! who will find you?" "They will find me; they will be sure to find me. Thank you, Piotr Petrovitch--I shall never forget your kindness; but now you must leave me; such is my fate, it seems." "Ah, Matrona, Matrona, I thought you were a girl of character!" And, indeed, she had a great deal of character.... She had a heart, a heart of gold! "Why should you be left here? It makes no difference; things can't be worse. Come, tell me--you've felt the bailiff's fists, eh?" Matrona fairly crimsoned, and her lips trembled. "But there'll be no living for my family on my account." "Why, your family now--will they send them for soldiers?" "Yes; they'll send my brother for a soldier." "And your father?" "Oh, they won't send father; he's the only good tailor among us."

'"There, you see; and it won't kill your brother." Would you believe it, I'd hard work to persuade her; she even brought forward a notion that I might have to answer for it. "But that's not your affair," said I.... However, I did carry her off... not that time, but another; one night I came with a light cart, and carried her off.'

'You carried her off?'

'Yes... Well, so she lived in my house. It was a little house, and I'd few servants. My people, I will tell you frankly, respected me; they wouldn't have betrayed me for any reward. I began to be as happy as a prince. Matrona rested and recovered, and I grew devoted to her.... And what a girl she was! It seemed to come by nature! She could sing, and dance, and play the guitar!... I didn't show her to my neighbours; I was afraid they'd gossip! But there was one fellow, my bosom friend, Gornostaev, Panteley--you don't know him? He was simply crazy about her; he'd kiss her hand as though she were a lady; he would, really. And I must tell you, Gornostaev was not like me; he was a cultivated man, had read all Pushkin; sometimes, he'd talk to Matrona and me so that we pricked up our ears to listen. He taught her to write; such a queer chap he was! And how I dressed her--better than the governor's wife, really; I had a pelisse made her of crimson velvet, edged with fur... Ah! how that pelisse suited her! It was made by a Moscow madame in a new fashion, with a waist. And what a wonderful creature Matrona was! Sometimes she'd fall to musing, and sit for hours together looking at the ground, without stirring a muscle; and I'd sit too, and look at her, and could never gaze enough, just as if I were seeing her for the first time.... Then she would smile, and my heart would give a jump as though someone were tickling me. Or else she'd suddenly fall to laughing, joking, dancing; she would embrace me so warmly, so passionately, that my head went round. From morning to evening I thought of nothing but how I could please her. And would you believe it? I gave her presents simply to see how pleased she would be, the darling! all blushing with delight! How she would try on my present; how she would come back with her new possession on, and kiss me! Her father, Kulik, got wind of it, somehow; the old man came to see us, and how he wept.... In that way we lived for five months, and I should have been glad to live with her for ever, but for my cursed ill-luck!'

Piotr Petrovitch stopped.

'What was it happened?' I asked him sympathetically. He waved his hand.

'Everything went to the devil. I was the ruin of her too. My little Matrona was passionately fond of driving in sledges, and she used to drive herself; she used to put on her pelisse and her embroidered Torzhok gloves, and cry out with delight all the way. We used to go out sledging always in the evening, so as not to meet any one, you know. So, once it was such a splendid day, you know, frosty and clear, and no wind... we drove out.

Matrona had the reins. I looked where she was driving. Could it be to Kukuyevka, her mistress's village? Yes, it was to Kukuyevka. I said to her, "You mad girl, where are you going?" She gave me a look over her shoulder and laughed. "Let me," she said, "for a lark." "Well," thought I, "come what may!..." To drive past her mistress's house was nice, wasn't it? Tell me yourself--wasn't it nice? So we drove on. The shaft-horse seemed to float through the air, and the trace-horses went, I can tell you, like a regular whirlwind. We were already in sight of Kukuyevka; when suddenly I see an old green coach crawling along with a groom on the footboard up behind.... It was the mistress--the mistress driving towards us! My heart failed me; but Matrona--how she lashed the horses with the reins, and flew straight towards the coach! The coachman, he, you understand, sees us flying to meet him, meant, you know, to move on one side, turned too sharp, and upset the coach in a snowdrift. The window was broken; the mistress shrieked, "Ai! ai! ai! ai! ai! ai!" The companion wailed, "Help! help!" while we flew by at the best speed we might. We galloped on, but I thought, "Evil will come of it. I did wrong to let her drive to Kukuyevka." And what do you think? Why, the mistress had recognised Matrona, and me too, the old wretch, and made a complaint against me. "My runaway serf-girl," said she, "is living at Mr. Karataev's"; and thereupon she made a suitable present. Lo and behold! the captain of police comes to me; and he was a man I knew, Stepan Sergyeitch Kuzovkin, a good fellow; that's to say, really a regular bad lot. So he came up and said this and that, and "How could you do so, Piotr Petrovitch?... The liability is serious, and the laws very distinct on the subject." I tell him, "Well, we'll have a talk about that, of course; but come, you'll take a little something after your drive." He agreed to take something, but he said, "Justice has claims, Piotr Petrovitch; think for yourself." "Justice, to be sure," said I, "of course... but, I have heard say you've a little black horse. Would you be willing to exchange it for my Lampurdos?... But there's no girl called Matrona Fedorovna in my keeping." "Come," says he, "Piotr Petrovitch, the girl's with you, we're not living in Switzerland, you know... though my little horse might be exchanged for Lampurdos; I might, to be sure, accept it in that way." However, I managed to get rid of him somehow that time. But the old lady made a greater fuss than ever; ten thousand roubles, she said, she wouldn't grudge over the business. You see, when she saw me, she suddenly took an idea into her head to marry me to her young lady companion in green; that I found out later; that was why she was so spiteful. What ideas won't these great ladies take into their heads!... It comes through being dull, I suppose. Things went badly with me: I didn't spare money, and I kept Matrona in hiding. No, they harassed me, and turned me this way and that: I got into debt; I lost my health.... So one night, as I lay in my bed, thinking, "My God, why should I suffer so? What am I to do, since I can't get over loving her?... There, I can't, and that's all about it!" into the room walked Matrona. I had hidden her for the time at a farmhouse a mile and a half from my house. I was frightened. "What? have they discovered you even there?" "No, Piotr Petrovitch," said she, "no one disturbs me at Bubnova; but will that last long? My heart," she said, "is torn, Piotr Petrovitch; I am sorry for you, my dear one; never shall I forget your goodness, Piotr Petrovitch, but now I've come to say good-bye to you." "What do you mean, what do you mean, you mad girl?... Good-bye, how good-bye?"... "Yes... I am going to give myself up." "But I'll lock you up in a garret, mad girl!... Do you mean to destroy me? Do you want to kill me, or what?" The girl was silent; she looked on the floor. "Come, speak, speak!" "I can't bear to cause you any more trouble, Piotr Petrovitch." Well, one might talk to her as one pleased... "But do you know, little fool, do you know, mad..."

And Piotr Petrovitch sobbed bitterly.

'Well, what do you think?' he went on, striking the table with his fist and trying to frown, while the tears still coursed down his flushed cheeks; 'the girl gave herself up.... She went and gave herself up...'

'The horses are ready,' the overseer cried triumphantly, entering the room.

We both stood up.

'What became of Matrona?' I asked.

Karataev waved his hand.

A year after my meeting with Karataev, I happened to go to Moscow. One day, before dinner, for some reason or other I went into a cafe in the Ohotny row--an original Moscow cafe . In the billiard-room, across clouds of smoke, I caught glimpses of flushed faces, whiskers, old-fashioned Hungarian coats, and new-fangled Slavonic costumes.

Thin little old men in sober surtouts were reading the Russian papers. The waiters flitted airily about with trays, treading softly on the green carpets. Merchants, with painful concentration, were drinking tea. Suddenly a man came out of the billiard-room, rather dishevelled, and not quite steady on his legs. He put his hands in his pockets, bent his head, and looked aimlessly about.

'Ba, ba, ba! Piotr Petrovitch!... How are you?'

Piotr Petrovitch almost fell on my neck, and, slightly staggering, drew me into a small private room.

'Come here,' he said, carefully seating me in an easy-chair; 'here you will be comfortable. Waiter, beer! No, I mean champagne! There, I'll confess, I didn't expect; I didn't expect... Have you been here long? Are you staying much longer? Well, God has brought us, as they say, together.'

'Yes, do you remember...'

'To be sure, I remember; to be sure, I remember!' he interrupted me hurriedly; 'it's a thing of the past...'

'Well, what are you doing here, my dear Piotr Petrovitch?'

'I'm living, as you can see. Life's first-rate here; they're a merry lot here. Here I've found peace.'

And he sighed, and raised his eyes towards heaven.

'Are you in the service?'

'No, I'm not in the service yet, but I think I shall enter. But what's the service?... People are the chief thing. What people I have got to know here!...'

A boy came in with a bottle of champagne on a black tray.

'There, and this is a good fellow.... Isn't that true, Vasya, that you're a good fellow? To your health!'

The boy stood a minute, shook his head, decorously smiled, and went out.

'Yes, there are capital people here,' pursued Piotr Petrovitch; 'people of soul, of feeling.... Would you like me to introduce you?--such jolly chaps.... They'll all be glad to know you. I say... Bobrov is dead; that's a sad thing.'

'What Bobrov?'

'Sergay Bobrov; he was a capital fellow; he took me under his wing as an ignoramus from the wilds. And Panteley Gornostaev is dead. All dead, all!'

'Have you been living all the time in Moscow? You haven't been away to the country?'

'To the country!... My country place is sold.'

'Sold?'

'By auction.... There! what a pity you didn't buy it.'

'What are you going to live on, Piotr Petrovitch?'

'I shan't die of hunger; God will provide when I've no money. I shall have friends. And what is money.... Dust and ashes! Gold is dust!'

He shut his eyes, felt in his pocket, and held out to me in the palm of his hand two sixpences and a penny.

'What's that? Isn't it dust and ashes' (and the money flew on the floor). 'But you had better tell me, have you read Polezhaev?'

'Yes.'

'Have you seen Motchalov in Hamlet?'

'No, I haven't.'

'You've not seen him, not seen him!...' (And Karataev's face turned pale; his eyes strayed uneasily; he turned away; a faint spasm passed over his lips.) 'Ah, Motchalov, Motchalov! "To die--to sleep!"' he said in a thick voice:

'No more; and by a sleep to say we end
The heart-ache and the thousand natural shocks
That flesh is heir to; 'tis a consummation
Devoutly to be wished. To die--to sleep!'

'To sleep--to sleep,' he muttered several times.
'Tell me, please,' I began; but he went on with fire:
'Who would bear the whips and scorns of time,
The oppressor's wrong, the proud man's contumely,
The insolence of office and the spurns
That patient merit of the unworthy takes
When he himself might his quietus make
With a bare bodkin? Nymph in thy orisons
Be all my sins remembered.'

And he dropped his head on the table. He began stammering and talking at random. 'Within a month'! he delivered with fresh fire:

'A little month, or ere those shoes were old,
With which she followed my poor father's body,
Like Niobe--all tears; why she, even she--
O God! a beast, that wants discourse of reason,
Would have mourned longer!'

He raised a glass of champagne to his lips, but did not drink off the wine, and went on:

'For Hecuba!
What's Hecuba to him, or he to Hecuba,
That he should weep for her?...
But I'm a dull and muddy mettled-rascal,
Who calls me coward? gives me the lie i' the throat?
... Why I should take it; for it cannot be,
But I am pigeon-livered and lack gall
To make oppression bitter.'

Karataev put down the glass and grabbed at his head. I fancied I understood him.

'Well, well,' he said at last, 'one must not rake up the past. Isn't that so?' (and he laughed). 'To your health!'

'Shall you stay in Moscow?' I asked him.

'I shall die in Moscow!'

'Karataev!' called a voice in the next room; 'Karataev, where are you? Come here, my dear fellow!'

'They're calling me,' he said, getting up heavily from his seat. 'Good-bye; come and see me if you can; I live in....'

But next day, through unforeseen circumstances, I was obliged to leave Moscow, and I never saw Piotr Petrovitch Karataev again.

XIX   THE TRYST

I was sitting in a birchwood in autumn, about the middle of September. From early morning a fine rain had been falling, with intervals from time to time of warm sunshine; the weather was unsettled. The sky was at one time overcast with soft white clouds, at another it suddenly cleared in parts for an instant, and then behind the parting clouds could be seen a blue, bright and tender as a beautiful eye. I sat looking about and listening. The leaves faintly rustled over my head; from the sound of them alone one could tell what time of year it was. It was not the gay laughing tremor of the spring, nor the subdued whispering, the prolonged gossip of the summer, nor the chill and timid faltering of late autumn, but a scarcely audible, drowsy chatter. A slight breeze was faintly humming in the tree-tops. Wet with the rain, the copse in its inmost recesses was for ever changing as the sun shone or hid behind a cloud; at one moment it was all a radiance, as though suddenly everything were smiling in it; the slender stems of the thinly-growing birch-trees took all at once the soft lustre of white silk, the tiny leaves lying on the earth were on a sudden flecked and flaring with purplish gold, and the graceful stalks of the high, curly bracken, decked already in their autumn colour, the hue of an over-ripe grape, seemed interlacing in endless tangling crisscross before one's eyes; then suddenly again everything around was faintly bluish; the glaring tints died away instantaneously, the birch-trees stood all white and lustreless, white as fresh-fallen snow, before the cold rays of the winter sun have caressed it; and slily, stealthily there began drizzling and whispering through the wood the finest rain. The leaves on the birches were still almost all green, though perceptibly paler; only here and there stood one young leaf, all red or golden, and it was a sight to see how it flamed in the sunshine when the sunbeams suddenly pierced with tangled flecks of light through the thick network of delicate twigs, freshly washed by the sparkling rain. Not one bird could be heard; all were in hiding and silent, except that at times there rang out the metallic, bell-like sound of the jeering tomtit. Before halting in this birch copse I had been through a wood of tall aspen-trees with my dog. I confess I have no great liking for that tree, the aspen, with its pale-lilac trunk and the greyish-green metallic leaves which it flings high as it can, and unfolds in a quivering fan in the air; I do not care for the eternal shaking of its round, slovenly leaves, awkwardly hooked on to long stalks. It is only fine on some summer evenings when, rising singly above low undergrowth, it faces the reddening beams of the setting sun, and shines and quivers, bathed from root to top in one unbroken yellow glow, or when, on a clear windy day, it is all rippling, rustling, and whispering to the blue sky, and every leaf is, as it were, taken by a longing to break away, to fly off and soar into the distance. But, as a rule, I don't care for the tree, and so, not stopping to rest in the aspen wood, I made my way to the birch-copse, nestled down under one tree whose branches started low down near the ground, and were consequently capable of shielding me from the rain, and after admiring the surrounding view a little, I fell into that sweet untroubled sleep only known to sportsmen.

I cannot say how long I was asleep, but when I opened my eyes, all the depths of the wood were filled with sunlight, and in all directions across the joyously rustling leaves there were glimpses and, as it were, flashes of intense blue sky; the clouds had vanished, driven away by the blustering wind; the weather had changed to fair, and there was that feeling of peculiar dry freshness in the air which fills the heart with a sense of boldness, and is almost always a sure sign of a still bright evening after a rainy day. I was just about to get up and try my luck again when suddenly my eyes fell on a motionless human figure. I looked attentively; it was a young peasant girl. She was sitting twenty paces off, her head bent in thought, and her hands lying in her lap; one of them, half-open, held a big nosegay of wild flowers, which softly stirred on her checked petticoat with every breath. Her clean white smock, buttoned up at the throat and wrists, lay in short soft folds about her figure; two rows of big yellow beads fell from her neck to her bosom. She was very pretty. Her thick fair hair of a lovely, almost ashen hue, was parted into two carefully combed semicircles, under the narrow crimson fillet, which was brought down almost on to her forehead, white as ivory; the rest of her face was faintly tanned that golden hue which is only taken by a delicate skin. I could not see her eyes--she did not raise them; but I saw her delicate high eye-brows, her long lashes; they were wet, and on one of her cheeks there shone in the sun the traces of quickly drying tears, reaching right down to her rather pale lips. Her little head was very charming altogether; even her rather thick and snub nose did not spoil her. I was especially taken with the expression of her face; it was so simple and gentle, so sad and so full of childish wonder at its own sadness. She was obviously waiting for some one; something made a faint crackling in the wood; she raised her head at once, and looked round; in the transparent shade I caught a rapid glimpse of her eyes, large, clear, and timorous, like a fawn's. For a few instants she listened, not moving her wide open eyes from the spot whence the faint sound had come; she sighed, turned her head slowly, bent still lower, and began sorting her flowers. Her eyelids turned red, her lips twitched faintly, and a fresh tear rolled from under her thick eyelashes, and stood brightly shining on her cheek. Rather a long while passed thus; the poor girl did not stir, except for a despairing movement of her hands now and then--and she kept listening, listening.... Again there was a crackling sound in the wood: she started. The sound did not cease, grew more distinct, and came closer; at last one could hear quick resolute footsteps. She drew herself up and seemed frightened; her intent gaze was all aquiver, all aglow with expectation. Through the thicket quickly appeared the figure of a man. She gazed at it, suddenly flushed, gave a radiant, blissful smile, tried to rise, and sank back again at once, turned white and confused, and only raised her quivering, almost supplicating eyes to the man approaching, when the latter stood still beside her.

I looked at him with curiosity from my ambush. I confess he did not make an agreeable impression on me. He was, to judge by external signs, the pampered valet of some rich young gentleman. His attire betrayed pretensions to style and fashionable carelessness; he wore a shortish coat of a bronze colour, doubtless from his master's wardrobe, buttoned up to the top, a pink cravat with lilac ends, and a black velvet cap with a gold ribbon, pulled forward right on to his eyebrows. The round collar of his white shirt mercilessly propped up his ears and cut his cheeks, and his starched cuffs hid his whole hand to the red crooked fingers, adorned by gold and silver rings, with turquoise forget-me-nots. His red, fresh, impudent-looking face belonged to the order of faces which, as far as I have observed, are almost always repulsive to men, and unfortunately are very often attractive to women. He was obviously trying to give a scornful and bored expression to his coarse features; he was incessantly screwing up his milky grey eyes--small enough at all times; he scowled, dropped the corners of his mouth, affected to yawn, and with careless, though not perfectly natural nonchalance, pushed back his modishly curled red locks, or pinched the yellow hairs sprouting on his thick upper lip--in fact, he gave himself insufferable airs. He began his antics directly he caught sight of the young peasant girl waiting for him; slowly, with a swaggering step, he went up to her, stood a moment shrugging his shoulders, stuffed both hands in his coat pockets, and barely vouchsafing the poor girl a cursory and indifferent glance, he dropped on to the ground.

'Well,' he began, still gazing away, swinging his leg and yawning, 'have you been here long?'

The girl could not at once answer.

'Yes, a long while, Viktor Alexandritch,' she said at last, in a voice hardly audible.

'Ah!' (He took off his cap, majestically passed his hand over his thick, stiffly curled hair, which grew almost down to his eyebrows, and looking round him with dignity, he carelessly covered his precious head again.) 'And I quite forgot all about it. Besides, it rained!' (He yawned again.) 'Lots to do; there's no looking after everything; and he's always scolding. We set off to-morrow....'

'To-morrow?' uttered the young girl. And she fastened her startled eyes upon him.

'Yes, to-morrow.... Come, come, come, please!' he added, in a tone of vexation, seeing she was shaking all over and softly bending her head; 'please, Akulina, don't cry.

You know, I can't stand that.' (And he wrinkled up his snub nose.) 'Else I'll go away at once.... What silliness--snivelling!'

'There, I won't, I won't!' cried Akulina, hurriedly gulping down her tears with an effort. 'You are starting to-morrow?' she added, after a brief silence: 'when will God grant that we see each other again, Viktor Alexandritch?'

'We shall see each other, we shall see each other. If not next year--then later. The master wants to enter the service in Petersburg, I fancy,' he went on, pronouncing his words with careless condescension through his nose; 'and perhaps we shall go abroad too.'

'You will forget me, Viktor Alexandritch,' said Akulina mournfully.

'No, why so? I won't forget you; only you be sensible, don't be a fool; obey your father.... And I won't forget you--no-o.' (And he placidly stretched and yawned again.)

'Don't forget me, Viktor Alexandritch,' she went on in a supplicating voice. 'I think none could, love you as I do. I have given you everything.... You tell me to obey my father, Viktor Alexandritch.... But how can I obey my father?...'

'Why not?' (He uttered these words, as it were, from his stomach, lying on his back with his hands behind his head.)

'But how can I, Viktor Alexandritch?--you know yourself...'

She broke off. Viktor played with his steel watch-chain.

'You're not a fool, Akulina,' he said at last, 'so don't talk nonsense. I desire your good--do you understand me? To be sure, you're not a fool--not altogether a mere rustic, so to say; and your mother, too, wasn't always a peasant. Still you've no education--so you ought to do what you're told.'

'But it's fearful, Viktor Alexandritch.'

'O-oh! that's nonsense, my dear; a queer thing to be afraid of! What have you got there?' he added, moving closer to her; 'flowers?'

'Yes,' Akulina responded dejectedly. 'That's some wild tansy I picked,' she went on, brightening up a little; 'it's good for calves. And this is bud-marigold--against the king's evil. Look, what an exquisite flower! I've never seen such a lovely flower before. These are forget-me-nots, and that's mother-darling.... And these I picked for you,' she added, taking from under a yellow tansy a small bunch of blue corn-flowers, tied up with a thin blade of grass.' Do you like them?'

Viktor languidly held out his hand, took the flowers, carelessly sniffed at them, and began twirling them in his fingers, looking upwards. Akulina watched him.... In her mournful eyes there was such tender devotion, adoring submission and love. She was afraid of him, and did not dare to cry, and was saying good-bye to him and admiring him for the last time; while he lay, lolling like a sultan, and with magnanimous patience and condescension put up with her adoration. I must own, I glared indignantly at his red face, on which, under the affectation of scornful indifference, one could discern vanity soothed and satisfied. Akulina was so sweet at that instant; her whole soul was confidingly and passionately laid bare before him, full of longing and caressing tenderness, while he... he dropped the corn-flowers on the grass, pulled out of the side pocket of his coat a round eye-glass set in a brass rim, and began sticking it in his eye; but however much he tried to hold it with his frowning eyebrow, his pursed-up cheek and nose, the eye-glass kept tumbling out and falling into his hand.

'What is it?' Akulina asked at last in wonder.

'An eye-glass,' he answered with dignity.

'What for?'

'Why, to see better.'

'Show me.'

Viktor scowled, but gave her the glass.

'Don't break it; look out.'

'No fear, I won't break it.' (She put it to her eye.) 'I see nothing,' she said innocently.

'But you must shut your eye,' he retorted in the tones of a displeased teacher. (She shut the eye before which she held the glass.)

'Not that one, not that one, you fool! the other!' cried Viktor, and he took away his eye-glass, without allowing her to correct her mistake.

Akulina flushed a little, gave a faint laugh, and turned away.

'It's clear it's not for the likes of us,' she said.

'I should think not, indeed!'

The poor girl was silent and gave a deep sigh.

'Ah, Viktor Alexandritch, what it will be like for me to be without you!' she said suddenly.

Victor rubbed the glass on the lappet of his coat and put it back in his pocket.

'Yes, yes,'he said at last, 'at first it will be hard for you, certainly.' (He patted her condescendingly on the shoulder; she softly took his hand from her shoulder and timidly kissed it.) 'There, there, you're a good girl, certainly,' he went on, with a complacent smile; 'but what's to be done? You can see for yourself! me and the master could never stay on here; it will soon be winter now, and winter in the country--you know yourself--is simply disgusting. It's quite another thing in Petersburg! There there are simply such wonders as a silly girl like you could never fancy in your dreams! Such horses and streets, and society, and civilisation--simply marvellous!...' (Akulina listened with devouring attention, her lips slightly parted, like a child.) 'But what's the use,' he added, turning over on the ground, 'of my telling you all this? Of course, you can't understand it!'

'Why so, Viktor Alexandritch! I understand; I understood everything.'

'My eye, what a girl it is!'

Akulina looked down.

'You used not to talk to me like that once, Viktor Alexandritch,' she said, not lifting her eyes.

'Once?... once!... My goodness!' he remarked, as though in indignation.

They both were silent.

'It's time I was going,' said Viktor, and he was already rising on to his elbow.

'Wait a little longer,' Akulina besought him in a supplicating voice.

'What for?... Why, I've said good-bye to you.'

'Wait a little,' repeated Akulina.

Viktor lay down again and began whistling. Akulina never took her eyes off him. I could see that she was gradually being overcome by emotion; her lips twitched, her pale cheeks faintly glowed.

'Viktor Alexandritch,' she began at last in a broken voice, 'it's too bad of you... it is too bad of you, Viktor Alexandritch, indeed it is!'

'What's too bad?' he asked frowning, and he slightly raised his head and turned it towards her.

'It's too bad, Viktor Alexandritch. You might at least say one kind word to me at parting; you might have said one little word to me, a poor luckless forlorn.'...

'But what am I to say to you?'

'I don't know; you know that best, Viktor Alexandritch. Here you are going away, and one little word.... What have I done to deserve it?'

'You're such a queer creature! What can I do?'

'One word at least.'

'There, she keeps on at the same thing,' he commented with annoyance, and he got up.

'Don't be angry, Viktor Alexandritch,' she added hurriedly, with difficulty suppressing her tears.

I'm not angry, only you're silly.... What do you want? You know I can't marry you, can I? I can't, can I? What is it you want then, eh?' (He thrust his face forward as though expecting an answer, and spread his fingers out.)

'I want nothing... nothing,' she answered falteringly, and she ventured to hold out her trembling hands to him; 'but only a word at parting.'

And her tears fell in a torrent.

'There, that means she's gone off into crying,' said Viktor coolly, pushing down his cap on to his eyes.

'I want nothing,' she went on, sobbing and covering her face with her hands; 'but what is there before me in my family? what is there before me? what will happen to me? what will become of me, poor wretch? They will marry me to a hateful... poor forsaken... Poor me!'

'Sing away, sing away,' muttered Viktor in an undertone, fidgeting with impatience as he stood.

'And he might say one word, one word.... He might say, "Akulina... I..."'

Sudden heart-breaking sobs prevented her from finishing; she lay with her face in the grass and bitterly, bitterly she wept.... Her whole body shook convulsively, her neck fairly heaved.... Her long-suppressed grief broke out in a torrent at last. Viktor stood over her, stood a moment, shrugged his shoulders, turned away and strode off.

A few instants passed... she grew calmer, raised her head, jumped up, looked round and wrung her hands; she tried to run after him, but her legs gave way under her--she fell on her knees.... I could not refrain from rushing up to her; but, almost before she had time to look at me, making a superhuman effort she got up with a faint shriek and vanished behind the trees, leaving her flowers scattered on the ground.

I stood a minute, picked up the bunch of cornflowers, and went out of the wood into the open country. The sun had sunk low in the pale clear sky; its rays too seemed to have grown pale and chill; they did not shine; they were diffused in an unbroken, watery light. It was within half-an-hour of sunset, but there was scarcely any of the glow of evening. A gusty wind scurried to meet me across the yellow parched stubble; little curled-up leaves, scudding hurriedly before it, flew by across the road, along the edge of the copse; the side of the copse facing the fields like a wall, was all shaking and lighted up by tiny gleams, distinct, but not glowing; on the reddish plants, the blades of grass, the straws on all sides, were sparkling and stirring innumerable threads of autumn spider-webs. I stopped... I felt sad at heart: under the bright but chill smile of fading nature, the dismal dread of coming winter seemed to steal upon me. High overhead flew a cautious crow, heavily and sharply cleaving the air with his wings; he turned his head, looked sideways at me, flapped his wings and, cawing abruptly, vanished behind the wood; a great flock of pigeons flew up playfully from a threshing floor, and suddenly eddying round in a column, scattered busily about the country. Sure sign of autumn! Some one came driving over the bare hillside, his empty cart rattling loudly....

I turned homewards; but it was long before the figure of poor Akulina faded out of my mind, and her cornflowers, long since withered, are still in my keeping.

XX   THE HAMLET OF THE SHTCHIGRI DISTRICT

On one of my excursions I received an invitation to dine at the house of a rich landowner and sportsman, Alexandr Mihalitch G----. His property was four miles from the small village where I was staying at the time. I put on a frock-coat, an article without which I advise no one to travel, even on a hunting expedition, and betook myself to Alexandr Mihalitch's. The dinner was fixed for six o'clock; I arrived at five, and found already a great number of gentlemen in uniforms, in civilian dress, and other nondescript garments. My host met me cordially, but soon hurried away to the butler's pantry. He was expecting a great dignitary, and was in a state of agitation not quite in keeping with his independent position in society and his wealth. Alexandr Mihalitch had never married, and did not care for women; his house was the centre of a bachelor society. He lived in grand style; he had enlarged and sumptuously redecorated his ancestral mansion, spent fifteen thousand roubles on wine from Moscow every year, and enjoyed the highest public consideration. Alexandr Mihalitch had retired from the service ages ago, and had no ambition to gain official honours of any kind. What could have induced him to go out of his way to procure a guest of high official position, and to be in a state of excitement from early morning on the day of the grand dinner? That remains buried in the obscurity of the unknown, as a friend of mine, an attorney, is in the habit of saying when he is asked whether he takes bribes when kindly-disposed persons offer them.

On parting from my host, I began walking through the rooms. Almost all the guests were utterly unknown to me: about twenty persons were already seated at the card-tables. Among these devotees of preference were two warriors, with aristocratic but rather battered countenances, a few civilian officials, with tight high cravats and drooping dyed moustaches, such as are only to be found in persons of resolute character and strict conservative opinions: these conservative persons picked up their cards with dignity, and, without turning their heads, glared sideways at everyone who approached; and five or six local petty officials, with fair round bellies, fat, moist little hands, and staid, immovable little legs. These worthies spoke in a subdued voice, smiled benignly in all directions, held their cards close up to their very shirt-fronts, and when they trumped did not flap their cards on the table, but, on the contrary, shed them with an undulatory motion on the green cloth, and packed their tricks together with a slight, unassuming, and decorous swish. The rest of the company were sitting on sofas, or hanging in groups about the doors or at the windows; one gentleman, no longer young, though of feminine appearance, stood in a corner, fidgeting, blushing, and twisting the seal of his watch over his stomach in his embarrassment, though no one was paying any attention to him; some others in swallow-tail coats and checked trousers, the handiwork of the tailor and Perpetual Master of the Tailors Corporation, Firs Klyuhin, were talking together with extraordinary ease and liveliness, turning their bald, greasy heads from side to side unconstrainedly as they talked; a young man of twenty, short-sighted and fair-haired, dressed from head to foot in black, obviously shy, smiled sarcastically....

I was beginning, however, to feel bored, when suddenly I was joined by a young man, one Voinitsin by name, a student without a degree, who resided in the house of Alexandr Mihalitch in the capacity of...it would be hard to say precisely, of what. He was a first-rate shot, and could train dogs. I had known him before in Moscow. He was one of those young men who at every examination 'played at dumb-show,' that is to say, did not answer a single word to the professor's questions. Such persons were also designated 'the bearded students.' (You will gather that this was in long past days.) This was how it used to be: they would call Voinitsin, for example. Voinitsin, who had sat upright and motionless in his place, bathed in a hot perspiration from head to foot, slowly and aimlessly looked about him, got up, hurriedly buttoned up his undergraduate's uniform, and edged up to the examiner's table. 'Take a paper, please,' the professor would say to him pleasantly. Voinitsin would stretch out his hand, and with trembling fingers fumble at the pile of papers. 'No selecting, if you please,' observed, in a jarring voice, an assistant-examiner, an irritable old gentleman, a professor in some other faculty, conceiving a sudden hatred for the unlucky bearded one. Voinitsin resigned himself to his fate, took a paper, showed the number on it, and went and sat down by the window, while his predecessor was answering his question. At the window Voinitsin never took his eyes off his paper, except that at times he looked slowly round as before, though he did not move a muscle. But his predecessor would finish at last, and would be dismissed with, 'Good! you can go,' or even 'Good indeed, very good!' according to his abilities. Then they call Voinitsin: Voinitsin gets up, and with resolute step approaches the table. 'Read your question,' they tell him. Voinitsin raises the paper in both hands up to his very nose, slowly reads it, and slowly drops his hands. 'Well, now, your answer, please,' the same professor remarks languidly, throwing himself backwards, and crossing his arms over his breast.

There reigns the silence of the tomb. 'Why are you silent?' Voinitsin is mute. The assistant-examiner begins to be restive. 'Well, say something!' Voinitsin is as still as if he were dead. All his companions gaze inquisitively at the back of his thick, close-cropped, motionless head. The assistant-examiner's eyes are almost starting out of his head; he positively hates Voinitsin. 'Well, this is strange, really,' observes the other examiner. 'Why do you stand as if you were dumb? Come, don't you know it? if so, say so.' 'Let me take another question,' the luckless youth articulates thickly. The professors look at one another.' Well, take one,' the head-examiner answers, with a wave of the hand. Voinitsin again takes a paper, again goes to the window, again returns to the table, and again is silent as the grave. The assistant-examiner is capable of devouring him alive. At last they send him away and mark him a nought. You would think, 'Now, at least, he will go.' Not a bit of it! He goes back to his place, sits just as immovably to the end of the examination, and, as he goes out, exclaims: 'I've been on the rack! what ill-luck!' and the whole of that day he wanders about Moscow, clutching every now and then at his head, and bitterly cursing his luckless fate. He never, of course, touched a book, and the next day the same story was repeated.

So this was the Voinitsin who joined me. We talked about Moscow, about sport.

'Would you like me,' he whispered to me suddenly, 'to introduce you to the first wit of these parts?'

'If you will be so kind.'

Voinitsin led me up to a little man, with a high tuft of hair on his forehead and moustaches, in a cinnamon-coloured frock-coat and striped cravat. His yellow, mobile features were certainly full of cleverness and sarcasm. His lips were perpetually curved in a flitting ironical smile; little black eyes, screwed up with an impudent expression, looked out from under uneven lashes. Beside him stood a country gentleman, broad, soft, and sweet--a veritable sugar-and-honey mixture--with one eye. He laughed in anticipation at the witticisms of the little man, and seemed positively melting with delight. Voinitsin presented me to the wit, whose name was Piotr Petrovitch Lupihin. We were introduced and exchanged the preliminary civilities.

'Allow me to present to you my best friend,' said Lupihin suddenly in a strident voice, seizing the sugary gentleman by the arm.

'Come, don't resist, Kirila Selifanitch,' he added; 'we're not going to bite you. I commend him to you,' he went on, while the embarrassed Kirila Selifanitch bowed with about as much grace as if he were undergoing a surgical operation; 'he's a most superior gentleman. He enjoyed excellent health up to the age of fifty, then suddenly conceived the idea of doctoring his eyes, in consequence of which he has lost one. Since then he doctors his peasants with similar success.... They, to be sure, repay with similar devotion...'

'What a fellow it is!' muttered Kirila Selifanitch. And he laughed.

'Speak out, my friend; eh, speak out!' Lupihin rejoined. 'Why, they may elect you a judge; I shouldn't wonder, and they will, too, you see. Well, to be sure, the secretaries will do the thinking for you, we may assume; but you know you'll have to be able to speak, anyhow, even if only to express the ideas of others. Suppose the governor comes and asks, "Why is it the judge stammers?" And they'd say, let's assume, "It's a paralytic stroke." "Then bleed him," he'd say. And it would be highly indecorous, in your position, you'll admit.'

The sugary gentleman was positively rolling with mirth.

'You see he laughs,' Lupihin pursued with a malignant glance at Kirila Selifanitch's heaving stomach. 'And why shouldn't he laugh?' he added, turning to me: 'he has enough to eat, good health, and no children; his peasants aren't mortgaged--to be sure, he doctors them--and his wife is cracked.' (Kirila Selifanitch turned a little away as though he were not listening, but he still continued to chuckle.) 'I laugh too, while my wife has eloped with a land-surveyor.' (He grinned.) 'Didn't you know that? What! Why, one fine day she ran away with him and left me a letter.

"Dear Piotr Petrovitch," she said, "forgive me: carried away by passion, I am leaving with the friend of my heart."... And the land-surveyor only took her fancy through not cutting his nails and wearing tight trousers. You're surprised at that? "Why, this," she said, "is a man with no dissimulation about him."... But mercy on us! Rustic fellows like us speak the truth too plainly. But let us move away a bit.... It's not for us to stand beside a future judge.'...

He took me by the arm, and we moved away to a window.

'I've the reputation of a wit here,' he said to me, in the course of conversation. 'You need not believe that. I'm simply an embittered man, and I do my railing aloud: that's how it is I'm so free and easy in my speech. And why should I mince matters, if you come to that; I don't care a straw for anyone's opinion, and I've nothing to gain; I'm spiteful--what of that? A spiteful man, at least, needs no wit. And, however enlightening it may be, you won't believe it.... I say, now, I say, look at our host! There! what is he running to and fro like that for? Upon my word, he keeps looking at his watch, smiling, perspiring, putting on a solemn face, keeping us all starving for our dinner! Such a prodigy! a real court grandee! Look, look, he's running again--bounding, positively, look!'

And Lupihin laughed shrilly.

'The only pity is, there are no ladies,' he resumed with a deep sigh; 'it's a bachelor party, else that's when your humble servant gets on. Look, look,' he cried suddenly: 'Prince Kozelsky's come--that tall man there, with a beard, in yellow gloves. You can see at once he's been abroad... and he always arrives as late. He's as heavy, I tell you, by himself, as a pair of merchant's horses, and you should see how condescendingly he talks with your humble servant, how graciously he deigns to smile at the civilities of our starving mothers and daughters!... And he sometimes sets up for a wit, but he is only here for a little time; and oh, his witticisms! It's for all the world like hacking at a ship's cable with a blunt knife. He can't bear me.... I'm going to bow to him.'

And Lupihin ran off to meet the prince.

'And here comes my special enemy,' he observed, turning all at once to me. 'Do you see that fat man with the brown face and the bristles on his head, over there, that's got his cap clutched in his hand, and is creeping along by the wall and glaring in all directions like a wolf? I sold him for 400 roubles a horse worth 1000, and that stupid animal has a perfect right now to despise me; though all the while he is so destitute of all faculty of imagination, especially in the morning before his tea, or after dinner, that if you say "Good morning!" to him, he'll answer, "Is it?" 'And here comes the general,' pursued Lupihin, 'the civilian general, a retired, destitute general. He has a daughter of beetroot-sugar, and a manufactory with scrofula.... Beg pardon, I've got it wrong... but there, you understand. Ah! and the architect's turned up here! A German, and wears moustaches, and does not understand his business--a natural phenomenon!... though what need for him to understand his business so long as he takes bribes and sticks in pillars everywhere to suit the tastes of our pillars of society!'

Lupihin chuckled again.... But suddenly a wave of excitement passed over the whole house. The grandee had arrived. The host positively rushed into the hall. After him ran a few devoted members of the household and eager guests.... The noisy talk was transformed into a subdued pleasant chat, like the buzzing of bees in spring within their hives. Only the turbulent wasp, Lupihin, and the splendid drone, Kozelsky, did not subdue their voices.... And behold, at last, the queen!--the great dignitary entered. Hearts bounded to meet him, sitting bodies rose; even the gentleman who had bought a horse from Lupihin poked his chin into his chest. The great personage kept up his dignity in an inimitable manner; throwing his head back, as though he were bowing, he uttered a few words of approbation, of which each was prefaced by the syllable er , drawled through his nose; with a sort of devouring indignation he looked at Prince Kozelsky's democratic beard, and gave the destitute general with the factory and the daughter the forefinger of his right hand. After a few minutes, in the course of which the dignitary had had time to observe twice that he was very glad he was not late for dinner, the whole company trooped into the dining-room, the swells first.

There is no need to describe to the reader how they put the great man in the most important place, between the civilian general and the marshal of the province, a man of an independent and dignified expression of face, in perfect keeping with his starched shirt-front, his expanse of waistcoat, and his round snuff-box full of French snuff; how our host bustled about, and ran up and down, fussing and pressing the guests to eat, smiling at the great man's back in passing, and hurriedly snatching a plate of soup or a bit of bread in a corner like a schoolboy; how the butler brought in a fish more than a yard long, with a nosegay in its mouth; how the surly-looking foot-men in livery sullenly plied every gentleman, now with Malaga, now dry Madeira; and how almost all the gentlemen, particularly the more elderly ones, drank off glass after glass with an air of reluctantly resigning themselves to a sense of duty; and finally, how they began popping champagne bottles and proposing toasts: all that is probably only too well known to the reader. But what struck me as especially noteworthy was the anecdote told us by the great man himself amid a general delighted silence. Someone--I fancy it was the destitute general, a man familiar with modern literature--referred to the influence of women in general, and especially on young men. 'Yes, yes,' chimed in the great man, 'that's true; but young men ought to be kept in strict subjection, or else, very likely, they'll go out of their senses over every petticoat.' (A smile of child-like delight flitted over the faces of all the guests; positive gratitude could be seen in one gentleman's eyes.) 'For young men are idiots.' (The great man, I suppose for the sake of greater impressiveness, sometimes changed the accepted accentuation of words.)

'My son, Ivan, for instance,' he went on; 'the fool's only just twenty--and all at once he comes to me and says: "Let me be married, father." I told him he was a fool; told him he must go into the service first.... Well, there was despair--tears... but with me... no nonsense.' (The words 'no nonsense' the great man seemed to enunciate more with his stomach than his lips; he paused and glanced majestically at his neighbour, the general, while he raised his eyebrows higher than any one could have expected. The civilian general nodded agreeably a little on one side, and with extraordinary rapidity winked with the eye turned to the great man.) 'And what do you think?' the great man began again: 'now he writes to me himself, and thanks me for looking after him when he was a fool.... So that's the way to act.' All the guests, of course, were in complete agreement with the speaker, and seemed quite cheered up by the pleasure and instruction they derived from him.... After dinner, the whole party rose and moved into the drawing-room with a great deal of noise--decorous, however; and, as it were, licensed for the occasion.... They sat down to cards.

I got through the evening somehow, and charging my coachman to have my carriage ready at five o'clock next morning, I went to my room. But I was destined, in the course of that same day, to make the acquaintance of a remarkable man.

In consequence of the great number of guests staying in the house, no one had a bedroom to himself. In the small, greenish, damp room to which I was conducted by Alexandr Mihalitch's butler, there was already another guest, quite undressed. On seeing me, he quickly ducked under the bed-clothes, covered himself up to the nose, turned a little on the soft feather-bed, and lay quiet, keeping a sharp look-out from under the round frill of his cotton night-cap. I went up to the other bed (there were only two in the room), undressed, and lay down in the damp sheets. My neighbour turned over in bed.... I wished him good-night.

Half-an-hour went by. In spite of all my efforts, I could not get to sleep: aimless and vague thoughts kept persistently and monotonously dragging one after another on an endless chain, like the buckets of a hydraulic machine.

'You're not asleep, I fancy?' observed my neighbour.

'No, as you see,' I answered. 'And you're not sleepy either, are you?'

'I'm never sleepy.'

'How's that?'

'Oh! I go to sleep--I don't know what for. I lie in bed, and lie in bed, and so get to sleep.'

'Why do you go to bed before you feel sleepy?'

'Why, what would you have me do?'

I made no answer to my neighbour's question.

'I wonder,' he went on, after a brief silence, 'how it is there are no fleas here? Where should there be fleas if not here, one wonders?'

'You seem to regret them,' I remarked.

'No, I don't regret them; but I like everything to be consecutive.'

'O-ho!' thought I; 'what words he uses.'

My neighbour was silent again.

'Would you like to make a bet with me?' he said again, rather loudly.

'What about?'

I began to be amused by him.

'Hm... what about? Why, about this: I'm certain you take me for a fool.'

'Really,' I muttered, astounded.

'For an ignoramus, for a rustic of the steppes.... Confess....'

'I haven't the pleasure of knowing you,' I responded. 'What can make you infer?...'

'Why, the sound of your voice is enough; you answer me so carelessly.... But I'm not at all what you suppose....'

'Allow me....'

'No, you allow me. In the first place, I speak French as well as you, and German even better; secondly, I have spent three years abroad--in Berlin alone I lived eight months. I've studied Hegel, honoured sir; I know Goethe by heart: add to that, I was a long while in love with a German professor's daughter, and was married at home to a consumptive lady, who was bald, but a remarkable personality. So I'm a bird of your feather; I'm not a barbarian of the steppes, as you imagine.... I too have been bitten by reflection, and there's nothing obvious about me.'

I raised my head and looked with redoubled attention at the queer fellow. By the dim light of the night-lamp I could hardly distinguish his features.

'There, you're looking at me now,' he went on, setting his night-cap straight, 'and probably you're asking yourself, "How is it I didn't notice him to-day?" I'll tell you why you didn't notice me: because I didn't raise my voice; because I get behind other people, hang about doorways, and talk to no one; because, when the butler passes me with a tray, he raises his elbow to the level of my shoulder.... And how is it all that comes about? From two causes: first, I'm poor; and secondly, I've grown humble.... Tell the truth, you didn't notice me, did you?'

'Certainly, I've not had the pleasure....'

'There, there,' he interrupted me, 'I knew that.'

He raised himself and folded his arms; the long shadow of his cap was bent from the wall to the ceiling.

'And confess, now,' he added, with a sudden sideway glance at me; 'I must strike you as a queer fellow, an original, as they say, or possibly as something worse: perhaps you think I affect to be original!'

'I must repeat again that I don't know you....'

He looked down an instant.

'Why have I begun talking so unexpectedly to you, a man utterly a stranger?--the Lord, the Lord only knows!' (He sighed.) 'Not through the natural affinity of our souls! Both you and I are respectable people, that's to say, egoists: neither of us has the least concern with the other; isn't it so? But we are neither of us sleepy... so why not chat? I'm in the mood, and that's rare with me. I'm shy, do you see? and not shy because I'm a provincial, of no rank and poor, but because I'm a fearfully vain person. But at times, under favourable circumstances, occasions which I could not, however, particularise nor foresee, my shyness vanishes completely, as at this moment, for instance. At this moment you might set me face to face with the Grand Lama, and I'd ask him for a pinch of snuff. But perhaps you want to go to sleep?'

'Quite the contrary,' I hastened to respond; 'it is a pleasure for me to talk to you.'

'That is, I amuse you, you mean to say.... All the better.... And so, I tell you, they call me here an original; that's what they call me when my name is casually mentioned, among other gossip. No one is much concerned about my fate.... They think it wounds me.... Oh, good Lord! if they only knew... it's just what's my ruin, that there is absolutely nothing original in me--nothing, except such freaks as, for instance, my conversation at this moment with you; but such freaks are not worth a brass farthing. That's the cheapest and lowest sort of originality.'

He turned facing me, and waved his hands.

'Honoured sir!' he cried, 'I am of the opinion that life on earth's only worth living, as a rule, for original people; it's only they who have a right to live. Man verre n'est pas grand, maisje bois dans mon verre, said someone. Do you see,' he added in an undertone, 'how well I pronounce French? What is it to one if one's a capacious brain, and understands everything, and knows a lot, and keeps pace with the age, if one's nothing of one's own, of oneself! One more storehouse for hackneyed commonplaces in the world; and what good does that do to anyone? No, better be stupid even, but in one's own way! One should have a flavour of one's own, one's individual flavour; that's the thing! And don't suppose that I am very exacting as to that flavour.... God forbid! There are no end of original people of the sort I mean: look where you will--there's an original: every live man is an original; but I am not to be reckoned among them!'

'And yet,' he went on, after a brief silence, 'in my youth what expectations I aroused! What a high opinion I cherished of my own individuality before I went abroad, and even, at first, after my return! Well, abroad I kept my ears open, held aloof from everyone, as befits a man like me, who is always seeing through things by himself, and at the end has not understood the A B C!'

'An original, an original!' he hurried on, shaking his head reproachfully....' They call me an original.... In reality, it turns out that there's not a man in the world less original than your humble servant. I must have been born even in imitation of someone else.... Oh, dear! It seems I am living, too, in imitation of the various authors studied by me; in the sweat of my brow I live: and I've studied, and fallen in love, and married, in fact, as it were, not through my own will--as it were, fulfilling some sort of duty, or sort of fate-- who's to make it out?'

He tore the nightcap off his head and flung it on the bed.

'Would you like me to tell you the story of my life?' he asked me in an abrupt voice; 'or, rather, a few incidents of my life?'

'Please do me the favour.'

'Or, no, I'd better tell you how I got married. You see marriage is an important thing, the touchstone that tests the whole man: in it, as in a glass, is reflected.... But that sounds too hackneyed.... If you'll allow me, I'll take a pinch of snuff.'

He pulled a snuff-box from under his pillow, opened it, and began again, waving the open snuff-box about.

'Put yourself, honoured sir, in my place.... Judge for yourself, what, now what, tell me as a favour: what benefit could I derive from the encyclopaedia of Hegel? What is there in common, tell me, between that encyclopaedia and Russian life? and how would you advise me to apply it to our life, and not it, the encyclopaedia only, but German philosophy in general.... I will say more--science itself?'

He gave a bound on the bed and muttered to himself, gnashing his teeth angrily.

'Ah, that's it, that's it!... Then why did you go trailing off abroad? Why didn't you stay at home and study the life surrounding you on the spot? You might have found out its needs and its future, and have come to a clear comprehension of your vocation, so to say.... But, upon my word,' he went on, changing his tone again as though timidly justifying himself, 'where is one to study what no sage has yet inscribed in any book? I should have been glad indeed to take lessons of her--of Russian life, I mean--but she's dumb, the poor dear. You must take her as she is; but that's beyond my power: you must give me the inference; you must present me with a conclusion. Here you have a conclusion too: listen to our wise men of Moscow--they're a set of nightingales worth listening to, aren't they? Yes, that's the pity of it, that they pipe away like Kursk nightingales, instead of talking as the people talk.... Well, I thought, and thought--

"Science, to be sure," I thought, "is everywhere the same, and truth is the same"--so I was up and off, in God's name, to foreign parts, to the heathen.... What would you have? I was infatuated with youth and conceit; I didn't want, you know, to get fat before my time, though they say it's healthy. Though, indeed, if nature doesn't put the flesh on your bones, you won't see much fat on your body!'

'But I fancy,' he added, after a moment's thought, 'I promised to tell you how I got married--listen. First, I must tell you that my wife is no longer living; secondly... secondly, I see I must give you some account of my youth, or else you won't be able to make anything out of it.... But don't you want to go to sleep?'

'No, I'm not sleepy.'

'That's good news. Hark!... how vulgarly Mr. Kantagryuhin is snoring in the next room! I was the son of parents of small property--I say parents, because, according to tradition, I had once had a father as well as a mother, I don't remember him: he was a narrow-minded man, I've been told, with a big nose, freckles, and red hair; he used to take snuff on one side of his nose only; his portrait used to hang in my mother's bedroom, and very hideous he was in a red uniform with a black collar up to his ears. They used to take me to be whipped before him, and my mother used always on such occasions to point to him, saying, "He would give it to you much more if he were here." You can imagine what an encouraging effect that had on me. I had no brother nor sister--that's to say, speaking accurately, I had once had a brother knocking about, with the English disease in his neck, but he soon died.... And why ever, one wonders, should the English disease make its way to the Shtchigri district of the province of Kursk? But that's neither here nor there. My mother undertook my education with all the vigorous zeal of a country lady of the steppes: she undertook it from the solemn day of my birth till the time when my sixteenth year had come.... You are following my story?'

'Yes, please go on.'

'All right. Well, when I was sixteen, my mother promptly dismissed my teacher of French, a German, Filipovitch, from the Greek settlement of Nyezhin. She conducted me to Moscow, put down my name for the university, and gave up her soul to the Almighty, leaving me in the hands of my uncle, the attorney Koltun-Babur, one of a sort well-known not only in the Shtchigri district. My uncle, the attorney Koltun-Babur, plundered me to the last half-penny, after the custom of guardians.... But again that's neither here nor there. I entered the university--I must do so much justice to my mother--rather well grounded; but my lack of originality was even then apparent. My childhood was in no way distinguished from the childhood of other boys; I grew up just as languidly and dully--much as if I were under a feather-bed--just as early I began repeating poetry by heart and moping under the pretence of a dreamy inclination... for what?--why, for the beautiful... and so on. In the university I went on in the same way; I promptly got into a "circle." Times were different then.... But you don't know, perhaps, what sort of thing a student's "circle" is? I remember Schiller said somewhere:

Gefaehrlich ist's den Leu zu wecken
Und schrecklich ist des Tigers Zahn,
Doch das schrecklichste der Schrecken
Das ist der Mensch in seinem Wahn!

He didn't mean that, I can assure you; he meant to say: Das ist ein circle in der Stadt Moskau !'

'But what do you find so awful in the circle?' I asked.

My neighbour snatched his cap and pulled it down on to his nose.

'What do I find so awful?' he shouted. 'Why, this: the circle is the destruction of all independent development; the circle is a hideous substitute for society, woman, life; the circle... oh, wait a bit, I'll tell you what a circle is! A circle is a slothful, dull living side by side in common, to which is attached a serious significance and a show of rational activity; the circle replaces conversation by debate, trains you in fruitless discussion, draws you away from solitary, useful labour, develops in you the itch for authorship--deprives you, in fact, of all freshness and virgin vigour of soul. The circle--why, it's vulgarity and boredom under the name of brotherhood and friendship! a concatenation of misunderstandings and cavillings under the pretence of openness and sympathy: in the circle--thanks to the right of every friend, at all hours and seasons, to poke his unwashed fingers into the very inmost soul of his comrade--no one has a single spot in his soul pure and undefiled; in the circle they fall down before the shallow, vain, smart talker and the premature wise-acre, and worship the rhymester with no poetic gift, but full of "subtle" ideas; in the circle young lads of seventeen talk glibly and learnedly of women and of love, while in the presence of women they are dumb or talk to them like a book--and what do they talk about? The circle is the hot-bed of glib fluency; in the circle they spy on one another like so many police officials.... Oh, circle! thou'rt not a circle, but an enchanted ring, which has been the ruin of many a decent fellow!'

'Come, you're exaggerating, allow me to observe,' I broke in.

My neighbour looked at me in silence.

'Perhaps, God knows, perhaps. But, you see, there's only one pleasure left your humble servant, and that's exaggeration--well, that was the way I spent four years in Moscow. I can't tell you, my dear sir, how quickly, how fearfully quickly, that time passed; it's positively painful and vexatious to remember. Some mornings one gets up, and it's like sliding downhill on little sledges.... Before one can look round, one's flown to the bottom; it's evening already, and already the sleepy servant is pulling on one's coat; one dresses, and trails off to a friend, and may be smokes a pipe, drinks weak tea in glasses, and discusses German philosophy, love, the eternal sunshine of the spirit, and other far-fetched topics. But even there I met original, independent people: however some men stultify themselves and warp themselves out of shape, still nature asserts itself; I alone, poor wretch, moulded myself like soft wax, and my pitiful little nature never made the faintest resistance! Meantime I had reached my twenty-first year. I came into possession of my inheritance, or, more correctly speaking, that part of my inheritance which my guardian had thought fit to leave me, gave a freed house-serf Vassily Kudryashev a warranty to superintend all my patrimony, and set off abroad to Berlin. I was abroad, as I have already had the pleasure of telling you, three years. Well. There too, abroad too, I remained the same unoriginal creature. In the first place, I need not say that of Europe, of European life, I really learnt nothing. I listened to German professors and read German books on their birthplace: that was all the difference. I led as solitary a life as any monk; I got on good terms with a retired lieutenant, weighed down, like myself, by a thirst for knowledge but always dull of comprehension, and not gifted with a flow of words; I made friends with slow-witted families from Penza and other agricultural provinces, hung about cafes , read the papers, in the evening went to the theatre. With the natives I associated very little; I talked to them with constraint, and never had one of them to see me at my own place, except two or three intrusive fellows of Jewish extraction, who were constantly running in upon me and borrowing money--thanks to der Russe's gullibility. A strange freak of chance brought me at last to the house of one of my professors. It was like this: I came to him to enter my name for a course of lectures, and he, all of a sudden, invited me to an evening party at his house. This professor had two daughters, of twenty-seven, such stumpy little things--God bless them!--with such majestic noses, frizzed curls and pale-blue eyes, and red hands with white nails. One was called Linchen and the other Minchen. I began to go to the professor's. I ought to tell you that the professor was not exactly stupid, but seemed, as it were, dazed: in his professorial desk he spoke fairly consecutively, but at home he lisped, and always had his spectacles on his forehead--he was a very learned man, though. Well, suddenly it seemed to me that I was in love with Linchen, and for six whole months this impression remained. I talked to her, it's true, very little--it was more that I looked at her; but I used to read various touching passages aloud to her, to press her hand on the sly, and to dream beside her in the evenings, gazing persistently at the moon, or else simply up aloft. Besides, she made such delicious coffee! One asks oneself--what more could one desire? Only one thing troubled me: at the very moments of ineffable bliss, as it's called, I always had a sort of sinking in the pit of the stomach, and a cold shudder ran down my back. At last I could not stand such happiness, and ran away. Two whole years after that I was abroad: I went to Italy, stood before the Transfiguration in Rome, and before the Venus in Florence, and suddenly fell into exaggerated raptures, as though an attack of delirium had come upon me; in the evenings I wrote verses, began a diary; in fact, there too I behaved just like everyone else. And just mark how easy it is to be original! I take no interest, for instance, in painting and sculpture.... But simply saying so aloud... no, it was impossible! I must needs take a cicerone, and run to gaze at the frescoes.'...

He looked down again, and again pulled off his nightcap.

'Well, I came back to my own country at last,' he went on in a weary voice. 'I went to Moscow. In Moscow a marvellous transformation took place in me. Abroad I was mostly silent, but now suddenly I began to talk with unexpected smartness, and at the same time I began to conceive all sorts of ideas of myself. There were kindly disposed persons to be found, to whom I seemed all but a genius; ladies listened sympathetically to my diatribes; but I was not able to keep on the summit of my glory. One fine morning a slander sprang up about me (who had originated it, I don't know; it must have been some old maid of the male sex--there are any number of such old maids in Moscow); it sprang up and began to throw off outshoots and tendrils like a strawberry plant. I was abashed, tried to get out of it, to break through its clinging toils--that was no good.... I went away. Well, in that too I showed that I was an absurd person; I ought to have calmly waited for the storm to blow over, just as one waits for the end of nettle-rash, and the same kindly-disposed persons would have opened their arms to me again, the same ladies would have smiled approvingly again at my remarks.... But what's wrong is just that I'm not an original person. Conscientious scruples, please to observe, had been stirred up in me; I was somehow ashamed of talk, talk without ceasing, nothing but talk--yesterday in Arbat, to-day in Truba, to-morrow in Sivtsevy-Vrazhky, and all about the same thing.... But if that is what people want of me? Look at the really successful men in that line: they don't ask its use; on the contrary, it's all they need; some will keep their tongues wagging twenty years together, and always in one direction.... That's what comes of self-confidence and conceit! I had that too, conceit--indeed, even now it's not altogether stifled.... But what was wrong was that--I say again, I'm not an original person--I stopped midway: nature ought to have given me far more conceit or none at all. But at first I felt the change a very hard one; moreover, my stay abroad too had utterly drained my resources, while I was not disposed to marry a merchant's daughter, young, but flabby as a jelly, so I retired to my country place. I fancy,' added my neighbour, with another glance sideways at me, 'I may pass over in silence the first impressions of country life, references to the beauty of nature, the gentle charm of solitude, etc.'

'You can, indeed,' I put in.

'All the more,' he continued, 'as all that's nonsense; at least, as far as I'm concerned. I was as bored in the country as a puppy locked up, though I will own that on my journey home, when I passed through the familiar birchwood in spring for the first time, my head was in a whirl and my heart beat with a vague, sweet expectation. But these vague expectations, as you're well aware, never come to pass; on the other hand, very different things do come to pass, which you don't at all expect, such as cattle disease, arrears, sales by auction, and so on, and so on. I managed to make a shift from day to day with the aid of my agent, Yakov, who replaced the former superintendent, and turned out in the course of time to be as great, if not a greater robber, and over and above that poisoned my existence by the smell of his tarred boots; suddenly one day I remembered a family I knew in the neighbourhood, consisting of the widow of a retired colonel and her two daughters, ordered out my droshky, and set off to see them. That day must always be a memorable one for me; six months later I was married to the retired colonel's second daughter!...'

The speaker dropped his head, and lifted his hands to heaven.

'And now,' he went on warmly, 'I couldn't bear to give you an unfavourable opinion of my late wife. Heaven forbid! She was the most generous, sweetest creature, a loving nature capable of any sacrifice, though I must between ourselves confess that if I had not had the misfortune to lose her, I should probably not be in a position to be talking to you to-day; since the beam is still there in my barn, to which I repeatedly made up my mind to hang myself!'

'Some pears,' he began again, after a brief pause, 'need to lie in an underground cellar for a time, to come, as they say, to their real flavour; my wife, it seems, belonged to a similar order of nature's works. It's only now that I do her complete justice. It's only now, for instance, that memories of some evenings I spent with her before marriage no longer awaken the slightest bitterness, but move me almost to tears. They were not rich people; their house was very old-fashioned and built of wood, but comfortable; it stood on a hill between an overgrown courtyard and a garden run wild. At the bottom of the hill ran a river, which could just be seen through the thick leaves. A wide terrace led from the house to the garden; before the terrace flaunted a long flower-bed, covered with roses; at each end of the flower-bed grew two acacias, which had been trained to grow into the shape of a screw by its late owner. A little farther, in the very midst of a thicket of neglected and overgrown raspberries, stood an arbour, smartly painted within, but so old and tumble-down outside that it was depressing to look at it. A glass door led from the terrace into the drawing-room; in the drawing-room this was what met the eye of the inquisitive spectator: in the various corners stoves of Dutch tiles, a squeaky piano to the right, piled with manuscript music, a sofa, covered with faded blue material with a whitish pattern, a round table, two what-nots of china and glass, knicknacks of the Catherine period; on the wall the well-known picture of a flaxen-haired girl with a dove on her breast and eyes turned upwards; on the table a vase of fresh roses. You see how minutely I describe it. In that drawing-room, on that terrace, was rehearsed all the tragi-comedy of my love. The colonel's wife herself was an ill-natured old dame, whose voice was always hoarse with spite--a petty, snappish creature. Of the daughters, one, Vera, did not differ in any respect from the common run of young ladies of the provinces; the other, Sofya, I fell in love with. The two sisters had another little room too, their common bedroom, with two innocent little wooden bedsteads, yellowish albums, mignonette, portraits of friends sketched in pencil rather badly (among them was one gentleman with an exceptionally vigorous expression of face and a still more vigorous signature, who had in his youth raised disproportionate expectations, but had come, like all of us, to nothing), with busts of Goethe and Schiller, German books, dried wreaths, and other objects, kept as souvenirs. But that room I rarely and reluctantly entered; I felt stifled there somehow. And, too, strange to say, I liked Sofya best of all when I was sitting with my back to her, or still more, perhaps, when I was thinking or dreaming about her in the evening on the terrace. At such times I used to gaze at the sunset, at the trees, at the tiny leaves, already in darkness, but standing out sharply against the rosy sky; in the drawing-room Sofya sat at the piano continually playing over and over again some favourite, passionately pathetic phrase from Beethoven; the ill-natured old lady snored peacefully, sitting on the sofa; in the dining-room, which was flooded by a glow of lurid light, Vera was bustling about getting tea; the samovar hissed merrily as though it were pleased at something; the cracknels snapped with a pleasant crispness, and the spoons tinkled against the cups; the canary, which trilled mercilessly all day, was suddenly still, and only chirruped from time to time, as though asking for something; from a light transparent cloud there fell a few passing drops of rain.... And I would sit and sit, listen, listen, and look, my heart would expand, and again it seemed to me that I was in love. Well, under the influence of such an evening, I one day asked the old lady for her daughter's hand, and two months later I was married. It seemed to me that I loved her.... By now, indeed, it's time I should know, but, by God, even now I don't know whether I loved Sofya. She was a sweet creature, clever, silent, and warm-hearted, but God only knows from what cause, whether from living too long in the country, or for some other reason, there was at the bottom of her heart (if only there is a bottom to the heart) a secret wound, or, to put it better, a little open sore which nothing could heal, to which neither she nor I could give a name. Of the existence of this sore, of course, I only guessed after marriage. The struggles I had over it... nothing availed! When I was a child I had a little bird, which had once been caught by the cat in its claws; it was saved and tended, but the poor bird never got right; it moped, it pined, it ceased to sing.... It ended by a cat getting into its open cage one night and biting off its beak, after which it made up its mind at last to die. I don't know what cat had caught my wife in its claws, but she too moped and pined just like my unlucky bird. Sometimes she obviously made an effort to shake herself, to rejoice in the open air, in the sunshine and freedom; she would try, and shrink up into herself again. And, you know she loved me; how many times has she assured me that she had nothing left to wish for?--oof! damn my soul! and the light was fading out of her eyes all the while. I wondered whether there hadn't been something in her past. I made investigations: there was nothing forthcoming. Well, you may form your own judgment; an original man would have shrugged his shoulders and heaved a sigh or two, perhaps, and would have proceeded to live his own life; but I, not being an original creature, began to contemplate a beam and halter. My wife was so thoroughly permeated by all the habits of an old maid--Beethoven, evening walks, mignonette, corresponding with her friends, albums, et cetera--that she never could accustom herself to any other mode of life, especially to the life of the mistress of a house; and yet it seemed absurd for a married woman to be pining in vague melancholy and singing in the evening: "Waken her not at the dawn!"'

'Well, we were blissful after that fashion for three years; in the fourth, Sofya died in her first confinement, and, strange to say, I had felt, as it were, beforehand that she would not be capable of giving me a daughter or a son--of giving the earth a new inhabitant. I remember how they buried her. It was in the spring. Our parish church was small and old, the screen was blackened, the walls bare, the brick floor worn into hollows in parts; there was a big, old-fashioned holy picture in each half of the choir. They brought in the coffin, placed it in the middle before the holy gates, covered it with a faded pall, set three candlesticks about it. The service commenced. A decrepit deacon, with a little shock of hair behind, belted low down with a green kerchief, was mournfully mumbling before a reading-desk; a priest, also an old man, with a kindly, purblind face, in a lilac cassock with yellow flowers on it, served the mass for himself and the deacon. At all the open windows the fresh young leaves were stirring and whispering, and the smell of the grass rose from the churchyard outside; the red flame of the wax-candles paled in the bright light of the spring day; the sparrows were twittering all over the church, and every now and then there came the ringing cry of a swallow flying in under the cupola. In the golden motes of the sunbeams the brown heads of the few peasants kept rising and dropping down again as they prayed earnestly for the dead; in a thin bluish stream the smoke issued from the holes of the censer. I looked at the dead face of my wife.... My God! even death--death itself-- had not set her free, had not healed her wound: the same sickly, timid, dumb look, as though, even in her coffin, she were ill at ease.... My heart was filled with bitterness. A sweet, sweet creature she was, and she did well for herself to die!'

The speaker's cheeks flushed, and his eyes grew dim.

'When at last,' he began again, 'I emerged from the deep depression which overwhelmed me after my wife's death, I resolved to devote myself, as it is called, to work. I went into a government office in the capital of the province; but in the great apartments of the government institution my head ached, and my eyesight too began to fail: other incidental causes came in.... I retired. I had thought of going on a visit to Moscow, but, in the first place, I hadn't the money, and secondly... I've told you already: I'm resigned. This resignation came upon me both suddenly and not suddenly. In spirit I had long ago resigned myself, but my brain was still unwilling to accept the yoke. I ascribed my humble temper and ideas to the influence of country life and happiness!... On the other side, I had long observed that all my neighbours, young and old alike, who had been frightened at first by my learning, my residence abroad, and my other advantages of education, had not only had time to get completely used to me, but had even begun to treat me half-rudely, half-contemptuously, did not listen to my observations, and, in talking to me, no longer made use of superfluous signs of respect. I forgot to tell you, too, that during the first year after my marriage, I had tried to launch into literature, and even sent a thing to a journal--a story, if I'm not mistaken; but in a little time I received a polite letter from the editor, in which, among other things, I was told that he could not deny I had intelligence, but he was obliged to say I had no talent, and talent alone was what was needed in literature. To add to this, it came to my knowledge that a young man, on a visit from Moscow--a most good-natured youth too--had referred to me at an evening party at the governor's as a shallow person, antiquated and behind the times. But my half-wilful blindness still persisted: I was unwilling to give myself a slap in the face, you know; at last, one fine morning, my eyes were opened. This was how it happened. The district captain of police came to see me, with the object of calling my attention to a tumble-down bridge on my property, which I had absolutely no money to repair. After consuming a glass of vodka and a snack of dried fish, this condescending guardian of order reproached me in a paternal way for my heedlessness, sympathising, however, with my position, and only advising me to order my peasants to patch up the bridge with some rubbish; he lighted a pipe, and began talking of the coming elections. A candidate for the honourable post of marshal of the province was at that time one Orbassanov, a noisy, shallow fellow, who took bribes into the bargain. Besides, he was not distinguished either for wealth or for family. I expressed my opinion with regard to him, and rather casually too: I regarded Mr. Orbassanov, I must own, as beneath my level. The police-captain looked at me, patted me amicably on the shoulder, and said good-naturedly: "Come, come, Vassily Vassilyevitch, it's not for you and me to criticise men like that--how are we qualified to? Let the shoemaker stick to his last." "But, upon my word," I retorted with annoyance, "whatever difference is there between me and Mr. Orbassanov?" The police-captain took his pipe out of his mouth, opened his eyes wide, and fairly roared. "Well, you're an amusing chap," he observed at last, while the tears ran down his cheeks: "what a joke to make!... Ah! you are a funny fellow!" And till his departure he never ceased jeering at me, now and then giving me a poke in the ribs with his elbow, and addressing me by my Christian name. He went away at last. This was enough: it was the last drop, and my cup was overflowing. I paced several times up and down the room, stood still before the looking-glass and gazed a long, long while at my embarrassed countenance, and deliberately putting out my tongue, I shook my head with a bitter smile. The scales fell from my eyes: I saw clearly, more clearly than I saw my face in the glass, what a shallow, insignificant, worthless, unoriginal person I was!'

He paused.

'In one of Voltaire's tragedies,' he went on wearily, 'there is some worthy who rejoices that he has reached the furthest limit of unhappiness. Though there is nothing tragic in my fate, I will admit I have experienced something of that sort. I have known the bitter transports of cold despair; I have felt how sweet it is, lying in bed, to curse deliberately for a whole morning together the hour and day of my birth. I could not resign myself all at once. And indeed, think of it yourself: I was kept by impecuniosity in the country, which I hated; I was not fitted for managing my land, nor for the public service, nor for literature, nor anything; my neighbours I didn't care for, and books I loathed; as for the mawkish and morbidly sentimental young ladies who shake their curls and feverishly harp on the word "life," I had ceased to have any attraction for them ever since I gave up ranting and gushing; complete solitude I could not face.... I began--what do you suppose?--I began hanging about, visiting my neighbours. As though drunk with self-contempt, I purposely exposed myself to all sorts of petty slights. I was missed over in serving at table; I was met with supercilious coldness, and at last was not noticed at all; I was not even allowed to take part in general conversation, and from my corner I myself used purposely to back up some stupid talker who in those days at Moscow would have ecstatically licked the dust off my feet, and kissed the hem of my cloak.... I did not even allow myself to believe that I was enjoying the bitter satisfaction of irony.... What sort of irony, indeed, can a man enjoy in solitude? Well, so I have behaved for some years on end, and so I behave now.'

'Really, this is beyond everything,' grumbled the sleepy voice of Mr. Kantagryuhin from the next room: 'what fool is it that has taken a fancy to talk all night?'

The speaker promptly ducked under the clothes and peeping out timidly, held up his finger to me warningly,

'Sh--sh--!' he whispered; and, as it were, bowing apologetically in the direction of Kantagryuhin's voice, he said respectfully: 'I obey, sir, I obey; I beg your pardon.... It's permissible for him to sleep; he ought to sleep,' he went on again in a whisper: 'he must recruit his energies--well, if only to eat his dinner with the same relish to-morrow. We have no right to disturb him. Besides, I think I've told you all I wanted to; probably you're sleepy too. I wish you good-night.'

He turned away with feverish rapidity and buried his head in the pillow.

'Let me at least know,' I asked, 'with whom I have had the pleasure....'

He raised his head quickly.

'No, for mercy's sake!' he cut me short, 'don't inquire my name either of me or of others. Let me remain to you an unknown being, crushed by fate, Vassily Vassilyevitch. Besides, as an unoriginal person, I don't deserve an individual name.... But if you really want to give me some title, call me... call me the Hamlet of the Shtchigri district. There are many such Hamlets in every district, but perhaps you haven't come across others.... After which, good-bye.'

He buried himself again in his feather-bed, and the next morning, when they came to wake me, he was no longer in the room. He had left before daylight.

XXI   TCHERTOP-HANOV AND NEDOPYUSKIN

One hot summer day I was coming home from hunting in a light cart; Yermolai sat beside me dozing and scratching his nose. The sleeping dogs were jolted up and down like lifeless bodies under our feet. The coachman kept flicking gadflies off the horses with his whip. The white dust rose in a light cloud behind the cart. We drove in between bushes. The road here was full of ruts, and the wheels began catching in the twigs. Yermolai started up and looked round.... 'Hullo!' he said; 'there ought to be grouse here. Let's get out.' We stopped and went into the thicket. My dog hit upon a covey. I took a shot and was beginning to reload, when suddenly there was a loud crackling behind me, and a man on horseback came towards me, pushing the bushes apart with his hands. 'Sir... pe-ermit me to ask,' he began in a haughty voice, 'by what right you are--er--shooting here, sir?' The stranger spoke extraordinarily quickly, jerkily and condescendingly. I looked at his face; never in my life have I seen anything like it. Picture to yourselves, gentle readers, a little flaxen-haired man, with a little turn-up red nose and long red moustaches. A pointed Persian cap with a crimson cloth crown covered his forehead right down to his eyebrows. He was dressed in a shabby yellow Caucasian overcoat, with black velveteen cartridge pockets on the breast, and tarnish silver braid on all the seams; over his shoulder was slung a horn; in his sash was sticking a dagger. A raw-boned, hook-nosed chestnut horse shambled unsteadily under his weight; two lean, crook-pawed greyhounds kept turning round just under the horse's legs. The face, the glance, the voice, every action, the whole being of the stranger, was expressive of a wild daring and an unbounded, incredible pride; his pale-blue glassy eyes strayed about with a sideway squint like a drunkard's; he flung back his head, puffed out his cheeks, snorted and quivered all over, as though bursting with dignity--for all the world like a turkey-cock. He repeated his question.

'I didn't know it was forbidden to shoot here,' I replied.

'You are here, sir,' he continued, 'on my land.'

'With your permission, I will go off it.'

'But pe-ermit me to ask,' he rejoined, 'is it a nobleman I have the honour of addressing?'

I mentioned my name.

'In that case, oblige me by hunting here. I am a nobleman myself, and am very pleased to do any service to a nobleman.... And my name is Panteley Tchertop-hanov.' He bowed, hallooed, gave his horse a lash on the neck; the horse shook its head, reared, shied, and trampled on a dog's paws. The dog gave a piercing squeal. Tchertop-hanov boiled over with rage; foaming at the mouth, he struck the horse with his fist on the head between the ears, leaped to the ground quicker than lightning, looked at the dog's paw, spat on the wound, gave it a kick in the ribs to stop its whining, caught on to the horse's forelock, and put his foot in the stirrup. The horse flung up its head, and with its tail in the air edged away into the bushes; he followed it, hopping on one leg; he got into the saddle at last, however, flourished his whip in a sort of frenzy, blew his horn, and galloped off. I had not time to recover from the unexpected appearance of Tchertop-hanov, when suddenly, almost without any noise, there came out of the bushes a stoutish man of forty on a little black nag. He stopped, took off his green leather cap, and in a thin, subdued voice he asked me whether I hadn't seen a horseman riding a chestnut? I answered that I had.

'Which way did the gentleman go?' he went on in the same tone, without putting on his cap.

'Over there.'

'I humbly thank you, sir.'

He made a kissing sound with his lips, swung his legs against his horse's sides, and fell into a jog-trot in the direction indicated. I looked after him till his peaked cap was hidden behind the branches. This second stranger was not in the least like his predecessor in exterior. His face, plump and round as a ball, expressed bashfulness, good-nature, and humble meekness; his nose, also plump and round and streaked with blue veins, betokened a sensualist. On the front of his head there was not a single hair left, some thin brown tufts stuck out behind; there was an ingratiating twinkle in his little eyes, set in long slits, and a sweet smile on his red, juicy lips. He had on a coat with a stand-up collar and brass buttons, very worn but clean; his cloth trousers were hitched up high, his fat calves were visible above the yellow tops of his boots.

'Who's that?' I inquired of Yermolai.

'That? Nedopyuskin, Tihon Ivanitch. He lives at Tchertop-hanov's.'

'What is he, a poor man?'

'He's not rich; but, to be sure, Tchertop-hanov's not got a brass farthing either.'

'Then why does he live with him?'

'Oh, they made friends. One's never seen without the other.... It's a fact, indeed-- where the horse puts its hoof, there the crab sticks its claw.'

We got out of the bushes; suddenly two hounds 'gave tongue' close to us, and a big hare bounded through the oats, which were fairly high by now. The dogs, hounds and harriers, leaped out of the thicket after him, and after the dogs flew out Tchertop-hanov himself. He did not shout, nor urge the dogs on, nor halloo; he was breathless and gasping; broken, senseless sounds were jerked out of his gaping mouth now and then; he dashed on, his eyes starting out of his head, and furiously lashed at his luckless horse with the whip. The harriers were gaining on the hare... it squatted for a moment, doubled sharply back, and darted past Yermolai into the bushes.... The harriers rushed in pursuit. 'Lo-ok out! lo-ok out!' the exhausted horseman articulated with effort, in a sort of stutter: 'lo-ok out, friend!' Yermolai shot... the wounded hare rolled head over heels on the smooth dry grass, leaped into the air, and squealed piteously in the teeth of a worrying dog. The hounds crowded about her. Like an arrow, Tchertop-hanov flew off his horse, clutched his dagger, ran straddling among the dogs with furious imprecations, snatched the mangled hare from them, and, creasing up his whole face, he buried the dagger in its throat up to the very hilt... buried it, and began hallooing. Tihon Ivanitch made his appearance on the edge of the thicket 'Ho-ho-ho-ho-ho-ho-ho-ho!' vociferated Tchertop-hanov a second time. 'Ho-ho-ho-ho,' his companion repeated placidly.

'But really, you know, one ought not to hunt in summer, 'I observed to Tchertop-hanov, pointing to the trampled-down oats.

'It's my field,' answered Tchertop-hanov, gasping.

He pulled the hare into shape, hung it on to his saddle, and flung the paws among the dogs. 'I owe you a charge, my friend, by the rules of hunting,' he said, addressing Yermolai. 'And you, dear sir,' he added in the same jerky, abrupt voice, 'my thanks.'

He mounted his horse.

'Pe-ermit me to ask... I've forgotten your name and your father's.'

Again I told him my name.

'Delighted to make your acquaintance. When you have an opportunity, hope you'll come and see me.... But where is that Fomka, Tihon Ivanitch?' he went on with heat; 'the hare was run down without him.'

'His horse fell down under him,' replied Tihon Ivanitch with a smile.

'Fell down! Orbassan fell down? Pugh! tut!... Where is he?'

'Over there, behind the copse.'

Tchertop-hanov struck his horse on the muzzle with his whip, and galloped off at a breakneck pace. Tihon Ivanitch bowed to me twice, once for himself and once for his companion, and again set off at a trot into the bushes.

These two gentlemen aroused my curiosity keenly. What could unite two creatures so different in the bonds of an inseparable friendship? I began to make inquiries. This was what I learned.

Panteley Eremyitch Tchertop-hanov had the reputation in the whole surrounding vicinity of a dangerous, crack-brained fellow, haughty and quarrelsome in the extreme. He had served a very short time in the army, and had retired from the service through 'difficulties' with his superiors, with that rank which is generally regarded as equivalent to no rank at all. He came of an old family, once rich; his forefathers lived sumptuously, after the manner of the steppes--that is, they welcomed all, invited or uninvited, fed them to exhaustion, gave out oats by the quarter to their guests' coachmen for their teams, kept musicians, singers, jesters, and dogs; on festive days regaled their people with spirits and beer, drove to Moscow in the winter with their own horses, in heavy old coaches, and sometimes were for whole months without a farthing, living on home-grown produce. The estate came into Panteley Eremyitch's father's hands in a crippled condition; he, in his turn, 'played ducks and drakes' with it, and when he died, left his sole heir, Panteley, the small mortgaged village of Bezsonovo, with thirty-five souls of the male, and seventy-six of the female sex, and twenty-eight acres and a half of useless land on the waste of Kolobrodova, no record of serfs for which could be found among the deceased's deeds. The deceased had, it must be confessed, ruined himself in a very strange way: 'provident management' had been his destruction. According to his notions, a nobleman ought not to depend on merchants, townsmen, and 'brigands' of that sort, as he called them; he set up all possible trades and crafts on his estate; 'it's both seemlier and cheaper,' he used to say: 'it's provident management'! He never relinquished this fatal idea to the end of his days; indeed, it was his ruin. But, then, what entertainment it gave him! He never denied himself the satisfaction of a single whim. Among other freaks, he once began building, after his own fancy, so immense a family coach that, in spite of the united efforts of the peasants' horses, drawn together from the whole village, as well as their owners, it came to grief and fell to pieces on the first hillside. Eremey Lukitch (the name of Panteley's father was Eremey Lukitch), ordered a memorial to be put up on the hillside, but was not, however, at all abashed over the affair. He conceived the happy thought, too, of building a church--by himself, of course--without the assistance of an architect. He burnt a whole forest in making the bricks, laid an immense foundation, as though for a provincial hall, raised the walls, and began putting on the cupola; the cupola fell down. He tried again-- the cupola again broke down; he tried the third time---the cupola fell to pieces a third time. Good Eremey Lukitch grew thoughtful; there was something uncanny about it, he reflected... some accursed witchcraft must have a hand in it... and at once he gave orders to flog all the old women in the village. They flogged the old women; but they didn't get the cupola on, for all that. He began reconstructing the peasants' huts on a new plan, and all on a system of 'provident management'; he set them three homesteads together in a triangle, and in the middle stuck up a post with a painted bird-cage and flag. Every day he invented some new freak; at one time he was making soup of burdocks, at another cutting his horses' tails off to make caps for his servants; at another, proposing to substitute nettles for flax, to feed pigs on mushrooms.... He had once read in the Moscow Gazette an article by a Harkov landowner, Hryak-Hrupyorsky, on the importance of morality to the well-being of the peasant, and the next day he gave forth a decree to all his peasants to learn off the Harkov landowner's article by heart at once. The peasants learnt the article; the master asked them whether they understood what was said in it? The bailiff replied-- that to be sure they understood it! About the same time he ordered all his subjects, with a view to the maintenance of order and provident management, to be numbered, and each to have his number sewn on his collar. On meeting the master, each was to shout, 'Number so-and-so is here!' and the master would answer affably: 'Go on, in God's name!'

In spite, however, of order and provident management, Eremey Lukitch got by degrees into a very difficult position; he began at first by mortgaging his villages, and then was brought to the sale of them; the last ancestral home, the village with the unfinished church, was sold at last for arrears to the Crown, luckily not in the lifetime of Eremey Lukitch--he could never have supported such a blow--but a fortnight after his death. He succeeded in dying at home in his own bed, surrounded by his own people, and under the care of his own doctor; but nothing was left to poor Panteley but Bezsonovo.

Panteley heard of his father's illness while he was still in the service, in the very heat of the 'difficulties' mentioned above. He was only just nineteen. From his earliest childhood he had not left his father's house, and under the guidance of his mother, a very good-natured but perfectly stupid woman, Vassilissa Vassilyevna, he grew up spoilt and conceited. She undertook his education alone; Eremey Lukitch, buried in his economical fancies, had no thoughts to spare for it. It is true, he once punished his son with his own hand for mispronouncing a letter of the alphabet; but Eremey Lukitch had received a cruel and secret blow that day: his best dog had been crushed by a tree. Vassilissa Vassilyevna's efforts in regard Panteley's education did not, however, get beyond one terrific exertion; in the sweat of her brow she engaged him a tutor, one Birkopf, a retired Alsatian soldier, and to the day of her death she trembled like a leaf before him. 'Oh,' she thought, 'if he throws us up--I'm lost! Where could I turn? Where could I find another teacher? Why, with what pains, what pains I enticed this one away from our neighbours!' And Birkopf, like a shrewd man, promptly took advantage of his unique position; he drank like a fish, and slept from morning till night. On the completion of his 'course of science,' Panteley entered the army. Vassilissa Vassilyevna was no more; she had died six months before that important event, of fright. She had had a dream of a white figure riding on a bear. Eremey Lukitch soon followed his better half.

At the first news of his illness, Panteley galloped home at breakneck speed, but he did not find his father alive. What was the amazement of the dutiful son when he found himself, utterly unexpectedly, transformed from a rich heir to a poor man! Few men are capable of bearing so sharp a reverse well. Panteley was embittered, made misanthropical by it. From an honest, generous, good-natured fellow, though spoilt and hot-tempered, he became haughty and quarrelsome; he gave up associating with the neighbours--he was too proud to visit the rich, and he disdained the poor--and behaved with unheard of arrogance to everyone, even to the established authorities. 'I am of the ancient hereditary nobility,' he would say. Once he had been on the point of shooting the police-commissioner for coming into the room with his cap on his head. Of course the authorities, on their side, had their revenge, and took every opportunity to make him feel their power; but still, they were rather afraid of him, because he had a desperate temper, and would propose a duel with knives at the second word. At the slightest retort Tchertop-hanov's eyes blazed, his voice broke.... Ah, er--er--er,' he stammered, 'damn my soul!'... and nothing could stop him. And, moreover, he was a man of stainless character, who had never had a hand in anything the least shady. No one, of course, visited him... and with all this he was a good-hearted, even a great-hearted man in his own way; acts of injustice, of oppression, he would not brook even against strangers; he stood up for his own peasants like a rock. 'What?' he would say, with a violent blow on his own head: 'touch my people, mine? My name's not Tchertop-hanov, if I...'

Tihon Ivanitch Nedopyuskin could not, like Panteley Eremyitch, pride himself on his origin. His father came of the peasant proprietor class, and only after forty years of service attained the rank of a noble. Mr. Nedopyuskin, the father, belonged to the number of those people who are pursued by misfortune with an obduracy akin to personal hatred. For sixty whole years, from his very birth to his very death, the poor man was struggling with all the hardships, calamities, and privations, incidental to people of small means; he struggled like a fish under the ice, never having enough food and sleep--cringing, worrying, wearing himself to exhaustion, fretting over every farthing, with genuine 'innocence' suffering in the service, and dying at last in either a garret or a cellar, in the unsuccessful struggle to gain for himself or his children a crust of dry bread. Fate had hunted him down like a hare.

He was a good-natured and honest man, though he did take bribes--from a threepenny bit up to a crown piece inclusive. Nedopyuskin had a wife, thin and consumptive; he had children too; luckily they all died young except Tihon and a daughter, Mitrodora, nicknamed 'the merchants' belle,' who, after many painful and ludicrous adventures, was married to a retired attorney. Mr. Nedopyuskin had succeeded before his death in getting Tihon a place as supernumerary clerk in some office; but directly after his father's death Tihon resigned his situation. Their perpetual anxieties, their heartrending struggle with cold and hunger, his mother's careworn depression, his father's toiling despair, the coarse aggressiveness of landladies and shopkeepers--all the unending daily suffering of their life had developed an exaggerated timidity in Tihon: at the mere sight of his chief he was faint and trembling like a captured bird. He threw up his office. Nature, in her indifference, or perhaps her irony, implants in people all sorts of faculties and tendencies utterly inconsistent with their means and their position in society; with her characteristic care and love she had moulded of Tihon, the son of a poor clerk, a sensuous, indolent, soft, impressionable creature--a creature fitted exclusively for enjoyment, gifted with an excessively delicate sense of smell and of taste...she had moulded him, finished him off most carefully, and set her creation to struggle up on sour cabbage and putrid fish! And, behold! the creation did struggle up somehow, and began what is called 'life.' Then the fun began. Fate, which had so ruthlessly tormented Nedopyuskin the father, took to the son too; she had a taste for them, one must suppose. But she treated Tihon on a different plan: she did not torture him; she played with him. She did not once drive him to desperation, she did not set him to suffer the degrading agonies of hunger, but she led him a dance through the whole of Russia from one end to the other, from one degrading and ludicrous position to another; at one time Fate made him 'majordomo' to a snappish, choleric Lady Bountiful, at another a humble parasite on a wealthy skinflint merchant, then a private secretary to a goggle-eyed gentleman, with his hair cut in the English style, then she promoted him to the post of something between butler and buffoon to a dog-fancier.... In short, Fate drove poor Tihon to drink drop by drop to the dregs the bitter poisoned cup of a dependent existence. He had been, in his time, the sport of the dull malignity and the boorish pranks of slothful masters. How often, alone in his room, released at last 'to go in peace,' after a mob of visitors had glutted their taste for horseplay at his expense, he had vowed, blushing with shame, chill tears of despair in his eyes, that he would run away in secret, would try his luck in the town, would find himself some little place as clerk, or die once for all of hunger in the street! But, in the first place, God had not given him strength of character; secondly, his timidity unhinged him; and thirdly, how could he get himself a place? whom could he ask? 'They'll never give it me,' the luckless wretch would murmur, tossing wearily in his bed, 'they'll never give it me!' And the next day he would take up the same degrading life again. His position was the more painful that, with all her care, nature had not troubled to give him the smallest share of the gifts and qualifications without which the trade of a buffoon is almost impossible. He was not equal, for instance, to dancing till he dropped, in a bearskin coat turned inside out, nor making jokes and cutting capers in the immediate vicinity of cracking whips; if he was turned out in a state of nature into a temperature of twenty degrees below freezing, as often as not, he caught cold; his stomach could not digest brandy mixed with ink and other filth, nor minced funguses and toadstools in vinegar. There is no knowing what would have become of Tihon if the last of his patrons, a contractor who had made his fortune, had not taken it into his head in a merry hour to inscribe in his will: 'And to Zyozo (Tihon, to wit) Nedopyuskin, I leave in perpetual possession, to him and his heirs, the village of Bezselendyevka, lawfully acquired by me, with all its appurtenances.' A few days later this patron was taken with a fit of apoplexy after gorging on sturgeon soup. A great commotion followed; the officials came and put seals on the property.

The relations arrived; the will was opened and read; and they called for Nedopyuskin: Nedopyuskin made his appearance. The greater number of the party knew the nature of Tihon Ivanitch's duties in his patron's household; he was greeted with deafening shouts and ironical congratulations. 'The landowner; here is the new owner!' shouted the other heirs. 'Well, really this,' put in one, a noted wit and humourist; 'well, really this, one may say... this positively is... really what one may call... an heir-apparent!' and they all went off into shrieks. For a long while Nedopyuskin could not believe in his good fortune. They showed him the will: he flushed, shut his eyes, and with a despairing gesture he burst into tears. The chuckles of the party passed into a deep unanimous roar. The village of Bezselendyevka consisted of only twenty-two serfs, no one regretted its loss keenly; so why not get some fun out of it? One of the heirs from Petersburg, an important man, with a Greek nose and a majestic expression of face, Rostislav Adamitch Shtoppel, went so far as to go up to Nedopyuskin and look haughtily at him over his shoulder. 'So far as I can gather, honoured sir,' he observed with contemptuous carelessness, 'you enjoyed your position in the household of our respected Fedor Fedoritch, owing to your obliging readiness to wait on his diversions?' The gentleman from Petersburg expressed himself in a style insufferably refined, smart, and correct. Nedopyuskin, in his agitation and confusion, had not taken in the unknown gentleman's words, but the others were all quiet at once; the wit smiled condescendingly. Mr. Shtoppel rubbed his hands and repeated his question. Nedopyuskin raised his eyes in bewilderment and opened his mouth. Rostislav Adamitch puckered his face up sarcastically.

'I congratulate you, my dear sir, I congratulate you,' he went on: 'it's true, one may say, not everyone would have consented to gain his daily bread in such a fashion; but de guslibus non est disputandum , that is, everyone to his taste.... Eh?'

Someone at the back uttered a rapid, decorous shriek of admiration and delight.

'Tell us,' pursued Mr. Shtoppel, much encouraged by the smiles of the whole party, 'to what special talent are you indebted for your good-fortune? No, don't be bashful, tell us; we're all here, so to speak, en famille . Aren't we, gentlemen, all here en famille ?'

The relation to whom Rostislav Adamitch chanced to turn with this question did not, unfortunately, know French, and so he confined himself to a faint grunt of approbation. But another relation, a young man, with patches of a yellow colour on his forehead, hastened to chime in, 'Wee, wee, to be sure.'

'Perhaps,' Mr. Shtoppel began again, 'you can walk on your hands, your legs raised, so to say, in the air?'

Nedopyuskin looked round in agony: every face wore a taunting smile, every eye was moist with delight.

'Or perhaps you can crow like a cock?'

A loud guffaw broke out on all sides, and was hushed at once, stifled by expectation.

'Or perhaps on your nose you can....'

'Stop that!' a loud harsh voice suddenly interrupted Rostislav Adamitch; 'I wonder you're not ashamed to torment the poor man!'

Everyone looked round. In the doorway stood Tchertop-hanov. As a cousin four times removed of the deceased contractor, he too had received a note of invitation to the meeting of the relations. During the whole time of reading the will he had kept, as he always did, haughtily apart from the others.

'Stop that!' he repeated, throwing his head back proudly.

Mr. Shtoppel turned round quickly, and seeing a poorly dressed, unattractive-looking man, he inquired of his neighbour in an undertone (caution's always a good thing):

'Who's that?' 'Tchertop-hanov--he's no great shakes,' the latter whispered in his ear.

Rostislav Adamitch assumed a haughty air.

'And who are you to give orders?' he said through his nose, drooping his eyelids scornfully; 'who may you be, allow me to inquire?--a queer fish, upon my word!'

Tchertop-hanov exploded like gunpowder at a spark. He was choked with fury.

'Ss--ss--ss!' he hissed like one possessed, and all at once he thundered: 'Who am I? Who am I? I'm Panteley Tchertop-hanov, of the ancient hereditary nobility; my forefathers served the Tsar: and who may you be?'

Rostislav Adamitch turned pale and stepped back. He had not expected such resistance.

'I--I--a fish indeed!'

Tchertop-hanov darted forward; Shtoppel bounded away in great perturbation, the others rushed to meet the exasperated nobleman.

'A duel, a duel, a duel, at once, across a handkerchief!' shouted the enraged Panteley, 'or beg my pardon--yes, and his too....'

'Pray beg his pardon!' the agitated relations muttered all round Shtoppel; 'he's such a madman, he'd cut your throat in a minute!'

'I beg your pardon, I beg your pardon, I didn't know,' stammered Shtoppel; 'I didn't know....'

'And beg his too!' vociferated the implacable Panteley.

'I beg your pardon too,' added Rostislav Adamitch, addressing Nedopyuskin, who was shaking as if he were in an ague.

Tchertop-hanov calmed down; he went up to Tihon Ivanitch, took him by the hand, looked fiercely round, and, as not one pair of eyes ventured to meet his, he walked triumphantly amid profound silence out of the room, with the new owner of the lawfully acquired village of Bezselendyevka.

From that day they never parted again. (The village of Bezselendyevka was only seven miles from Bezsonovo.) The boundless gratitude of Nedopyuskin soon passed into the most adoring veneration. The weak, soft, and not perfectly stainless Tihon bowed down in the dust before the fearless and irreproachable Panteley. 'It's no slight thing,' he thought to himself sometimes, 'to talk to the governor, look him straight in the face.... Christ have mercy on us, doesn't he look at him!'

He marvelled at him, he exhausted all the force of his soul in his admiration of him, he regarded him as an extraordinary man, as clever, as learned. And there's no denying that, bad as Tchertop-hanov's education might be, still, in comparison with Tihon's education, it might pass for brilliant. Tchertop-hanov, it is true, had read little Russian, and knew French very badly--so badly that once, in reply to the question of a Swiss tutor: ' Vous parlez francais, monsieur? ' he answered: ' Je ne comprehend ' and after a moment's thought, he added pa ; but any way he was aware that Voltaire had once existed, and was a very witty writer, and that Frederick the Great, king of Prussia, had been distinguished as a great military commander. Of Russian writers he respected Derzhavin, but liked Marlinsky, and called Ammalat-Bek the best of the pack....

A few days after my first meeting with the two friends, I set off for the village of Bezsonovo to see Panteley Eremyitch. His little house could be seen a long way off; it stood out on a bare place, half a mile from the village, on the 'bluff,' as it is called, like a hawk on a ploughed field. Tchertop-hanov's homestead consisted of nothing more than four old tumble-down buildings of different sizes--that is, a lodge, a stable, a barn, and a bath-house. Each building stood apart by itself; there was neither a fence round nor a gate to be seen. My coachman stopped in perplexity at a well which was choked up and had almost disappeared. Near the barn some thin and unkempt puppies were mangling a dead horse, probably Orbassan; one of them lifted up the bleeding nose, barked hurriedly, and again fell to devouring the bare ribs. Near the horse stood a boy of seventeen, with a puffy, yellow face, dressed like a Cossack, and barelegged; he looked with a responsible air at the dogs committed to his charge, and now and then gave the greediest a lash with his whip.

'Is your master at home?' I inquired.

'The Lord knows!' answered the lad; 'you'd better knock.'

I jumped out of the droshky, and went up to the steps of the lodge.

Mr. Tchertop-hanov's dwelling presented a very cheerless aspect; the beams were blackened and bulging forward, the chimney had fallen off, the corners of the house were stained with damp, and sunk out of the perpendicular, the small, dusty, bluish windows peeped out from under the shaggy overhanging roof with an indescribably morose expression: some old vagrants have eyes that look like that. I knocked; no one responded. I could hear, however, through the door some sharply uttered words:

'A, B, C; there now, idiot!' a hoarse voice was saying: 'A, B, C, D... no! D, E, E, E!... Now then, idiot!'

I knocked a second time.

The same voice shouted: 'Come in; who's there?'...

I went into the small empty hall, and through the open door I saw Tchertop-hanov himself. In a greasy oriental dressing-gown, loose trousers, and a red skull-cap, he was sitting on a chair; in one hand he gripped the face of a young poodle, while in the other he was holding a piece of bread just above his nose.

'Ah!' he pronounced with dignity, not stirring from his seat: 'delighted to see you. Please sit down. I am busy here with Venzor.... Tihon Ivanitch,' he added, raising his voice, 'come here, will you? Here's a visitor.'

'I'm coming, I'm coming,' Tihon Ivanitch responded from the other room. 'Masha, give me my cravat.'

Tchertop-hanov turned to Venzor again and laid the piece of bread on his nose. I looked round. Except an extending table much warped with thirteen legs of unequal length, and four rush chairs worn into hollows, there was no furniture of any kind in the room; the walls, which had been washed white, ages ago, with blue, star-shaped spots, were peeling off in many places; between the windows hung a broken tarnished looking-glass in a huge frame of red wood. In the corners stood pipestands and guns; from the ceiling hung fat black cobwebs.

'A, B, C, D,' Tchertop-hanov repeated slowly, and suddenly he cried furiously: ' E! E! E! E! ... What a stupid brute!...'

But the luckless poodle only shivered, and could not make up his mind to open his mouth; he still sat wagging his tail uneasily and wrinkling up his face, blinked dejectedly, and frowned as though saying to himself: 'Of course, it's just as you please!'

'There, eat! come! take it!' repeated the indefatigable master.

'You've frightened him,' I remarked.

'Well, he can get along, then!'

He gave him a kick. The poor dog got up softly, dropped the bread off his nose, and walked, as it were, on tiptoe to the hall, deeply wounded. And with good reason: a stranger calling for the first time, and to treat him like that!

The door from the next room gave a subdued creak, and Mr. Nedopyuskin came in, affably bowing and smiling.

I got up and bowed.

'Don't disturb yourself, don't disturb yourself,' he lisped.

We sat down. Tchertop-hanov went into the next room.

'You have been for some time in our neighbourhood,' began Nedopyuskin in a subdued voice, coughing discreetly into his hand, and holding his fingers before his lips from a feeling of propriety.

'I came last month.'

'Indeed.'

We were silent for a little.

'Lovely weather we are having just now,' resumed Nedopyuskin, and he looked gratefully at me as though I were in some way responsible for the weather: 'the corn, one may say, is doing wonderfully.'

I nodded in token of assent. We were silent again.

'Panteley Eremyitch was pleased to hunt two hares yesterday,' Nedopyuskin began again with an effort, obviously wishing to enliven the conversation; 'yes, indeed, very big hares they were, sir.'

'Has Mr. Tchertop-hanov good hounds?'

'The most wonderful hounds, sir!' Nedopyuskin replied, delighted; 'one may say, the best in the province, indeed.' (He drew nearer to me.) 'But, then, Panteley Eremyitch is such a wonderful man! He has only to wish for anything--he has only to take an idea into his head--and before you can look round, it's done; everything, you may say, goes like clockwork. Panteley Eremyitch, I assure you....'

Tchertop-hanov came into the room. Nedopyuskin smiled, ceased speaking, and indicated him to me with a glance which seemed to say, 'There, you will see for yourself.' We fell to talking about hunting.

'Would you like me to show you my leash?' Tchertop-hanov asked me; and, not waiting for a reply, he called Karp.

A sturdy lad came in, in a green nankin long coat, with a blue collar and livery buttons.

'Tell Fomka,' said Tchertop-hanov abruptly, 'to bring in Ammalat and Saiga, and in good order, do you understand?'

Karp gave a broad grin, uttered an indefinite sound, and went away. Fomka made his appearance, well combed and tightly buttoned up, in boots, and with the hounds. From politeness, I admired the stupid beasts (harriers are all exceedingly stupid). Tchertop-hanov spat right into Ammalat's nostrils, which did not, however, apparently afford that dog the slightest satisfaction. Nedopyuskin, too, stroked Ammalat from behind. We began chatting again. By degrees Tchertop-hanov unbent completely, and no longer stood on his dignity nor snorted defiantly; the expression of his face changed. He glanced at me and at Nedopyuskin....

'Hey!' he cried suddenly; 'why should she sit in there alone? Masha! hi, Masha! come in here!'

Some one stirred in the next room, but there was no answer. 'Ma-a-sha!' Tchertop-hanov repeated caressingly; 'come in here. It's all right, don't be afraid.'

The door was softly opened, and I caught sight of a tall and slender girl of twenty, with a dark gypsy face, golden-brown eyes, and hair black as pitch; her large white teeth gleamed between full red lips. She had on a white dress; a blue shawl, pinned close round her throat with a gold brooch, half hid her slender, beautiful arms, in which one could see the fineness of her race. She took two steps with the bashful awkwardness of some wild creature, stood still, and looked down.

'Come, let me introduce,' said Panteley Eremyitch; 'wife she is not, but she's to be respected as a wife.'

Masha flushed slightly, and smiled in confusion. I made her a low bow. I thought her very charming. The delicate falcon nose, with distended, half-transparent nostrils; the bold sweep of her high eyebrows, the pale, almost sunken cheeks--every feature of her face denoted wilful passion and reckless devilry. From under the coil of her hair two rows of little shining hairs ran down her broad neck--a sign of race and vigour.

She went to the window and sat down. I did not want to increase her embarrassment, and began talking with Tchertop-hanov. Masha turned her head slyly, and began peeping from under her eyelids at me stealthily, shyly, and swiftly. Her glance seemed to flash out like a snake's sting. Nedopyuskin sat beside her, and whispered something in her ear. She smiled again. When she smiled, her nose slightly puckered up, and her upper lip was raised, which gave her face something of the expression of a cat or a lion....

'Oh, but you're one of the "hands off!" sort,' I thought, in my turn stealing a look at her supple frame, her hollow breast, and her quick, angular movements.

'Masha,' Tchertop-hanov asked, 'don't you think we ought to give our visitor some entertainment, eh?'

'We've got some jam,' she replied.

'Well, bring the jam here, and some vodka, too, while you're about it. And, I say, Masha,' he shouted after her, 'bring the guitar in too.'

'What's the guitar for? I'm not going to sing.'

'Why?'

'I don't want to.'

'Oh, nonsense; you'll want to when....'

'What?' asked Masha, rapidly knitting her brows.

'When you're asked,' Tchertop-hanov went on, with some embarrassment.

'Oh!'

She went out, soon came back with jam and vodka, and again sat by the window. There was still a line to be seen on her forehead; the two eyebrows rose and drooped like a wasp's antennae.... Have you ever noticed, reader, what a wicked face the wasp has? 'Well,' I thought, 'I'm in for a storm.' The conversation flagged. Nedopyuskin shut up completely, and wore a forced smile; Tchertop-hanov panted, turned red, and opened his eyes wide; I was on the point of taking leave.... Suddenly Masha got up, flung open the window, thrust out her head, and shouted lustily to a passing peasant woman, 'Aksinya!' The woman started, and tried to turn round, but slipped down and flopped heavily on to a dung-heap. Masha threw herself back and laughed merrily; Tchertop-hanov laughed too; Nedopyuskin shrieked with delight. We all revived. The storm had passed off in one flash of lightning... the air was clear again.

Half-an-hour later, no one would have recognised us; we were chatting and frolicking like children. Masha was the merriest of all; Tchertop-hanov simply could not take his eyes off her. Her face grew paler, her nostrils dilated, her eyes glowed and darkened at the same time. It was a wild creature at play. Nedopyuskin limped after her on his short, fat little legs, like a drake after a duck. Even Venzor crawled out of his hiding-place in the hall, stood a moment in the doorway, glanced at us, and suddenly fell to jumping up into the air and barking. Masha flitted into the other room, fetched the guitar, flung off the shawl from her shoulders, seated herself quickly, and, raising her head, began singing a gypsy song. Her voice rang out, vibrating like a glass bell when it is struck; it flamed up and died away.... It filled the heart with sweetness and pain.... Tchertop-hanov fell to dancing. Nedopyuskin stamped and swung his legs in tune. Masha was all a-quiver, like birch-bark in the fire; her delicate fingers flew playfully over the guitar, her dark-skinned throat slowly heaved under the two rows of amber. All at once she would cease singing, sink into exhaustion, and twang the guitar, as it were involuntarily, and Tchertop-hanov stood still, merely working his shoulders and turning round in one place, while Nedopyuskin nodded his head like a Chinese figure; then she would break out into song like a mad thing, drawing herself up and holding up her head, and Tchertop-hanov again curtsied down to the ground, leaped up to the ceiling, spun round like a top, crying 'Quicker!...'

'Quicker, quicker, quicker!' Nedopyuskin chimed in, speaking very fast.

It was late in the evening when I left Bezsonovo....

XXII   THE END OF TCHERTOP-HANOV

I

It was two years after my visit that Panteley Eremyitch's troubles began--his real troubles. Disappointments, disasters, even misfortunes he had had before that time, but he had paid no attention to them, and had risen superior to them in former days. The first blow that fell upon him was the most heartrending for him. Masha left him.

What induced her to forsake his roof, where she seemed to be so thoroughly at home, it is hard to say. Tchertop-hanov to the end of his days clung to the conviction that a certain young neighbour, a retired captain of Uhlans, named Yaff, was at the root of

Masha's desertion. He had taken her fancy, according to Panteley Eremyitch, simply by constantly curling his moustaches, pomading himself to excess, and sniggering significantly; but one must suppose that the vagrant gypsy blood in Masha's veins had more to do with it. However that may have been, one fine summer evening Masha tied up a few odds and ends in a small bundle, and walked out of Tchertop-hanov's house.

For three days before this she had sat crouched up in a corner, huddled against the wall, like a wounded fox, and had not spoken a word to any one; she had only turned her eyes about, and twitched her eyebrows, and faintly gnashed her teeth, and moved her arms as though she were wrapping herself up. This mood had come upon her before, but had never lasted long: Tchertop-hanov knew that, and so he neither worried himself nor worried her. But when, on coming in from the kennels, where, in his huntsman's words, the last two hounds 'had departed,' he met a servant girl who, in a trembling voice, informed him that Marya Akinfyevna sent him her greetings, and left word that she wished him every happiness, but she was not coming back to him any more; Tchertop-hanov, after reeling round where he stood and uttering a hoarse yell, rushed at once after the runaway, snatching up his pistol as he went.

He overtook her a mile and a half from his house, near a birch wood, on the high-road to the district town. The sun was sinking on the horizon, and everything was suddenly suffused with purple glow--trees, plants, and earth alike.

'To Yaff! to Yaff!' groaned Tchertop-hanov directly he caught sight of Masha. 'Going to Yaff!' he repeated, running up to her, and almost stumbling at every step.

Masha stood still, and turned round facing him.

She stood with her back to the light, and looked all black, as though she had been carved out of dark wood; only the whites of her eyes stood out like silvery almonds, but the eyes themselves--the pupils--were darker than ever.

She flung her bundle aside, and folded her arms. 'You are going to Yaff, wretched girl!' repeated Tchertop-hanov, and he was on the point of seizing her by the shoulder, but, meeting her eyes, he was abashed, and stood uneasily where he was.

'I am not going to Mr. Yaff, Panteley Eremyitch,' replied Masha in soft, even tones; 'it's only I can't live with you any longer.'

'Can't live with me? Why not? Have I offended you in some way?'

Masha shook her head. 'You've not offended me in any way, Panteley Eremyitch, only my heart is heavy in your house.... Thanks for the past, but I can't stay--no!'

Tchertop-hanov was amazed; he positively slapped his thighs, and bounced up and down in his astonishment.

'How is that? Here she's gone on living with me, and known nothing but peace and happiness, and all of a sudden--her heart's heavy! and she flings me over! She goes and puts a kerchief on her head, and is gone. She received every respect, like any lady.'

'I don't care for that in the least,' Masha interrupted.

'Don't care for it? From a wandering gypsy to turn into a lady, and she doesn't care for it! How don't you care for it, you low-born slave? Do you expect me to believe that? There's treachery hidden in it--treachery!'

He began frowning again.

'There's no treachery in my thoughts, and never has been,' said Masha in her distinct, resonant voice; 'I've told you already, my heart was heavy.'

'Masha!' cried Tchertop-hanov, striking himself a blow on the chest with his fist; 'there, stop it; hush, you have tortured me... now, it's enough! O my God! think only what Tisha will say; you might have pity on him, at least!'

'Remember me to Tihon Ivanitch, and tell him...'

Tchertop-hanov wrung his hands. 'No, you are talking nonsense--you are not going! Your Yaff may wait for you in vain!'

'Mr. Yaff,' Masha was beginning....

'A fine Mister Yaff!' Tchertop-hanov mimicked her. 'He's an underhand rascal, a low cur--that's what he is--and a phiz like an ape's!'

For fully half-an-hour Tchertop-hanov was struggling with Masha. He came close to her, he fell back, he shook his fists at her, he bowed down before her, he wept, he scolded.

...'I can't,' repeated Masha; 'I am so sad at heart... devoured by weariness.'

Little by little her face assumed such an indifferent, almost drowsy expression, that Tchertop-hanov asked her if they had not drugged her with laudanum.

'It's weariness,' she said for the tenth time.

'Then what if I kill you?' he cried suddenly, and he pulled the pistol out of his pocket.

Masha smiled; her face brightened.

'Well, kill me, Panteley Eremyitch; as you will; but go back, I won't.'

'You won't come back?' Tchertop-hanov cocked the pistol.

'I won't go back, my dearie. Never in my life will I go back. My word is steadfast.'

Tchertop-hanov suddenly thrust the pistol into her hand, and sat down on the ground.

'Then, you kill me! Without you I don't care to live. I have grown loathsome to you--and everything's loathsome for me!'

Masha bent down, took up her bundle, laid the pistol on the grass, its mouth away from Tchertop-hanov, and went up to him.

'Ah, my dearie, why torture yourself? Don't you know what we gypsy girls are? It's our nature; you must make up your mind to it. When there comes weariness the divider, and calls the soul away to strange, distant parts, how is one to stay here? Don't forget your Masha; you won't find such another sweetheart, and I won't forget you, my dearie; but our life together's over!'

'I loved you, Masha,' Tchertop-hanov muttered into the fingers in which he had buried his face....

'And I loved you, little friend Panteley Eremyitch.'

'I love you, I love you madly, senselessly--and when I think now that you, in your right senses, without rhyme or reason, are leaving me like this, and going to wander over the face of the earth--well, it strikes me that if I weren't a poor penniless devil, you wouldn't be throwing me over!'

At these words Masha only laughed.

'And he used to say I didn't care for money,' she commented, and she gave Tchertop-hanov a vigorous thump on the shoulder.

He jumped up on to his feet.

'Come, at least you must let me give you some money--how can you go like this without a halfpenny? But best of all: kill me! I tell you plainly: kill me once for all!'

Masha shook her head again. 'Kill you? Why get sent to Siberia, my dearie?'

Tchertop-hanov shuddered. 'Then it's only from that--from fear of penal servitude.'

He rolled on the grass again.

Masha stood over him in silence. 'I'm sorry for you, dear,' she said with a sigh: 'you're a good fellow... but there's no help for it: good-bye!'

She turned away and took two steps. The night had come on by now, and dim shadows were closing in on all sides. Tchertop-hanov jumped up swiftly and seized Masha from behind by her two elbows.

'You are going away like this, serpent, to Yaff!'

'Good-bye!' Masha repeated sharply and significantly; she tore herself away and walked off.

Tchertop-hanov looked after her, ran to the place where the pistol was lying, snatched it up, took aim, fired.... But before he touched the trigger, his arm twitched upwards; the ball whistled over Masha's head. She looked at him over her shoulder without stopping, and went on, swinging as she walked, as though in defiance of him.

He hid his face--and fell to running.

But before he had run fifty paces he suddenly stood still as though turned to stone. A well-known, too well-known voice came floating to him. Masha was singing. 'It was in the sweet days of youth,' she sang: every note seemed to linger plaintive and ardent in the evening air. Tchertop-hanov listened intently. The voice retreated and retreated; at one moment it died away, at the next it floated across, hardly audible, but still with the same passionate glow.

'She does it to spite me,' thought Tchertop-hanov; but at once he moaned, 'oh, no! it's her last farewell to me for ever,'--and he burst into floods of tears.

The next day he appeared at the lodgings of Mr. Yaff, who, as a true man of the world, not liking the solitude of the country, resided in the district town, 'to be nearer the young ladies,' as he expressed it. Tchertop-hanov did not find Yaff; he had, in the words of his valet, set off for Moscow the evening before.

'Then it is so!' cried Tchertop-hanov furiously; 'there was an arrangement between them; she has run away with him... but wait a bit!'

He broke into the young cavalry captain's room in spite of the resistance of the valet. In the room there was hanging over the sofa a portrait in oils of the master, in the Uhlan uniform. 'Ah, here you are, you tailless ape!' thundered Tchertop-hanov; he jumped on to the sofa, and with a blow of his fist burst a big hole in the taut canvas.

'Tell your worthless master,' he turned to the valet, 'that, in the absence of his own filthy phiz, the nobleman Tchertop-hanov put a hole through the painted one; and if he cares for satisfaction from me, he knows where to find the nobleman Tchertop-hanov! or else I'll find him out myself! I'll fetch the rascally ape from the bottom of the sea!'

Saying these words, Tchertop-hanov jumped off the sofa and majestically withdrew.

But the cavalry captain Yaff did not demand satisfaction from him--indeed, he never met him anywhere--and Tchertop-hanov did not think of seeking his enemy out, and no scandal followed. Masha herself soon after this disappeared beyond all trace. Tchertop-hanov took to drink; however, he 'reformed' later. But then a second blow fell upon him.

II

This was the death of his bosom friend Tihon Ivanovitch Nedopyuskin. His health had begun to fail two years before his death: he began to suffer from asthma, and was constantly dropping asleep, and on waking up could not at once come to himself; the district doctor maintained that this was the result of 'something rather like fits.' During the three days which preceded Masha's departure, those three days when 'her heart was heavy,' Nedopyuskin had been away at his own place at Bezselendyevka: he had been laid up with a severe cold. Masha's conduct was consequently even more unexpected for him; it made almost a deeper impression on him than on Tchertop-hanov himself. With his natural sweetness and diffidence, he gave utterance to nothing but the tenderest sympathy with his friend, and the most painful perplexity... but it crushed and made havoc of everything in him. 'She has torn the heart out of me,' he would murmur to himself, as he sat on his favourite checked sofa and twisted his fingers. Even when Tchertop-hanov had got over it, he, Nedopyuskin, did not recover, and still felt that 'there was a void within him.' 'Here,' he would say, pointing to the middle of his breast above his stomach. In that way he lingered on till the winter. When the frosts came, his asthma got better, but he was visited by, not 'something rather like a fit' this time, but a real unmistakable fit. He did not lose his memory at once; he still knew Tchertop-hanov and his friend's cry of despair, 'How can you desert me, Tisha, without my consent, just as Masha did?' He even responded with faltering, uncertain tongue, 'O--P--a--ey--E--e--yitch, I will o--bey you.'

This did not, however, prevent him from dying the same day, without waiting for the district doctor, who (on seeing the hardly cold body) found nothing left for him to do, but with a melancholy recognition of the instability of all things mortal, to ask for 'a drop of vodka and a snack of fish.' As might have been anticipated, Tihon Ivanitch had bequeathed his property to his revered patron and generous protector, Panteley Eremyitch Tchertop-hanov; but it was of no great benefit to the revered patron, as it was shortly after sold by public auction, partly in order to cover the expense of a sepulchral monument, a statue, which Tchertop-hanov (and one can see his father's craze coming out in him here) had thought fit to put up over the ashes of his friend. This statue, which was to have represented an angel praying, was ordered by him from Moscow; but the agent recommended to him, conceiving that connoisseurs in sculpture were not often to be met with in the provinces, sent him, instead of an angel, a goddess Flora, which had for many years adorned one of those neglected gardens near Moscow, laid out in the days of Catherine. He had an excellent reason for doing so, since this statue, though highly artistic, in the rococo style, with plump little arms, tossing curls, a wreath of roses round the bare bosom, and a serpentine figure, was obtained by him, the agent, for nothing. And so to this day the mythological goddess stands, with one foot elegantly lifted, above the tomb of Tihon Ivanovitch, and with a genuinely Pompadour simper, gazes at the calves and sheep, those invariable visitors of our village graveyards, as they stray about her.

III

On the loss of his faithful friend, Tchertop-hanov again took to drink, and this time far more seriously. Everything went utterly to the bad with him. He had no money left for sport; the last of his meagre fortune was spent; the last of his few servants ran away. Panteley Eremyitch's isolation became complete: he had no one to speak a word to even, far less to open his heart to. His pride alone had suffered no diminution. On the contrary, the worse his surroundings became, the more haughty and lofty and inaccessible he was himself. He became a complete misanthrope in the end. One distraction, one delight, was left him: a superb grey horse, of the Don breed, named by him Malek-Adel, a really wonderful animal.

This horse came into his possession in this fashion.

As he was riding one day through a neighbouring village, Tchertop-hanov heard a crowd of peasants shouting and hooting before a tavern. In the middle of the crowd stalwart arms were continually rising and falling in exactly the same place.

'What is happening there?' he asked, in the peremptory tone peculiar to him, of an old peasant woman who was standing on the threshold of her hut. Leaning against the doorpost as though dozing, the old woman stared in the direction of the tavern. A white-headed urchin in a print smock, with a cypress-wood cross on his little bare breast, was sitting with little outstretched legs, and little clenched fists between her bast slippers; a chicken close by was chipping at a stale crust of rye-bread.

'The Lord knows, your honour,' answered the old woman. Bending forward, she laid her wrinkled brown hand on the child's head. 'They say our lads are beating a Jew.'

'A Jew? What Jew?'

'The Lord knows, your honour. A Jew came among us; and where he's come from--who knows? Vassya, come to your mammy, sir; sh, sh, nasty brute!'

The old woman drove away the chicken, while Vassya clung to her petticoat.

'So, you see, they're beating him, sir.'

'Why beating him? What for?'

'I don't know, your honour. No doubt, he deserves it. And, indeed, why not beat him? You know, your honour, he crucified Christ!'

Tchertop-hanov uttered a whoop, gave his horse a lash on the neck with the riding-whip, flew straight towards the crowd, and plunging into it, began with the same riding-whip thrashing the peasants to left and to right indiscriminately, shouting in broken tones: 'Lawless brutes! lawless brutes! It's for the law to punish, and not pri-vate per-sons! The law! the law! the law!'

Before two minutes had passed the crowd had beaten a retreat in various directions; and on the ground before the tavern door could be seen a small, thin, swarthy creature, in a nankin long coat, dishevelled and mangled... a pale face, rolling eyes, open mouth.... What was it?... deadly terror, or death itself?

'Why have you killed this Jew?' Tchertop-hanov shouted at the top of his voice, brandishing his riding-whip menacingly.

The crowd faintly roared in response. One peasant was rubbing his shoulder, another his side, a third his nose.

'You're pretty free with your whip!' was heard in the back rows.

'Why have you killed the Jew, you christened Pagans?' repeated Tchertop-hanov.

But, at this point, the creature lying on the ground hurriedly jumped on to its feet, and, running up to Tchertop-hanov, convulsively seized hold of the edge of the saddle.

'Alive!' was heard in the background.

'He's a regular cat!'

'Your ex-shelency, defend me, save me!' the unhappy Jew was faltering meanwhile, his whole body squeezed up against Tchertop-hanov's foot; 'or they will murder me, they will murder me, your ex-shelency!'

'What have they against you?' asked Tchertop-hanov.

'I can't tell, so help me God! Some cow hereabouts died... so they suspect me... but I...' 'Well, that we'll go into later!' Tchertop-hanov interrupted; 'but now, you hold on to the saddle and follow me. And you!' he added, turning to the crowd,' do you know me?-- I'm the landowner Panteley Tchertop-hanov. I live at Bezsonovo,--and so you can take proceedings against me, when you think fit--and against the Jew too, while you're about it!'

'Why take proceedings?' said a grey-bearded, decent-looking peasant, bowing low, the very picture of an ancient patriarch. (He had been no whit behind the others in belabouring the Jew, however). 'We know your honour, Panteley Eremyitch, well; we thank your honour humbly for teaching us better!'

'Why take proceedings?' chimed in the others.

'As to the Jew, we'll take it out of him another day! He won't escape us! We shall be on the look-out for him.'

Tchertop-hanov pulled his moustaches, snorted, and went home at a walking pace, accompanied by the Jew, whom he had delivered from his persecutors just as he had once delivered Tihon Nedopyuskin.

IV

A few days later the one groom who was left to Tchertop-hanov announced that someone had come on horseback and wanted to speak to him. Tchertop-hanov went out on to the steps and recognised the Jew, riding a splendid horse of the Don breed, which stood proud and motionless in the middle of the courtyard. The Jew was bareheaded; he held his cap under his arm, and had thrust his feet into the stirrup-straps, not into the stirrups themselves; the ragged skirts of his long coat hung down on both sides of the saddle. On seeing Tchertop-hanov, he gave a smack with his lips, and ducked down with a twitch of the elbows and a bend of the legs. Tchertop-hanov, however, not only failed to respond to his greeting, but was even enraged by it; he was all on fire in a minute: a scurvy Jew dare to ride a magnificent horse like that!... It was positively indecent!

'Hi, you Ethiopian fright!' he shouted; 'get off at once, if you don't want to be flung off into the mud!'

The Jew promptly obeyed, rolled off the horse like a sack, and keeping hold of the rein with one hand, he approached Tchertop-hanov, smiling and bowing.

'What do you want?' Panteley Eremyitch inquired with dignity.

'Your ex-shelency, deign to look what a horse!' said the Jew, never ceasing to bow for an instant.

'Er... well... the horse is all right. Where did you get it from? Stole it, I suppose?'

'How can you say that, your ex-shelency! I'm an honest Jew. I didn't steal it, but I obtained it for your ex-shelency--really! And the trouble, the trouble I had to get it? But, then, see what a horse it is! There's not another horse like it to be found in all the Don country! Look, your ex-shelency, what a horse it is! Here, kindly step this way! Wo!... wo!... turn round, stand sideways! And we'll take off the saddle. What do you think of him, your ex-shelency?'

'The horse is all right,' repeated Tchertop-hanov with affected indifference, though his heart was beating like a sledge-hammer in his breast. He was a passionate lover of 'horse-flesh,' and knew a good thing when he saw it.

'Only take a look at him, your ex-shelency! Pat him on the neck! yes, yes, he-he-he-he! like this, like this!'

Tchertop-hanov, with apparent reluctance, laid his hand on the horse's neck, gave it a pat or two, then passed his fingers from the forelock along the spine, and when he had reached a certain spot above the kidneys, like a connoisseur, he lightly pressed that spot. The horse instantly arched its spine, and looking round suspiciously at Tchertop-hanov with its haughty black eye, snorted and moved its hind legs.

The Jew laughed and faintly clapped his hands. 'He knows his master, your ex-shelency, his master!'

'Don't talk nonsense,' Tchertop-hanov interrupted with vexation. 'To buy this horse from you... I haven't the means, and as for presents, I not only wouldn't take them from a Jew; I wouldn't take a present from Almighty God Himself!'

'As though I would presume to offer you a present, mercy upon me!' cried the Jew: 'you buy it, your ex-shelency... and as to the little sum--I can wait for it.'

Tchertop-hanov sank into thought.

'What will you take for it?' he muttered at last between his teeth.

The Jew shrugged his shoulders.

'What I paid for it myself. Two hundred roubles.'

The horse was well worth twice---perhaps even three times that sum.

Tchertop-hanov turned away and yawned feverishly.

'And the money... when?' he asked, scowling furiously and not looking at the Jew.

'When your ex-shelency thinks fit.'

Tchertop-hanov flung his head back, but did not raise his eyes. 'That's no answer. Speak plainly, son of Herod! Am I to be under an obligation to you, hey?'

'Well, let's say, then,' the Jew hastened to add, 'in six months' time... Do you agree?'

Tchertop-hanov made no reply.

The Jew tried to get a look at his face. 'Do you agree? You permit him to be led to your stable?'

'The saddle I don't want,' Tchertop-hanov blurted out abruptly. 'Take the saddle--do you hear?'

'To be sure, to be sure, I will take it,' faltered the delighted Jew, shouldering the saddle.

'And the money,' Tchertop-hanov pursued... 'in six months. And not two hundred, but two hundred and fifty. Not a word! Two hundred and fifty, I tell you! to my account.'

Tchertop-hanov still could not bring himself to raise his eyes. Never had his pride been so cruelly wounded.

'It's plain, it's a present,' was the thought in his mind; 'he's brought it out of gratitude, the devil!' And he would have liked to kiss the Jew, and he would have liked to beat him.

'Your ex-shelency,' began the Jew, gaining a little courage, and grinning all over his face, 'should, after the Russian fashion, take from hand to hand....'

'What next? what an idea! A Hebrew... and Russian customs! Hey! you there! Take the horse; lead him to the stable. And give him some oats. I'll come myself and look after him. And his name is to be--Malek-Adel!'

Tchertop-hanov turned to go up the steps, but turning sharply back, and running up to the Jew, he pressed his hand warmly. The latter was bending down to kiss his hand, but Tchertop-hanov bounded back again, and murmuring, 'Tell no one!' he vanished through the door.

V

From that very day the chief interest, the chief occupation, the chief pleasure in the life of Tchertop-hanov, was Malek-Adel. He loved him as he had not loved even Masha; he became more attached to him than even to Nedopyuskin. And what a horse it was! All fire--simply explosive as gunpowder--and stately as a boyar! Untiring, enduring, obedient, whatever you might put him to; and costing nothing for his keep; he'd be ready to nibble at the ground under his feet if there was nothing else. When he stepped at a walking pace, it was like being lulled to sleep in a nurse's arms; when he trotted, it was like rocking at sea; when he galloped, he outstripped the wind! Never out of breath, perfectly sound in his wind. Sinews of steel: for him to stumble was a thing never recorded! To take a ditch or a fence was nothing to him--and what a clever beast! At his master's voice he would run with his head in the air; if you told him to stand still and walked away from him, he would not stir; directly you turned back, a faint neigh to say, 'Here I am.' And afraid of nothing: in the pitch-dark, in a snow-storm he would find his way; and he would not let a stranger come near him for anything; he would have had his teeth in him! And a dog dare never approach him; he would have his fore-leg on his head in a minute! and that was the end of the beast. A horse of proper pride, you might flourish a switch over him as an ornament--but God forbid you touched him! But why say more?--a perfect treasure, not a horse!

If Tchertop-hanov set to describing his Malek-Adel, he could not find words to express himself. And how he petted and pampered him! His coat shone like silver--not old, but new silver--with a dark polish on it; if one passed one's hand over it, it was like velvet! His saddle, his cloth, his bridle--all his trappings, in fact, were so well-fitted, in such good order, so bright--a perfect picture! Tchertop-hanov himself--what more can we say?--with his own hands plaited his favourite's forelocks and mane, and washed his tail with beer, and even, more than once, rubbed his hoofs with polish. Sometimes he would mount Malek-Adel and ride out, not to see his neighbours--he avoided them, as of old--but across their lands, past their homesteads... for them, poor fools, to admire him from a distance! Or he would hear that there was to be a hunt somewhere, that a rich landowner had arranged a meet in some outlying part of his land: he would be off there at once, and would canter in the distance, on the horizon, astounding all spectators by the swiftness and beauty of his horse, and not letting any one come close to him. Once some hunting landowner even gave chase to him with all his suite; he saw Tchertop-hanov was getting away, and he began shouting after him with all his might, as he galloped at full speed: 'Hey, you! Here! Take what you like for your horse! I wouldn't grudge a thousand! I'd give my wife, my children! Take my last farthing!'

Tchertop-hanov suddenly reined in Malek-Adel. The hunting gentleman flew up to him. 'My dear sir!' he shouted, 'tell me what you want? My dear friend!'

'If you were the Tsar,' said Tchertop-hanov emphatically (and he had never heard of Shakespeare), 'you might give me all your kingdom for my horse; I wouldn't take it!' He uttered these words, chuckled, drew Malek-Adel up on to his haunches, turned him in the air on his hind legs like a top or teetotum, and off! He went like a flash over the stubble. And the hunting man (a rich prince, they said he was) flung his cap on the ground, threw himself down with his face in his cap, and lay so for half an hour.

And how could Tchertop-hanov fail to prize his horse? Was it not thanks to him, he had again an unmistakable superiority, a last superiority over all his neighbours?

VI

Meanwhile time went by, the day fixed for payment was approaching; while, far from having two hundred and fifty roubles, Tchertop-hanov had not even fifty. What was to be done? how could it be met? 'Well,' he decided at last, 'if the Jew is relentless, if he won't wait any longer, I'll give him my house and my land, and I'll set off on my horse, no matter where! I'll starve before I'll give up Malek-Adel!' He was greatly perturbed and even downcast; but at this juncture Fate, for the first and last time, was pitiful and smiled upon him; some distant kinswoman, whose very name was unknown to Tchertop-hanov, left him in her will a sum immense in his eyes--no less than two thousand roubles! And he received this sum in the very nick, as they say, of time; the day before the Jew was to come. Tchertop-hanov almost went out of his mind with joy, but he never even thought of vodka; from the very day Malek-Adel came into his hands he had not touched a drop.

He ran into the stable and kissed his favourite on both sides of his face above the nostrils, where the horse's skin is always so soft. 'Now we shall not be parted!' he cried, patting Malek-Adel on the neck, under his well-combed mane. When he went back into the house, he counted out and sealed up in a packet two hundred and fifty roubles. Then, as he lay on his back and smoked a pipe, he mused on how he would lay out the rest of the money--what dogs he would procure, real Kostroma hounds, spot and tan, and no mistake! He even had a little talk with Perfishka, to whom he promised a new Cossack coat, with yellow braid on all the seams, and went to bed in a blissful frame of mind.

He had a bad dream: he dreamt he was riding out, hunting, not on Malek-Adel, but on some strange beast of the nature of a unicorn; a white fox, white as snow, ran to meet him.... He tried to crack his whip, tried to set the dogs on her--but instead of his riding-whip, he found he had a wisp of bast in his hand, and the fox ran in front of him, putting her tongue out at him. He jumped off, his unicorn stumbled, he fell... and fell straight into the arms of a police-constable, who was taking him before the Governor-General, and whom he recognised as Yaff....

Tchertop-hanov waked up. The room was dark; the cocks were just crowing for the second time.... Somewhere in the far, far distance a horse neighed. Tchertop-hanov lifted up his head.... Once more a faint, faint neigh was heard.

'That's Malek-Adel neighing!' was his thought.... 'It's his neigh. But why so far away? Bless us and save us!... It can't be...'

Tchertop-hanov suddenly turned chill all over; he instantly leaped out of bed, fumbled after his boots and his clothes, dressed himself, and, snatching up the stable-door key from under his pillow, he dashed out into the courtyard.

VII

The stable was at the very end of the courtyard; one wall faced the open country. Tchertop-hanov could not at once fit the key into the lock--his hands were shaking--and he did not immediately turn the key.... He stood motionless, holding his breath; if only something would stir inside! 'Malek! Malek!' he cried, in a low voice: the silence of death! Tchertop-hanov unconsciously jogged the key; the door creaked and opened.... So, it was not locked. He stepped over the threshold, and again called his horse; this time by his full name, Malek-Adel! But no response came from his faithful companion; only a mouse rustled in the straw. Then Tchertop-hanov rushed into one of the three horse-boxes in the stable in which Malek-Adel was put. He went straight to the horse-box, though it was pitch-dark around.... Empty! Tchertop-hanov's head went round; it seemed as though a bell was booming in his brain. He tried to say something, but only brought out a sort of hiss; and fumbling with his hands above, below, on all sides, breathless, with shaking knees, he made his way from one horse-box to another... to a third, full almost to the top with hay; stumbled against one wall, and then the other; fell down, rolled over on his head, got up, and suddenly ran headlong through the half-open door into the courtyard....

'Stolen! Perfishka! Perfishka! Stolen!' he yelled at the top of his voice.

The groom Perfishka flew head-over-heels out of the loft where he slept, with only his shirt on....

Like drunk men they ran against one another, the master and his solitary servant, in the middle of the courtyard; like madmen they turned round each other. The master could not explain what was the matter; nor could the servant make out what was wanted of him. 'Woe! woe!' wailed Tchertop-hanov. 'Woe! woe!' the groom repeated after him. 'A lantern!

here! light a lantern! Light! light!' broke at last from Tchertop-hanov's fainting lips. Perfishka rushed into the house.

But to light the lantern, to get fire, was not easy; lucifer matches were regarded as a rarity in those days in Russia; the last embers had long ago gone out in the kitchen; flint and steel were not quickly found, and they did not work well. Gnashing his teeth, Tchertop-hanov snatched them out of the hands of the flustered Perfishka, and began striking a light himself; the sparks fell in abundance, in still greater abundance fell curses, and even groans; but the tinder either did not catch or went out again, in spite of the united efforts of four swollen cheeks and lips to blow it into a flame! At last, in five minutes, not sooner, a bit of tallow candle was alight at the bottom of a battered lantern; and Tchertop-hanov, accompanied by Perfishka, dashed into the stable, lifted the lantern above his head, looked round....

All empty!

He bounded out into the courtyard, ran up and down it in all directions--no horse anywhere! The hurdle-fence, enclosing Panteley Eremyitch's yard, had long been dilapidated, and in many places was bent and lying on the ground.... Beside the stable, it had been completely levelled for a good yard's width. Perfishka pointed this spot out to Tchertop-hanov.

'Master! look here; this wasn't like this to-day. And see the ends of the uprights sticking out of the ground; that means someone has pulled them out.'

Tchertop-hanov ran up with the lantern, moved it about over the ground....

'Hoofs, hoofs, prints of horse-shoes, fresh prints!' he muttered, speaking hurriedly.' They took him through here, through here!'

He instantly leaped over the fence, and with a shout, 'Malek-Adel! Malek-Adel!' he ran straight into the open country.

Perfishka remained standing bewildered at the fence. The ring of light from the lantern was soon lost to his eyes, swallowed up in the dense darkness of a starless, moonless night.

Fainter and fainter came the sound of the despairing cries of Tchertop-hanov....

VIII

It was daylight when he came home again. He hardly looked like a human being. His clothes were covered with mud, his face had a wild and ferocious expression, his eyes looked dull and sullen. In a hoarse whisper he drove Perfishka away, and locked himself in his room. He could hardly stand with fatigue, but he did not lie on his bed, but sat down on a chair by the door and clutched at his head.

'Stolen!... stolen!...'

But in what way had the thief contrived by night, when the stable was locked, to steal Malek-Adel? Malek-Adel, who would never let a stranger come near him even by day--steal him, too, without noise, without a sound? And how explain that not a yard-dog had barked? It was true there were only two left--two young puppies--and those two probably burrowing in rubbish from cold and hunger--but still!

'And what am I to do now without Malek-Adel?' Tchertop-hanov brooded. 'I've lost my last pleasure now; it's time to die. Buy another horse, seeing the money has come? But where find another horse like that?'

'Panteley Eremyitch! Panteley Eremyitch!' he heard a timid call at the door.

Tchertop-hanov jumped on to his feet.

'Who is it?' he shouted in a voice not his own.

'It's I, your groom, Perfishka.'

'What do you want? Is he found? has he run home?'

'No, Panteley Eremyitch; but that Jew chap who sold him.'...

'Well?'

'He's come.'

'Ho-ho-ho-ho-ho!' yelled Tchertop-hanov, and he at once flung open the door. 'Drag him here! drag him along!'

On seeing the sudden apparition of his 'benefactor's' dishevelled, wild-looking figure, the Jew, who was standing behind Perfishka's back, tried to give them the slip; but Tchertop-hanov, in two bounds, was upon him, and like a tiger flew at his throat.

'Ah! he's come for the money! for the money!' he cried as hoarsely as though he were being strangled himself instead of strangling the Jew; 'you stole him by night, and are come by day for the money, eh? Eh? Eh?'

'Mercy on us, your ex-shelency,' the Jew tried to groan out.

'Tell me, where's my horse? What have you done with him? Whom have you sold him to? Tell me, tell me, tell me!'

The Jew by now could not even groan; his face was rapidly turning livid, and even the expression of fear had vanished from it. His hands dropped and hung lifeless, his whole body, furiously shaken by Tchertop-hanov, waved backwards and forwards like a reed.

'I'll pay you your money, I'll pay it you in full to the last farthing,' roared Tchertop-hanov, 'but I'll strangle you like any chicken if you don't tell me at once!'...

'But you have strangled him already, master,' observed the groom Perfishka humbly.

Then only Tchertop-hanov came to his senses.

He let go of the Jew's neck; the latter fell heavily to the ground. Tchertop-hanov picked him up, sat him on a bench, poured a glass of vodka down his throat, and restored him to consciousness. And having restored him to consciousness, he began to talk to him.

It turned out that the Jew had not the slightest idea that Malek-Adel had been stolen. And, indeed, what motive could he have to steal the horse which he had himself procured for his 'revered Panteley Eremyitch.'

Then Tchertop-hanov led him into the stable.

Together they scrutinised the horse-boxes, the manger, and the lock on the door, turned over the hay and the straw, and then went into the courtyard. Tchertop-hanov showed the Jew the hoofprints at the fence, and all at once he slapped his thighs.

'Stay!' he cried. 'Where did you buy the horse?'

'In the district of Maloarchangel, at Verhosensky Fair,' answered the Jew.

'Of whom?'

'A Cossack.'

Stay! This Cossack; was he a young man or old?'

'Middle-aged--a steady man.'

'And what was he like? What did he look like? A cunning rascal, I expect?'

'Sure to have been a rascal, your ex-shelency.'

'And, I say, what did he say, this rascal?--had he had the horse long?'

'I recollect he said he'd had it a long while.'

'Well, then, no one could have stolen him but he! Consider it yourself, listen, stand here!... What's your name?'

The Jew started and turned his little black eyes upon Tchertop-hanov.

'What's my name?'

'Yes, yes; what are you called?'

'Moshel Leyba.'

'Well, judge then, Moshel Leyba, my friend--you're a man of sense--whom would Malek-Adel have allowed to touch him except his old master? You see he must have saddled him and bridled him and taken off his cloth--there it is lying on the hay!... and made all his arrangements simply as if he were at home! Why, anyone except his master, Malek-Adel would have trampled under foot! He'd have raised such a din, he'd have roused the whole village? Do you agree with me?'

'I agree, I agree, your ex-shelency.'...

'Well, then, it follows that first of all we must find this Cossack!'

'But how are we to find him, your ex-shelency? I have only seen him one little time in my life, and where is he now, and what's his name? Alack, alack!' added the Jew, shaking the long curls over his ears sorrowfully.

'Leyba!' shouted Tchertop-hanov suddenly; 'Leyba, look at me! You see I've lost my senses; I'm not myself!... I shall lay hands on myself if you don't come to my aid!'

'But how can I?'...

'Come with me, and let us find the thief.'

'But where shall we go?'

'We'll go to the fairs, the highways and by-ways, to the horse-stealers, to towns and villages and hamlets--everywhere, everywhere! And don't trouble about money; I've come into a fortune, brother! I'll spend my last farthing, but I'll get my darling back! And he shan't escape us, our enemy, the Cossack! Where he goes we'll go! If he's hidden in the earth we'll follow him! If he's gone to the devil, we'll follow him to Satan himself!'

'Oh, why to Satan?' observed the Jew; 'we can do without him.'

'Leyba!' Tchertop-hanov went on; 'Leyba, though you're a Jew, and your creed's an accursed one, you've a soul better than many a Christian soul! Have pity on me! I can't go alone; alone I can never carry the thing through. I'm a hot-headed fellow, but you've a brain--a brain worth its weight in gold! Your race are like that; you succeed in everything without being taught! You're wondering, perhaps, where I could have got the money? Come into my room--I'll show you all the money. You may take it, you may take the cross off my neck, only give me back Malek-Adel; give him me back again!'

Tchertop-hanov was shivering as if he were in a fever; the sweat rolled down his face in drops, and, mingling with his tears, was lost in his moustaches. He pressed Leyba's hands, he besought him, he almost kissed him.... He was in a sort of delirium. The Jew tried to object, to declare that it was utterly impossible for him to get away; that he had business.... It was useless! Tchertop-hanov would not even hear anything. There was no help for it; the poor Jew consented.

The next day Tchertop-hanov set out from Bezsonovo in a peasant cart, with Leyba. The Jew wore a somewhat troubled aspect; he held on to the rail with one hand, while all his withered figure bounded up and down on the jolting seat; the other hand he held pressed to his bosom, where lay a packet of notes wrapped up in newspaper. Tchertop-hanov sat like a statue, only moving his eyes about him, and drawing in deep breaths; in his sash there was stuck a dagger.

'There, the miscreant who has parted us must look out for himself now!' he muttered, as they drove out on the high-road.

His house he left in the charge of Perfishka and an old cook, a deaf old peasant woman, whom he took care of out of compassion.

'I shall come back to you on Malek-Adel,' he shouted to them at parting, 'or never come back at all!'

'You might as well be married to me at once!' jested Perfishka, giving the cook a dig in the ribs with his elbow. 'No fear! the master'll never come back to us; and here I shall be bored to death all alone!'

IX

A year passed... a whole year: no news had come of Panteley Eremyitch. The cook was dead, Perfishka himself made up his mind to abandon the house and go off to town, where he was constantly being persuaded to come by his cousin, apprenticed to a barber; when suddenly a rumour was set afloat that his master was coming back. The parish deacon got a letter from Panteley Eremyitch himself, in which he informed him of his intention of arriving at Bezsonovo, and asked him to prepare his servant to be ready for his immediate return. These words Perfishka understood to mean that he was to sweep up the place a bit. He did not, however, put much confidence in the news; he was convinced, though, that the deacon had spoken the truth, when a few days later Panteley Eremyitch in person appeared in the courtyard, riding on Malek-Adel.

Perfishka rushed up to his master, and, holding the stirrup, would have helped him to dismount, but the latter got off alone, and with a triumphant glance about him, cried in a loud voice: 'I said I would find Malek-Adel, and I have found him in spite of my enemies, and of Fate itself!' Perfishka went up to kiss his hand, but Tchertop-hanov paid no attention to his servant's devotion. Leading Malek-Adel after him by the rein, he went with long strides towards the stable. Perfishka looked more intently at his master, and his heart sank. 'Oh, how thin and old he's grown in a year; and what a stern, grim face!' One would have thought Panteley Eremyitch would have been rejoicing, that he had gained his end; and he was rejoicing, certainly... and yet Perfishka's heart sank: he even felt a sort of dread. Tchertop-hanov put the horse in its old place, gave him a light pat on the back, and said, 'There! now you're at home again; and mind what you're about.' The same day he hired a freedman out of work as watchman, established himself again in his rooms, and began living as before....

Not altogether as before, however... but of that later...

The day after his return, Panteley Eremyitch called Perfishka in to him, and for want of anyone else to talk to, began telling him--keeping up, of course, his sense of his own dignity and his bass voice--how he had succeeded in finding Malek-Adel. Tchertop-hanov sat facing the window while he told his story, and smoked a pipe with a long tube while Perfishka stood in the doorway, his hands behind his back, and, respectfully contemplating the back of his master's head, heard him relate how, after many fruitless efforts and idle expeditions, Panteley Eremyitch had at last come to the fair at Romyon by himself, without the Jew Leyba, who, through weakness of character, had not persevered, but had deserted him; how, on the fifth day, when he was on the point of leaving, he walked for the last time along the rows of carts, and all at once he saw between three other horses fastened to the railings--he saw Malek-Adel! How he knew him at once, and how Malek-Adel knew him too, and began neighing, and dragging at his tether, and scraping the earth with his hoof.

'And he was not with the Cossack,' Tchertop-hanov went on, still not turning his head, and in the same bass voice, 'but with a gypsy horse-dealer; I, of course, at once took hold of my horse and tried to get him away by force, but the brute of a gypsy started yelling as if he'd been scalded, all over the market, and began swearing he'd bought the horse off another gypsy--and wanted to bring witnesses to prove it.... I spat, and paid him the money: damn the fellow! All I cared for was that I had found my favourite, and had got back my peace of mind. Moreover, in the Karatchevsky district, I took a man for the Cossack--I took the Jew Leyba's word for it that he was my thief--and smashed his face for him; but the Cossack turned out to be a priest's son, and got damages out of me--a hundred and twenty roubles. Well, money's a thing one may get again, but the great thing is, I've Malek-Adel back again! I'm happy now--I'm going to enjoy myself in peace. And I've one instruction to give you, Perfishka: if ever you, which God forbid, catch sight of the Cossack in this neighbourhood, run the very minute without saying a word, and bring me my gun, and I shall know what to do!'

This was what Panteley Eremyitch said to Perfishka: this was how his tongue spoke; but at heart he was not so completely at peace as he declared.

Alas! in his heart of hearts he was not perfectly convinced that the horse he had brought back was really Malek-Adel!

X

Troubled times followed for Panteley Eremyitch. Peace was just the last thing he enjoyed. He had some happy days, it is true; the doubt stirring within him would seem to him all nonsense; he would drive away the ridiculous idea, like a persistent fly, and even laugh at himself; but he had bad days too: the importunate thought began again stealthily gnawing and tearing at his heart, like a mouse under the floor, and he existed in secret torture. On the memorable day when he found Malek-Adel, Tchertop-hanov had felt nothing but rapturous bliss... but the next morning, when, in a low-pitched shed of the inn, he began saddling his recovered joy, beside whom he had spent the whole night, he felt for the first time a certain secret pang.... He only shook his head, but the seed was sown. During the homeward journey (it lasted a whole week) doubts seldom arose in him; they grew stronger and more distinct directly he was back at Bezsonovo, directly he was home again in the place where the old authentic Malek-Adel had lived.... On the road home he had ridden at a quiet, swinging pace, looking in all directions, smoking a short pipe, and not reflecting at all, except at times the thought struck him: 'When the Tchertop-hanovs want a thing, they get it, you bet!' and he smiled to himself; but on his return home it was a very different state of things. All this, however, he kept to himself; vanity alone would have prevented him from giving utterance to his inner dread. He would have torn anyone to pieces who had dropped the most distant hint that the new Malek-Adel was possibly not the old one; he accepted congratulations on his 'successful recovery of his horse,' from the few persons whom he happened to meet; but he did not seek such congratulations; he avoided all contact with people more than ever--a bad sign! He was almost always putting Malek-Adel through examinations, if one may use the expression; he would ride him out to some point at a little distance in the open country, and put him to the proof, or would go stealthily into the stable, lock the door after him, and standing right before the horse's head, look into his eyes, and ask him in a whisper, 'Is it you? Is it you? You?'... or else stare at him silently and intently for hours together, and then mutter, brightening up: 'Yes! it's he! Of course it's he!' or else go out with a puzzled, even confused look on his face. Tchertop-hanov was not so much confused by the physical differences between this Malek-Adel and that one... though there were a few such differences: that one's tail and mane were a little thinner, and his ears more pointed, and his pasterns shorter, and his eyes brighter--but all that might be only fancy; what confounded Tchertop-hanov most were, so to say, the moral differences. The habits of that one had been different: all his ways were not the same. For instance, that Malek-Adel had looked round and given a faint neigh every time Tchertop-hanov went into the stable; while this one went on munching hay as though nothing had happened, or dozed with his head bent. Both of them stood still when their master leaped out of the saddle; but that one came at once at his voice when he was called, while this one stood stock still. That one galloped as fast, but with higher and longer bounds; this one went with a freer step and at a more jolting trot, and at times 'wriggled' with his shoes--that is, knocked the back one against the front one; that one had never done anything so disgraceful--God forbid! This one, it struck Tchertop-hanov, kept twitching his ears in such a stupid way, while with that one it was quite the contrary; he used to lay one ear back, and hold it so, as though on the alert for his master! That one, directly he saw that it was dirty about him, would at once knock on the partition of his box with his hind-leg, but this one did not care if the dung was heaped up to his belly. That one if, for instance, he were set facing the wind, would take deep breaths and shake himself, this one simply snorted; that one was put out by the rain, this one cared nothing for it.... This was a coarser beast--coarser! And there wasn't the gentleness in it, and hard in the mouth it was--no denying it! That horse was a darling, but this....

This was what Tchertop-hanov sometimes thought, and very bitter were such thoughts to him. At other times he would set his horse at full gallop over some newly ploughed field, or would make him leap down to the very bottom of a hollow ravine, and leap out again at the very steepest point, and his heart would throb with rapture, a loud whoop would break from his lips, and he would know, would know for certain, that it was the real, authentic Malek-Adel he had under him; for what other horse could do what this one was doing?

However, there were sometimes shortcomings and misfortunes even here. The prolonged search for Malek-Adel had cost Tchertop-hanov a great deal of money; he did not even dream of Kostroma hounds now, and rode about the neighbourhood in solitude as before. So one morning, four miles from Bezsonovo, Tchertop-hanov chanced to come upon the same prince's hunting party before whom he had cut such a triumphant figure a year and a half before. And, as fate would have it, just as on that day a hare must go leaping out from the hedge before the dogs, down the hillside! Tally-ho! Tally-ho! All the hunt fairly flew after it, and Tchertop-hanov flew along too, but not with the rest of the party, but two hundred paces to one side of it, just as he had done the time before. A huge watercourse ran zigzagging across the hillside, and as it rose higher and higher got gradually narrower, cutting off Tchertop-hanov's path. At the point where he had to jump it, and where, eighteen months before, he actually had jumped it, it was eight feet wide and fourteen feet deep. In anticipation of a triumph--a triumph repeated in such a delightful way--Tchertop-hanov chuckled exultantly, cracked his riding-whip; the hunting party were galloping too, their eyes fixed on the daring rider; his horse whizzed along like a bullet, and now the watercourse was just under his nose--now, now, at one leap, as then!... But Malek-Adel pulled up sharply, wheeled to the left, and in spite of Tchertop-hanov's tugging him to the edge, to the watercourse, he galloped along beside the ravine.

He was afraid, then; did not trust himself!

Then Tchertop-hanov, burning with shame and wrath, almost in tears, dropped the reins, and set the horse going straight forward, down the hill, away, away from the hunting party, if only not to hear them jeering at him, to escape as soon as might be from their damnable eyes!

Covered with foam, his sides lashed unmercifully, Malek-Adel galloped home, and Tchertop-hanov at once locked himself into his room.

'No, it's not he; it's not my darling! He would have broken his neck before he would have betrayed me!'

XI

What finally 'did for,' as they say, Tchertop-hanov was the following circumstance. One day he sauntered, riding on Malek-Adel, about the back-yards of the priest's quarters round about the church of the parish in which is Bezsonovo. Huddled up, with his Cossack fur cap pulled down over his eyes, and his hands hanging loose on the saddle-bow, he jogged slowly on, a vague discontent in his heart. Suddenly someone called him.

He stopped his horse, raised his head, and saw his correspondent, the deacon. With a brown, three-cornered hat on his brown hair, which was plaited in a pig-tail, attired in a yellowish nankin long coat, girt much below the waist by a strip of blue stuff, the servant of the altar had come out into his back-garden, and, catching sight of Panteley Eremyitch, he thought it his duty to pay his respects to him, and to take the opportunity of doing so to ask him a question about something. Without some such hidden motive, as we know, ecclesiastical persons do not venture to address temporal ones.

But Tchertop-hanov was in no mood for the deacon; he barely responded to his bow, and, muttering something between his teeth, he was already cracking his whip, when....

'What a magnificent horse you have!' the deacon made haste to add: 'and really you can take credit to yourself for it. Truly you're a man of amazing cleverness, simply a lion indeed!'

His reverence the deacon prided himself on his fluency, which was a great source of vexation to his reverence the priest, to whom the gift of words had not been vouchsafed; even vodka did not loosen his tongue.

'After losing one animal by the cunning of evil men,' continued the deacon, 'you did not lose courage in repining; but, on the other hand, trusting the more confidently in Divine Providence, procured yourself another, in no wise inferior, but even, one may say, superior, since....'

'What nonsense are you talking?' Tchertop-hanov interrupted gloomily; 'what other horse do you mean? This is the same one; this is Malek-Adel.... I found him. The fellow's raving!'....

'Ay! ay! ay!' responded the deacon emphatically with a sort of drawl, drumming with his fingers in his beard, and eyeing Tchertop-hanov with his bright eager eyes: 'How's that, sir? Your horse, God help my memory, was stolen a fortnight before Intercession last year, and now we're near the end of November.'

'Well, what of that?'

The deacon still fingered his beard.

'Why, it follows that more than a year's gone by since then, and your horse was a dapple grey then, just as it is now; in fact, it seems even darker. How's that? Grey horses get a great deal lighter in colour in a year.'

Tchertop-hanov started... as though someone had driven a dagger into his heart. It was true: the grey colour did change! How was it such a simple reflection had never occurred to him?

'You damned pigtail! get out!' he yelled suddenly, his eyes flashing with fury, and instantaneously he disappeared out of the sight of the amazed deacon.

Well, everything was over!

Now, at last, everything was really over, everything was shattered, the last card trumped. Everything crumbled away at once before that word 'lighter'!

Grey horses get lighter in colour! 'Gallop, gallop on, accursed brute! You can never gallop away from that word!'

Tchertop-hanov flew home, and again locked himself up.

XII

That this worthless jade was not Malek-Adel; that between him and Malek-Adel there was not the smallest resemblance; that any man of the slightest sense would have seen this from the first minute; that he, Tchertop-hanov, had been taken in in the vulgarest way--no! that he purposely, of set intent, tricked himself, blinded his own eyes--of all this he had not now the faintest doubt!

Tchertop-hanov walked up and down in his room, turning monotonously on his heels at each wall, like a beast in a cage. His vanity suffered intolerably; but he was not only tortured by the sting of wounded vanity; he was overwhelmed by despair, stifled by rage, and burning with the thirst for revenge. But rage against whom? On whom was he to be revenged? On the Jew, Yaff, Masha, the deacon, the Cossack-thief, all his neighbours, the whole world, himself? His brain was giving way. The last card was trumped! (That simile gratified him.) And he was again the most worthless, the most contemptible of men, a common laughing-stock, a motley fool, a damned idiot, an object for jibes--to a deacon!... He fancied, he pictured vividly how that loathsome pig-tailed priest would tell the story of the grey horse and the foolish gentleman.... O damn!! In vain Tchertop-hanov tried to check his rising passion, in vain he tried to assure himself that this... horse, though not Malek-Adel, was still... a good horse, and might be of service to him for many years to come; he put this thought away from him on the spot with fury, as though there were contained in it a new insult to that Malek-Adel whom he considered he had wronged so already.... Yes, indeed! this jade, this carrion he, like a blind idiot, had put on a level with him, Malek-Adel! And as to the service the jade could be to him!... as though he would ever deign to get astride of him? Never! on no consideration!!... He would sell him to a Tartar for dog's meat--it deserved no better end.... Yes, that would be best!'

For more than two hours Tchertop-hanov wandered up and down his room.

'Perfishka!' he called peremptorily all of a sudden, 'run this minute to the tavern; fetch a gallon of vodka! Do you hear? A gallon, and look sharp! I want the vodka here this very second on the table!'

The vodka was not long in making its appearance on Panteley Eremyitch's table, and he began drinking.

XIII

If anyone had looked at Tchertop-hanov then; if anyone could have been a witness of the sullen exasperation with which he drained glass after glass--he would inevitably have felt an involuntary shudder of fear. The night came on, the tallow candle burnt dimly on the table. Tchertop-hanov ceased wandering from corner to corner; he sat all flushed, with dull eyes, which he dropped at one time on the floor, at another fixed obstinately on the dark window; he got up, poured out some vodka, drank it off, sat down again, again fixed his eyes on one point, and did not stir--only his breathing grew quicker and his face still more flushed. It seemed as though some resolution were ripening within him, which he was himself ashamed of, but which he was gradually getting used to; one single thought kept obstinately and undeviatingly moving up closer and closer, one single image stood out more and more distinctly, and under the burning weight of heavy drunkenness the angry irritation was replaced by a feeling of ferocity in his heart, and a vindictive smile appeared on his lips.

'Yes, the time has come!' he declared in a matter-of-fact, almost weary tone. 'I must get to work.'

He drank off the last glass of vodka, took from over his bed the pistol--the very pistol from which he had shot at Masha--loaded it, put some cartridges in his pocket--to be ready for anything--and went round to the stables.

The watchman ran up to him when he began to open the door, but he shouted to him: 'It's I! Are you blind? Get out!' The watchman moved a little aside. 'Get out and go to bed!' Tchertop-hanov shouted at him again: 'there's nothing for you to guard here! A mighty wonder, a treasure indeed to watch over!' He went into the stable. Malek-Adel... the spurious Malek-Adel, was lying on his litter. Tchertop-hanov gave him a kick, saying, 'Get up, you brute!' Then he unhooked a halter from a nail, took off the horsecloth and flung it on the ground, and roughly turning the submissive horse round in the box, led it out into the courtyard, and from the yard into the open country, to the great amazement of the watchman, who could not make out at all where the master was going off to by night, leading an unharnessed horse. He was, of course, afraid to question him, and only followed him with his eyes till he disappeared at the bend in the road leading to a neighbouring wood.

XIV

Tchertop-hanov walked with long strides, not stopping nor looking round. Malek-Adel--we will call him by that name to the end--followed him meekly. It was a rather clear night; Tchertop-hanov could make out the jagged outline of the forest, which formed a black mass in front of him. When he got into the chill night air, he would certainly have thrown off the intoxication of the vodka he had drunk, if it had not been for another, stronger intoxication, which completely over-mastered him. His head was heavy, his blood pulsed in thuds in his throat and ears, but he went on steadily, and knew where he was going.

He had made up his mind to kill Malek-Adel; he had thought of nothing else the whole day.... Now he had made up his mind!

He went out to do this thing not only calmly, but confidently, unhesitatingly, as a man going about something from a sense of duty. This 'job' seemed a very 'simple' thing to him; in making an end of the impostor, he was quits with 'everyone' at once--he punished himself for his stupidity, and made expiation to his real darling, and showed the whole world (Tchertop-hanov worried himself a great deal about the 'whole world') that he was not to be trifled with.... And, above all, he was making an end of himself too with the impostor--for what had he to live for now? How all this took shape in his brain, and why, it seemed to him so simple--it is not easy to explain, though not altogether impossible; stung to the quick, solitary, without a human soul near to him, without a halfpenny, and with his blood on fire with vodka, he was in a state bordering on madness, and there is no doubt that even in the absurdest freaks of mad people there is, to their eyes, a sort of logic, and even justice. Of his justice Tchertop-hanov was, at any rate, fully persuaded; he did not hesitate, he made haste to carry out sentence on the guilty without giving himself any clear definition of whom he meant by that term.... To tell the truth, he reflected very little on what he was about to do. 'I must, I must make an end,' was what he kept stupidly and severely repeating to himself; 'I must make an end!'

And the guiltless guilty one followed in a submissive trot behind his back.... But there was no pity for him in Tchertop-hanov's heart.

XV

Not far from the forest to which he was leading his horse there stretched a small ravine, half overgrown with young oak bushes. Tchertop-hanov went down into it.... Malek-Adel stumbled and almost fell on him.

'So you would crush me, would you, you damned brute!' shouted Tchertop-hanov, and, as though in self-defence, he pulled the pistol out of his pocket. He no longer felt furious exasperation, but that special numbness of the senses which they say comes over a man before the perpetration of a crime. But his own voice terrified him—it sounded so wild and strange under the cover of dark branches in the close, decaying dampness of the forest ravine! Moreover, in response to his exclamation, some great bird suddenly fluttered in a tree-top above his head... Tchertop-hanov shuddered. He had, as it were, roused a witness to his act—and where? In that silent place where he should not have met a living creature....

'Away with you, devil, to the four winds of heaven!' he muttered, and letting go Malek-Adel's rein, he gave him a violent blow on the shoulder with the butt end of the pistol. Malek-Adel promptly turned back, clambered out of the ravine... and ran away. But the thud of his hoofs was not long audible. The rising wind confused and blended all sounds together.

Tchertop-hanov too slowly clambered out of the ravine, reached the forest, and made his way along the road homewards. He was ill at ease with himself; the weight he had felt in his head and his heart had spread over all his limbs; he walked angry, gloomy, dissatisfied, hungry, as though some one had insulted him, snatched his prey, his food from him....

The suicide, baffled in his intent, must know such sensations.

Suddenly something poked him behind between his shoulder blades. He looked round.... Malek-Adel was standing in the middle of the road. He had walked after his master; he touched him with his nose to announce himself.

'Ah!' shouted Tchertop-hanov,' of yourself, of yourself you have come to your death! So, there!'

In the twinkling of an eye he had snatched out his pistol, drawn the trigger, turned the muzzle on Malek-Adel's brow, fired....

The poor horse sprung aside, rose on its haunches, bounded ten paces away, and suddenly fell heavily, and gasped as it writhed upon the ground....

Tchertop-hanov put his two hands over his ears and ran away. His knees were shaking under him. His drunkenness and revenge and blind self-confidence—all had flown at once. There was left nothing but a sense of shame and loathing—and the consciousness, unmistakeable, that this time he had put an end to himself too.

XVI

Six weeks later, the groom Perfishka thought it his duty to stop the commissioner of police as he happened to be passing Bezsonovo.

'What do you want?' inquired the guardian of order.

'If you please, your excellency, come into our house,' answered the groom with a low bow.

'Panteley Eremyitch, I fancy, is about to die; so that I'm afraid of getting into trouble.'

'What? die?' queried the commissioner.

'Yes, sir. First, his honour drank vodka every day, and now he's taken to his bed and got very thin. I fancy his honour does not understand anything now. He's lost his tongue completely.'

The commissioner got out of his trap.

'Have you sent for the priest, at least? Has your master been confessed? Taken the sacrament?'

'No, sir!'

The commissioner frowned. 'How is that, my boy? How can that be--hey? Don't you know that for that... you're liable to have to answer heavily--hey?'

'Indeed, and I did ask him the day before yesterday, and yesterday again,' protested the intimidated groom. "Wouldn't you, Panteley Eremyitch," says I, "let me run for the priest, sir?" "You hold your tongue, idiot," says he; "mind your own business." But to-day, when I began to address him, his honour only looked at me, and twitched his moustache.'

'And has he been drinking a great deal of vodka?' inquired the commissioner.

'Rather! But if you would be so good, your honour, come into his room.'

'Well, lead the way!' grumbled the commissioner, and he followed Perfishka.

An astounding sight was in store for him. In a damp, dark back-room, on a wretched bedstead covered with a horsecloth, with a rough felt cloak for a pillow, lay Tchertop-hanov. He was not pale now, but yellowish green, like a corpse, with sunken eyes under leaden lids and a sharp, pinched nose--still reddish--above his dishevelled whiskers. He lay dressed in his invariable Caucasian coat, with the cartridge pockets on the breast, and blue Circassian trousers. A Cossack cap with a crimson crown covered his forehead to his very eyebrows. In one hand Tchertop-hanov held his hunting whip, in the other an embroidered tobacco pouch--Masha's last gift to him. On a table near the bed stood an empty spirit bottle, and at the head of the bed were two water-colour sketches pinned to the wall; one represented, as far as could be made out, a fat man with a guitar in his hand-- probably Nedopyuskin; the other portrayed a horseman galloping at full speed.... The horse was like those fabulous animals which are sketched by children on walls and fences; but the carefully washed-in dappling of the horse's grey coat, and the cartridge pocket on the rider's breast, the pointed toes of his boots, and the immense moustaches, left no room for doubt--this sketch was meant to represent Panteley Eremyitch riding on Malek-Adel.

The astonished commissioner of police did not know how to proceed. The silence of death reigned in the room. 'Why, he's dead already!' he thought, and raising his voice, he said, 'Panteley Eremyitch! Eh, Panteley Eremyitch!'

Then something extraordinary occurred. Tchertop-hanov's eyelids slowly opened, the eyes, fast growing dim, moved first from right to left, then from left to right, rested on the commissioner--saw him.... Something gleamed in their dull whites, the semblance of a flash came back to them, the blue lips were gradually unglued, and a hoarse, almost sepulchral, voice was heard.

'Panteley Eremyitch of the ancient hereditary nobility is dying: who can hinder him? He owes no man anything, asks nothing from any one.... Leave him, people! Go!'

The hand holding the whip tried to lift it... In vain! The lips cleaved together again, the eyes closed, and as before Tchertop-hanov lay on his comfortless bed, flat as an empty sack, and his feet close together.

'Let me know when he dies,' the commissioner whispered to Perfishka as he went out of the room; 'and I suppose you can send for the priest now. You must observe due order; give him extreme unction.'

Perfishka went that same day for the priest, and the following morning he had to let the commissioner know: Panteley Eremyitch had died in the night.

When they buried him, two men followed his coffin; the groom Perfishka and Moshel Leyba. The news of Tchertop-hanov's death had somehow reached the Jew, and he did not fail to pay this last act of respect to his benefactor.

XXIII   A LIVING RELIC

'O native land of long suffering,
Land of the Russian people.'

F. TYUTCHEV.

A French proverb says that 'a dry fisherman and a wet hunter are a sorry sight.' Never having had any taste for fishing, I cannot decide what are the fisherman's feelings in fine bright weather, and how far in bad weather the pleasure derived from the abundance of fish compensates for the unpleasantness of being wet. But for the sportsman rain is a real calamity. It was to just this calamity that Yermolai and I were exposed on one of our expeditions after grouse in the Byelevsky district. The rain never ceased from early morning. What didn't we do to escape it? We put macintosh capes almost right over our heads, and stood under the trees to avoid the raindrops.... The waterproof capes, to say nothing of their hindering our shooting, let the water through in the most shameless fashion; and under the trees, though at first, certainly, the rain did not reach us, afterwards the water collected on the leaves suddenly rushed through, every branch dripped on us like a waterspout, a chill stream made its way under our neck-ties, and trickled down our spines.... This was 'quite unpleasant,' as Yermolai expressed it. 'No, Piotr Petrovitch,' he cried at last; 'we can't go on like this....There's no shooting to-day. The dogs' scent is drowned. The guns miss fire....Pugh! What a mess!'

'What's to be done?' I queried.

'Well, let's go to Aleksyevka. You don't know it, perhaps--there's a settlement of that name belonging to your mother; it's seven miles from here. We'll stay the night there, and to-morrow....'

'Come back here?'

'No, not here....I know of some places beyond Aleksyevka...ever so much better than here for grouse!'

I did not proceed to question my faithful companion why he had not taken me to those parts before, and the same day we made our way to my mother's peasant settlement, the existence of which, I must confess, I had not even suspected up till then. At this settlement, it turned out, there was a little lodge. It was very old, but, as it had not been inhabited, it was clean; I passed a fairly tranquil night in it.

The next day I woke up very early. The sun had only just risen; there was not a single cloud in the sky; everything around shone with a double brilliance--the brightness of the fresh morning rays and of yesterday's downpour. While they were harnessing me a cart, I went for a stroll about a small orchard, now neglected and run wild, which enclosed the little lodge on all sides with its fragrant, sappy growth. Ah, how sweet it was in the open air, under the bright sky, where the larks were trilling, whence their bell-like notes rained down like silvery beads! On their wings, doubtless, they had carried off drops of dew, and their songs seemed steeped in dew. I took my cap off my head and drew a glad deep breath.... On the slope of a shallow ravine, close to the hedge, could be seen a beehive; a narrow path led to it, winding like a snake between dense walls of high grass and nettles, above which struggled up, God knows whence brought, the pointed stalks of dark-green hemp.

I turned along this path; I reached the beehive. Beside it stood a little wattled shanty, where they put the beehives for the winter. I peeped into the half-open door; it was dark, still, dry within; there was a scent of mint and balm. In the corner were some trestles fitted together, and on them, covered with a quilt, a little figure of some sort.... I was walking away....

'Master, master! Piotr Petrovitch!' I heard a voice, faint, slow, and hoarse, like the whispering of marsh rushes.

I stopped.

'Piotr Petrovitch! Come in, please!' the voice repeated. It came from the corner where were the trestles I had noticed.

I drew near, and was struck dumb with amazement. Before me lay a living human being; but what sort of a creature was it?

A head utterly withered, of a uniform coppery hue--like some very ancient holy picture, yellow with age; a sharp nose like a keen-edged knife; the lips could barely be seen--only the teeth flashed white and the eyes; and from under the kerchief some thin wisps of yellow hair straggled on to the forehead. At the chin, where the quilt was folded, two tiny hands of the same coppery hue were moving, the fingers slowly twitching like little sticks. I looked more intently; the face, far from being ugly, was positively beautiful, but strange and dreadful; and the face seemed the more dreadful to me that on it--on its metallic cheeks--I saw, struggling...struggling, and unable to form itself--a smile.

'You don't recognise me, master?' whispered the voice again: it seemed to be breathed from the almost unmoving lips. 'And, indeed, how should you? I'm Lukerya....Do you remember, who used to lead the dance at your mother's, at Spasskoye?... Do you remember, I used to be leader of the choir too?'

'Lukerya!' I cried. 'Is it you? Can it be?'

'Yes, it's I, master--I, Lukerya.'

I did not know what to say, and gazed in stupefaction at the dark motionless face with the clear, death-like eyes fastened upon me. Was it possible? This mummy Lukerya--the greatest beauty in all our household--that tall, plump, pink-and-white, singing, laughing, dancing creature! Lukerya, our smart Lukerya, whom all our lads were courting, for whom I heaved some secret sighs--I, a boy of sixteen!

'Mercy, Lukerya!' I said at last; 'what is it has happened to you?'

'Oh, such a misfortune befel me! But don't mind me, sir; don't let my trouble revolt you; sit there on that little tub--a little nearer, or you won't be able to hear me....I've not much of a voice now-a-days!... Well, I am glad to see you! What brought you to Aleksyevka?'

Lukerya spoke very softly and feebly, but without pausing.

'Yermolai, the huntsman, brought me here. But you tell me...'

'Tell you about my trouble? Certainly, sir. It happened to me a long while ago now--six or seven years. I had only just been betrothed then to Vassily Polyakov--do you remember, such a fine-looking fellow he was, with curly hair?--he waited at table at your mother's. But you weren't in the country then; you had gone away to Moscow to your studies. We were very much in love, Vassily and me; I could never get him out of my head; and it was in the spring it all happened. Well, one night...not long before sunrise, it was...I couldn't sleep; a nightingale in the garden was singing so wonderfully sweet!... I could not help getting up and going out on to the steps to listen. It trilled and trilled... and all at once I fancied some one called me; it seemed like Vassya's voice, so softly, "Lusha!"... I looked round, and being half asleep, I suppose, I missed my footing and fell straight down from the top-step, and flop on to the ground! And I thought I wasn't much hurt, for I got up directly and went back to my room. Only it seems something inside me--in my body--was broken.... Let me get my breath...half a minute... sir.'

Lukerya ceased, and I looked at her with surprise. What surprised me particularly was that she told her story almost cheerfully, without sighs and groans, not complaining nor asking for sympathy.

'Ever since that happened,' Lukerya went on, 'I began to pine away and get thin; my skin got dark; walking was difficult for me; and then--I lost the use of my legs altogether; I couldn't stand or sit; I had to lie down all the time. And I didn't care to eat or drink; I got worse and worse. Your mamma, in the kindness of her heart, made me see doctors, and sent me to a hospital. But there was no curing me. And not one doctor could even say what my illness was. What didn't they do to me?--they burnt my spine with hot irons, they put me in lumps of ice, and it was all no good. I got quite numb in the end....

So the gentlemen decided it was no use doctoring me any more, and there was no sense in keeping cripples up at the great house... well, and so they sent me here--because I've relations here. So here I live, as you see.'

Lukerya was silent again, and again she tried to smile.

'But this is awful--your position!' I cried... and not knowing how to go on, I asked: 'and what of Vassily Polyakov?' A most stupid question it was.

Lukerya turned her eyes a little away.

'What of Polyakov? He grieved--he grieved for a bit--and he is married to another, a girl from Glinnoe. Do you know Glinnoe? It's not far from us. Her name's Agrafena. He loved me dearly--but, you see, he's a young man; he couldn't stay a bachelor. And what sort of a helpmeet could I be? The wife he found for himself is a good, sweet woman-- and they have children. He lives here; he's a clerk at a neighbour's; your mamma let him go off with a passport, and he's doing very well, praise God.'

'And so you go on lying here all the time?' I asked again.

'Yes, sir, I've been lying here seven years. In the summer-time I lie here in this shanty, and when it gets cold they move me out into the bath-house: I lie there.'

'Who waits on you? Does any one look after you?'

'Oh, there are kind folks here as everywhere; they don't desert me. Yes, they see to me a little. As to food, I eat nothing to speak of; but water is here, in the pitcher; it's always kept full of pure spring water. I can reach to the pitcher myself: I've one arm still of use. There's a little girl here, an orphan; now and then she comes to see me, the kind child. She was here just now.... You didn't meet her? Such a pretty, fair little thing. She brings me flowers. We've some in the garden--there were some--but they've all disappeared. But, you know, wild flowers too are nice; they smell even sweeter than garden flowers. Lilies of the valley, now... what could be sweeter?'

'And aren't you dull and miserable, my poor Lukerya?'

'Why, what is one to do? I wouldn't tell a lie about it. At first it was very wearisome; but later on I got used to it, I got more patient--it was nothing; there are others worse off still.'

'How do you mean?'

'Why, some haven't a roof to shelter them, and there are some blind or deaf; while I, thank God, have splendid sight, and hear everything--everything. If a mole burrows in the ground--I hear even that. And I can smell every scent, even the faintest! When the buckwheat comes into flower in the meadow, or the lime-tree in the garden--I don't need to be told of it, even; I'm the first to know directly. Anyway, if there's the least bit of a wind blowing from that quarter. No, he who stirs God's wrath is far worse off than me. Look at this, again: anyone in health may easily fall into sin; but I'm cut off even from sin. The other day, father Aleksy, the priest, came to give me the sacrament, and he says: "There's no need," says he, "to confess you; you can't fall into sin in your condition, can you?" But I said to him; "How about sinning in thought, father?" "Ah, well," says he, and he laughed himself, "that's no great sin."

'But I fancy I'm no great sinner even in that way, in thought,' Lukerya went on, 'for I've trained myself not to think, and above all, not to remember. The time goes faster.'

I must own I was astonished. 'You're always alone, Lukerya: how can you prevent the thoughts from coming into your head? or are you constantly asleep?'

'Oh, no, sir! I can't always sleep. Though I've no great pain, still I've an ache, there, right inside, and in my bones too; it won't let me sleep as I ought. No... but there, I lie by myself; I lie here and lie here, and don't think: I feel that I'm alive, I breathe; and I put myself all into that. I look and listen. The bees buzz and hum in the hive; a dove sits on the roof and coos; a hen comes along with her chickens to peck up crumbs; or a sparrow flies in, or a butterfly--that's a great treat for me. Last year some swallows even built a nest over there in the corner, and brought up their little ones. Oh, how interesting it was! One would fly to the nest, press close, feed a young one, and off again. Look again: the other would be in her place already. Sometimes it wouldn't fly in, but only fly past the open door; and the little ones would begin to squeak, and open their beaks directly....I was hoping for them back again the next year, but they say a sportsman here shot them with his gun. And what could he gain by it? It's hardly bigger, the swallow, than a beetle....What wicked men you are, you sportsmen!'

'I don't shoot swallows,' I hastened to remark.

'And once, Lukerya began again, 'it was comical, really. A hare ran in, it did really! The hounds, I suppose, were after it; anyway, it seemed to tumble straight in at the door!... It squatted quite near me, and sat so a long while; it kept sniffing with its nose, and twitching its whiskers--like a regular officer! and it looked at me. It understood, to be sure, that I was no danger to it. At last it got up, went hop-hop to the door, looked round in the doorway; and what did it look like? Such a funny fellow it was!'

Lukerya glanced at me, as much as to say, 'Wasn't it funny?' To satisfy her, I laughed. She moistened her parched lips.

'Well, in the winter, of course, I'm worse off, because it's dark: to burn a candle would be a pity, and what would be the use? I can read, to be sure, and was always fond of reading, but what could I read? There are no books of any kind, and even if there were, how could I hold a book? Father Aleksy brought me a calendar to entertain me, but he saw it was no good, so he took and carried it away again. But even though it's dark, there's always something to listen to: a cricket chirps, or a mouse begins scratching somewhere. That's when it's a good thing--not to think!'

'And I repeat the prayers too,' Lukerya went on, after taking breath a little; 'only I don't know many of them---the prayers, I mean. And besides, why should I weary the Lord God? What can I ask Him for? He knows better than I what I need. He has laid a cross upon me: that means that He loves me. So we are commanded to understand. I repeat the Lord's Prayer, the Hymn to the Virgin, the Supplication of all the Afflicted, and I lie still again, without any thought at all, and am all right!' Two minutes passed by. I did not break the silence, and did not stir on the narrow tub which served me as a seat. The cruel stony stillness of the living, unlucky creature lying before me communicated itself to me; I too turned, as it were, numb.

'Listen, Lukerya,' I began at last; 'listen to the suggestion I'm going to make to you. Would you like me to arrange for them to take you to a hospital--a good hospital in the town? Who knows, perhaps you might yet be cured; anyway, you would not be alone'...

Lukerya's eyebrows fluttered faintly. 'Oh, no, sir,' she answered in a troubled whisper; 'don't move me into a hospital; don't touch me. I shall only have more agony to bear there! How could they cure me now?... Why, there was a doctor came here once; he wanted to examine me. I begged him, for Christ's sake, not to disturb me. It was no use. He began turning me over, pounding my hands and legs, and pulling me about. He said, "I'm doing this for Science; I'm a servant of Science--a scientific man! And you," he said, "really oughtn't to oppose me, because I've a medal given me for my labours, and it's for you simpletons I'm toiling." He mauled me about, told me the name of my disease--some wonderful long name--and with that he went away; and all my poor bones ached for a week after. You say "I'm all alone; always alone." Oh, no, I'm not always; they come to see me--I'm quiet--I don't bother them. The peasant girls come in and chat a bit; a pilgrim woman will wander in, and tell me tales of Jerusalem, of Kiev, of the holy towns. And I'm not afraid of being alone. Indeed, it's better--ay, ay! Master, don't touch me, don't take me to the hospital.... Thank you, you are kind; only don't touch me, there's a dear!'

'Well, as you like, as you like, Lukerya. You know, I only suggested it for your good.'

'I know, master, that it was for my good. But, master dear, who can help another? Who can enter into his soul? Every man must help himself! You won't believe me, perhaps. I lie here sometimes so alone...and it's as though there were no one else in the world but me. As if I alone were living! And it seems to me as though something were blessing me....I'm carried away by dreams that are really marvellous!'

'What do you dream of, then, Lukerya?'

'That, too, master, I couldn't say; one can't explain. Besides, one forgets afterwards. It's like a cloud coming over and bursting, then it grows so fresh and sweet; but just what it was, there's no knowing! Only my idea is, if folks were near me, I should have nothing of that, and should feel nothing except my misfortune.'

Lukerya heaved a painful sigh. Her breathing, like her limbs, was not under her control.

'When I come to think, master, of you,' she began again, 'you are very sorry for me. But you mustn't be too sorry, really! I'll tell you one thing; for instance, I sometimes, even now.... Do you remember how merry I used to be in my time? A regular madcap!... So do you know what? I sing songs even now.'

'Sing?... You?'

'Yes; I sing the old songs, songs for choruses, for feasts, Christmas songs, all sorts! I know such a lot of them, you see, and I've not forgotten them. Only dance songs I don't sing. In my state now, it wouldn't suit me.'

'How do you sing them?...to yourself?'

'To myself, yes; and aloud too. I can't sing loud, but still one can understand it. I told you a little girl waits on me. A clever little orphan she is. So I have taught her; four songs she has learnt from me already. Don't you believe me? Wait a minute, I'll show you directly....'

Lukerya took breath.... The thought that this half-dead creature was making ready to begin singing raised an involuntary feeling of dread in me. But before I could utter a word, a long-drawn-out, hardly audible, but pure and true note, was quivering in my ears... it was followed by a second and a third. 'In the meadows,' sang Lukerya. She sang, the expression of her stony face unchanged, even her eyes riveted on one spot. But how touchingly tinkled out that poor struggling little voice, that wavered like a thread of smoke: how she longed to pour out all her soul in it!... I felt no dread now; my heart throbbed with unutterable pity.

'Ah, I can't!' she said suddenly. 'I've not the strength. I'm so upset with joy at seeing you.'

She closed her eyes.

I laid my hand on her tiny, chill fingers.... She glanced at me, and her dark lids, fringed with golden eyelashes, closed again, and were still as an ancient statue's. An instant later they glistened in the half-darkness.... They were moistened by a tear.

As before, I did not stir.

'How silly I am!' said Lukerya suddenly, with unexpected force, and opened her eyes wide: she tried to wink the tears out of them. 'I ought to be ashamed! What am I doing? It's a long time since I have been like this... not since that day when Vassya-Polyakov was here last spring. While he sat with me and talked, I was all right; but when he had gone away, how I did cry in my loneliness! Where did I get the tears from? But, there! we girls get our tears for nothing. Master,' added Lukerya, 'perhaps you have a handkerchief.... If you won't mind, wipe my eyes.'

I made haste to carry out her desire, and left her the handkerchief. She refused it at first.... 'What good's such a gift to me?' she said. The handkerchief was plain enough, but clean and white. Afterwards she clutched it in her weak fingers, and did not loosen them again. As I got used to the darkness in which we both were, I could clearly make out her features, could even perceive the delicate flush that peeped out under the coppery hue of her face, could discover in the face, so at least it seemed to me, traces of its former beauty.

'You asked me, master,' Lukerya began again, 'whether I sleep. I sleep very little, but every time I fall asleep I've dreams--such splendid dreams! I'm never ill in my dreams; I'm always so well, and young.... There's one thing's sad: I wake up and long for a good stretch, and I'm all as if I were in chains. I once had such an exquisite dream! Shall I tell it you? Well, listen. I dreamt I was standing in a meadow, and all round me was rye, so tall, and ripe as gold!... and I had a reddish dog with me--such a wicked dog; it kept trying to bite me. And I had a sickle in my hands; not a simple sickle; it seemed to be the moon itself--the moon as it is when it's the shape of a sickle. And with this same moon I had to cut the rye clean. Only I was very weary with the heat, and the moon blinded me, and I felt lazy; and cornflowers were growing all about, and such big ones! And they all turned their heads to me. And I thought in my dream I would pick them; Vassya had promised to come, so I'd pick myself a wreath first; I'd still time to plait it. I began picking cornflowers, but they kept melting away from between my fingers, do what I would. And I couldn't make myself a wreath. And meanwhile I heard someone coming up to me, so close, and calling, "Lusha! Lusha!"... "Ah," I thought, "what a pity I hadn't time!" No matter, I put that moon on my head instead of cornflowers. I put it on like a tiara, and I was all brightness directly; I made the whole field light around me. And, behold! over the very top of the ears there came gliding very quickly towards me, not Vassya, but Christ Himself! And how I knew it was Christ I can't say; they don't paint Him like that--only it was He! No beard, tall, young, all in white, only His belt was golden; and He held out His hand to me. "Fear not," said He; "My bride adorned, follow Me; you shall lead the choral dance in the heavenly kingdom, and sing the songs of Paradise." And how I clung to His hand! My dog at once followed at my heels... but then we began to float upwards! He in front.... His wings spread wide over all the sky, long like a sea-gull's--and I after Him! And my dog had to stay behind. Then only I understood that that dog was my illness, and that in the heavenly kingdom there was no place for it.'

Lukerya paused a minute.

'And I had another dream, too,' she began again; 'but may be it was a vision. I really don't know. It seemed to me I was lying in this very shanty, and my dead parents, father and mother, come to me and bow low to me, but say nothing. And I asked them, "Why do you bow down to me, father and mother?" "Because," they said, "you suffer much in this world, so that you have not only set free your own soul, but have taken a great burden from off us too. And for us in the other world it is much easier. You have made an end of your own sins; now you are expiating our sins." And having said this, my parents bowed down to me again, and I could not see them; there was nothing but the walls to be seen. I was in great doubt afterwards what had happened with me. I even told the priest of it in confession. Only he thinks it was not a vision, because visions come only to the clerical gentry.'

'And I'll tell you another dream,' Lukerya went on. 'I dreamt I was sitting on the high-road, under a willow; I had a stick, had a wallet on my shoulders, and my head tied up in a kerchief, just like a pilgrim woman! And I had to go somewhere, a long, long way off, on a pilgrimage. And pilgrims kept coming past me; they came along slowly, all going one way; their faces were weary, and all very much like one another. And I dreamt that moving about among them was a woman, a head taller than the rest, and wearing a peculiar dress, not like ours--not Russian. And her face too was peculiar--a worn face and severe. And all the others moved away from her; but she suddenly turns, and comes straight to me. She stood still, and looked at me; and her eyes were yellow, large, and clear as a falcon's. And I ask her, "Who are you?" And she says to me, "I'm your death." Instead of being frightened, it was quite the other way. I was as pleased as could be; I crossed myself! And the woman, my death, says to me: "I'm sorry for you, Lukerya, but I can't take you with me. Farewell!" Good God! how sad I was then!... "Take me," said I, "good mother, take me, darling!" And my death turned to me, and began speaking to me.... I knew that she was appointing me my hour, but indistinctly, incomprehensibly. "After St. Peter's day," said she.... With that I awoke.... Yes, I have such wonderful dreams!'

Lukerya turned her eyes upwards... and sank into thought....

'Only the sad thing is, sometimes a whole week will go by without my getting to sleep once. Last year a lady came to see me, and she gave me a little bottle of medicine against sleeplessness; she told me to take ten drops at a time. It did me so much good, and I used to sleep; only the bottle was all finished long ago. Do you know what medicine that was, and how to get it?'

The lady had obviously given Lukerya opium. I promised to get her another bottle like it, and could not refrain from again wondering aloud at her patience.

'Ah, master!' she answered, 'why do you say so? What do you mean by patience? There, Simeon Stylites now had patience certainly, great patience; for thirty years he stood on a pillar! And another saint had himself buried in the earth, right up to his breast, and the ants ate his face.... And I'll tell you what I was told by a good scholar: there was once a country, and the Ishmaelites made war on it, and they tortured and killed all the inhabitants; and do what they would, the people could not get rid of them. And there appeared among these people a holy virgin; she took a great sword, put on armour weighing eighty pounds, went out against the Ishmaelites and drove them all beyond the sea. Only when she had driven them out, she said to them: "Now burn me, for that was my vow, that I would die a death by fire for my people." And the Ishmaelites took her and burnt her, and the people have been free ever since then! That was a noble deed, now! But what am I!'

I wondered to myself whence and in what shape the legend of Joan of Arc had reached her, and after a brief silence, I asked Lukerya how old she was.

'Twenty-eight... or nine.... It won't be thirty. But why count the years! I've something else to tell you....'

Lukerya suddenly gave a sort of choked cough, and groaned....

'You are talking a great deal,' I observed to her; 'it may be bad for you.'

'It's true,' she whispered, hardly audibly; 'it's time to end our talk; but what does it matter! Now, when you leave me, I can be silent as long as I like. Any way, I've opened my heart....'

I began bidding her good-bye. I repeated my promise to send her the medicine, and asked her once more to think well and tell me--if there wasn't anything she wanted?'

'I want nothing; I am content with all, thank God!' she articulated with very great effort, but with emotion; 'God give good health to all! But there, master, you might speak a word to your mamma--the peasants here are poor--if she could take the least bit off their rent! They've not land enough, and no advantages.... They would pray to God for you.... But I want nothing; I'm quite contented with all.'

I gave Lukerya my word that I would carry out her request, and had already walked to the door.... She called me back again.

'Do you remember, master,' she said, and there was a gleam of something wonderful in her eyes and on her lips, 'what hair I used to have? Do you remember, right down to my knees! It was long before I could make up my mind to it.... Such hair as it was! But how could it be kept combed? In my state!... So I had it cut off.... Yes.... Well, good-bye, master! I can't talk any more.'...

That day, before setting off to shoot, I had a conversation with the village constable about Lukerya. I learnt from him that in the village they called Lukerya the 'Living Relic'; that she gave them no trouble, however; they never heard complaint or repining from her. 'She asks nothing, but, on the contrary, she's grateful for everything; a gentle soul, one must say, if any there be. Stricken of God,' so the constable concluded, 'for her sins, one must suppose; but we do not go into that. And as for judging her, no--no, we do not judge her. Let her be!'

A few weeks later I heard that Lukerya was dead. So her death had come for her... and 'after St. Peter's day.' They told me that on the day of her death she kept hearing the sound of bells, though it was reckoned over five miles from Aleksyevka to the church, and it was a week-day. Lukerya, however, had said that the sounds came not from the church, but from above! Probably she did not dare to say--from heaven.

XXIV   THE RATTLING OF WHEELS

'I've something to tell you,' observed Yermolai, coming into the hut to see me. I had just had dinner, and was lying down on a travelling bed to rest a little after a fairly successful but fatiguing day of grouse-shooting--it was somewhere about the 10th of July, and the heat was terrific.... 'I've something to tell you: all our shot's gone.'

I jumped off the bed.

'All gone? How's that? Why, we took pretty nearly thirty pounds with us from the village--a whole bag!'

'That's so; and a big bag it was: enough for a fortnight. But there's no knowing! There must have been a hole come in it, or something; anyway, there's no shot... that's to say, there's enough for ten charges left.'

'What are we to do now? The very best places are before us--we're promised six coveys for to-morrow....'

'Well, send me to Tula. It's not so far from here; only forty miles. I'll fly like the wind, and bring forty pounds of shot if you say the word.'

'But when would you go?'

'Why, directly. Why put it off? Only, I say, we shall have to hire horses.'

'Why hire horses? Why not our own?'

'We can't drive there with our own. The shaft horse has gone lame... terribly!'

'Since when's that?'

'Well, the other day, the coachman took him to be shod. So he was shod, and the blacksmith, I suppose, was clumsy. Now, he can't even step on the hoof. It's a front leg. He lifts it up... like a dog.'

'Well? they've taken the shoe off, I suppose, at least?'

'No, they've not; but, of course, they ought to take it off. A nail's been driven right into the flesh, I should say.'

I ordered the coachman to be summoned. It turned out that Yermolai had spoken the truth: the shaft-horse really could not put its hoof to the ground. I promptly gave orders for it to have the shoe taken off, and to be stood on damp clay.

'Then do you wish me to hire horses to go to Tula?' Yermolai persisted.

'Do you suppose we can get horses in this wilderness?' I exclaimed with involuntary irritation. The village in which we found ourselves was a desolate, God-forsaken place; all its inhabitants seemed to be poverty-stricken; we had difficulty in discovering one hut, moderately roomy, and even that one had no chimney.

'Yes,' replied Yermolai with his habitual equanimity; 'what you said about this village is true enough; but there used to be living in this very place one peasant--a very clever fellow! rich too! He had nine horses. He's dead, and his eldest son manages it all now. The man's a perfect fool, but still he's not had time to waste his father's wealth yet. We can get horses from him. If you say the word, I will fetch him. His brothers, I've heard say, are smart chaps...but still, he's their head.'

'Why so?'

'Because--he's the eldest! Of course, the younger ones must obey!' Here Yermolai, in reference to younger brothers as a class, expressed himself with a vigour quite unsuitable for print.

'I'll fetch him. He's a simple fellow. With him you can't fail to come to terms.'

While Yermolai went after his 'simple fellow' the idea occurred to me that it might be better for me to drive into Tula myself. In the first place, taught by experience, I had no very great confidence in Yermolai: I had once sent him to the town for purchases; he had promised to get through all my commissions in one day, and was gone a whole week, drank up all the money, and came back on foot, though he had set off in my racing droshky. And, secondly, I had an acquaintance in Tula, a horsedealer; I might buy a horse off him to take the place of the disabled shaft-horse.

'The thing's decided!' I thought; 'I'll drive over myself; I can sleep just as well on the road--luckily, the coach is comfortable.'

'I've brought him!' cried Yermolai, rushing into the hut a quarter of an hour later. He was followed by a tall peasant in a white shirt, blue breeches, and bast shoes, with white eyebrows and short-sighted eyes, a wedge-shaped red beard, a long swollen nose, and a gaping mouth. He certainly did look 'simple.'

'Here, your honour,' observed Yermolai, 'he has horses--and he's willing.'

'So be, surely, I'... the peasant began hesitatingly in a rather hoarse voice, shaking his thin wisps of hair, and drumming with his fingers on the band of the cap he held in his hands.... 'Surely, I....'

'What's your name?' I inquired.

The peasant looked down and seemed to think deeply. 'My name?'

'Yes; what are you called?'

'Why my name 'ull be--Filofey.'

'Well, then, friend Filofey; I hear you have horses. Bring a team of three here--we'll put them in my coach--it's a light one--and you drive me in to Tula. There's a moon now at night; it's light, and it's cool for driving. What sort of a road have you here?'

'The road? There's naught amiss with the road. To the main road it will be sixteen miles--not more.... There's one little place... a bit awkward; but naught amiss else.'

'What sort of little place is it that's awkward?'

'Well, we'll have to cross the river by the ford.'

'But are you thinking of going to Tula yourself?' inquired Yermolai.

'Yes.'

'Oh!' commented my faithful servant with a shake of his head. 'Oh-oh!' he repeated; then he spat on the floor and walked out of the room.

The expedition to Tula obviously no longer presented any features of interest to him; it had become for him a dull and unattractive business.

'Do you know the road well?' I said, addressing Filofey.

'Surely, we know the road! Only, so to say, please your honour, can't... so on the sudden, so to say...'

It appeared that Yermolai, on engaging Filofey, had stated that he could be sure that, fool as he was, he'd be paid... and nothing more! Filofey, fool as he was--in Yermolai's words--was not satisfied with this statement alone. He demanded, of me fifty roubles--an exorbitant price; I offered him ten--a low price. We fell to haggling; Filofey at first was stubborn; then he began to come down, but slowly. Yermolai entering for an instant began assuring me, 'that fool--('He's fond of the word, seemingly!' Filofey remarked in a low voice)--'that fool can't reckon money at all,' and reminded me how twenty years ago a posting tavern established by my mother at the crossing of two high-roads came to complete grief from the fact that the old house-serf who was put there to manage it positively did not understand reckoning money, but valued sums simply by the number of coins--in fact, gave silver coins in change for copper, though he would swear furiously all the time.

'Ugh, you Filofey! you're a regular Filofey!' Yermolai jeered at last--and he went out, slamming the door angrily.

Filofey made him no reply, as though admitting that to be called Filofey was--as a fact--not very clever of him, and that a man might fairly be reproached for such a name, though really it was the village priest was to blame in the matter for not having done better by him at his christening.

At last we agreed, however, on the sum of twenty roubles. He went off for the horses, and an hour later brought five for me to choose from. The horses turned out to be fairly good, though their manes and tails were tangled, and their bellies round and taut as drums. With Filofey came two of his brothers, not in the least like him. Little, black-eyed, sharp-nosed fellows, they certainly produced the impression of 'smart chaps'; they talked a great deal, very fast--'clacked away,' as Yermolai expressed it--but obeyed the elder brother.

They dragged the coach out of the shed and were busy about it and the horses for an hour and a half; first they let out the traces, which were of cord, then pulled them too tight again! Both brothers were very much set on harnessing the 'roan' in the shafts, because 'him can do best going down-hill'; but Filofey decided for 'the shaggy one.' So the shaggy one was put in the shafts accordingly.

They heaped the coach up with hay, put the collar off the lame shaft-horse under the seat, in case we might want to fit it on to the horse to be bought at Tula.... Filofey, who had managed to run home and come back in a long, white, loose, ancestral overcoat, a high sugar-loaf cap, and tarred boots, clambered triumphantly up on to the box. I took my seat, looking at my watch: it was a quarter past ten. Yermolai did not even say good-bye to me--he was engaged in beating his Valetka--Filofey tugged at the reins, and shouted in a thin, thin voice: 'Hey! you little ones!'

His brothers skipped away on both sides, lashed the trace-horses under the belly, and the coach started, turned out of the gates into the street, the shaggy one tried to turn off towards his own home, but Filofey brought him to reason with a few strokes of the whip, and behold! we were already out of the village, and rolling along a fairly even road, between close-growing bushes of thick hazels.

It was a still, glorious night, the very nicest for driving. A breeze rustled now and then in the bushes, set the twigs swinging and died away again; in the sky could be seen motionless, silvery clouds; the moon stood high and threw a bright light on all around. I stretched myself on the hay, and was just beginning to doze... but I remembered the 'awkward place,' and started up.

'I say, Filofey, is it far to the ford?'

'To the ford? It'll be near upon seven miles.'

'Seven miles!' I mused. 'We shan't get there for another hour. I can have a nap meanwhile. Filofey, do you know the road well?' I asked again.

'Surely; how could I fail to know it? It's not the first time I've driven.'

He said something more, but I had ceased to listen.... I was asleep.

I was awakened not, as often happens, by my own intention of waking in exactly an hour, but by a sort of strange, though faint, lapping, gurgling sound at my very ear. I raised my head....

Wonderful to relate! I was lying in the coach as before, but all round the coach, half a foot, not more, from its edge, a sheet of water lay shining in the moonlight, broken up into tiny, distinct, quivering eddies. I looked in front. On the box, with back bowed and head bent, Filofey was sitting like a statue, and a little further on, above the rippling water, I saw the curved arch of the yoke, and the horses' heads and backs. And everything as motionless, as noiseless, as though in some enchanted realm, in a dream--a dream of fairyland.... 'What does it mean?' I looked back from under the hood of the coach.... 'Why, we are in the middle of the river!'... the bank was thirty paces from us.

'Filofey!' I cried.

'What?' he answered.

'What, indeed! Upon my word! Where are we?'

'In the river.'

'I see we're in the river. But, like this, we shall be drowned directly. Is this how you cross the ford? Eh? Why, you're asleep, Filofey! Answer, do!'

'I've made a little mistake,' observed my guide;

'I've gone to one side, a bit wrong, but now we've got to wait a bit.'

'Got to wait a bit? What ever are we going to wait for?'

'Well, we must let the shaggy one look about him; which way he turns his head, that way we've got to go.'

I raised myself on the hay. The shaft-horse's head stood quite motionless. Above the head one could only see in the bright moonlight one ear slightly twitching backwards and forwards.

'Why, he's asleep too, your shaggy one!'

'No,' responded Filofey,' 'he's sniffing the water now.'

And everything was still again; there was only the faint gurgle of the water as before. I sank into a state of torpor.

Moonlight, and night, and the river, and we in it....

'What is that croaking noise?' I asked Filofey.

'That? Ducks in the reeds... or else snakes.'

All of a sudden the head of the shaft-horse shook, his ears pricked up; he gave a snort, began to move. 'Ho-ho, ho-ho-o!' Filofey began suddenly bawling at the top of his voice; he sat up and brandished the whip. The coach was at once tugged away from where it had stuck, it plunged forward, cleaving the waters of the river, and moved along, swaying and lurching from side to side.... At first it seemed to me we were sinking, getting deeper; however, after two or three tugs and jolts, the expanse of water seemed suddenly lower.... It got lower and lower, the coach seemed to grow up out of it, and now the wheels and the horses' tails could be seen, and now stirring with a mighty splashing of big drops, scattering showers of diamonds--no, not diamonds--sapphires in the dull brilliance of the moon, the horses with a spirited pull all together drew us on to the sandy bank and trotted along the road to the hill-side, their shining white legs flashing in rivalry.

'What will Filofey say now?' was the thought that glanced through my mind; 'you see I was right!' or something of that sort. But he said nothing. So I too did not think it necessary to reproach him for carelessness, and lying down in the hay, I tried again to go to sleep.

But I could not go to sleep, not because I was not tired from hunting, and not because the exciting experience I had just been through had dispelled my sleepiness: it was that we were driving through such very beautiful country. There were liberal, wide-stretching, grassy riverside meadows, with a multitude of small pools, little lakes, rivulets, creeks overgrown at the ends with branches and osiers--a regular Russian scene, such as Russians love, like the scenes amid which the heroes of our old legends rode out to shoot white swans and grey ducks. The road we were driven along wound in a yellowish ribbon, the horses ran lightly--and I could not close my eyes. I was admiring! And it all floated by, softened into harmony under the kindly light of the moon. Filofey--he too was touched by it.

'Those meadows are called St. Yegor's,' he said, turning to me. 'And beyond them come the Grand Duke's; there are no other meadows like them in all Russia.... Ah, it's lovely!' The shaft-horse snorted and shook itself.... 'God bless you,' commented Filofey gravely in an undertone. 'How lovely!' he repeated with a sigh; then he gave a long sort of grunt. 'There, mowing time's just upon us, and think what hay they'll rake up there!--regular mountains!--And there are lots of fish in the creeks. Such bream!' he added in a sing-song voice. 'In one word, life's sweet--one doesn't want to die.'

He suddenly raised his hand.

'Hullo! look-ee! over the lake... is it a crane standing there? Can it be fishing at night? Bless me! it's a branch, not a crane. Well, that was a mistake! But the moon is always so deceptive.'

So we drove on and on.... But now the end of the meadows had been reached, little copses and ploughed fields came into view; a little village flashed with two or three lights on one side--it was only four miles now to the main road. I fell asleep.

Again I did not wake up of my own accord. This time I was roused by the voice of Filofey.

'Master!... hey, master!'

I sat up. The coach was standing still on level ground in the very middle of the high-road. Filofey, who had turned round on the box, so as to face me, with wide-open eyes (I was positively surprised at them; I couldn't have imagined he had such large eyes), was whispering with mysterious significance:

'A rattle!... a rattle of wheels!'

'What do you say?'

'I say, there's a rattling! Bend down and listen. Do you hear it?'

I put my head out of the coach, held my breath, and did catch, somewhere in the distance, far behind us, a faint broken sound, as of wheels rolling.

'Do you hear it?' repeated Filofey.

'Well, yes,' I answered. 'Some vehicle is coming.'

'Oh, you don't hear... shoo! The tambourines... and whistling too....Do you hear? Take off your cap... you will hear better.'

I didn't take off my cap, but I listened.

'Well, yes... perhaps. But what of it?'

Filofey turned round facing the horses.

'It's a cart coming... lightly; iron-rimmed wheels,' he observed, and he took up the reins. 'It's wicked folks coming, master; hereabouts, you know, near Tula, they play a good many tricks.'

'What nonsense! What makes you suppose it's sure to be wicked people?'

'I speak the truth... with tambourines... and in an empty cart.... Who should it be?'

'Well... is it much further to Tula?'

'There's twelve miles further to go, and not a habitation here.'

'Well, then, get on quicker; it's no good lingering.'

Filofey brandished the whip, and the coach rolled on again.

Though I did not put much faith in Filofey, I could not go to sleep. 'What if it really is so?' A disagreeable sensation began to stir in me. I sat up in the coach--till then I had lain down--and began looking in all directions. While I had been asleep, a slight fog had come over, not the earth, but the sky; it stood high, the moon hung a whitish patch in it, as though in smoke. Everything had grown dim and blended together, though it was clearer near the ground. Around us flat, dreary country; fields, nothing but fields--here and there bushes and ravines--and again fields, mostly fallow, with scanty, dusty grass. A wilderness... deathlike! If only a quail had called!

We drove on for half an hour. Filofey kept constantly cracking his whip and clicking with his lips, but neither he nor I uttered a word. So we mounted the hillside.... Filofey pulled up the horses, and promptly said again:

'It is a rattle of wheels, master; yes, it is!'

I poked my head out of the coach again, but I might have stayed under the cover of the hood, so distinctly, though still from a distance, the sound reached me of cart-wheels, men whistling, the jingling of tambourines, and even the thud of horses' hoofs; I even fancied I could hear singing and laughter. The wind, it is true, was blowing from there, but there was no doubt that the unknown travellers were a good mile, perhaps two, nearer us. Filofey and I looked at one another; he only gave his hat a tweak forward from behind, and at once, bending over the reins, fell to whipping up the horses. They set off at a gallop, but they could not gallop for long, and fell back into a trot again. Filofey continued to whip them. We must get away!

I can't account for the fact that, though I had not at first shared Filofey's apprehensions, about this time I suddenly gained the conviction that we really were being followed by highwaymen.... I had heard nothing new: the same tambourines, the same rattle of a cart without a load, the same intermittent whistling, the same confused uproar.... But now I had no doubt. Filofey could not have made a mistake!

And now twenty minutes more had gone by.... During the last of these twenty minutes, even through the clatter and rumble of our own carriage, we could hear another clatter and another rumbling....

'Stop, Filofey,' I said; 'it's no use--the end's the same!'

Filofey uttered a faint-hearted 'wo'! The horses instantaneously stopped, as though delighted at the chance of resting!

Mercy upon us! the tambourines were simply booming away just behind our backs, the cart was rattling and creaking, the men were whistling, shouting, and singing, the horses were snorting and thumping on the ground with their hoofs.... They had overtaken us!

'Bad luck,' Filofey commented, in an emphatic undertone; and, clicking to the horses irresolutely, he began to urge them on again. But at that very instant there was a sort of sudden rush and whizz, and a very big, wide cart, harnessed with three lean horses, cut sharply at a rush up to us, galloped in front, and at once fell into a walking pace, blocking up the road.

'A regular brigand's trick!' murmured Filofey. I must own I felt a cold chill at my heart.... I fell to staring before me with strained attention in the half-darkness of the misty moonlight. In the cart in front of us were--half-lying, half-sitting--six men in shirts, and in unbuttoned rough overcoats; two of them had no caps on; huge feet in boots were swinging and hanging over the cart-rail, arms were rising and falling helter-skelter... bodies were jolting backwards and forwards.... It was quite clear--a drunken party. Some were bawling at random; one was whistling very correctly and shrilly, another was swearing; on the driver's seat sat a sort of giant in a cape, driving. They went at a walking pace, as' though paying no attention to us.

What was to be done? We followed them also at a walking pace... we could do nothing else.

For a quarter of a mile we moved along in this manner. The suspense was torturing.... To protect, to defend ourselves, was out of the question! There were six of them; and I hadn't even a stick! Should we turn back? But they would catch us up directly. I remembered the line of Zhukovsky (in the passage where he speaks of the murder of field-marshal Kamensky):

'The scoundrel highwayman's vile axe!...'

Or else--strangling with filthy cord... flung into a ditch...there to choke and struggle like a hare in a trap....

Ugh, it was horrid!

And they, as before, went on at a walking pace, taking no notice of us.

'Filofey!' I whispered,'just try, keep more to the right; see if you can get by.'

Filofey tried--kept to the right... but they promptly kept to the right too... It was impossible to get by.

Filofey made another effort; he kept to the left.... But there, again, they did not let him pass the cart. They even laughed aloud. That meant that they wouldn't let us pass.

'Then they are a bad lot,' Filofey whispered to me over his shoulder.

'But what are they waiting for?' I inquired, also in a whisper.

'To reach the bridge--over there in front--in the hollow--above the stream.... They'll do for us there! That's always their way... by bridges. It's a clear case for us, master.' He added with a sigh: 'They'll hardly let us go alive; for the great thing for them is to keep it all dark. I'm sorry for one thing, master; my horses are lost, and my brothers won't get them!'

I should have been surprised at the time that Filofey could still trouble about his horses at such a moment; but, I must confess, I had no thoughts for him.... 'Will they really kill me?' I kept repeating mentally. 'Why should they? I'll give them everything I have....'

And the bridge was getting nearer and nearer; it could be more and more clearly seen.

Suddenly a sharp whoop was heard; the cart before us, as it were, flew ahead, dashed along, and reaching the bridge, at once stopped stock-still a little on one side of the road. My heart fairly sank like lead.

'Ah, brother Filofey,' I said, 'we are going to our death. Forgive me for bringing you to ruin.'

'As though it were your fault, master! There's no escaping one's fate! Come, Shaggy, my trusty little horse,' Filofey addressed the shaft-horse; 'step on, brother! Do your last bit of service! It's all the same...'

And he urged his horses into a trot We began to get near the bridge--near that motionless, menacing cart.... In it everything was silent, as though on purpose. Not a single halloo! It was the stillness of the pike or the hawk, of every beast of prey, as its victim approaches. And now we were level with the cart.... Suddenly the giant in the cape sprang out of the cart, and came straight towards us!

He said nothing to Filofey, but the latter, of his own accord, tugged at the reins.... The coach stopped. The giant laid both arms on the carriage door, and bending forward his shaggy head with a grin, he uttered the following speech in a soft, even voice, with the accent of a factory hand:

'Honoured sir, we are coming from an honest feast--from a wedding; we've been marrying one of our fine fellows--that is, we've put him to bed; we're all young lads, reckless chaps--there's been a good deal of drinking, and nothing to sober us; so wouldn't your honour be so good as to favour us, the least little, just for a dram of brandy for our mate? We'd drink to your health, and remember your worship; but if you won't be gracious to us--well, we beg you not to be angry!'

'What's the meaning of this?' I thought.... 'A joke?... a jeer?'

The giant continued to stand with bent head. At that very instant the moon emerged from the fog and lighted up his face. There was a grin on the face, in the eyes, and on the lips. But there was nothing threatening to be seen in it... only it seemed, as it were, all on the alert... and the teeth were so white and large....

'I shall be pleased... take this...' I said hurriedly, and pulling my purse out of my pocket, I took out two silver roubles--at that time silver was still circulating in Russia--'here, if that's enough?'

'Much obliged!' bawled the giant, in military fashion; and his fat fingers in a flash snatched from me--not the whole purse--but only the two roubles: 'much obliged!' He shook his hair back, and ran up to the cart.

'Lads!' he shouted, 'the gentleman makes us a present of two silver roubles!' They all began, as it were, gabbling at once.... The giant rolled up on to the driver's seat....

'Good luck to you, master!'

And that was the last we saw of them. The horses dashed on, the cart rumbled up the hill; once more it stood out on the dark line separating the earth from the sky, went down, and vanished.

And now the rattle of the wheels, the shouts and tambourines, could not be heard....

There was a death-like silence.

Filofey and I could not recover ourselves all at once.

'Ah, you're a merry fellow!' he commented at last, and taking off his hat he began crossing himself. 'Fond of a joke, on my word,' he added, and he turned to me, beaming all over. 'But he must be a capital fellow--on my word! Now, now, now, little ones, look alive! You're safe! We are all safe! It was he who wouldn't let us get by; it was he who drove the horses. What a chap for a joke! Now, now! get on, in God's name!'

I did not speak, but I felt happy too. 'We are safe!' I repeated to myself, and lay down on the hay. 'We've got off cheap!'

I even felt rather ashamed that I had remembered that line of Zhukovsky's.

Suddenly an idea occurred to me.

'Filofey!'

'What is it?'

'Are you married?'

'Yes.'

'And have you children?'

'Yes.'

'How was it you didn't think of them? You were sorry for your horses: weren't you sorry for your wife and children?'

'Why be sorry for them? They weren't going to fall into the hands of thieves, you know. But I kept them in my mind all the while, and I do now... surely.' Filofey paused.... 'May be... it was for their sake Almighty God had mercy on us.'

'But if they weren't highwaymen?'

'How can we tell? Can one creep into the soul of another? Another's soul, we know, is a dark place. But, with the thought of God in the heart, things are always better.... No, no!... I'd my family all the time.... Gee... gee-up! little ones, in God's name!'

It was already almost daylight; we began to drive into Tula. I was lying, dreamy and half-asleep.

'Master,' Filofey said to me suddenly, 'look: there they're stopping at the tavern... their cart.'

I raised my head... there they were, and their cart and horses. In the doorway of the drinking-house there suddenly appeared our friend, the giant in the cape. 'Sir!' he shouted, waving his cap, 'we're drinking your health!--Hey, coachman,' he added, wagging his head at Filofey; 'you were a bit scared, I shouldn't wonder, hey?'

'A merry fellow!' observed Filofey when we had driven nearly fifty yards from the tavern.

We got into Tula at last: I bought shot, and while I was about it, tea and spirits, and even got a horse from the horse-dealer.

At mid-day we set off home again. As we drove by the place where we first heard the rattle of the cart behind us, Filofey, who, having had something to drink at Tula, turned out to be very talkative--he even began telling me fairy-tales--as he passed the place, suddenly burst out laughing.

'Do you remember, master, how I kept saying to you, "A rattle... a rattle of wheels," I said!'

He waved his hand several times. This expression struck him as most amusing. The same evening we got back to his village.

I related the adventure that had befallen us to Yermolai. Being sober, he expressed no sympathy; he only gave a grunt--whether of approval or reproach, I imagine he did not know himself. But two days later he informed me, with great satisfaction, that the very night Filofey and I had been driving to Tula, and on the very road, a merchant had been robbed and murdered. I did not at first put much faith in this, but later on I was obliged to believe it: it was confirmed by the police captain, who came galloping over in consequence.

Was not that perhaps the 'wedding' our brave spirits were returning from?--wasn't that the 'fine fellow' they had 'put to bed,' in the words of the jocose giant? I stayed five days longer in Filofey's village. Whenever I meet him I always say to him: 'A rattle of wheels? Eh?'

'A merry fellow!' he always answers, and bursts out laughing.

EPILOGUE   THE FOREST AND THE STEPPE

'And slowly something began to draw him,
Back to the country, to the garden dark,
Where lime-trees are so huge, so full of shade,
And lilies of the valley, sweet as maids,
Where rounded willows o'er the water's edge
Lean from the dyke in rows, and where the oak
Sturdily grows above the sturdy field,
Amid the smell of hemp and nettles rank...
There, there, in meadows stretching wide,
Where rich and black as velvet is the earth,
Where the sweet rye, far as the eye can see,
Moves noiselessly in tender, billowing waves,
And where the heavy golden light is shed
From out of rounded, white, transparent clouds:
There it is good....'
(From a poem, devoted to the flames.)

The reader is, very likely, already weary of my sketches; I hasten to reassure him by promising to confine myself to the fragments already printed; but I cannot refrain from saying a few words at parting about a sportman's life.

Hunting with a dog and a gun is delightful in itself, *fuer sich* , as they used to say in old days; but let us suppose you were not born a sportsman, but are fond of nature all the same; you cannot then help envying us sportsmen.... Listen.

Do you know, for instance, the delight of setting off before daybreak in spring? You come out on to the steps.... In the dark grey sky stars are twinkling here and there; a damp breeze in faint gusts flies to meet you now and then; there is heard the secret, vague whispering of the night; the trees faintly rustle, wrapt in darkness. And now they pull the hood over the cart, and lay a box with the samovar at your feet. The trace-horses move restlessly, snort, and daintily paw the ground; a couple of white geese, only just awake, waddle slowly and silently across the road. On the other side of the hedge, in the garden, the watchman is snoring peacefully; every sound seems to stand still in the frozen air-- suspended, not moving. You take your seat; the horses start at once; the cart rolls off with a loud rumble.... You drive--drive past the church, downhill to the right, across the dyke.... The pond is just beginning to be covered with mist. You are rather chilly; you cover your face with the collar of your fur cloak; you doze. The horse's hoofs splash sonorously through the puddles; the coachman begins to whistle. But by now you have driven over three miles... the rim of the sky flushes crimson; the jackdaws are heard, fluttering clumsily in the birch-trees; sparrows are twittering about the dark hayricks. The air is clearer, the road more distinct, the sky brightens, the clouds look whiter, and the fields look greener. In the huts there is the red light of flaming chips; from behind gates comes the sound of sleepy voices. And meanwhile the glow of dawn is beginning; already streaks of gold are stretching across the sky; mists are gathering in clouds over the ravines; the larks are singing musically; the breeze that ushers in the dawn is blowing; and slowly the purple sun floats upward. There is a perfect flood of light; your heart is fluttering like a bird. Everything is fresh, gay, delightful! One can see a long way all round. That way, beyond the copse, a village; there, further, another, with a white church, and there a birch-wood on the hill; behind it the marsh, for which you are bound.... Quicker, horses, quicker!

Forward at a good trot!... There are three miles to go—not more. The sun mounts swiftly higher; the sky is clear.... It will be a glorious day. A herd of cattle comes straggling from the village to meet us. You go up the hill.... What a view! The river winds for ten miles, dimly blue through the mist; beyond it meadows of watery green; beyond the meadows sloping hills; in the distance the plovers are wheeling with loud cries above the marsh; through the moist brilliance suffused in the air the distance stands out clearly... not as in the summer. How freely one drinks in the air, how quickly the limbs move, how strong is the whole man, clasped in the fresh breath of spring!...

And a summer morning—a morning in July! Who but the sportsman knows how soothing it is to wander at daybreak among the underwoods? The print of your feet lies in a green line on the grass, white with dew. You part the drenched bushes; you are met by a rush of the warm fragrance stored up in the night; the air is saturated with the fresh bitterness of wormwood, the honey sweetness of buckwheat and clover; in the distance an oak wood stands like a wall, and glows and glistens in the sun; it is still fresh, but already the approach of heat is felt. The head is faint and dizzy from the excess of sweet scents. The copse stretches on endlessly.... Only in places there are yellow glimpses in the distance of ripening rye, and narrow streaks of red buckwheat. Then there is the creak of cart-wheels; a peasant makes his way among the bushes at a walking-pace, and sets his horse in the shade before the heat of the day.... You greet him, and turn away; the musical swish of the scythe is heard behind you. The sun rises higher and higher. The grass is speedily dry. And now it is quite sultry. One hour passes another.... The sky grows dark over the horizon; the still air is baked with piercing heat.... 'Where can one get a drink here, brother?' you inquire of the mower. 'Yonder, in the ravine's a well.' Through the thick hazel-bushes, tangled by the clinging grass, you drop down to the bottom of the ravine. Right under the cliff a little spring is hidden; an oak bush greedily spreads out its twigs like great fingers over the water; great silvery bubbles rise trembling from the bottom, covered with fine velvety moss. You fling yourself on the ground, you drink, but you are too lazy to stir. You are in the shade, you drink in the damp fragrance, you take your ease, while the bushes face you, glowing, and, as it were, turning yellow in the sun. But what is that? There is a sudden flying gust of wind; the air is astir all about you: was not that thunder? Is it the heat thickening? Is a storm coming on?... And now there is a faint flash of lightning.... Ah, this is a storm! The sun is still blazing; you can still go on hunting. But the storm-cloud grows; its front edge, drawn out like a long sleeve, bends over into an arch. The grass, the bushes, everything around grows dark.... Make haste! over there you think you catch sight of a hay barn... make haste!... You run there, go in.... What rain! What flashes of lightning! The water drips in through some hole in the thatch-roof on to the sweet-smelling hay.... But now the sun is shining bright again. The storm is over; you come out. My God, the joyous sparkle of everything! the fresh, limpid air, the scent of raspberries and mushrooms! And then the evening comes on. There is the blaze of fire glowing and covering half the sky. The sun sets: the air near has a peculiar transparency as of crystal; over the distance lies a soft, warm-looking haze; with the dew a crimson light is shed on the fields, lately plunged in floods of limpid gold; from trees and bushes and high stacks of hay run long shadows.... The sun has set: a star gleams and quivers in the fiery sea of the sunset... and now it pales; the sky grows blue; the separate shadows vanish; the air is plunged in darkness. It is time to turn homewards to the village, to the hut, where you will stay the night. Shouldering your gun, you move briskly, in spite of fatigue.... Meanwhile, the night comes on: now you cannot see twenty paces from you; the dogs show faintly white in the dark. Over there, above the black bushes, there is a vague brightness on the horizon.... What is it?—a fire?... No, it is the moon rising. And away below, to the right, the village lights are twinkling already.... And here at last is your hut. Through the tiny window you see a table, with a white cloth, a candle burning, supper....

Another time you order the racing droshky to be got out, and set off to the forest to shoot woodcock. It is pleasant making your way along the narrow path between two high walls of rye. The ears softly strike you in the face; the cornflowers cling round your legs; the quails call around; the horse moves along at a lazy trot. And here is the forest, all shade and silence. Graceful aspens rustle high above you; the long-hanging branches of the birches scarcely stir; a mighty oak stands like a champion beside a lovely lime-tree. You go along the green path, streaked with shade; great yellow flies stay suspended, motionless, in the sunny air, and suddenly dart away; midges hover in a cloud, bright in the shade, dark in the sun; the birds are singing peacefully; the golden little voice of the warbler sings of innocent, babbling joyousness, in sweet accord with the scent of the lilies of the valley. Further, further, deeper into the forest... the forest grows more dense.... An unutterable stillness falls upon the soul within; without, too, all is still and dreamy. But now a wind has sprung up, and the tree-tops are booming like falling waves. Here and there, through last year's brown leaves, grow tall grasses; funguses stand apart under their wide-brimmed hats. All at once a hare skips out; the dog scurries after it with a resounding bark....

And how fair is this same forest in late autumn, when the snipe are on the wing! They do not keep in the heart of the forest; one must look for them along the outskirts. There is no wind, and no sun; no light, no shade, no movement, no sound: the autumn perfume, like the perfume of wine, is diffused in the soft air; a delicate haze hangs over the yellow fields in the distance. The still sky is a peacefully untroubled white through the bare brown branches; in parts, on the limes, hang the last golden leaves. The damp earth is elastic under your feet; the high dry blades of grass do not stir; long threads lie shining on the blanched turf, white with dew. You breathe tranquilly; but there is a strange tremor in the soul. You walk along the forest's edge, look after your dog, and meanwhile loved forms, loved faces dead and living, come to your mind; long, long slumbering impressions unexpectedly awaken; the fancy darts off and soars like a bird; and all moves so clearly and stands out before your eyes. The heart at one time throbs and beats, plunging passionately forward; at another it is drowned beyond recall in memories. Your whole life, as it were, unrolls lightly and rapidly before you: a man at such times possesses all his past, all his feelings and his powers--all his soul; and there is nothing around to hinder him--no sun, no wind, no sound....

And a clear, rather cold autumn day, with a frost in the morning, when the birch, all golden like some tree in a fairy tale, stands out picturesquely against the pale blue sky; when the sun, standing low in the sky, does not warm, but shines more brightly than in summer; the small aspen copse is all a-sparkle through and through, as though it were glad and at ease in its nakedness; the hoar-frost is still white at the bottom of the hollows; while a fresh wind softly stirs up and drives before it the falling, crumpled leaves; when blue ripples whisk gladly along the river, lifting rhythmically the heedless geese and ducks; in the distance the mill creaks, half-hidden by the willows; and with changing colours in the clear air the pigeons wheel in swift circles above it....

Sweet, too, are dull days in summer, though the sportsmen do not like them. On such days one can't shoot the bird that flutters up from under your very feet, and vanishes at once in the whitish dark of the hanging fog. But how peaceful, how unutterably peaceful it is everywhere! Everything is awake, and everything is hushed. You pass by a tree: it does not stir a leaf; it is musing in repose. Through the thin steamy mist, evenly diffused in the air, there is a long streak of black before you. You take it for a neighbouring copse close at hand; you go up--the copse is transformed into a high row of wormwood in the boundary-ditch. Above you, around you, on all sides--mist.... But now a breeze is faintly astir; a patch of pale-blue sky peeps dimly out; through the thinning, as it were, smoky mist, a ray of golden yellow sunshine breaks out suddenly, flows in a long stream, strikes on the fields and in the copse--and now everything is overcast again. For long this struggle is drawn out, but how unutterably brilliant and magnificent the day becomes when at last light triumphs and the last waves of the warmed mist here unroll and are drawn out over the plains, there wind away and vanish into the deep, tenderly shining heights....

Again you set off into outlying country, to the steppe. For some ten miles you make your way over cross-roads, and here at last is the high-road. Past endless trains of waggons, past wayside taverns, with the hissing samovar under a shed, wide-open gates and a well, from one hamlet to another; across endless fields, alongside green hempfields, a long, long time you drive. The magpies flutter from willow to willow; peasant women with long rakes in their hands wander in the fields; a man in a threadbare nankin overcoat, with a wicker pannier over his shoulder, trudges along with weary step; a heavy country coach, harnessed with six tall, broken-winded horses, rolls to meet you. The corner of a cushion is sticking out of a window, and on a sack up behind, hanging on to a string, perches a groom in a fur-cloak, splashed with mud to his very eyebrows. And here is the little district town with its crooked little wooden houses, its endless fences, its empty stone shops, its old-fashioned bridge over a deep ravine.... On, on!... The steppe country is reached at last. You look from a hill-top: what a view! Round low hills, tilled and sown to their very tops, are seen in broad undulations; ravines, overgrown with bushes, wind coiling among them; small copses are scattered like oblong islands; from village to village run narrow paths; churches stand out white; between willow-bushes glimmers a little river, in four places dammed up by dykes; far off, in a field, in a line, an old manor-house, with its outhouses, fruit-garden, and threshing-floor, huddles close up to a small lake. But on, on you go. The hills are smaller and ever smaller; there is scarcely a tree to be seen. Here it is at last--the boundless, untrodden steppe!

And on a winter day to walk over the high snowdrifts after hares; to breathe the keen frosty air, while half-closing the eyes involuntarily at the fine blinding sparkle of the soft snow; to admire the emerald sky above the reddish forest!... And the first spring day when everything is shining, and breaking up, when across the heavy streams, from the melting snow, there is already the scent of the thawing earth; when on the bare thawed places, under the slanting sunshine, the larks are singing confidingly, and, with glad splash and roar, the torrents roll from ravine to ravine....

But it is time to end. By the way, I have spoken of spring: in spring it is easy to part; in spring even the happy are drawn away to the distance.... Farewell, reader! I wish you unbroken prosperity.

The End

Made in the USA
Middletown, DE
18 March 2017